BEYOND
MAGIC

BEYOND MAGIC

A Collection of Novellas

Susan Kearney

Elaine Cunningham

Kassandra Sims

TOR®
paranormal romance

A TOM DOHERTY ASSOCIATES BOOK
NEW YORK

This is a work of fiction. All the characters, organizations, and events portrayed in this novel are either products of the author's imagination or are used fictitiously.

BEYOND MAGIC

Copyright © 2008 by Tom Doherty Associates, LLC

"The Shimmering" copyright © 2008 by Hair Express, Inc.
"Beyond Dreams" copyright © 2008 by Elaine Cunningham
"Hill and Sky" copyright © 2008 by Kassandra Sims

All rights reserved.

A Tor Book
Published by Tom Doherty Associates, LLC
175 Fifth Avenue
New York, NY 10010

www.tor-forge.com

Tor® is a registered trademark of Tom Doherty Associates, LLC.

ISBN-13: 978-0-7653-5527-0
ISBN-10: 0-7653-5527-2

First Edition: September 2008

Printed in the United States of America

0 9 8 7 6 5 4 3 2 1

Contents

THE SHIMMERING

Susan Kearney

Prologue

Sandra Lowell tossed in her bed, half-asleep, her dream too delicious to wake up from. Without opening her eyes, she flung her hand toward the ringing alarm clock, hit the snooze button, and slipped back into the arms of her dream lover. And oh . . . wow. Her dream man had powerful biceps that sported a two-headed serpent symbol that twisted around his forearms, a chest as wide as a Kodiak bear's, and the arrogant features of a Viking, except for his dark hair. Perfect lips. Perfect cheekbones. Perfect fingers that wrapped around her neck and drew her mouth to his for a kiss that ravished, seduced, stroked.

Yum. Threading her hands into his hair, she tugged him closer and breathed in his exotic scent, an alien and erotic scent that caused her heart to pound. She leaned into his kiss, arched into his touch, ground her hips into his. He traced a path from her mouth to her collarbone, and in anticipation of him going lower, her breasts tingled.

Her alarm clock shrilled again and she wakened, pulse pounding, heart jolting. Her arms clutching . . . her pillow.

Breathing in deeply and exhaling slowly, Sandra groaned. Another minute. She'd only needed one more damn minute to find release. Instead, she'd overslept and had no time to take off the edge herself. When it came to men, her social life was nonexistent. So it figured she'd run out of time and wake up from her dream—just when things were turning deliciously interesting.

With a sigh of frustration, she ripped back the sheet and padded toward the bathroom. Even in her dreams she'd never been that lucky.

Chapter One

"You think the astral projection machine is legit?"

At Dr. Liza Mancuso's question, Sandra halted on the concrete steps of the Psychophysical Research Institute, shaded her eyes from the Florida sunshine, and frowned at her best friend. "Do I think a machine can sling someone's mind into an out-of-body experience? Of course not."

Really, how could Liz even seriously consider the possibility? The chances of Sandra having an out-of-body experience were no more likely than bumping into her dream man as they approached the institute's front doors.

Setting down her medical bag on the steps, Liza wrinkled her brow in confusion. "Then why don't we just forget it?"

If only Sandra *could* forget it. This silly assignment was not at the top of her make-a-difference in the world list. Nor was it even on the page. But reporters had to work their way to the top within a hierarchy of corporate politics. Until Sandra was one of the lucky few who could choose their assignments, she had to take the stories her editor handed out.

As Sandra answered Liza she ticked off points on her fingers. "I'm a reporter. My boss believes that astral projection is newsworthy, if only for its quirkiness. He assigned this story to me. So here I am to uncover the facts, while you protect me from becoming a medical malpractice victim." She refrained from mentioning her boss was currently none too pleased with her after she'd taken a few risks while covering a celebrity murder trial last month. She'd gotten her story, but word had gotten back to corporate that she'd impersonated a book editor to gather background material and apparently that was a no-no. Of course, if one of her male colleagues had pulled the same trick, he'd be accepting free drinks in the bar for a month. Her reward after putting the follow-up to bed was this bizarre assignment, a definite comedown. "Come on." She glanced at her watch. "I'm on deadline."

Liza hesitated, her warm brown eyes filled with concern. "You're supposed to report the stories, not become the experiment yourself."

"A little risk comes with the job." Especially if Sandra wanted to get ahead. When she started as a cub reporter three years ago, she'd made up her mind to stand out from the others in the fiercely competitive world of journalism. An A student in college, she'd also worked on the student paper full time. When a slot opened at the *Sun,* a professor had recommended her. Sandra had made herself available nights, weekends, and triple shifts, determined to get ahead. And she refused to give up because of a minor setback. If she had to write soft news, she'd search for a different angle to make the story fresh and riveting. And if she had to try astral projection for the sake of her work, she was up for that, too.

Liza's tone had an edge of Southern-accented disapproval. "Was it your job to skydive out of that helicopter and break your leg?"

Sandra flexed her limb. "You fixed me up good, doc."

"Was it your job to volunteer as a hostage when those crazy kids robbed Citibank? I had to remove a bullet from your arm that time. Another four inches over and it would have been your heart. And remember when—"

"I'll be careful," Sandra sighed. It wasn't as if she had a family to worry about her. No parents, grandparents, aunts, uncles. Not even a lover. Being alone had advantages. She could do what she wished. What if she took risks to get ahead, prudent risks to kick her career into high gear? However, Liza worried so Sandra did her best to ally her fears. "If I put in another medical claim, my boss has threatened to demote me to writing classifieds." Yet, despite his annoyance and Liza's worries over the risks Sandra had taken, she recalled with satisfaction how her investigative pieces *had* made page one.

She enjoyed her career too much to turn down this assignment. Or to give it up for a family. Sure, someday she'd have a guy like the one in her dreams—but not yet. Nothing pleased her more than uncovering the layers to a story, learning secrets, and finding the truth. The sense of satisfaction as she gathered bits and pieces of a puzzle until she had the entire story kept her working long after her colleagues went home to their families. The only downside was she'd sacrificed her social life. She had a crazy schedule—it wouldn't be fair to ask anyone to put up with her eighty-hour work week. Plus, she was too young to make commitments to anyone since she yearned for her career to soar. *Damn.* She didn't need a shrink to tell her why her unconscious was inundating her with lusty fantasies. Three times this week, the same lover with the exotic serpent symbol had invaded her dreams, leaving an impression that splashed over into her waking hours.

"Here we go again." Rolling her eyes, Liza's words pulled Sandra's attention back to the conversation.

Sandra shrugged. "There's no real danger involved this time, because nothing's going to happen. The astral projection machine is a hoax."

"How can you ignore all those people you interviewed who claim they've left their bodies?"

Three years as a reporter had left her cynical. Sandra might still want to make a difference, but she was no longer dewy eyed and innocent.

"Maybe they're kooks. A few centuries ago, hundreds of people reported abduction by fairies. Or maybe they hyperventilated. Lack of oxygen causes hallucinations. Look how many people claim to have been visited by aliens."

"Maybe they have."

She winked at Liza. "That's why I need you. If anything does go wrong, you'll patch me up like always."

"Don't count on it. I'm a general practitioner, not a soul catcher—and this experiment is way outside my field of expertise. Perhaps—"

"Dr. Flores earned a Harvard medical degree and completed his residency at Johns Hopkins. I highly doubt he's going to harm me. Just make sure he doesn't slip me a hallucinogen or put me in a hypnotic trance, okay?" Despite Liza's reservations, she was obviously as curious to see the machine as Sandra—which is why she'd so easily talked her into taking the afternoon off from her busy medical practice.

They hurried up the steps to Dr. Flores's imposing steel building. A revolving door spun soundlessly, depositing them in a vast foyer, decorated with all the personality of a gloomy cave. The hushed air smelled stale . . . like the interior of the county jail. They crossed the foyer toward the elevators, the only sound the click of their heels on the black marble floor.

Surely the chilly air, not the idea of astral projection or the unnatural silence, caused the goose bumps to rise on her neck. They stepped into the elevator, and she jabbed the button for the top floor. They rose smoothly, but Sandra's stomach somersaulted like a gymnast's. According to her research many Eastern cults accepted astral travel as an everyday matter. Supposedly, the mind or astral spirit could separate itself from the body.

But then thousands of people believed in Roswell and little green men, too.

The elevator doors opened directly into a murky room with dozens of widely spaced reclining leather chairs with headphone attachments. Carpeting muffled the footsteps of attendants who checked blinking monitors above their patients, who lay with eyes closed, gentle music lending a soothing sound to the still atmosphere.

"What kind of laboratory is this?" Liza whispered.

Before Sandra could respond, a smallish man in a lab

coat a size too big strode forward with an eager grin plastered across his cherubic face. His benevolent smile, his guileless eyes, and his rosy cheeks seemed so compassionate and out of place that Sandra found it hard to believe he was Dr. Flores, the head of the institute.

He pumped her hand enthusiastically, blue eyes twinkling behind a set of bifocals. "Thanks for visiting. Are you ready for the experience of a lifetime?"

"I have a few questions I'd like to ask first, please." Sandra almost hoped he'd refuse to answer. It would be a good indication he had something to hide.

No such luck. Instead he dismissed an assistant before leading them to his private sanctum, a surprisingly cozy office with oriental furniture and tapestries on the paneled walls. He offered sweetened ice tea with lemon slices and delicate sugar cookies. Sandra placed the recorder on Flores's immaculate desk, so she could quote him exactly. She might not believe in his theory, but as always she was determined to report the facts—not her opinion.

Leaning over his desk, his gaze directly on her, he spoke right into the microphone. "What would you like to know?"

"Tell me about your invention." She'd begin by accumulating background information with an open-ended question.

Resting his elbows on the desk, he propped his chin in his palm. "Very simply, my astral machine allows the mind to leave the body."

"How?"

"Let me back up a second. Before my invention, it took years of study to attain the necessary level of relaxation needed for the mind to separate from the body. One must relax to the point of 'hearing' silence and 'listening' to the inner workings of one's mind."

Yeah, right.

Three years as a reporter made it easy for Sandra to keep her face blank, her disbelief hidden.

"To ensure the astral spirit is free to leave the body," he continued, "extraordinary relaxation is required. During the process a slow paralysis creeps over the body. However, fear of that very paralysis is a great deterrent to out-of-body experiences. Untrained people tense, stopping them from successfully freeing the mind from the body."

She raised an eyebrow. Was he going to claim in advance that it was her fault, her fear, if the machine didn't work as designed? "Go on, please."

"My techniques eliminate the fear, but not the paralysis."

Okay, he had the fear angle covered. But paralysis? Sandra exchanged a long glance with Liza, a silent urging for her to ask the medical questions.

Liza didn't disappoint. "Wouldn't a sedative take away fear?"

"Yes. Of course. But eliminating the fear is only the first step in the process." Flores popped a cookie into his mouth, chewed and swallowed. "Once the subject relaxes, my machine boosts the patient out of his or her body."

Sandra tried to keep the skepticism from her face. "Your machine works every time?"

"Every time." Dr. Flores beamed.

"Do you administer drugs?" Liza asked.

"Only a minor relaxant. My machines' vibrations do the rest. If you decide to go ahead and try the process," he said to Sandra, "your friend is free to observe the procedure."

Sandra nodded. "Have you had any difficulties?"

At the question, the happy expression on Dr. Flores's face dimmed, and he stood, drawing himself up to his full five feet of height. "Our past experiments are not a secret. There's someone you should see."

Sandra grabbed her recorder, and she and Liza followed the quick-stepping doctor to a curtained-off cubicle in the corner of the lab. At the hissing and sucking noises behind the screen, Sandra experienced a sudden twinge of apprehension and dryness in her mouth.

Doctor Flores yanked back the curtain. A handsome man lay in bed, hooked to a respirator. At their rude interruption,

Sandra half-expected his eyes to fly open, but he remained completely still, the only indication of life being the rise and fall of his chest beneath a crisp cream-colored sheet. His unlined, pale face didn't so much as twitch a muscle— not his sensuously full lips, not his masculine nostrils, not his ultra-long eyelashes. If he'd been healthy, he'd have been as handsome as her dream man.

"You're keeping him alive with the machine?" Liza asked.

The hiss of air pumping oxygen into the man's lungs grated on Sandra's nerves. She fumbled and switched on the recorder. True, she wanted a story, but even she would only go so far. "What happened to him?"

"He didn't choose to come back."

He didn't choose? "Excuse me?"

"It's the truth." Flores tucked the blanket more snugly around his patient's feet. "After he paid for this entire wing, I saw no reason to refuse his request to try my machine. Before he astral projected, he made out his will, named an executor, and signed power of attorney over to his chief accountant."

"Does he have a name?"

"He's a wealthy Romanian prince. Telling you his name would violate doctor–patient confidentiality."

A wealthy Romanian prince? If Sandra were at her computer, she'd have his identity within a few keystrokes. Instinct prompted her next question. "There's more to his story than choosing not to return, isn't there?"

"He specified in a living will that if his mind didn't rejoin with his body, the institute was not to keep him alive by artificial means."

"Then why all this?" Liza pointed to the machines surrounding the patient.

Dr. Flores sighed. "Before he left on his astral journey, the prince turned over the day-to-day operations of his financial empire to others. Rather than accept new management and forfeit huge salaries, private jets, and luxurious yachts, his lawyers and accountants prefer to run the companies themselves. They overturned his will and as long as he lives, they can run his companies. A court order prevents me from shutting down the machines that breathe for him. There's nothing I can do."

Sandra studied the handsome prince in wary fascination. If only he could speak, what would he say? Had he really left? Or had the machine forced him into a coma-like state? And if he'd gone, why hadn't he returned? Or had he changed his mind and couldn't find his way back? Most important of all, could the same thing happen to her?

She inhaled deeply to steady her nerves. "How long has he been like that?"

"Several years. He's my *only* deviation from the norm. I assure you, Ms. Lowell, my machine is perfectly safe."

Sandra looked to Liza, who perused the monitors. "He's in a vegetative state—almost no brain activity. Sandra, I have a bad feeling. You should reconsider."

"Nonsense." Dr. Flores patted Liza's shoulder. "Your concern for your friend is admirable but unwarranted. At first, I blamed the prince's predicament on my machine, too. We stopped the astral projections, double and triple checked our data. But it wasn't our error or a technological malfunction."

"How do you know?" Sandra asked, still skeptical.

"We received a letter dated before the prince left, stating the unequivocal fact that he didn't intend to return to an existence trapped inside a body." He handed her a note. "This is a copy. Read for yourself. Experts verified the handwriting. It was his choice not to return, not any fault of my machine."

"And what's to prevent this fiasco from recurring?" Liza asked.

Flores didn't appear to take offense. "We screen our candidates more carefully now, and we also subject everyone to the same exhaustive battery of psychological tests Sandra took last week."

Sandra sighed. Flores had impeccable credentials. And

the fact that he'd openly admitted one failure was to his credit. "Am I a good candidate?"

He didn't flinch. "You're perfect. Now come. It's time to experience my invention for yourself."

They followed Dr. Flores down a long corridor, and Liza whispered in Sandra's ear. "You don't have to do this. No job is worth ending up like that."

Sandra ignored her suggestion. "I have a few more questions, Dr. Flores. Why is the Romanian at the institute instead of a hospital?"

"If we move his body, the astral spirit won't know where to return—if he should so choose."

Since Flores's sincere tone reflected complete frankness, Sandra swallowed her disbelief. His spirit refused to return? She found it much more likely that the guy had had a mental breakdown. Flores had sent her a DVD of background material about astral projection. She'd watched a patient sit in a chair, his heart rate slowing a bit on the monitor. Breathing deepened. Then absolutely nothing happened for twenty minutes until the patient returned and made all sorts of unverifiable claims.

Perhaps the *Sun*'s experts could discredit Flores's machine, if not his theories. "Could you describe the mechanism behind your invention?"

"Later. I'll explain everything once you experience astral travel for yourself." His tone implied she'd be more receptive later. Didn't he know reporters lived to poke holes in other people's theories?

Dr. Flores opened a door into a well-lit room. If not the same room, it was a twin to the one she'd viewed on the tape. A reclining chair in the middle of the floor eclipsed the rest of the equipment. Overhead, a brown box hung from the ceiling.

"Have a seat, please," he gestured to the chair, his tone confident. "Don't worry. I've done this thousands of times."

Sandra handed Liza her purse and ignored her friend's disapproving frown. Flores must have noticed Liza's dubious expression because he redoubled his assurances. "I'd hardly invite the press to a demonstration if I hadn't worked out the bugs, now, would I?"

"Of course not." Sandra settled back in the chair and grinned at Liza, reminding herself that the larger and more outrageous the scientific scam, the bigger the headline.

She took a deep breath. "I'm ready. Let's do it."

Chapter Two

The planet Farii
Central Milky Way Galaxy

Sire, have you signed the document?"

Daveck Gorait, head warrior of West Farii, strode across his ruling chamber to glare down at the parchment in his chief counsel's hands—a document he didn't want to look at, never mind sign. But even he couldn't delay much longer. Backed into a defensive stance he'd never wanted, he restrained his annoyance. It wasn't his advisor's fault that after Daveck had poured so much credit into spies, he still hadn't found where his enemy, Maglek, had hidden the *Zorash,* an ancient totem that protected their world from climate changes.

Twenty years ago, Maglek had betrayed the entire warrior caste by stealing the *Zorash* to use the totem's powers to amass private wealth. Ever since the *Zorash* had vanished, hurricane activity had increased by a factor of fifteen. Disturbing volcanic lava flows disrupted trade routes that had previously been open for centuries. Those people who didn't freeze during the chaotic winter storms starved through the spring drought.

Despite Daveck's vast resources, he had been unable to right the wrong, recover the totem, and return the *Zorash* to its rightful place on the ancient pedestal and restore their climate. With the *Zorash* missing and storms worsening every season, the need to reverse the climatic upheaval grew more dire by the day.

Daveck kept his tone even. "An alliance is my only option?"

"Not necessarily." Dinar folded his hands within the sleeves of his robe. "It's possible the lady doesn't even know about her father's theft."

"This alliance is the only way I can make a legal search of her property?"

"We could go to war with the East," Dinar suggested.

Daveck sighed. "War will only breed mistrust. Farii knows I'm not eager to wed, but we need cooperation."

"An alliance with that traitor's family—" Dinar practically spat the words, "will only build a false trust."

"If a false trust works, I will have done my duty. This alliance is only a means to recovering the *Zorash*."

"So it comes to you sacrificing . . . all."

"There is no other viable option." Daveck's voice dropped and he rubbed the serpent brand on his arm to remind himself of his duty. His people had suffered enough. War was not the answer. So what if he abhorred the idea of marriage? Lightning flashed outside his office window, reminding him that his personal preferences were nothing compared to the empty bellies of starving children. Daveck picked up the pen. With a bold flourish, he signed the document.

Earth

Dr. Flores taped the round pad dangling from the overhead astral machine to Sandra's forehead. He flicked a switch, and the box hummed. "It'll take a moment to warm up. Meanwhile, a mild tranquilizer will help you relax."

Flores removed a hermetically sealed bottle of pills from a cabinet and handed it to Liza. "Please give her one of these pills."

After checking the label, Liza broke open the factory-packaged medicine and popped the lid, and Flores handed Sandra a sealed water bottle. Sandra washed down the bitter pill with the water and disregarded Liza's brows knitted with worry. The soft sounds of a classical symphony drifted down from overhead speakers. The lights dimmed.

Sandra fought the urge to fidget, and averted her gaze from Liza, unwilling to reveal any apprehension. Nothing was going to happen. But what if it did? What if she left her body and freaked, or couldn't find her way back?

"What do I do?"

Flores checked his machine. "Relax."

"Relax? Like going to sleep and dreaming?"

He shook his head.

Too bad. She wouldn't have minded another bout with her dream man. At the memory of her dream lover, she squirmed in her seat. Then again, for that kind of dream, she'd require privacy.

"The drifting–tingling sensation is different from anything you've experienced. You'll remain alert, abnormally awake, and serene. If anything frightens you, your astral spirit will immediately return to your body. But most patients report only peacefulness."

His explanation reassured her—which was silly because if she didn't believe she could astral project, she shouldn't have felt any relief from his words. *Stop analyzing. Close your eyes.*

Eyes closed, the man from her dream last night—all tall, handsome, and glaring at her as if she'd done something wrong—branded himself on the inside of her eyelids. She gripped the chair, tension settling into her shoulders. *Let it go. It was only a dream.*

"Breathe evenly," the doctor instructed in a sing-song voice.

The comfortable chair cradled her, supporting her neck and spine. Tension eased out of her muscles and peace engulfed her. She drifted, her thoughts focusing on the most pleasant part of her day—her morning dream. Her lover's eyes glimmered with promise. His lips curved into a haunting smile.

Her skin felt weird . . . like a silk handkerchief being tugged out of a pocket. At first she attributed the odd sensation to her daydream. But when she suddenly opened her eyes, she appeared to be about two inches from the ceiling. Oh . . . my . . . sweet lord. She was looking down on her physical body from overhead. From the freakin' ceiling. Below her, she could see her body in the chair with her eyes still closed, hands relaxed. She appeared to be in a deep trance or sleeping—just like the patient in the DVD.

Only she was floating by the ceiling.

Her mind had actually separated from her body. She was astral projecting. And somehow the drug kept the calm washing through her free-floating mind, bathing her in peace, as she drifted on a current of air.

So the good doctor wasn't a fraud after all. Amazing. Awesome. What a story she would write. Except if she wrote the truth, who would believe her?

Below her astral spirit, she watched Liza work on the physical plane. Liza lifted Sandra's wrist and checked her pulse, smoothed back her short hair from her cheekbones, seemingly unaware Sandra had left her body. Flores hummed off-tune.

Okay. She was doing it. Astral projecting. How far could she go?

Drifting like a ghost through the ceiling and past steel girders, Sandra peered at the skyscrapers of downtown Tampa. The university's minarets, onion-shaped towers of silver, glinted across the Hillsborough River. In Ybor City the trolleys ferrying tourists appeared no larger than toy cars, and the interstate was a thin ribbon heading west across the bay.

Gliding higher through the scattered cirrus clouds, Sandra tested the limits of her newfound freedom over the splendor of the Florida coastline. How easy it was to soar across the state and the country in a mere moment. The blue-green waters of the coast merged with the deep sapphire of the Gulf Stream, the green of the Ozarks, the flooding Mississippi, the snow-capped Alaskan peaks—awe-inspiring images of nature's grandeur flew by in an instant.

The Pacific Ocean and Hawaii beckoned, but her career called—she had a story to write. A story so fantastic, so shocking, so controversial, it might be just what she needed to rocket her career, if anyone believed her. Still, she had to try. She wasn't hallucinating. This was real. Reversing direction, Sandra began a downward spiral and steered gently toward Tampa.

She floated calmly, certain of finding her way back to her body. Then like a huge, invisible hand, a force reached out. Grabbed her.

What the hell? It was as if something had ripped the steering wheel from her hands. And she was caught in the force. Trapped. Terribly out of control.

Darkness engulfed her in a silent, starry womb—but oddly, she felt only calm, not terror, as a vortex sucked her into a spinning, twisting turbulence of slashing color and darting light.

Sandra spun forward, backward, through a dark vacuum pierced by streams of color. But where was her fear of falling into chaos? Panic should have crashed over her in waves. According to Flores, fright should cause the automatic return of her astral spirit to her body. But despite her desire to return, she couldn't summon fear—only a sense of marvel at stars streaming by.

Whatever force had her strengthened its grasp. She floated past the moon in absolute silence, savored the sights of Mars, Jupiter, and Pluto. The sun shrank behind her until it appeared like other stars, a glittering pinpoint in an obsidian sky. Her reporter's mind cataloged the details, a calm counterpoint to her unnaturally suppressed fear of the unknown. Cold black emptiness surrounded her. Sandra told herself to go back. But she couldn't. Star after star sped past. Time lost meaning.

Finally, her speed declined, and one orange star grew larger and brighter in the vacuum. Something wrenched her toward this sun's fourth planet, a turquoise ball rotating under three moons. She spied three hurricanes lined up over the ocean, and a volcano erupting south of the equator. Questions tumbled in her mind, but the world rushed to meet her too quickly to sort through her myriad impressions.

The horizon sped toward her, revealing a small continent. As if this was her fate and final destination, a force other than gravity tugged her downward, over rounded icecapped mountains jutting through fierce snow storms and desert sands of whirling dust devils. Signs of civilization—square fields, silver roads, and golden skyscrapers—flashed by.

A domed structure with a crystal roof perched on a hillside at the end of a row of similar structures. Sandra plummeted through the brilliant roof. Inside, windows of pink-colored glass rose from the dusky marble-like floor to the domed ceiling high above. The proportions of the tables and chairs seemed wrong, the legs too long and thin. A spectacular carpet of changing iridescent colors lit the room, causing odd reflections to dance over the walls and onto the people inside.

As once Sandra had watched her own body from the astral plane, she now watched another woman who was lying on a circular crimson bed. The woman screamed. Sandra hovered above. What was going on? The woman screamed again, but no one spoke to ask what was wrong.

What had happened? What was this place? Why was she here? And how could she return to Earth and her body? On Earth, when she'd astral projected, she'd easily chosen her own direction, soaring out of Flores's facility, but here a force held her in place. Captured, wary, and beginning to fear that she might never find her way home, Sandra tried to focus on what was happening on this strange planet.

The woman below clutched the crimson coverlet and

her screams ebbed into great sobbing shudders. For a moment Sandra feared she'd frightened the poor lady. But no one paid the slightest attention to Sandra. She must be invisible in her astral state.

Surrounded by a group of attendants, the black-haired woman collapsed in the pillows, her eyes swollen and red from weeping. Sandra glimpsed two arms, two legs, a face with all the proper features of a human and supposed she should consider herself lucky. She could have found herself on a planet of giant roaches or spiders.

Oddly, the shrill wailing stopped suddenly but for no reason she could discern. Yet, in the space of a breath, the woman's expression had changed from hysterical sobbing to vacant-eyed serenity.

Oh my. The woman was leaving her body, astral projecting.

The stranger's aura ascended from her body and floated toward Sandra, explaining the sudden silence of the body below them. As much as Sandra welcomed company, she had to warn the stranger to return before the peculiar force also pulled her away from her home, her world, and everything she held dear.

Go back while you still can.

I prefer to risk this existence than to remain on Farii.

The other's thoughts conveyed a grim hopelessness wrapped in overwhelming grief. Her golden aura flickered, then vanished through the crystalline roof, her telepathic communication leaving no doubt of her intentions. Like the Romanian prince, she'd given up, moved on, abandoned life.

Sandra had no time to mourn her passing or to dwell on what had so saddened the woman. The same relentless force that had propelled Sandra across the galaxy tugged her toward the spiritless body. Closer.

What the hell was happening, now?

The force shoved, pushed, tugged, and Sandra's astral spirit merged with the alien woman's flesh.

Sandra screamed in a low-pitched voice she didn't recognize as her own. With vision sharper than any she'd ever possessed, Sandra stared at a roomful of females, some crying, others patting her back or arms in consoling gestures. Outside the room, the wind keened and rain pattered on the roof. Lightning lit up the skies and reflected through the windows. Thunder clapped and the acrid taste of terror welled in her mouth as she registered the physical sensations of strange fibers rubbing against her skin and breathed in the corky aroma of dry air, licked the strange shape of her own unfamiliarly full lips.

The gravity seemed too light, the air too thin and pungent. Every sense seemed skewed, alien, as disturbing as the violent storm raging outside.

A long-nosed woman slapped Sandra across the face and spoke harshly. The stinging blow stopped her screaming and allowed the lyrical sounds of an alien language to chime in her ears. Sandra couldn't understand them. But then why should she? By God, she'd traveled to the end of the universe and expected to hear English?

Stifling a hysterical giggle, she breathed deeply, trying to steady the rising panic. She let the thin air out with a slow hiss and forced her reeling thoughts into a semblance of order.

She was alive. Mostly unhurt. And surrounded by immaculately dressed women who all wore their hair down to their waists and who flinched at every clap of thunder as if unaccustomed to storms.

The woman who'd slapped her stared down her long nose at Sandra. Her expression revealed she was considering doing so again, to stop Sandra from pitching a freakin' fit. Her jumbled thoughts swirled, making her dizzy. She dropped her gaze to see unfamiliar hands—her hands—twisting the too-soft blanket. She couldn't draw enough air into her oxygen-starved lungs and despite her now tall size and lack of muscles, her every movement was too big, the gravity too light. Fear soured her breath and the acrid scent of cork increased her light-headedness.

Questions hammered inside her head. Would she ever see Earth and Liza again? Had Flores tricked her somehow? Sandra's fingers clenched the blanket until her palms ached. Could she simply be hallucinating? She didn't think so.

It was so real. She simply didn't have this kind of imagination. And both the pill she'd taken and the water had come from sealed bottles. But something had gone horribly wrong. Dr. Flores had claimed fear would return her to her body. Yet this one certainly wasn't hers.

She needed to go home. But how? Could she leave this body? Astral project back to Earth without Flores's machine?

Ignoring the fear that even if she managed to leave this body, she might not know the way home, Sandra shut her eyes and hung onto sanity with the hope that whatever force had sent her here might send her home—that she didn't need Flores's machine to astral project. He'd told her the key was relaxation.

Relax.

She could do this.

Relax.

Instead of obeying, every muscle tightened. After what had happened, relaxing was impossible. She sat up from the pillows abruptly. Her pulse raced. Her hands were icy. Except it wasn't *her* hands that were cold, or her heart that raced, or her long hair that stuck to the back of her clammy neck.

Had she gone crazy? Was this a bad dream? A side effect of Dr. Flores's machine? An accident? She recalled the force pulling her here and doubted it could have been coincidence. There were limits beyond which a rational person stopped believing in coincidence. She was supposed to believe she'd used Flores's machine and then, by accident, a nameless force flung her across the galaxy and just happened to find her a suitable body? No way. No time, no how.

She didn't understand what had happened or why. But

her journey here was no coincidence—of that she was certain. She only had to stay calm, put the pieces together, and find a way home.

The woman who had slapped her frowned, and Sandra scooted back out of reach, in case she intended to hit her again. But all the woman did was to set a glass with liquid on a table beside her. Then she shooed the others out the door of the over-sized bedroom, decorated with rich draperies and carpets but no televisions, phones, or computers that Sandra could see. The building appeared modern though, and she thought perhaps the devices might simply have been hidden. The room was brightly lit through ceiling panels but she had no idea what powered them . . . or if she was free to leave or was a prisoner.

The frowning woman spoke to one younger girl who'd tarried behind the others. This time, Sandra understood the word "go." And the murmured reply, "Yes, Fexel."

The lyrical speech of the people exiting the room shifted Sandra's scrambled brains—as if a hundred rubber bands snapped inside her head. Slumping, she covered her eyes with her hands, and let the alien language inundate her.

She could discern the words! In addition to the gift of her body, the departing woman had given her a knowledge of the language. Sandra merely had to look at an object to know its name, think a thought and the correct phrases popped into her mind—as if she'd been born to the alien tongue. Testing for limits to her ability, she searched for personal memories. Being orphaned at age five in a car accident that took both her parents but left her without a scratch. Graduating first in her journalism class. Her first page one story. But she found none that didn't belong to her life on Earth.

Sandra sat on the bed and trembled from head to foot. She counted her long fingers and when she reached ten, counted her bare toes.

Noting the little differences of the other woman's body that was now hers, Sandra took in her buffed white nails, her soft, uncalloused palms, her long hair that hung heavy over her shoulders and cascaded to her waist, and sought to steady her trembling. All the while she considered her situation, she told herself to assess and analyze. She didn't have time to panic. Her life might depend on what she did next.

After a plane crash or a mudslide, a person's very first decision often determined if they lived or died. Last year, she'd interviewed a woman who'd confronted a bear while camping. She could have held still or fled. Instead, she'd run straight at the bear, waving her hands and howling. The bear had run away—and she'd lived to tell Sandra her tale.

Come on, damn it. *Think*. Things could be worse. She could still be drifting in space. Lightning could have struck her. She could be dead.

Obviously, she'd landed on another world, but everyone here believed she was the same woman they'd always known. While asking a dozen questions appealed to Sandra, logic told her to wait, to listen, to try and figure out what was going on before she revealed her true self.

The sharp-eyed woman, Fexel, shut the door and dusted her hands. Obviously, she held some position of importance here and she seemed less concerned about the stormy weather than about what was happening inside. She could be the mother of the woman whose body Sandra now inhabited—or she could be her jailor. She could be a friend or an enemy and until Sandra knew for certain, she would remain very, very careful.

But one thing she did know. Someone here had made the woman whose body she inhabited miserable enough to abandon her life and live as an astral spirit. And although the other woman had claimed she was never returning, perhaps she would—if Sandra could make her life better. She liked thinking she was here to do some good.

Fexel pulled a fragile chair over to the bed, and Sandra studied her. Her long grayish hair was tinged with blue, and Fexel had tied it at her nape in a severe knot, drawing the skin around her face taut. "You're too old for hysterics, young lady."

Sandra understood Fexel's every word. But she remained silent, not yet willing to speak.

Fexel's voice sharpened, more than necessary to be heard above the storm. "Haven't I raised you better?"

Raised her? Was Fexel mother, nursemaid, teacher? Her sharp words didn't sound loving. Sandra guessed Fexel could be old enough to be a mother. Although tempted to explain she wasn't the woman Fexel thought her to be, she'd best be careful, or she could end up in this planet's equivalent of a mental institution or worse. Until Sandra found a way to return to Earth, she'd ease slowly and carefully into this society.

Fexel arched her eyebrow and waited for her response.

"I'm sorry," Sandra spoke, her tongue twisting around the alien words with ease.

"Sorry won't stop the gossip. And when *he* hears about your antics, you may be sure he won't be pleased."

"He?" Was Fexel referring to her father? Her boss?

"Lira, you can't go on pretending."

"Pretending?" Sandra prodded for information and hoped Fexel didn't notice she sounded like a parrot. At least, she'd discovered her new name: Lira.

"Young lady, you cannot make believe your contract to *him* doesn't exist." Thunder rolled as if to punctuate her words.

"Why not?"

Fexel shook her finger in Sandra's face, her eyes narrowed with suspicion. "You little fool. Have you truly lost your wits? You've been sobbing for days on end and now you claim to not even remember why?"

A sensation as ominous as the stormy skies outside prickled down her spine as Sandra recalled Lira's last words, Lira's preference to depart everything she'd known for the astral plane. Not only had Sandra made Fexel suspicious by not remembering whatever was so upsetting, Sandra still didn't have a clue what was going on. But since more questions would alert Fexel to the fact that she was not Lira, she had to be patient.

And now, as if Sandra didn't have enough to deal with by landing in a stranger's body on the alien world, she would have to face Lira's fate. Lira could be a virgin about to be sacrificed to their god, or a criminal facing the death sentence. Sandra could only hope she had more intelligence, more spunk than Lira. But she was a stranger here and Lira had resources she never would—knowledge, friends, family. Whatever. Sandra had decided she was here to help Lira and she would do it before she went home.

Preferring to let Fexel be suspicious rather than risk the unknown, she tilted her chin and looked the other woman in the eye. "Just tell me what you want me to do."

Chapter Three

"Sire?" Dinar bowed his head and waited.

Daveck paused in his sword practice and turned off the holosimulator. "Has word of the alliance been made known?"

"Yes. The daughter of Maglek has taken to her quarters in tears since the high priest announced the document signing."

"Perhaps tears will make her more pliable."

"In my experience, only a happy woman is amenable to her lord's wishes."

Daveck glared at Dinar. "I wouldn't know." His first marriage had been a disaster. No one dared speak of it. And in truth, Daveck knew little of women beyond his sisters, both intelligent, one a healer and the other an artist of renown, both so emotional that he had difficulty understanding their complexity. He much preferred the simple company of warriors. But with the new alliance with the East, he'd not only break his sacred vow to remain solitary, he'd have to make other sacrifices as well. He couldn't waver. Just that morning, Ysandro, a fertile town to the south, had flooded with tidal flow from a hurricane. And if he didn't soon recover the *Zorash* and restore the stolen artifact to its sacred place, more deaths would rest on his conscience.

SHOVING BACK HER chair, Fexel walked to the curved wall, and opened a pocket door. She reached inside a closet filled with brightly colored clothing and withdrew a scarlet garment.

Drawing a deep breath, Sandra concentrated on one simple detail at a time as if it were the most important thing in her existence. In desperation, she locked her gaze onto the garment. Then she added details, slowly, so she wouldn't be overwhelmed by the alien perceptions bombarding her frazzled senses.

From the waist up, the outfit reminded Sandra of a kimono. A hood hung from the back and in front the deep V-neck plunged to the navel, meeting a six-inch girdle that would cinch tight at the waist. The full-length skirt divided into two parts and gathered at the ankles.

Fexel laid out panties that tied with a cord at the waist. Apparently the women here didn't wear the equivalent of a bra. Which could be a problem, especially since Lira's breasts were much more voluptuous than Sandra's own. Women would pay thousands of dollars for implants like these. Sandra used to fantasize about having large breasts and now that she had them, they felt cumbersome, but lovely. Oh, yeah. She could get used to these curves, no problem.

"Hurry," Fexel ordered.

"What's the rush?"

"Don't sass me, young lady. The upcoming ceremony is important."

While Sandra hastily dressed behind a screen, she examined her body with appreciation. She now possessed long legs, trim ankles, and dainty feet. Sandra had been careful not to let the sun burn her fair skin back in Florida, but now she couldn't help but appreciate this body's glamorous golden tan. Her wide hips and ample bustline filled out the garment to perfection, and she wished for a mirror to examine her face.

What kind of woman was Lira? It wouldn't be easy keeping up the charade without someone realizing a new person had taken over Lira's body. Sandra could ask only limited questions without arousing suspicion. But no way could she rein back her normal curiosity forever. Besides, somehow she must find out all she could about this place without revealing her true identity. For all she knew her very survival, not just finding a way back home, might depend upon her ability to adapt.

Compared with the clothing the others had worn, Lira's was of higher quality, with detailing that revealed extra work and cost. Sandra guessed Lira had been the lady of the house and a woman of means. But was she kind? Intelligent? Personable? What would happen if Sandra couldn't bluff her way through the upcoming ceremony without giving herself away?

Perhaps she could draw Fexel out with chitchat. "Is the ceremony really that important?"

Outside the rain turned to hail and tiny balls of ice battered the windows. Fexel paid no attention. "All lives on Farii hinge on it. He's coming. Hurry."

Sandra wanted to ask who was coming, but she remained silent, fairly certain she should already know the answer. Instead, she rushed to dress in the rest of the unfamiliar garb. Over the scarlet ensemble, she donned a gold, cropped vest which served to emphasize her cleavage. Sandra tugged the plummeting neckline closed, but when she removed her fingers, the material eased back, again showing off too much of Lira's magnificent chest for Sandra's sense of modesty. To avoid revealing even more, she must remember to stand very straight.

She slipped into a pair of sandals. Around her neck, Fexel placed an animal-shaped pendant with its tail wound about a spherical, celadon-green gemstone that was a tiny replica of Farii. Fexel handed her a matching ring, and Sandra slipped it onto her left hand.

Fexel frowned. "Do you mean to insult *him*?"

Why did the woman keep emphasizing *him*? Sandra longed to ask and clear up her confusion, but the scowl of irritation on Fexel's face made her more cautious. "Huh?"

"Put the ring on your right hand, and no more of your antics."

While Sandra switched the ring to her other hand, Fexel led her to a thin-legged chair. After she sat, Fexel twisted Sandra's long hair into loops and braided tiny button ornaments into her tresses. Somehow she managed her coiffure while keeping an eye on the door.

Fexel scolded a woman as she entered the doorway. "Yala, it's about time you got here." Judging by Yala's servile manner, she was an assistant. Head bowed, eyes downcast, Yala hurried into the room. After dipping her hands into the pocket of her plain brown frock, she removed a sprig of tiny lavender flowers.

She bowed deeper to Sandra, but spoke to Fexel in an anxious whisper. "He's almost here!"

While the frightened servant spoke, Yala pressed the tips of her fingers together, then touched her fingers to forehead, lips, and breast in a movement that reminded Sandra of Christians crossing themselves. Fexel copied the ritual, and when Sandra didn't follow suit, both women's eyes widened and stared at her, which strung her nerves taut.

She hurriedly copied the movement but Fexel's eyes narrowed in suspicion. "Keep your wits about you, girl. We all know you've been called to make a great sacrifice and you must appear courageous to uphold our honor. Do you understand?"

No. But she'd set herself a part to play. "Of course."

The idea of making a sacrifice sent a chill down her spine. What must she face that had so upset Lira that she'd left this world for the astral plane? Fexel had said lives were at stake. Sandra could only hope they weren't about to sacrifice Lira to their gods by slitting her throat. Yet she dared not ask for fear of arousing their suspicions.

Her ignorance of the customs on this world might get her killed. Sandra vowed to be more observant than usual. Even then it would be all too easy to fail. She had no idea of Lira's preferences in food, friends, or what she did for a living. The task of impersonation seemed daunting, but what choice did she have? She wished she knew more about the ceremony in which she was to take part, wished she knew more about the mysterious *him.* Back on Earth Sandra's social life might not be on par with other women her age, but she'd dabbled with men and wasn't a sexual neophyte. She always got out of the relationship before a guy expected her to turn up on a regular basis. However, her experience covering politics, crime, and arson had allowed her to see men in their element, wielding power and authority as if they were born to rule. She could deal with that.

"She's not herself today," Fexel explained Sandra's apparently odd behavior.

"In her place, I'd act the same. To have to face *him* . . ." Yala paled and her forehead perspired. Again she touched forehead, lips, and breast, giving the impression of warding off evil. This time Sandra and Fexel repeated the ritual almost at the same time.

"Go about your duties," Fexel said. "I alone will make certain Lira looks beautiful."

Sandra might not understand what the women discussed but she didn't like their condescending attitudes or the way they chattered around her. "Please, stop talking about me as if I'm not here," she snapped.

Fexel turned to stare, her jaw dropping open to reveal several missing teeth. Yala sucked in air, her cheeks pinched, her eyes dark with terror before she scurried out the door, her hand again touching forehead, lips, and breast.

What had Sandra said to cause such reactions in the servant? Was Lira so meek she allowed others to treat her like a child?

Fexel recovered from her surprise without responding to Sandra's request. She dusted off her hands and shook a finger at Sandra. "What you do or say will make no difference. Now let's go."

Sandra had never backed down from someone so arrogant and pompous and she never would. To make sure Fexel understood, she folded her arms across her chest. "I'm not going anywhere until you explain—"

Trumpets blared. A drum roll sounded. Cries from outside came to her clearly. Through the rose-tinted glass, she heard the townspeople and realized the hail had stopped, the thunderstorm had ended, or at least lightened so that she could no longer hear rain battering the building.

"It's *him.*"

"Murderer."

"Hush! He comes."

"Don't look him in the eye or he'll slice you in half."

Fexel clutched her arm, her obvious fear giving strength to her trembling grasp. "It's time. Be brave. Maglek, your dear father, would want that."

Sandra didn't know how to interpret the things she'd heard. If whoever was coming was a murderer, why wasn't he locked up? And why did she need to be brave? Couldn't Maglek protect her? Or was Maglek dead? From Fexel's icy demeanor, she'd concluded the woman wouldn't help her. Sandra's throat closed, and her heart pounded in time to the staccato beat of the drums.

Soon, she would meet—*him.*

FEXEL DREW HER along a tiled hall through an arched doorway. The orange sun was setting in a dun-colored sky. Already two of the planet's three moons rose to her left. A wall of fierce thunderclouds scudded away in the distance, the previous rainstorm leaving behind an electric excitement in the air. But it was the procession down the dirt street lined with glass buildings and milling crowds that drew Sandra's gaze.

Kangaroo-like animals, *gangras,* about the size and color of elephants, hopped in giant leaps down the street and shook the ground in thunderous waves. Dust swirled. The hind limbs of the *gangras* were greatly enlarged, and the crowd gave the lethal tails extra room. The first *gangra* in the herd carried a midnight blue banner that hung limp in the still air. When the animal bounded closer, she could see an odd harness with reins leading downward without any sign of a rider or a saddle on its sloping back. Could the *him* everyone so feared be this giant kangaroo demanding human sacrifice? Was this creature the reason Lira had fled her body?

Sandra reached for her shoulder bag and recorder to take notes, then remembered her strange journey. She wasn't on assignment, and she couldn't leap to conclusions. Studying the animal's wild brown eyes, she couldn't discern any hint of intelligence and that alarmed her more than the *gangra*'s bared teeth, or its alert ears, which pivoted back and forth in response to the jeering shouts of the crowd.

The drum roll increased in tempo and volume. Fexel squeezed Sandra's arm tight, but whether to hold her up, encourage her, or prevent her from running, Sandra didn't know.

Once the group stopped before the *gangras,* Fexel fell back, leaving Sandra to face Lira's fate alone. One of the *gangras* fed on some giant leafy trees. Sandra took small comfort in confirming that the big animals were vegetarian. At least she wasn't their supper.

When rope ladders unfurled from the animals' pouches, and two men of military bearing climbed down, Sandra fought against dropping her lower jaw in surprise. Relief washed through her that she had to deal with only the men—not a beast.

Pulling back to give the newcomers a wide berth, the crowd hushed and many dropped to their knees and touched their foreheads, lips, and chests with their hands, their faces rigid with terror. Sandra's gaze darted to one of the military men, then to the other, and suddenly she had no doubt who *he* was. His name traveled through the masses like a dirge.

"Daveck."

The crowd's whispers escalated to an angry cacophony that clashed with the ominous beat of the drums, vibrated the glass houses along the street, and blared Daveck's name across the village. Fear hung in the air as thick as the cloying dust, and Sandra was no more immune to the threat he emanated than were the others.

Overhead a green bird cawed, circled, and swooped down to hide in a kaydon tree. At the same time the sun plummeted below the horizon and the drums ceased, leaving the town in eerie, heart-thudding silence. Mouth dry, hands shaking, Sandra waited.

Where minutes before the sky had been clear, now violet lightning sizzled as if to announce Daveck's presence. Thick sapphire storm clouds scudded overhead, and the wind bellowed like a huge, injured beast. Her clothes caught in the gusts and Sandra swallowed hard, wondering what this man wanted from her.

She had no doubt he'd demand something. She recognized his aura of power from history books more than personal experience. He reminded her of Churchill, Roosevelt, Patton. He carried himself with an Alexander-the-Great attitude that suggested he expected immediate obedience. And while she realized it would be foolish to challenge him before she'd taken his measure and learned why they were all here, she was determined to set the tone that Lira was no pushover, either.

Recalling that she wanted to help Lira, Sandra lifted her chin, squared her shoulders. And willed her knees not to shake as she spied the wicked sword sheathed at his side.

Daveck strode toward her in clothes of deep midnight

blue so dark he might have worn black. He didn't look left or right, nor did he wait for his men. He advanced alone, seemingly unconcerned by the crowd's fear or hostility. A hood hid his face and a long cape cloaked his powerful physique. However, clothing could not disguise his height or the way his crackling vitality transfixed the crowd.

Waiting for Daveck to near, Sandra wondered if Lira had ever met this man. Although she had no idea if he was enemy, friend, or brother, he was a man—and she tried to take courage from the idea it would be better to deal with him than one of those gigantic *gangra* beasts.

Daveck stopped before her, and despite the fact she stood on a dais on the sidewalk, he was still an inch or two taller than her. Like everyone else on this world, his clothes were immaculate and fit him as if custom made to his powerful frame. There was an intense quality to his stillness, wary, coiled, intractable, that imparted a message of strength and power.

Ignoring Fexel, who dropped to her knees and made that sign of abasement, Sandra peered into the shadows of his hood but could not make out the man's features. "Welcome."

"You do not fear me, my lady?" Daveck's velvety soft tone was strangely cutting.

"Should I?" she hedged and stood straighter, all too aware of the low-cut V-neckline of her outfit and, for the moment, unwilling to give him a more revealing view than necessary.

In one smooth and deliberate motion, he swept back his hood. A baby cried. A beast howled. Around her, people gasped. From the reactions in the crowd, she'd almost expected him to reveal a deformity, but that was not the case at all.

She stared, shocked that she recognized him—this Daveck was the man she'd dreamed about back on Earth. It was impossible. Yet when his cape fluttered in a gust of wind, revealing the two-headed symbol on his bicep, she couldn't deny it was him, right down to the familiar sexual tug that rocked her.

He had a face she'd never forget. And she had to grit her teeth to prevent her lower jaw from dropping as she compared the man before her with the one she recalled so vividly from her lusty dreams. His cheekbones were noticeably sharp and clearly drawn in a tanned complexion. Heavy brows arched to accentuate the bridge of his slightly aquiline nose. He wore his black hair long, tied back with a strip of leather.

But it was his wide-set eyes that seized her attention. His frosty blue-black eyes bore into her with hypnotic intensity, mercilessly, as if penetrating her very being. Hoping to hide her nervousness, she held his stare and refused to squirm under his steady gaze. He kept his demeanor calm and poised, but she sensed a dynamic nature behind the façade.

Before their locked stares became a contest of wills, she darted a glance at the crowd before once again meeting his gaze. Not even a telltale blink of satisfaction cracked his cool composure. She suspected Daveck would never betray his feelings unless it suited his purpose, and she envied such mastery of emotion.

"Will you keep me standing in the street, dear lady?"

Should she ask him in? For all her hysterics and fears, Lira still may have invited him here. Sandra had no way of knowing, but a private discussion would be better than making a public spectacle, especially since the first drops of icy rain had just cascaded out of the night sky.

"Fexel, fetch refreshments for our guest." As the woman nodded, Sandra's gaze shifted to one of the glassy-eyed servants trying to shrink into the shadows. While Daveck watched warily, Sandra stood straighter, prouder, and issued orders with a confidence she didn't feel. "See that everyone is fed and given quarters, and have the men care for their mounts."

Spinning on her heel, Sandra walked back into the building, Fexel following close behind. Although her words had sounded suitably authoritative, she felt as if she'd stepped into a movie where everyone else knew their lines but no one had given her a script.

Sandra turned the opposite way from the bedroom and hoped the long hallway led into a formal or living area and not a laundry closet. Daveck followed, his boots padding silently on the tile floor. From the corner of her eye, she tried to take the man's measure, but he didn't give much away. There was that stillness about him, and yet she sensed a cauldron of emotions bubbling and seething beneath the surface.

The hall widened into an airy conservatory. Blossoming flowers in a variety of spectacular orange and gold hues permeated the air with their pungent bouquet. Glowing pink crystal lamps placed at intervals along the walls gave the room an intimate ambiance. Overhead a trellis supported a multitude of purplish-green vines. If this had been her house, she would have confiscated this room for her office. But she was no longer a reporter and had to keep her mind firmly on the fact that she must act like Lira. This was her house, her people, her world.

Sandra led her guest over to a thatched gazebo with several lounge chairs conveniently placed next to a gurgling waterfall. Daveck refused to sit, but stood and studied her with his back to the water, his arms crossed over his wide chest.

"My lady, how is it that I dreamed of your face last night?" he asked.

"Did you?" Stunned that apparently they'd dreamed of one another, Sandra lowered her eyes to fuss with her skirt and to hide her thoughts. She'd dreamed of him and he of her. Had an outside force dragged her across the galaxy to meet him?

"If you think to use sorcery on me—"

"Sorcery?" She laughed. "Surely you don't believe in—"

"My beliefs are not your concern."

Had she insulted him? His tone remained so stiff and polite, his demeanor so formal, she had no sense of his true feelings.

Interrupting the awkward silence, Fexel carried in a tray filled with tempting appetizers, one hexagonal glass, and a carafe of amber liquid. Sandra didn't know whether bringing only one glass was an oversight or custom but she could use a drink to cool her parched throat. "Please bring another glass. I'll join my guest in a refreshment."

Fexel looked as if she wanted to protest but didn't dare. Instead she glanced at Daveck who stood motionless, his expression hooded. When he didn't contradict Sandra's order, Fexel scuttled away, wariness and fear tightening her features.

Why were Fexel and her people so panic-stricken around this man? Daveck might be physically intimidating, but his stillness did nothing to warrant such reactions—until she recalled someone in the crowd calling him a murderer. But that could be gossip. It was more likely these people sensed the same dangerous and forbidding undercurrents churning beneath his cool exterior that she did.

Daveck's low voice mocked her. "Is that where you find the courage to face me? In a decanter?"

"Why would I need courage to face you?" Sandra answered his question with a question, a reporter's trick.

At her response, surprise and a touch of admiration glinted in his eyes. "I'd been told to expect a hysterical woman."

"Sorry to disappoint you." Her words might be flippant but she managed to keep the sarcasm from her tone. Was she leery of him and his world? Yes. Worried? Definitely. But it would take more than a Viking-sized warrior with a compelling symbol in her living room to drive her into hysterics.

"Would you like a sweet cake?" she offered.

"No." His eyes narrowed as if she might have poisoned the food, and then he finally added a grudging, "No, thank-you."

To prove his suspicion wrong, she popped a pastry into her mouth and savored the mouth-watering sweet. After licking her bottom lip and watching his eyes focus on her mouth, she poured him a glass of wine and offered it to him, wondering again if his dreams had been as erotic as hers.

He accepted the glass and sipped in silence. Since Daveck didn't seem inclined to start a conversation, she searched for a neutral topic. Lightning streaked across the sky and brought the glass room into stark relief. Thunder boomed almost immediately, indicating the storm's closeness.

"Do you think the storm will last long?"

A foil to the tempest outside, his face reflected glacial calm. "The increasingly severe weather pattern is the primary reason I'm here."

"Really?" She didn't dare say more and risk revealing she had no idea of Farii's normal climate. She reminded herself to express the proper concern, pretend this world and its people were hers. But, the stormy weather didn't worry her as much as the controlled power of this man or her immediate attraction to him. Yikes. What was going on here? Was it simple sexual chemistry?

It had been too long since she'd had a fling. But was it coincidence this guy mirrored her dream man? She thought not. And yet she couldn't think how any of this made a lick of sense.

However, one thing she knew for certain. She no longer had a job. At least she didn't on this planet. And that gave her a certain freedom to maneuver. She certainly didn't have to play fair with this dude. If she got caught up with him in a relationship and then disappeared, she couldn't be blamed for playing with his emotions.

So what if he looked tough? He was damn attractive. And although she planned to be careful, she didn't have her normal rules to hold her back.

While his rigid command of his facial features and his stillness displayed muscles coiled tight as a cougar about to spring, she wasn't yet certain if she wanted to acknowledge or explore the instinctive chemistry that drew her taut and kept her on edge.

"These severe climatic changes are ruining Farii crops and causing flooding that carries away the fertile topsoil, leaving future generations to starve. Glaciers in both hemispheres are melting, and the polar caps have shrunk, creating flooding along the coast."

He cared about his people, a good thing. She could read his concerns in his eyes, hear it in his tone.

During his explanation, Sandra had allowed her shoulders to relax and the front of her gown gaped slightly, exposing the curve of her breasts and drawing Daveck's gaze. Hmm. She could use this body to her advantage. However, she was fairly certain Lira wouldn't have employed such a brazenly feminine tactic and she put the idea on hold since she didn't want to explain that she wasn't Lira. Sandra straightened and resisted the urge to allow the neckline to gape. Still, once again she couldn't help wondering if his dream about her had been as erotic as hers about him.

Sandra might be half way across the galaxy in a different body, but her proximity to the delicious warrior had caused the heat from her dream to return—along with an edge she'd never satisfied. Heat curled in her core and she decided there was no reason not to at least test the chemistry between them to find out what he wanted from her. While Lira might have been reluctant to get close to this man, Sandra found him engaging, exciting. In fact, she very much wanted to discover if he was as good a lover in person as he'd been in her dreams.

Too bad she didn't know the customs here. For all she knew, lovemaking was a crime. Or might commit her to him for life. However, a little flirting couldn't do any harm. Or could it?

She reminded herself that Lira had been in tears, desperate to avoid Daveck—so she couldn't exactly come on to him . . . at least not overtly. However, a woman could send signals. Relaxing her shoulders, she allowed her vest to part a bit—giving him an eyeful. And when Daveck's gaze dropped again, she couldn't quite restrain a grin of satisfaction.

Chapter Four

Daveck's spies had led him to expect a cringing, weeping woman who would plead with him to tear up the document. Yet Lira was far from tears. Although her luxurious black hair, braided into patrician loops, and wide mouth matched the holocube he'd acquired, her ability to talk to him without cowering rocked him back on his heels. She'd actually looked him in the eye when she'd spoken. Had she so little sense that she didn't fear him like the rest of the populus? Did she think the stories about his first wife's death were fiction? Or did she simply find the idea of his past so unconscionable that she couldn't bear to stay in the same room with him—unless she pretended ignorance of the fact that he'd murdered Ciel?

He hadn't missed either her subtlety in tapping him for information, or the delightful flush coloring her creamy cheeks. Was she really as opposed to him as his spies had reported, or was she now faking her interest? Perhaps her traitorous father had told her to manage Daveck with feminine wiles.

Several shouts and a loud thud sounded in the hallway. Unannounced, the old woman dashed into the room, the extra requested wineglass clutched in her hand. Sliding to a halt in front of her mistress, she spoke in outrage. "His men are ransacking your house!"

Lira calmly took the glass, poured herself a small amount, and sipped. Then the intelligent gaze of Maglek's daughter narrowed on Daveck. To her credit, Lira didn't raise her voice. "What are you doing? What are you looking for?"

At Lira's direct questions, the maid dropped to her knees and bowed. Her mistress stood defiant, green eyes flashing as if unaware that questioning him in such a manner was not only rude, but dangerous: men had lost their lives for lesser slights.

And yet, despite her defiance, Daveck admired Lira's courage and intelligence, though not her judgment in confronting him. Odd how a woman without any knowledge of military discipline had correctly concluded his men would not have entered her home without his direct order, and again how she'd deduced they'd come not to steal, but to search. It was unfortunate he had to resort to ransacking her home, but too many people's lives were at stake for him to cater to her sensibilities. Perhaps it was foolish, but he still hoped to find the *Zorash* before he was forced to make their contract permanent. Surely she'd be better off in a gutted house than in a forced alliance with him, or maybe dead, which is what would happen to her if he didn't find what he sought.

At the sound of breaking glass, her fingers clenched tight. Her chest heaved, exposing one creamy curve, and even with the distraction of tempting flesh, he sensed she was trying to restrain her temper, not hold back fear.

When he didn't answer, Lira asked more questions. "Why have you come into my home? You owe me that much of an explanation."

The maid scuttled back, her eyes bulging in an ashen face. Daveck flicked his thumb toward the door. "Leave us."

He expected Lira to protest being left alone with his anger. She didn't.

Once the servant departed, he turned to face his enemy's daughter, eager to gauge her reaction to his next words. "My men are looking for the *Zorash* your father stole over twenty-nine years ago."

"Zorash?" She looked puzzled for a moment, as if she'd never heard the word, then recalled it with a light of comprehension. "But isn't the idol just a legend?"

"The *Zorash* is real enough and so is her control of the weather."

Thunder boomed and echoed across the village. Hail tapped against the glass. The lady facing him cocked her head to one side as if considering her next question with care. "So why isn't the *Zorash* doing her job?"

"Do not mock the goddess. She's been taken from her rightful place and is without her normal powers."

"Is that so?"

Her intelligent and questioning gaze sought his, but he wouldn't be fooled so easily into thinking she knew nothing about the stolen totem. As leader of the Sanroyai warriors sworn to protect the *Zorash,* Daveck had access to the facts—facts that pointed directly to her father, Maglek's, guilt. But how much did she know? His spies had determined that she still sent messages to Maglek but had been unable to intercept any of the missives.

Daveck decided to test her. "Maglek was almost a Sanroyai. We trusted him, and he betrayed us. After he stole the *Zorash* from her rightful place at the base of the megalith and hid her from the world, the idol lost the power to maintain Farii's weather."

"You're talking about the three hurricanes coming in off the water?"

He raised a suspicious eyebrow. "Three hurricanes? How do you know about them?"

Sandra ignored his question. "If the idol is powerless unless she's at the base of the megalith, why would anyone steal her?"

Her logic was flawless for someone who knew nothing about the past. But how could she have lived here all her life and not have heard the legends about the *Zorash*? Even tiny children learned about the idol's powers from their mother's lullabies. He recalled Lira's mother had died in childbirth—so it might somehow be possible she wasn't lying—but he doubted it.

He explained anyway. "It's true the *Zorash* cannot tap her full powers since she has been weakened, but even separated from the source of her strength, she has limited abilities. Your father has been using the idol to create wealth and power."

She folded her arms under her chest. "How?"

"When the idol takes her place at the base of the megalith, she controls Farii's weather worldwide. When she's not in her proper place, she can only regulate local climate. Maglek has used her to give good weather to townships on the borders, allowing their crops to prosper while there are droughts or floods everywhere else. Prices go up, profits are huge, and he rakes in a huge cut off the top."

Puzzlement furrowed her brow. "Why are you telling me this?"

"I need your help." He carefully measured his words. "Since the megalith of the *Zorash* is a holy site where only full-blooded Sanroyai warriors have access, the civilian masses have no knowledge that our most valuable treasure's been stolen, but I cannot keep the secret much longer. Even a blind beggar knows the storms grow worse."

"I have no idea where the *Zorash* is, but if I did, I would give it to you."

She oozed sincerity, but her attitude must be a ruse to be rid of him. He couldn't imagine any daughter of Maglek handing over the idol without a fight.

He hardened his tone. "Where is Maglek?"

He expected her to flinch and drop her gaze. Instead, her spine stiffened and she raised her chin. "I don't know."

"Liar." Not many men would dare to defy him so boldly and for a woman to do so was inexplicable. But he should have known Maglek's daughter would be extraordinarily cunning.

"Some things are not what they seem."

Although she'd spoken calmly, she sounded disappointed that he'd accused her of lying. He'd expected her to rage, cry, and deny his every accusation, and that she could hold her emotions in check, showing unexpected maturity, irritated and angered him. But habit forced him to subdue his temper before she bolted—just like every other woman who'd fled his temper since that nightmarish day that he'd killed Ciel. Of course, Lira's fleeing wasn't one of her options—but she didn't seem to realize that yet.

So for now, he made his tone reasonable. "While I've done my best to conceal your family's dishonor, time is running out."

"What are you saying?"

He saw no harm in revealing part of the truth. "Unless the *Zorash* is found and returned to her place at the base of the megalith, Farii's weather will deteriorate until life on this world ceases to exist."

A loud crash from the hallway jerked her to her feet. She tossed one loop of hair over her squared shoulders, straightened her spine, and assumed an air of innocence. "I have nothing else to say."

She wasn't going to cooperate. He'd have to force her to tell him what he needed to know. She locked gazes with him, as if daring him to call her bluff, more formidable than any woman he'd ever known. To say he hadn't expected such behavior would be a vast understatement. Not even Sanroyai princes spoke to him like this.

Odd though, that now he'd glimpsed her inner fire, he looked forward to her yielding to him as she had in his dream. He'd been too long without a woman. It was just his bad luck that the first female he'd found attractive in years was going to bring out his worst side.

From down the hall, shrieks mingled with the crash of drawers overturning and the tinkle of glass shattering. Although he thought it unlikely that the destruction of her property would convince the woman to cooperate, he'd had to try. Besides, there was always the chance his men would find a clue to the *Zorash*'s location.

Daveck stepped close enough that Sandra was forced to tilt her head back to look at him. He held absolutely still. He didn't utter one word, and yet she trembled as if sensing the palpable heat of his interest.

She leaned back as if to retreat a step. Before she could move, he reached up, clenched her loops of hair and dragged her head back. His breath caught as he saw a spark in her eyes that matched his. Perhaps if she had a taste of what was to come, she'd consider telling him the truth. Angry that she'd reduced him into trying to frighten her made his heart race. Lira had denied any knowledge of the crime committed before her birth, but her father must have spoken of the source of his wealth. "In your twenty-five years, you must have heard a whisper, a rumor about the *Zorash*."

"I haven't."

"Your defiance may result in the death of all people on Farii. And still you seek to protect Maglek?"

"Why would I defy you?" She rolled her eyes at the ceiling, and spoke in a sultry voice that mocked him, even as it shot ripples of interest down his spine.

He tugged her closer, until her chest pressed against his. "You could make this easy on yourself. Give me what I want—"

"You can take anything I have." Again she mocked him. The little she-feline had claws.

"—or I'll do this the hard way." His head dipped until mere inches separated their lips.

"Maybe I prefer . . . hard."

He almost choked. She couldn't have meant . . . but when he caught the sparkle in her eyes, he knew for certain she was toying with him. *Him*. Wife killer.

"You won't like my methods."

"Maybe I will." Her palms rested against his shoulders, but she didn't attempt to push him away. She provocatively licked her bottom lip with her pink tongue. "You intend to . . ."

"Most certainly." He turned up the corners of his mouth in a sardonic smile.

She leaned closer. "Let's see if there's more to you than idle boasts."

Maglek's daughter was daring him to kiss her. Was she insane? He did not know. He only knew that she fascinated him, and while he held her body against his, she acted as if she was the one in charge. She acted as if she wanted his kiss.

His smile hardened. His fingers clenched tighter in her hair, trapping her in his arms. The pulse at Lira's throat beat wildly. Her scent rose up to tease his nostrils. And then, as if she couldn't wait another second, she threaded her fingers into his hair and pulled his head closer.

Hot and sultry, Lira wasn't unaffected by his nearness. She trembled, a deep shudder racked through her, but her lips parted beneath his. Daveck hadn't kissed another woman since he'd killed Ciel. No woman had wanted him and force disgusted him. All his pent-up passion was damn dangerous. So was Lira's heat.

He'd intended to threaten her with sexuality in order to make her talk. But she didn't view kissing as torment. She didn't fear him. There could be no doubting the soft welcome of her kiss, the arching of her spine as she melted into him, or the ripe hardness of her nipples.

If she wasn't careful, she could unleash a storm he wouldn't be able to control. And by the *Zorash*, the woman could kiss. As her seething eagerness penetrated his defenses, his ears roared, his senses stirred into overdrive, and he yearned . . . for more. Before she tugged him under and he drowned, he pulled away.

Stepping back, he frowned at her. "What kind of tricks are you playing?"

"Who said I was playing?" she teased.

"If you think only a kiss will satisfy me, you're wrong. By tomorrow, I'll have the right to take even more."

She cocked a haughty eyebrow. "I'd hardly call it taking when I'm willing to give."

Certain her words were no more than bravado, he chuckled, not out of amusement but from the desire to give such a courageous woman one last chance to avoid her fate. "Dear lady, don't tell me you have forgotten our contract of marriage?"

Chapter Five

Marriage contract? Her heart thumped so fast, blood pounded in her temples. Her throat tightened. Daveck might be a hunk she was more than willing to spend a night with—okay, several nights or days or even a week—but marriage with a total stranger was *not* an option she wanted to consider. Obviously, for reasons of her own, Lira hadn't wanted to go there, either, and the impending nuptials was probably the reason she'd left.

Sandra had to settle down and think. She needed to squeeze more information out of him to find out why two strangers were forming a union.

Focused on the determined face just inches from hers, she wondered why he'd signed such a contract. He obviously believed that once Lira was his wife that she'd tell him where the *Zorash* was. But surely these Farii women could lie as easily to their husbands as to a lover? Perhaps their husbands drugged them or tortured them into telling the truth. Or perhaps truth telling was mere tradition.

He held Sandra fast by the loops in her hair. If only she could draw back and think clearly. If only she wasn't breathing in his spicy male scent and pumping all kinds of make-love-now endorphins into her system, she might think of a way to draw more information from him.

He was close. Too close. His huge body dominated the room. He'd towered over others when he'd walked down the street. He had only to suggest that Fexel leave and the woman had scurried to do his bidding. Clearly this man was a master of his world, a leader of his people. But was he kind? Did he care about Lira?

Gazing back at him and keeping her wits about her took effort. His mouth parted in a hard grin. He oozed masculinity in a way she'd never experienced or imagined. His intent look, his staring right at her made the peach fuzz hairs on the back of her neck stand on end, electrifying her nerve endings and making her want to throw caution to the alien skies and just go with the flow.

While inhaling his musky male scent mixed with the peppery aroma of an exotic spice, she had difficulty remembering that Lira had been frightened of this man, and Sandra really knew little about him except what her senses told her. She was very much alone on this alien world, without one friend to bounce her ideas off of. He could do whatever he wanted to her, but somehow that thought only made her more eager to test him.

His voice vibrated with barely suppressed challenge. "Tomorrow you will be my wife."

Not so fast, dude. She should be afraid. But, somehow, she wasn't. While Daveck might win the Farii equivalent of the Mr. America Contest, she wouldn't let that sway her. She wasn't the kind of woman to marry a man because of his stunning good looks or his sexual chemistry. She might have a fling, or begin a relationship, but marriage was way too permanent for her liking. She didn't want to go there. She had a career and it wasn't fair to commit to a man when her heart was in her job.

She wasn't ready. On Earth, compromising her dreams for a man was not in her plans and coming to Farii hadn't changed her mind. She was going back to Earth. She didn't know how or when, but she wanted nothing that would tie her here.

Lust would not trap her.

Trying to ignore the flutter in her stomach, she reminded herself she had no proof Daveck had spoken the truth, nor had she any intention of taking his word about a marriage contract. Although he'd sounded so certain, most contracts had an escape clause, and she'd search for it in this one.

Shattering glass rained down on them, interrupting her thoughts and stinging her flesh with a dozen tiny cuts. Armed men on rappel lines dropped from the ceiling.

What was going on now? She had no idea, but adrenaline

kicked in. She'd covered enough dangerous situations to know that leaving fast was her number one priority.

Before her feet responded to the urge to flee, Daveck grabbed her hand. "We're under attack. Run."

Armed intruders, definitely not Daveck's men, had just invaded Lira's home, but it would be sheer stupidity to ask questions now. Sprinting side by side, they raced down the hallway that led to Lira's bedroom. Heart hammering her ribs, stomach knotting, she sprinted beside Daveck, struggling to match his long stride. Cursing her attire that allowed her breasts to bounce painfully, she flung her free hand over her chest for support. And all the while questions whirled like a weed eater. Who were these men? Were the intruders after her or him? Or both of them?

Behind them, shots fired and splintered the wood next to her head. Daveck yanked her into the bedroom, slammed the door behind them. Together they pushed a heavy wardrobe chest in front of the door.

She took a moment to catch her breath. Outside, men pounded the door and shouted. A moment later the sound of an ax blade biting into the wooden door warned her they wouldn't be safe much longer.

There were no windows on the floor level. The only way out was to squeeze through one of the tiny skylights near the roof. And even if they could climb up there, she doubted she could fit through—Daveck certainly couldn't, not with his broad shoulders.

"We're trapped," she muttered. "Who's after us?"

Daveck drew a weapon that looked like a plastic gun with lethal smooth lines. He twisted the nozzle, aimed at the door, and shooting flames melted the metal hardware. But the ax kept slashing into the door itself.

"That's not going to stop them." She approached Daveck and held out her hand. "If you give me your gun—"

"What?"

Her gaze dropped to his sheathed sword. "I don't know how to use a sword, but I can shoot as well as the next girl."

Her words drew as much suspicion as if she'd grown a second head. His voice rose in disbelief. "*You* know how to use a laser pistol?"

She hadn't expected their weapons to be so sophisticated and the idiosyncrasy bothered her—the weapons seemed more advanced than the other technology she'd seen here. But now was not the time to worry over the rate of technological advances. "What's so hard? Point and shoot. Just show me where the trigger is."

"Here." He placed the weapon into her hand and gently pressed her index finger on a button. "Here's the trigger. The more pressure, the more firepower."

"Got it." She sounded much more competent than she felt. Inside she shook. There had to be at least six men out there gunning for them. And the room had no cover. No place to flee.

She was going to die. And she didn't even know why. But with too many things she still wanted to do with her life, she intended to fight with every precious breath.

The men cutting down the door made so much noise that the attack through another wall took her by surprise. An explosion, smoke, followed by plaster dust had her spinning and shooting.

But she had to stop firing for fear of burning Daveck. He'd advanced quickly, slashing and stabbing one man with his sword, taking a second down fast and hard, then he scooped up a second weapon and thrust it into his shirt.

"Come on." He tugged her through the blast hole. "This way out."

Hope of escape raised her spirits. The crewmen with the ax was through the door and shoving aside the wardrobe chest. It toppled and crashed to the floor behind them just as they crawled out of the room through the blast hole.

Eyes tearing from the dust, smoke choking her, Sandra scooted through on her hands and knees. And blundered into a pair of shiny black boots. Damn.

Tilting back her head, she looked up from the boots to

see an armed intruder aiming a laser pistol at her head. And to either side of him were two more attackers, both fully armed and ready to shoot.

Seeing the furious faces of the men, Sandra shook, certain she was about to die. In the distance, she heard the pops of gunfire and the clash of swords, but Daveck's men would never reach them in time.

Daveck had crawled through the hole after her, taken in the situation, and tossed his sword away and held out his empty hands, but he didn't give up the laser pistol he'd hidden under his shirt. But surely, if they didn't shoot immediately, they'd frisk him?

Daveck placed an arm around her waist. "You got us. Now what?"

"Place your hands behind your—"

Still on her hands and knees, she felt Daveck's hand tug her waist, turning her, flipping her against his side. What now?

Space . . . shifted . . . shimmered.

She blinked in total confusion. Was she hallucinating?

One moment they'd been on hands and knees, armed men aiming weapons at them, then as she took another breath the armed men were gone and she seemed to be inside . . . a shimmering black coffin.

Lying on her side, her back pressed against Daveck, her mouth turned dry with fear. "Oh . . . my . . . God. Am I dead?"

"Are you hurt?" Daveck asked.

"I can't see. I'm blind." There was not even a shadow to guide her. She tried to reach out, but Daveck firmly clasped her hands in his. "Don't move. Are you in pain?"

"I can't see."

"But your arms and legs and feet are . . . okay?"

"It's just my eyes."

"Your eyes are fine. There's no light in the Shimmering."

The Shimmering—a place in the world, yet beyond, the definition came straight from Lira's language memories but Sandra didn't understand the meaning. Her pounding heart made her ears roar. "Where is here?"

"I've put up the Shimmering to protect us until my men arrive. You can't see inside. And you can't move, either."

"Why not?"

"The shield cuts off light. If you place a limb through the Shimmering, the edge will slice it off."

"Are you insane?"

"I'm trying to save our lives."

She breathed a calming breath: in through her nose, out through her mouth. It didn't work. She closed her eyes, pretending the Shimmering wasn't there, pretending she could see if she opened them.

But despite her fright, she couldn't ignore how tightly he was holding her against him. With the back of her head against his chest, her butt snuggled into his groin, she could not only feel his every breath, she also felt his arousal. She didn't budge, not with his frightful reminder to remain still lodged in her mind—she had no intention of lopping off a leg.

"So how will we know when it's safe to come out?" she asked, trying to keep the panic from her tone. She couldn't see or hear anything that was outside the force field and the sensory deprivation was making her claustrophobic.

"We'll have to estimate when it'll be safe. But it won't take my men much longer to fight their way here."

If he'd meant his words to reassure her, he hadn't. "Is it my imagination or is the air growing stuffy?"

"We're running out. Talk less. Use less air."

"Now you tell me." Sandra saved air and said no more. She should be thinking about what was going on outside, about when his men would reach them, about whether the air would run out before it was safe to drop the shield, and exactly how long the Shimmering would protect them.

But with his hand curved around her waist, with her nestled so intimately against him, she preferred to think about the last thing he'd told her before they'd been attacked.

Apparently, if she lived, she was about to marry this man. And she suspected they might have been attacked because someone wanted to stop their alliance. As usual, she didn't have enough facts to reach a valid conclusion. But of one thing she was very certain—Daveck wanted her. He'd saved her life. And he was attracted to her.

Sandra was willing to have a fling . . . but marriage was just too restricting . . . too permanent.

Chapter Six

"May I see this marriage contract?" she asked Daveck. A half hour ago he'd disintegrated the Shimmering to find his men had disposed of their attackers. There'd been no time for Sandra and Daveck to talk privately. Instead she'd remained quiet as he took charge and ordered his men to find out who had attacked them and why. He'd also summoned workers to restore order to her rooms and carpenters, masons, and plasterers were busy repairing the walls, even as women cleaned up the mess in her quarters. And Daveck had also posted more guards around her home.

Making himself at ease in her dining room, he brought a wineglass to his lips, took a leisurely sip, and eyed her over the brim. "Surely after all that has happened you can't question that you require my protection?"

"Until we know who attacked us and why, I can't assume anything. For all I know, those men wanted you dead and I was simply an innocent caught in the crossfire."

A muscle flicked in his jaw. His expression wasn't as stoic as she'd first thought. While he'd mastered unruffled and dangerous, if she looked hard enough, small signs of uncertainty appeared in his square jaw and wide forehead.

"I don't remember signing a contract," she commented.

Throwing back his head, he laughed, and the rich sound washed over her in harsh waves.

She glared at him. "What's so amusing?"

Gently, forcefully, he tugged her closer, trapping her against the rippling warmth of his chest. His easy way of drawing her into his arms excited her—it shouldn't—but judging by the electricity arcing between them, she'd bet her next meal that she'd find his lovemaking even more thrilling than her first skydive. The butterflies in her stomach were certainly stronger every time he touched her.

With his long arms wrapping around her back and his hands in her hair keeping her snugly in place, fighting him didn't appeal to her in the least. She'd much prefer he kiss her again.

But what would Lira want? While Sandra had decided to improve Lira's unfortunate situation so the woman might one day return to her body, Sandra simply couldn't understand why any woman would flee from Daveck.

"Your signature isn't required on a marriage contract. Only your father's and mine are necessary. And I suspect Maglek signed it just to set a trap for me—it was his men who attacked us."

"Why would my father want to . . . ?"

"Capture me? To stop me from going after the *Zorash*."

She shut her mouth to prevent her jaw falling to her toes. What kind of world was this where a man could unilaterally decide to take a wife and her father would betray his daughter? Sandra decided Lira wasn't a delicate rose to be plucked on a whim. She was about to refuse but decided to be prudent and first consider the consequences.

"And if I refuse?" she asked between gritted teeth.

Her question wiped the remnants of laughter from Daveck's eyes. He stared down at her with a probing, uneasy stare. "You would undergo *sharcrit*."

Until he spoke the word, she had no knowledge of the barbarian custom of *sharcrit*. The word had no translation in English, but Lira's language memories flooded her. If a woman refused to wed the man who chose her, the wedding guests killed the unwilling bride with heavy granite-like stones, piling one crushing slab atop another, slowly pulverizing the reluctant-to-wed woman to death. Anger surged through her. Now she understood Lira's reason for leaving her body. Rather than marry a man she found objectionable, she'd preferred to depart for the astral plane. Remaining silent, Sandra pressed her lips tight, trying to think of a way out of her predicament.

Daveck's firm grip drew her back from her thoughts. "Have you decided?"

"It's difficult to believe that a man who just saved my life would put me through *sharcrit*."

He shrugged, then traced a fingertip over her cheek in a caress, his sensual gesture underscoring his reply. "Do not seek to make me feel guilt when the choice is yours to make."

But a man like Daveck didn't marry a woman on a whim. "Why did you choose me? Why did you save me?"

His voice sharpened with impatience. "I already told you. Maglek stole the *Zorash*. I want it back."

He could pretend all he wanted that this was a business deal, but she'd seen the flare of interest in his gaze, felt his arousal when he held her in his arms. "But what does that have to do with me?"

His finger tipped up her chin, then stroked the side of her neck. "Once we are wed, you will not lie to me about where your father keeps the *Zorash*."

His words made no sense. After they wed, she could still lie to him. There must be a vital piece of information that she was missing.

When he traced her collarbone with his finger, he didn't just distract her but sent a delicious shiver of anticipation to her core. And once again she remembered that the wide V-slit in her bodice allowed his fingertips easy access to her breasts.

Sandra knew he wouldn't believe her, but she still had to try. "I'm not lying to you. There's no sense in making both of us miserable for the rest of our lives. Call off the marriage—or at least delay until we know one another better," she suggested.

"The climate is rapidly deteriorating. We can't delay."

At his refusal, she searched for another way out. "I don't suppose you've heard of the civilized custom of divorce?" *Divorce* came out in English. His finger hesitated its downward progress, but she already knew Farii had no Earthly equivalent.

"Di—vorce?"

"Ending a marriage."

"There can be only one end to a marriage—death." His words turned harsh. His scrutiny scraped her nerves, causing more uncertainty than she'd ever known. Or maybe it was the hard length of him pressed against her, inundating her with his blazing masculinity. If he chose to take her, right here, right now, she'd willingly agree.

His hand paused again in its relentless caress, a caress she leaned into as he just barely stroked the curve of her breasts. Triumph flashed in his eyes, which signaled he knew exactly what he was doing to her and exactly how she was responding—with desire.

When he leaned down and the warmth of his breath teased her earlobe, sane thinking became impossible. And when the heat of his hand made tiny circles in the hollow between her breasts, she sighed in pleasure.

As he stroked her flesh, he whispered into her ear. "I won't permit your arguments to delay our marriage but another few minutes."

She gasped. "You want to marry . . . now?"

He nodded. "You *are* wearing your wedding finery. The tabernacle is ready and the high priest has arrived."

Thoughts spinning, knowing she couldn't think clearly when all her hormones were flooding her with seduce-him-right-now demands—probably a reaction to almost dying during that attack—she swallowed hard. "We're strangers."

"Think of our marriage as a way to get acquainted."

"Mmm . . . is that what you call it." She couldn't focus on anything except how much she wanted to rip off his clothes and damn the consequences. But this might be her entire future they were talking about. She had to get a grip, pull herself together. "I'm not ready for marriage."

"Why not?"

"Marriage requires commitment. Compromise. I'm not that kind of woman." Especially since in her world the woman did the compromising and it seemed no better on Farii.

His midnight-blue irises dilated, smoldering with indefinable emotion. His body went taut, and she sensed she'd somehow insulted him. Then the tense set of his broad shoulders eased as if he'd mastered his annoyance, leaving her to wonder if she'd imagined his fleeting reaction.

He drew her closer, his voice intense. "I'll give you one last chance to avoid taking final vows. Tell me where Maglek hid the *Zorash*."

Damn him. She didn't know squat about the *Zorash*, but he'd never believe that. His attempt to intimidate her with his seductive tactics might have worked if she'd been Lira. But Sandra had enough experience with men not to capitulate to his sexy taunting.

She wished she had access to Lira's memories as well as her language ability. But she didn't, so she'd have to make do with the information she had. Except Daveck wouldn't give her time to think. He took her silence for a refusal to give him the answer he sought. His hand went to the small of her back, the other tightened slightly in her damn long hair.

For an instant she considered doing what she wanted—kissing him. Surely just one more kiss wouldn't hurt her and it would temper his anger. But it would give him the wrong idea.

"The longer you make me wait, my lady, the more impatient I become. It would be better if you cooperated."

"Better for whom?"

His eyes darkened with anger. A tiny muscle ticked in

the taut shadow of his jaw. But he sounded as curious as he did irritated. "Where does such defiance come from? The wish for independence? The courage to shoot a laser pistol like a warrior? Don't you know that I murdered my first wife for committing much less of an outrage?"

"What?" He'd murdered his wife? Her gut churned and her thoughts careened out of control. Surely her choices couldn't come down to marrying a murderer or being squashed to death. But even worse, she'd done a lot of crazy things in her life, but she'd never have thought she was far gone enough to consider a fling with a man who'd killed his wife.

Seeing her shock and distaste, rage darkened in his eyes, his mouth thinned to a sneer. "You didn't know?" he demanded. "How could you *not* know?"

"Because no one told me," she snapped. And then she stared into his eyes, searching for answers. "What exactly happened . . . to your wife?"

"We were dining when the border tribe attacked. I put up the Shimmering to protect her and it killed her."

"But the Shimmering protected me."

"Yes."

She didn't understand. "Did the force field device malfunction?"

"It's not a device. I trigger the force field with mental thought."

"So if it killed her, why didn't it kill me?"

"She panicked."

"So you didn't know the force field would kill her?"

"Of course not."

Relief washed over her. "Then it was an accident—not murder."

"She died because of my failure to protect her. That's murder."

Farii had a weird definition of murder. "But your intention—"

"Does not matter. I took a vow to protect her. She died by my hand. Facts are facts."

Drawing a deep breath, she made a futile attempt to steady her trembling nerves.

He spoke with little emotion, as if holding everything inside. "Let me be clear. After we wed, there will be more attacks—"

"Why?" She didn't understand why Lira's father would put his own daughter in danger.

"Do you think Maglek and the border tribes are my only enemies?"

"So you're a real popular guy," she teased.

He didn't crack a smile. "During an attack, I'll be forced to engage my shield. Like Ciel, you too may die."

"I survived once, I will survive again."

"Maybe not. This time I took extra seconds to make certain I wrapped all of you in the force field, I may not always have time to do so. But if you tell me where the *Zorash* is now—"

"I don't know," she repeated, fisting her hands in frustration.

"—I will tear up the marriage contract. It's a good offer, my lady. Think long and hard before you refuse—"

She pounded his chest with her fist. "You big, ignorant bastard. Why won't you listen to me. I don't know where your precious *Zorash* is."

His hand closed over her fist. "Enough. I will have what I came for. It is time to wed, my lady."

"And I tire of your threats. Perhaps you think the *Zorash* is on my person. Would you care to search me?"

His eyes narrowed, and he let go of her as fast as if he'd singed his hands on a hot stove. What had she said to make him react that way? He'd turned on his heel, so she couldn't see his face, and when he pivoted back, face stoic, she couldn't read him at all.

Had her boldness turned him off? Or turned him on?

"I plan to search you quite thoroughly . . . after we're married." He held out his hand. "Ready?"

"Now?" Her mouth went dry, her knees weakened.

"Right now."

Chapter Seven

S he stared at his hand as if she wanted to slap it away.
Although he'd never claimed to understand women,
this one seemed almost . . . unstable. She'd just invited
him to search her, as if forgetful they weren't wed, as if
she didn't have the modesty of a maiden. She seemed eager for lovemaking, yet not for marriage.

When they'd fought, she'd actually been ready to shoot
a weapon, yet she did so without losing one iota of her
feminine side. She hadn't panicked when enemies shot at
them or when his aroused *kaladon* had nuzzled her back-
side, and she'd been more furious about *sharcrit* than about
his kiss—a liberty he should never have taken until after
the marriage ceremony.

Zorash help him, he couldn't begin to fathom what or
how she thought. Couldn't begin to follow her reasoning
process or why she'd denied her knowledge of the idol. It
was almost as if she wasn't aware that after the wedding ceremony a wife couldn't lie to her husband, as if she wasn't
aware that the *Zorash*—even in her weakened state—didn't
allow married couples to lie to one another. For Lira to believe otherwise was foolish.

When she didn't place her hand in his, he reached over
and took it and was surprised to find her flesh icy cold. "At
least you've already experienced the Shimmering—so you
won't panic during the ceremony."

"Look, I didn't want to tell you . . ." She licked her bottom lip and couldn't quite meet his gaze.

"Yes?" Finally she was going to tell him about the *Zorash*. They wouldn't have to marry. Tension and excitement washed over him—as well as disappointment that, in
all likelihood, they'd never see one another again. It surprised him that he wanted to know more about her. She'd
held out on him for far longer than he'd expected, but once

she'd understood that he fully intended to wed, she'd accepted at last that she had no choice. Either way, he would learn the *Zorash*'s location.

"I'm not who you think."

"What?" He'd been so certain she'd been about to tell him where to find the *Zorash* that his tone came out sharper than he'd planned. Alarmed by his tone, his bodyguards leaned through the doorway for a room check, but Daveck waved them back to give them privacy.

"I'm not Lira. My name is Sandra and I come from a planet called Earth."

She was making no sense. Stalling. He'd been so certain she was intelligent, surely she could have come up with a more entertaining or believable story. "Stop lying. It will do you no good."

"You're missing the important point. I'm not Lira. The woman you intended to wed left me her language skills, but Maglek's daughter departed this body for the astral plane."

He snorted his disbelief. "And after we wed, I'm going to grow a pouch and turn into a *gangra*." He placed his palm in the small of her back and urged her toward the reception area where they were to wed. "My lady, please. No more delays."

She planted her feet, but her weight was no match for his mass and she stumbled forward. "You must listen to me. You're going to ruin our lives for nothing."

How dare she insult him? He didn't know whether to laugh or yell at her, but with determination, he kept them both advancing. "Are you saying marriage to me will ruin your life?"

"I'm saying . . . I'm . . . *not* . . . Lira. And only Lira can give you the information about the Kabash."

"*Zorash*," he corrected her automatically. "Now stop delaying. There's no more time to waste. The high priest is ready. Your people and my men are all waiting for us in the tabernacle."

He pulled her forward and she almost fell, glared at

him, then gave in, showing some good sense in the end. Together they left her home and entered the private tabernacle built in the rear quarter of the garden. At least once she understood that for the good of his people he would stand as immovable as a mountain, she didn't waste her limited strength or embarrass them with more antics before his men, who guarded their path, or the guests who milled in the garden, waiting for their arrival.

But once they entered the double front doors of the charming house of worship, she whispered, "You are impossible. You must listen—"

"Silence." He squeezed her hand for emphasis. "I do not wish to air our argument in public."

"It's going to be very public when all the people of Farii are dying because of your mistake," she hissed.

The high priest approached and finally, resentfully, she stopped talking. Her gaze focused past the priest to the *sharcrit* slabs by the altar and her face paled, alarming him. If she refused to take the marriage vows and accepted *sharcrit* instead, he would never learn what he needed. Besides, one woman's death on his conscience was already more than enough for any warrior to bear.

Now that witnesses had arrived, it was too late to turn back. The high priest gestured for them to approach. Witnesses stood in their hooded robes, the distinguishing features of their faces hidden by black netting.

His men stood guard along the tabernacle's stone-walled perimeter and the guests turned somber and silent. An organist played the traditional wedding song. Children threw flower petals in their path and incense scented the air with a sickening sweetness that forced him to take in air through his mouth in measured breaths.

Daveck had no idea what to expect from his bride. She might weep, beg, or try to flee and he held her hand firmly, hoping to lend her his strength so she wouldn't embarrass herself. Many women dreaded their wedding day, fearing the marriage bed and the Shimmering, but he already knew that was not her problem.

His glowering bride seemed to value her . . . independence. And the oddness of that notion disturbed him at a level he didn't comprehend. Because women of Farii didn't think that way. But if she was from Earth as she'd claimed, he imagined that she would certainly have different ways of looking at the world.

According to the ancients, the *Zorash* supposedly possessed many powers but modern-day Farii scholars considered the ancient tales mostly legends. However, one of the early tales foretold of a time when the *Zorash* would go missing, creating climate-wide havoc. Supposedly, one otherworldly soul was the key to the *Zorash*'s survival.

Otherworldly—he'd thought the term referred to a high priest or the pure heart of a warrior. But now as he knelt before the high priest and the man spouted the ritual incantations, Daveck wondered if Lira had heard of the ancient legend and tried to use it against him by coming up with such a fantastic tale.

Because if she spoke the truth—then he was marrying her for no reason. If she wasn't Lira, she wouldn't know where Maglek had hidden the *Zorash*. But there was only one way to be certain—complete the ceremony. And talk about truth checking—what were the chances that the daughter of his lying, cheating, selfish enemy was telling the truth?

Still, Lira had qualities he'd never seen in a woman. She had unusual courage—sweet *Zorash,* she argued with him like an equal. While he admired her spirit, he frowned. He certainly wasn't looking forward to the next few decades of fierce arguments—but if he didn't go through with the ceremony, there wouldn't be much time left for any of them.

Finally the priest finished and handed them the ritual wine. Daveck held the cup to Lira's mouth and she sipped, her eyes seeking his over the brim. Her wine-stained lips might have looked tempting enough to taste, but her eyes glared unbridled fire. But when he placed the wineglass in her hands, she offered a sip to him, doing her part.

She wasn't going to object. Until that moment he hadn't been certain. Oh, she was still clearly raging with anger, but she would live and relief lightened his shoulders . . . and his heart.

"You will now seek the *Zorash*'s blessing and become one in the Shimmering," the high priest intoned.

Daveck stood and helped Lira to her feet. Together, they walked out of the tabernacle toward the pavilion that had been set up in the garden for their wedding ceremony. If he'd thought her hands cold before, they were now icy.

"Aren't we staying to dine?" she asked as they strolled past the guests who helped themselves to food from tables laden with food and drink.

"We have other obligations." His tone thickened.

She must have noted the heat in his voice because she drew herself up so straight her spine cracked. "The Shimmering is part of the ceremony?"

"That's an odd way of putting it."

"It's an odd custom. Are you saying every man here can project a force field at will?"

"The *Zorash* gives only Sanroyai warriors that power and we employ it to protect our women during vulnerable moments."

Banking her annoyance, she grinned. "Like during love-making?"

He nodded.

Her voice turned low and husky, provocative. "You mean we're finally going to consummate the marriage?"

"The *Zorash* demands husband and wife must become one in body and spirit."

"I understand our bodies becoming one. Tell me about the spirit part."

They walked down a stone path lined with flowering shrubs and past sculptures made of flower petals. None of the guests dared approach. His men, inconspicuous but armed, guarded them from a distance.

"Earlier, during the attack when I created the Shimmering, you didn't join me. This time you will."

"I don't understand."

"No woman does . . . not until her wedding day."

She gave him a compassionate look. "Did Ciel survive her wedding day?"

"She did not. We were attacked and I didn't have time to explain what she must do. She panicked, touched the force field and . . ." Blood. So much blood. At least she'd died quickly, but he'd never forget her look of pain and horror or the damning accusation in her eyes before they'd closed for the final time.

Lira wrapped her hand in his. "Your men will protect us. You'll have all the time you need to prepare."

Her words stopped him, drew him right out of the past into the present. *She* was trying to comfort *him*. It made no sense and yet . . . it was true. This woman he'd forced to wed, this woman who appeared horrified that she had no choice, was trying to reassure him when it should have been the other way around. He swallowed hard, wondering if the *Zorash* was signaling him that he was on the correct path to be so lucky.

He peered down into her eyes. "Do you not fear the joining of our bodies?"

"Of course not." She grinned at him, her head at a cocky angle. "Unless you're into kink."

"Kink?"

"Pain. I'm not into pain."

"The first time can hurt but I will go—"

"Damn. I hadn't thought of that."

"What?"

"I'm a . . . virgin?"

"You don't know?" He stared at her. Either Lira was a mental case or . . . he sighed. He'd find out soon enough if she was lying to him.

She shrugged. "We'll be fine. This body is . . . responsive. Wait until you see the size of my chest," she teased.

"Are you trying to make my heart explode?" If she'd intended to shock him into forgetting his past marriage disaster she was succeeding. He'd never heard of a woman quite so forward. But then he was a simple warrior who was regaining his balance and confidence.

"Actually, I was thinking more along the lines of an explosion right here." Looking straight into his eyes, she palmed his growing *kaladon* with a boldness he was beginning to appreciate.

She felt good. Too good. Gritting his teeth, he grabbed her wrist to tug her away. "You must stop."

"Why?"

"Someone might . . . come along."

She chuckled. "I'll take the chance. And if I'd known how cute you are—"

"Cute?" he snorted.

"—at just the mention of sex—"

"My lady, you're doing a hell of a lot more than talking."

"—I'd have married you sooner." She returned to stroking him boldly, clearly enjoying herself. His *kaladon* strained and thinking about anything besides having her naked became a huge effort. Still, he tried to keep up the conversation.

He sputtered, "I gave you no choice about the date."

"Maybe you should have," she purred—and *winked* at him.

"For once, we're in agreement."

Chapter Eight

Daveck let out a whoop and scooped her into his arms, carrying her toward the pavilion. Heart thumping, Sandra placed her arms around his neck and snuggled against his chest.

Making love in Lira's body was going to be . . . interesting. Making love to Daveck . . . excited and intrigued her.

The man seemed one giant bundle of contradictions.

One moment he was demanding and arrogant, the next tender and uncertain, but she suspected that while making love, the real Daveck would show up. Would he be gentle with his "virgin bride"? Would he take the time needed to ensure her enjoyment? Or would he be so eager to enjoy his own pleasure and to complete his mission that he would show no concern for her?

Thank God, Lira's virgin body was reacting to Sandra's eagerness to make love. As Sandra thought about tearing off Daveck's clothes, her breasts swelled, her nipples hardened, and moisture seeped between her thighs. And she couldn't wait to see Daveck's reactions to her voluptuous breasts.

Daveck carried her past the pavilion's tent flap, yanking it closed behind them. Scented candles surrounded a circular mattress with soft tangerine-colored sheets. Fruits, cheeses, and sweetmeats sat in a variety of bowls, dishes, and trays on a sideboard. A frosted crystal decanter held wine, and beside it were two long-stemmed glasses with fragile etchings.

Daveck sat on the bed, keeping her in his lap. "Would you care for something to eat?"

"No, thanks."

"How about some wine?"

"After."

"Wine might make . . . this go . . . easier for you."

She released a low chuckle and tugged his head down toward hers. "I'm not expecting any trouble."

"You aren't?" He gazed at her with confusion in his eyes. "But your mother died when you were born. Did someone tell you what to expect?"

"From you?" She shook her head. "But you're going to be good to me."

"How can you be so sure?"

She nibbled along his jaw, breathing in his delicious scent, a mix of male essence and tangy heat. "Can't you feel what's happening between us?"

"You mean the Shimmering?"

She shook her head. "I'm talking about chemistry. Passion." She nipped his neck and let her hand slide to his jaw. "You want me."

"Yes."

"And I want you. It's simple. Really."

His hand clasped hers. "There's nothing simple about you, and I've never heard of a bride acting so boldly on her wedding bed."

"You're shocked but you don't really disapprove." She pressed herself against his *kaladon* and he couldn't deny the evidence.

He shot her a mocking glance but spoiled the effect as he began to smile. "So now you can read my mind?"

"If you didn't appreciate my feminine side, you wouldn't be so"—she swiveled her bottom against his hard sex— "aroused."

"For a lady who grew up without siblings or a mother, you certainly know a lot about men."

"But I did have a mother and—"

"Don't start." He kissed her lips, stopping her from saying anything about her life back on Earth. She sighed into his mouth, disappointed that he refused to believe her. But then if their situations were reversed, she wouldn't believe her story, either.

And once his tongue found hers, she no longer cared so much that he believed he was kissing Lira. His mouth might have angled down boldly over hers, but his tongue teased and taunted. He took his time, kissing her with a thoroughness that revved her pulse, heated her core, and made her fingers unfasten his shirt—seemingly of their own accord.

Unfamiliar with his wide, knobby buttons, she twisted around to face him, straddling his thighs. She fumbled at first, but then figured out she had to twist the buttons sideways through loops to free the fasteners. And all the while she worked on his shirt, he continued to kiss her—as if he had all the time in Farii.

Finally, she unfastened the last button and smoothed her

palms over his chest. He possessed only a light dusting of hair that stretched between his pectoral muscles and then narrowed at his hips. Flattening her palms over his warm flesh, she learned that his abs were cut like a six-pack and he carried no spare flesh on him.

But it was his heat that impressed her most. That and how his flesh rippled under her touch. The man had one fantastic body and touching his smooth skin pleased her as much as his kiss. If he'd been an athlete on Earth, he'd have been offered a slew of endorsements. If he'd been an actor, he would have had plenty of work. And if he'd simply walked down the street, female heads would have turned.

But it wasn't just his good looks that had her eager to make love. He possessed a presence that exuded . . . a noble determination, and she was certain that whatever he attempted, he would do to the best of his ability. And right now, all his delicious attention was focused on her.

A simple knotted cord held up his pants. When she reached to untie the knot, one of his big hands captured both her wrists, stopping her from exploring further.

And then it was his turn to remove her vest. But he simply parted the V to expose her breasts. Half dressed, sitting on his lap, the outside curves of her breasts squeezed by the material, she felt decidedly wanton.

When he released her hands and cupped her breasts as if testing their weight, she grinned. "Nice, huh?"

"Very nice," he agreed, using the pads of his thumbs to circle her nipples.

"Umm. You feel good."

"You like my touch?" he asked, sounding surprised and pleased.

"Even better, I'd like your mouth right there."

He didn't need a second invitation. He drew her nipple into his mouth, pulling hard. His deep, lingering tug caused her to go slick with desire.

She squirmed, again reached for the tie on his pants.

He tweaked one nipple with his teeth, the other with his fingers.

"Ah . . ." she released a soft moan and when she could think, she realized he'd once again captured her wrists in one hand. With his free hand and his mouth, he played with her breasts. And she'd never felt anything so lovely in her entire life. "Oh . . . oh . . . my . . . argh." She spread her thighs and pumped her hips, invited him to delve lower.

He placed her hands on his thighs. "Keep them here."

And then he went back to kissing her breast, taunting her other breast with one hand, while finally, ever so slowly, he teased and dipped below her waistband.

Legs folded under her and parted by his thighs, she waited impatiently for him to remove her vest and girdle around her waist. But he didn't bother. His hand slipped through the material to a slit between her thighs and then he had full access to her.

Ever so gently he parted her folds. She shivered with impatience. She was so ready for him. And yet he seemed determined to advance at a snail's pace. Keeping her hands on his thighs while he teased her breasts and taunted her was erotic and frustrating and . . . hot.

When she thought she could not wait another second . . . he pulled back. "I must be certain you understand what comes next."

She ground her teeth. "I . . . know . . . what . . . comes next."

He inserted his finger deep between her legs as he stared at her. "You have never made love before."

"This body has never . . . oh, what does it matter? I'm ready." He lightly touched the spot where all her nerve endings centered. "More than ready. Can we please lose the clothes?"

His eyes widened and he broke into a grin. "You don't mind . . . ?"

In one smooth movement, she lifted the vest over her head and shrugged her arms out of the V-necked blouse, letting it drop to her waist. "Better?"

"Oh, yes. You are lovely." A flush rose up his bronzed cheeks.

She leaned toward his chest, brushing her breasts against him. Rocking forward, she increased the pressure of the finger inside her and it was her turn to flush. She thought he'd have to release her so she could completely disrobe, but he ripped away the rest of the garment, leaving her naked, sitting on his lap with her legs parted, his finger probing her slick heat.

"Your turn." Once again, her hand went to the cord of his pants. This time, he didn't stop her.

It wasn't easy with him caressing her, but she took her time, loosening the knot and playing with the flesh at his waistband. She let the material slide down, stroking each inch of newly revealed skin.

When he placed his palms on her bottom and stood, his pants dropped to the floor. He lifted her onto his sex, and she wrapped her legs behind his back, positioned herself over his tip and slowly lowered herself onto him.

"You're . . . going to be . . . a tight . . . fit," she murmured, pleased by his fullness.

"Am I hurting you?" He gripped her bottom. Sweat beaded on his forehead.

"Sit on the bed. Play with me," she demanded.

"Where?"

She took his hand and placed it between her thighs. And as he stroked, she raised her hips, lowered herself onto him, taking in another inch of flesh.

"Careful," he warned.

She lifted her mouth for a kiss. His tongue and hands danced and teased and taunted. Again, she lifted her hips, and this time she dropped, taking all of him into her. A brief pain melted into the pleasure of his caresses and then she was tilting her hips, riding him, taking them both where she wanted to go.

Incredible friction. Incredible heat. And a need for completion robbed her of all thoughts but one.

As her body peaked, rolled, and exploded with her pleasure, the Shimmering shield popped into place. It was her explosion that fed into him that seemed to release the force field. This time the Shimmering was shiny, brighter, tightly woven—and as if their pleasure had transformed the shield, she could see through it.

And as he exploded into her and she found her pleasure—the shattering freed her astral mind from her body. As the last tingles of pleasure receded from her mind, she was aware she was no longer in her body. He was no longer in his, either.

Somehow, on the astral plane their spirits had merged into one. His thoughts swirled. His memories entered her head as if they were her own.

What's going on? she asked, as his thoughts and memories streamed through her—memories of his parents, a boyhood filled with loving approval and a big happy family, years of worrying about the *Zorash,* and guilt over Ciel's death.

It's the Shimmering.

This didn't happen last time. Last time, they'd remained in the dark, behind a force field. Last time she hadn't felt his mind in hers and hers in his. She saw his best boyhood friend as a child, a fellow student and a warrior who now had a family of his own. After Ciel's death, Daveck had denied himself any chance of normalcy. His honorable nature had coped with her death by punishing himself with harsh years of warrior training, and he'd dedicated himself to become a Sanroyai, despite the personal costs. The deep horror and guilt over Ciel's death permeated his waking thoughts, cloaking his sunny disposition in sadness. She felt his determination to make a new life and his commitment to Sanroyai training, only to have the disturbing weather patterns bring him to his search for the *Zorash* . . . and her.

And now she knew why he'd believed she would have to tell him the truth after marriage. There could be no lying to a person when they linked minds within the Shimmering.

Last time we weren't married. He tensed, both fascinated and dismayed. *You told me the truth. You are* . . . *Sandra. How can this be?*

I suspect the Zorash brought me here, but I'm only guessing. You believe me now, don't you?

She needed to hear him admit that she wasn't crazy. That somehow the impossible had happened. She needed to hear him think it for her own sanity.

Yes. I believe you. But I still must find the Zorash.

Talk about determination. *I would tell you—if I knew. You could see it in my mind if I knew.*

I know that now. Soothing peace bathed her. She didn't know if she was at peace with her past or if he'd calmed her because *he* was at peace. They had merged so that she wasn't sure what was her thought or emotion and what was his.

But now that she was back in the astral state, this might be her opportunity to go home.

Obviously he picked right up on that thought. *You cannot leave. You must help me find the Zorash or all on Farii will die.*

But as you now know, I don't know where your precious Zorash is. Damn it. There was a down side to not being able to keep one's thoughts to oneself. *If Lira knew, she took the knowledge with her when she left.*

Then we must find Lira.

How? Already she could feel them losing the astral state, being drawn back to their bodies. Perhaps her fear of never going home was drawing her there. Or perhaps his failure to find the Zorash was tugging them back to their bodies. But as their astral spirits parted, his disappointment and determination to find the Zorash stayed with her.

His will, his strength of purpose, astounded her. Daveck was a man so strong that he was almost beyond petty concerns. So strong that he could overlook their cultural differences. So strong he could accept that she might follow her own will, her own path. His strength freed her to be herself.

And that changed everything. Because he'd seen her true self, her workaholic tendencies, her need to make a difference in the world with her journalism career, and he'd accepted. She'd actually felt his every reaction, shock and wonderful approval. And she knew deep in her mind and whatever this body had for a heart that this man would never seek to limit her dreams.

He might actually support them. Now there was a novel idea. Because Daveck wanted his people to change, too. But first that required stability, finding the *Zorash* and replacing the idol.

After the joining of souls she'd just experienced, Sandra committed herself to his cause. No way could she leave without helping him. His mission had somehow become her own.

Chapter Nine

"I'm sorry I didn't believe you." Daveck paced her bedroom, his long strides taking him from the closed door back to the bed in just a few steps.

"It's okay." She couldn't be angry with the man—not after sharing his past, his character, his very self. She knew how much his responsibility to his people weighed on him and couldn't help but admire his commitment. She understood his entire purpose was tied into saving Farii. And to do that, he'd do whatever he must, even sacrifice any chance of his own personal happiness, to find the *Zorash*.

Before she'd shared his spirit, she'd been attracted to Daveck, but in their one joining she'd learned more about him than she knew about any other being. And she couldn't help respecting his determination.

"Tell me more about the *Zorash*. I had the impression it was a religious idol, but . . . to you it's so much more, isn't it?"

"Sanroyai warriors believe the idol is an ancient device constructed a millennium ago by beings who have moved on to the astral plane. Before they left, they built the *Zorash* to watch over those who stayed behind to live on Farii. The idol's placement at the base of the sacred megalith allows it to tap vast resources we do not comprehend. It's a sacrilege against all our people for Maglek to use it for his own greed." He paced, stopped, and rested his hands on his hips. "If we make love again, the Shimmering might let us search for Lira."

"Where would we look? We have no idea where she went."

"She's our only lead."

"No. She's not." She peered at him, watched his head jerk up, his nostrils flare. Clearly, he was not a man accustomed to others openly disagreeing with him. But perhaps he'd seen as much of her as she'd seen of him and understood she wouldn't abide being treated as less than an equal. "Maglek stole the *Zorash* and has it still. Why don't we go to him?"

"He uses the *Zorash* against anyone who tries to take it."

"Even against his own daughter?" she asked, her heart pounding at the idea of impersonating Lira. But even if the father knew his daughter better than anyone, he wouldn't suspect Sandra was now inhabiting his daughter's body—unless the *Zorash* passed on the information. Doubts filled her, but so did a certainty that this was the right course of action. The *Zorash* had pulled her to Farii for a reason. Why would the idol betray her now? She could feel a bright light of confidence urging her on, much stronger than her own good instincts when she was on the trail of a story. This feeling was intense, powerful and warming, and so strong in uplifting emotions that she wondered if the *Zorash* had suggestive powers. Was the idol leading her to it? Or fooling her into thinking what Maglek wanted her to?

But even if the *Zorash* had no extraordinary powers at

all, could she trick Maglek about her true identity long enough to find the *Zorash*? She did not know. But it seemed as if the *Zorash* might have brought her to Farii for this very reason. And that frightened her as much as it excited her. On Earth, she'd become a reporter because she wanted to make a difference. On Farii, if she and Daveck succeeded, they could change the fate of all who lived here.

Daveck's big hands clenched and unclenched as he eyed her. "You would face Maglek—even knowing he uses the *Zorash* for his own evil?"

"Maglek thinks I'm his daughter, Lira," she reminded him. "To convince him I'm Lira shouldn't be that difficult. Let's just hope the *Zorash* hasn't shared Lira's disappearance with Maglek."

"You would be walking straight into danger."

"Tell me something I don't know," she muttered.

"My lady, I'm not certain if your words are courageous . . . or reckless—"

"Probably both."

"—but I will not let you go alone." His solid voice comforted her.

She appreciated his sentiment. She'd like nothing better than his company as she faced his enemy. "But surely Maglek will recognize you and be suspicious?"

"I will tell him that I am displeased with my wife. That I will sell you to the border tribes as is my right—unless he makes me a better offer."

Daveck would never sell her to the border raiders. Now that she'd been inside his head she understood he was too honorable for such a deed, but Maglek wouldn't know that. "Maglek doesn't care about Lira's welfare or he wouldn't have used her to get to you. And if you walk right into his trap, he will kill you."

He shook his head. "Maglek only wants to capture and confine me. Not even your father would dare to kill a San-royai warrior, a guardian of the *Zorash,* without violent provocation—if he did, the *Zorash* would have the power to turn against him."

"He could take you prisoner."

"I'm counting on his locking me in his dungeons." He held her gaze and shrugged. "His doing so will give you time to search his household."

"Surely he will not give me the freedom to search where I please."

"I'm certain he won't." Daveck gave her a strained, apologetic look. "However, when he sees the way I treat you—I'll have to be harsh—I hope he'll believe you hate me as he does. If you are careful and cunning, you might make him believe you are on his side."

She shivered, the knowledge that Maglek wouldn't kill him but could nevertheless do him great harm worrying her. "And what good can you do from a dungeon?"

"I will find a way out. Even if I don't escape, Maglek will focus his thoughts on me . . . not you."

She saw certainty in his eyes that he would be forced to suffer before he shut down his emotions. Perhaps she wouldn't have been able to read him so easily if not for the sharing of his mind. But she understood that he believed he had no choice.

"Perhaps I can bribe a guard to free you. Or do so myself."

He shook his head. "You must not attempt to help me— not until you find the *Zorash*." His voice rasped across her heart and she shivered.

"I understand."

He gripped her shoulders. "I will have your promise. You will not free me until you have found the *Zorash*."

"I don't make promises I may not be able to keep."

He folded his arms across his chest. "Then we stay here, make love, and use the Shimmering to search for Lira."

His suggestion that they make love again sounded so appealing that she almost agreed. But she recalled her long journey from Earth as well as the vast expanses of Farii's lands and oceans and realized the hopelessness of finding one astral spirit.

Placing her hands behind her back, she crossed her fingers. "All right. I promise to find the *Zorash* before I attempt to free you."

Relief and pain filled his eyes as if he realized how hard it had been for her to say the words. "Thank-you."

"You may not be thanking me if you are forced to languish in his dungeons," she warned.

"And you might be pleased I'm there after I'm forced to publicly humiliate you."

"Why would you—?"

"A spectacle will cause gossip to travel far and wide, all the way to Maglek, that all is not well with his daughter's marriage. It will make us showing up on his doorstep more believable."

Her mouth went dry. "What do you want me to do?"

"It will be better if you don't know. Just remember, that outwardly I can give you no signal that my actions will cause my heart to weep at what I do."

She understood the need to plant seeds of discord between them. And in truth, if she hadn't shared his noble spirit she was not sure she could have trusted him enough to go through with his plan. "All right. Tell me what the *Zorash* looks like."

"I can do better." From a pocket he withdrew an artist's ink rendering.

She stared at the *Zorash*. A black cube on the bottom served as a base for a sphere that resembled Farii from space. "How big is it?"

Daveck gestured with his hands, indicating the *Zorash* was about the dimensions of a hardback book and could easily be hidden in a medium-sized purse. She stared at the drawing and noticed the artist had drawn something that looked like an aura around the *Zorash*. "What's that?"

"The Shimmering. According to legend, the *Zorash* instigates Sanroyai warriors' abilities to use the Shimmering. We don't know if it's true or how it works. But thousands of years ago, our civilization was more technological. Some of us left this world to colonize. Others stayed behind to guard the *Zorash*."

"Why are you less technologically advanced now?" she asked.

He released a long sigh. "There was a revolution. A shift from a society that depended on one dictator to many lesser leaders. During that time, much was lost . . . but we gained many freedoms—some of which led to the selfishness and greed that allowed Maglek to use the *Zorash* for his own purposes." He handed her a new set of clothes. "Tomorrow we leave on our journey. It is time to begin to plant the rumors."

Wishing she had a choice, she dressed and placed her hand in his. "Where are we going?"

"To the square. It's where men declare their displeasure with their wives."

"And where do wives declare their displeasure with their husbands?" she asked, already suspecting she wasn't going to like the answer.

"All husbands are perfect." A smile revealed he was teasing and his eyes danced with humor.

"It's a good thing I no longer have a weapon in my hand," she growled.

"Actually, women have the same right to complain about their husbands," he admitted—before her blood pressure shot up dangerously high.

"So we're going to the square to have a public fight?" She gave him a sidelong glance, worried that he didn't want to explain. "While you were sifting through my mind, did you come across the fact I was on my high school debate team? Or that when I'm cornered I tend to use a lot of sarcasm?"

"Feel free to insult me as much as you like."

Her nerves drew taut. She really didn't like the confidence in his tone. And the fact that this was a mock fight, only reassured her . . . a little.

But she squared her shoulders and held her chin high, determined to play her part.

DAVECK TUGGED SANDRA into the public square. His men guarded the perimeter, watching over the uneasy crowd that had come to watch the spectacle. Although Maglek's daughter was one of their own, Lira was from an old and wealthy house. She'd been privately schooled, didn't have to work, never went hungry and wore only the finest of clothes. And many people here would enjoy what Daveck would do—however, he was not one of them.

His stomach churned. He reminded himself that his task was necessary, minor in the face of the gathering thunderstorms that flooded the land and ruined their crops. And as the ground itself shuddered beneath his feet, he knew he couldn't delay.

They climbed the steps to the platform. Lights focused on them. Cameras would record her every expression and blow it up on giant screens for the masses outside who couldn't all squeeze within the square.

He hadn't spoken of what he must do because he needed her emotions to read true. And though her Earth customs would make the humiliation easier for her to bear than for a woman of Farii, it still would be difficult. Best to get it done.

Placing a hand on her shoulder, he forced her to her knees. Eyes wide, head high, she stared at the crowd, unblinking. Waiting.

Not wanting to miss one word, the crowd hushed.

Daveck waited an extra few beats of silence, allowing the tension to gather. Pulling a dagger from his belt, he stated loudly. "My wife does not please me."

"And my husband does not please me," Sandra spoke up. At her words, several women in the crowd gasped. Men cursed and snorted to show their outrage.

Daveck restrained a grin. This woman was the most independent thinker he'd ever known. When he'd been inside her head, if she hadn't been so feminine and filled with bright emotions, he might have mistaken her thoughts for those of . . . a warrior. After all, she'd fought many battles—with words.

"Maglek's poison has infested his daughter."

"Prove it," she demanded, raising an eyebrow.

"She did not come to the marriage joining with a pure heart."

"And how would you know the purity of my heart?" she countered.

"See how she questions me? There is no trust in her."

"Trust must be earned."

"As a Sanroyai warrior, I speak the truth. This lady is unfit." He raised his blade for all to see, and then held it to her neck. "As I made the ritual tribute, I renounce your wifely privileges."

"As far as I can see, being your wife has no privileges."

He raised the knife to her hair, slashed through the ties. Her long hair fell over her shoulders, rippled down her back, cascaded to her waist. Gathering her hair roughly in one hand, he lifted it from her neck, and then slashed it off at her nape. Sandra didn't move. Didn't utter a word of protest.

The crowd went strangely silent.

Then several women began to weep. Others murmured.

Her beautiful hair fell to the dirt and she stared straight ahead unblinking, stoic. He hoped the crowd believed her reaction was shock.

When he reached under her arm to lift her to her feet, she had no difficulty standing. Very careful not to so much as scratch her flesh, he tore the sleeves from her garment. He slashed several tears across the material—a sign of dishonor and humiliation.

She didn't move. And then she held out her hand, eyes glinting with annoyance. "My turn."

"I don't understand."

"It's my turn to use the knife."

She was going too far. But then it was his fault. Perhaps he should have explained. Maybe then she could have squeezed out a fake tear. For in reality, she looked much closer to stabbing him than she did to crying.

"You ask for too much," he refused her.

"I'm not asking. Are you afraid I might draw blood?"

By the *Zorash,* she was magnificent. And he'd wanted a spectacle—well, she'd given him one. If she'd wept like every other disgraced wife, it would never have caused the gossip to spread as far and wide as her bold behavior. He only prayed that those who knew Lira wouldn't suspect that Sandra was an imposter.

He handed her the knife, hilt first. For one second he thought she might request that he kneel. She didn't. Instead she lifted her arms, placed the knife by his neck, and neatly cut off one lock. Unlike him, she didn't let it fall to the ground. She captured his hair in her palm, clenched it tightly between her fingers.

"I renounce your husbandly privileges," she spoke clearly, then resheathed his knife in his belt and walked away, back straight, head high, shoulders squared.

And as he watched her leave, he had to fight back a smile. After sharing her mind during the Shimmering, he'd known she was his match in every way. What surprised him . . . was that her courage stole his breath, healed old scars, and assuaged his soul.

And he was about to let this woman—whom he admired more than any other—walk straight into danger.

Chapter Ten

During the two-week journey to Maglek's residence, Sandra learned how to ride a *gangra*. The giant marsupials covered about eight miles an hour, even during slashing rainstorms that turned the roads into mud pits, and their steady gait made riding in their pouches an experience to which she'd soon adjusted. And the passing towns and villages with their odd combinations of modern sewage systems and wide boulevards and old-fashioned transportation fascinated her.

The Farii people had no computers, phones, or fax machines, but generated electricity for heating and lighting. Daveck told her factories were underground and mostly automated, bringing resources from mines by maglev trains to manufacture many household goods. And yet she also saw children playing simple ball games with sticks, sheeplike creatures roaming the streets, and farmers carting their produce to local markets.

After their public fight, she and Daveck both remained careful to retain an icy demeanor in the public inns where they spent their nights. But once alone, Daveck treated her so well that she was already dreading when her time on Farii would end.

How ironic that she'd never found a man on Earth she'd gotten along so well with and then, on another planet, she'd met an alien who seemed to understand what she needed before she knew herself. Perhaps their mind-sharing during the Shimmering had brought them much closer. Perhaps it was their isolation from others during their journey. Or perhaps it was their sometimes tender, sometimes wild, but always wondrous lovemaking. She was falling for Daveck—falling hard.

And the compromise that she'd always thought would stifle her independence wasn't a problem very often. Daveck had a knack for discerning which Farii customs would irritate her and which she could accept, making the journey more of an adventure than a hardship. Commitment to his cause and to him was easier than she'd believed possible since his quest to find the *Zorash* had become her own—especially after she'd experienced fierce storms of fist-sized hail, water spouts that sucked sea creatures from the deep and rained them down upon the travelers miles inland. She'd seen fields of stunted crops, the flooded lowlands, the mudslides in the hills that ruined the valleys below. Seen the city folk fighting over the few foodstuffs that were for sale at exorbitant prices. Tears came to her eyes at the sight of children so gaunt, their eyes seemed too mature for their sad faces.

But as they neared Maglek's residence, the scenery changed along with the weather. Armed patrols kept the masses from entering and only Lira's status as Maglek's daughter allowed them to pass where most others were turned back at the city gates. In the border lands, the skies grew sunny with predictable and gentle morning showers. Daveck told her that all of Farii had once been as prosperous—before the weather had changed. The land turned green, the crops thrived, and the children's faces glowed—and yet, she sensed a fear in these people, a failure to greet strangers or look them in the eye, almost as if they were ashamed of their own prosperity when the rest of Farii suffered.

And as they traveled, Sandra's certainty that the *Zorash* was near grew stronger. It was almost as if she shared a connection with the alien totem and that it called to her on a level she didn't understand but couldn't deny. The compulsion to find the *Zorash* drove her so strongly that sometimes she wondered if her mind sharing during the Shimmering had caused Daveck's quest to root into her brain. And sometimes she believed she alone had a direct connection to the *Zorash*—that the ancient device had chosen her and drawn her across the galaxy for a purpose all its own. When they finally arrived at Maglek's residence perched on the peak of a mountain that overlooked a tiny town, she filled with excitement, fear, and a sense of destiny—that she was meant to be here on this world, in this time and place.

Soldiers guarded the only route to Maglek's residence, a gated road too steep for the *gangras* to travel. The soldiers disarmed Daveck, who handed over his weapons without protest. From this point they would walk, escorted by Maglek's men, who clearly had no fondness for the Sanroyai warrior, and their suspicion of him worried her.

The three-story residence made of concrete-like material and silver reflective glass looked surprisingly modern, with sweeping balconies that overlooked the prosperous lands and cities in a panoramic view. Maglek's soldiers directed them to an elevator on the lower level of the home, then left them alone.

Sandra steeled herself to meet Lira's father, wishing she had more information about their relationship. However, not even Fexel had been able to shed much light on when father and daughter had last seen one another—never mind any history between them. And while her sense of the *Zorash* was stronger than ever since her journey began, she also sensed a darkness, a dampening of the *Zorash,* almost as if Maglek cast a black shadow over the totem's essence.

When the elevator door opened with a swish, a short man with dark gray hair and a goatee, black eyes, and untamed eyebrows waited for them to exit. Maglek. Even if she hadn't recognized him from a portrait, Sandra would have known his identity from the aura of power that emanated from the man, a power so strong he didn't bother keeping his guards close—as if he possessed a mental superiority that could overpower Daveck's warrior skills. Which meant he was probably drawing on power from the *Zorash.*

With her pulse fluttering, it wasn't difficult to make her voice sound frantic. "Father. Thank you for—"

"Why have you come?" Maglek's intelligent eyes dismissed her and settled on Daveck.

Daveck kept his tone impersonal. "As prescribed by Farii law, I'm offering her to you before I sell her to the border tribes."

"Her mother brought me no pleasure. I'm not surprised her whelp is no different." Maglek insulted her and yet, Sandra glimpsed anger there, enough to raise her hopes that Maglek might take Lira's side and allow her to stay long enough to search for the *Zorash*.

Daveck didn't so much as glance in her direction and kept his tone impersonal. "With the credits from her sale, I will be able to buy badly needed food for my people."

"Idiot. You've brought me damaged goods. With her hair shorn, I'll have to keep her for years before I can sell her for a decent price." Maglek motioned for his guards to step forward. "Take the Sanroyai to rot in my dungeons."

Daveck raised an eyebrow. "I came here according to our law. You have no right to make me a prisoner."

Maglek glowered. "Did you think I would not guess at your plan to force me into an alliance by marrying my daughter? Well, Maglek isn't interested in sharing his power or his wealth with the likes of a Sanroyai warrior. Take him away so Maglek doesn't have to look at him."

Sandra kept her eyes down so Maglek couldn't read her roiling emotions. If he recognized her anger and attributed it to its true cause, a woman's worth being measured by the length of her hair, he might suspect all was not as it seemed. Their plan was working and Maglek seemingly had no clue of the real reason for their marriage. His odd way of speaking of himself in the third person annoyed her, but she was relieved that he seemed to be accepting their story that the marriage was unsuccessful.

Sandra reminded herself not to grow too confident. Maglek hadn't achieved his position of power by acting stupidly. She couldn't afford to assume that greed and cunning detracted from his intelligence. And with Daveck locked up, she was on her own, at least physically—but mentally she sensed a link of support that didn't diminish as the guards escorted him to the dungeons.

"Thank you, Father."

"Silence." Maglek back-handed her across the face so hard, he split her lip and she tasted blood. "Say another word and I'll give you to the first passing beggar for his own personal slave."

It took every ounce of determination not to spit her blood in his face. Instead, she hung her head, kept her eyes downcast, sick that this monster would treat his own daughter with such brutality. No wonder Lira had left.

I'm still here. Lira's aura appeared to Sandra as clearly as the day she'd arrived on Farii.

Sandra wondered if she'd finally lost it. After being dragged from Earth, finding herself in a new body, wedding Daveck, and facing Maglek, she'd finally gone insane.

You've done better than I could have done, Lira assured her. *The Zorash is in the garden. Tonight during Maglek's evening meal, you must steal the Zorash.*

It can't be that simple.

Fail and you will die.

Lira disappeared, but her message stayed with Sandra as Maglek roughly gripped her arm, shoving her into a room so hard she fell and cracked her knee against the stone floor. He slammed the door behind her, arrogantly assuming that she'd follow his orders. But as soon as the pain in her knee receded, she scrambled to the door, tested her situation. He hadn't bothered to lock it.

Even if her knee swelled to twice its size, even if she had to crawl and drag her leg behind her, tonight, she would go to the garden. In his arrogance, Maglek had made a mistake. He'd underestimated his "daughter."

Chapter Eleven

Daveck trudged with his shoulders slumped in defeat, dragged his steps and kept his head down, hoping his body attitude would convey meekness to his guards. However, after he heard Maglek strike Sandra, mastering his fury and maintaining his submissive demeanor took every speck of Sanroyai control. He vowed Maglek would pay a hundredfold for every pain he caused Sandra.

And meanwhile he harnessed his rage, waiting for the opportunity to take out his guards. He couldn't allow them to lock him inside the dungeons. Because once there—escape would become much more difficult.

They took a stairwell and he tensed to make his move, but a contingent of men entered the steps from another level and Daveck delayed his attack. The two groups passed, the other group of men avoiding Daveck's gaze—as if his bad luck could rub off on them.

Patience.

He waited until they left the stairwell and headed down a long hallway with dim lighting and many closed doors. The stale air reeked of unwashed bodies, urine, and . . . fear. Behind a door he heard a muffled high-pitched scream. Beside him, the guards didn't so much as flinch, as if torture and misery were a common occurrence.

Up ahead, two more guards stood outside a massive metal-barred door. Once they locked Daveck inside, escape would be impossible. With four armed men against his two bare fists, he had to make securing a weapon his first priority. Yet, there was no place to take cover. Nowhere to duck and hide. No weapon to steal.

He had no choice. If he was going to make a move—it would have to be now. Daveck called upon his Sanroyai skills, automatically forming a battle stance that allowed him to shift, attack, or defend with minimal effort. With fingers extended and curled slightly to parry or slice, he spun, kicked, and took out one guard with his foot, another with his left hand, the third with his right. But the fourth guard slammed in a blow to Daveck's head. Luckily the guard didn't go for his blaster. A mistake. Daveck ducked with the force of the blow, deflecting most of the damage, then caught the guy with a hammer strike to the temple.

AT FIRST SANDRA worried she wouldn't know when the dinner hour arrived. No one brought her any food, but then she smelled the scent of cooking meat and concluded she should soon begin her search for the *Zorash*.

Before she could exit her room, her door opened. Her pulse rocketed. And fear tightened her throat at the thought that she'd waited too long and lost her opportunity.

She raised her eyes to see Daveck. Relief and happiness lightened her spirit. She hadn't realized how much she'd hated the idea of leaving this room and exploring on her own until he'd showed up sporting a black eye and several cuts. He'd never looked so good.

Ignoring the pain in her injured knee, Sandra hobbled over to him, flung her arms around him, nestled against his chest, and took comfort from the strong beat of his heart and the solid feel of his powerful body. His arms closed around her and despite their dangerous circumstances, for one moment, she felt safe, as if she'd come home and belonged.

"You all right?" They both asked one another at the same time.

She recovered first, pulling back and wincing at the sight of an ugly, oozing gash behind his ear. "I banged up my knee but I can walk. You look like you've been in a war."

He pressed a hand gun into her palm. "I escaped shortly after I left you, but I had to hide in a closet until the shift change. We need to go now—before they discover I'm not locked up."

"The *Zorash* is in the garden," she told him.

"Maglek let you see it?"

"Lira's astral spirit told me where to go." After sharing her mind, she knew instinctively that no matter how impossible her words sounded, he'd believe her and she took great comfort in his immediate trust.

"Lira also told me where to find you," he admitted.

Wow. Lira's astral spirit had contacted him, too. Considering she'd left her body to avoid Daveck, she'd come a long way as an astral spirit. And Daveck had changed as well.

Sandra was pleased he'd handed her a weapon, and felt so much better now that she didn't have to search the garden for the *Zorash* alone. She staggered after Daveck, who headed straight down a hallway, through the back of the foyer, and into a courtyard open to a twilight sky of deep dusky rose.

Maglek's residence surrounded the courtyard on four sides and reminded her of the architecture in New Orleans. However, there was no Southern charm here. Many of the plants looked dead. The earth was black. They had no difficulty finding the *Zorash*. The idol sat on a marble-like pedestal in the center of a sand garden.

Daveck had shown her a picture of the *Zorash* before— a black cube base that supported a replica of Farii from space. But she hadn't expected the outside to be clear crystal or the insides to look like computer circuitry. He'd told her the ancients had built the device, but she'd expected a religious icon—not a supercomputer chip.

I am much more than a computer chip. The thought from the *Zorash* flowed into her head.

And like recognizing a familiar voice, she knew immediately that the thought came from the idol. *What are you? Why did you bring me to Farii? Why did you let Maglek use you for ill purposes?*

Like your computers, I must follow my programs. I cannot cause harm through action—

You caused harm through inaction, she countered, wondering if Daveck were privy to this telepathic communication.

I brought you here to save Farii. Your reward is . . . love.

What? Stunned, her thoughts swirled. She'd always believed that something had brought her here and the idol had just confirmed her suspicions. The astral projection machine hadn't allowed her to return to Earth because the *Zorash* had grabbed her, led her to Lira's body.

And her reward was love? Angry, scared, shocked, Sandra wished she could think with a clear head. Was the *Zorash* right? Did she love Daveck?

They might not have known one another for long, but she'd shared his mind. Knew him better than she'd ever known anyone. And she'd liked what she'd seen. She'd admired his cause from the start, but she'd also learned that along with his determination he was generous, protective, loving. And he'd accepted her as an equal, a partner.

She didn't know when she'd fallen for him, maybe during the Shimmering. But she had fallen for him. Hard.

She loved Daveck. A Sanroyai soldier. A warrior. An alien.

Before she could think through the ramifications of what her feelings meant to her future, Daveck placed his hand on her shoulder and approached the *Zorash*. "We need to leave."

"Too late." Maglek stalked into the garden, a scowl knotting his brow, his mouth a tight line, his eyes lit with a combination of fanaticism and power. Twenty armed men spread out around the perimeter, surrounding them.

Once again they were trapped. If Daveck had a getaway plan he'd failed to mention it to her.

"Ready weapons," Maglek ordered.

The soldiers aimed their guns at Sandra and Daveck like a firing squad. Sandra's mouth went dry, her knees shook. Automatically she stepped closer to Daveck and closed her eyes. If she was to die in this body, she wanted Daveck to know how she felt. "I love you."

Daveck swept Sandra up next to the *Zorash* and snapped the Shimmering shield around the *Zorash*, Sandra, and him. In her surprise and fear, she'd forgotten his ability to protect her. For the moment, they were safe, but the clear shield reminded her they were trapped, surrounded by Maglek and his soldiers. And this time, Daveck's own men weren't coming to rescue them.

"So what's the escape plan?" she asked, remembering to hold still. The Shimmering might protect them but she didn't want to lose a limb by touching it.

"According to ancient texts, the *Zorash* protects Sanroyai warriors above all others."

"That's it?" He'd just bet their lives on an ancient text?

"Fire," Maglek ordered.

Bullets rained on the Shimmering. She held her breath, but the shield held. And then a bolt of electricity flashed from the *Zorash* to the Shimmering and . . . for a second the shield crackled with silvery electrical energy. And then metal objects, knives, and swords flew toward the Shimmering. With a clang, the metal objects attached themselves to the shield, and she suspected the *Zorash* had magnetized the shield.

Release me, the *Zorash* demanded.

"How?" she asked.

"I didn't . . ." Daveck answered her, obviously thinking she'd asked about how he caused the shield's strange affinity for metal, then frowned. "The Shimmering is changing. It's losing integrity."

"Hold on," she pleaded.

Release me.

How?

Release me. Hurry. He can't hold the shield much longer.

Tell me what to do. As she pleaded with the idol for more information, the shield thinned, weakening. Beside her Daveck trembled, straining with effort, putting out tremendous mental energies. Sweat beaded on his brow and neck. His heavy corded thighs quivered and his shoulders tensed as if he carried an enormous weight.

Release me.

Sandra traced her fingers over the idol's spherical crystal, followed the smooth lines to the cool black base of the cube. Her finger slipped into a notch. She tugged.

The Shimmering thickened. The idol appeared to levitate into her hands, weighing almost nothing, as if gravity didn't affect it. And the Shimmering shield, with them and the *Zorash* inside, began to rise off the ground.

"Stop them," Maglek shouted, voice bellowing, lips spitting spray as his fury raged. But his men cowered back in fear of the idol, their eyes wide with terror and awe. Some of them made a religious gesture, touching forehead, lips, and breast.

What's happening? she asked.

Tell Daveck to maintain the shield.

She repeated the *Zorash*'s command to Daveck, although she didn't think it necessary. Daveck maintained his efforts, despite their strange ascent. Sweat trickled over his brow and his breath came in great, shuddering gasps.

His voice cracked with his effort. "I can't keep this up much longer."

The shield with them inside rose higher, perhaps a full meter above the ground. Then they started to spin. At first they spun slowly, then faster and faster until Sandra's head ached with dizziness.

"Nooo," Maglek screamed. "You won't escape." Like a maddened bull, he charged the sphere, jumping into the air, hands grasping at the spinning shield. He managed to cling to a sword that stuck to the shield due to the magnetic forces.

As if the added weight made the task more difficult, Daveck shuddered. Sandra's gut tightened against the nausea.

And then the world . . . shifted.

One moment they were in the garden, the next they were spinning so fast she couldn't see past the shield. Luckily for her churning stomach, the spinning didn't last long, slowing as suddenly as it had begun. And when she could once again focus, she saw they were no longer at Maglek's residence but in a desolate valley filled with a sweeping vista of trees and grasslands. Outside the shield, gray clouds swirled in tornado-like patterns, picking up leaves, branches, tree trunks, and car-sized boulders before tossing the debris hundreds of yards away.

In the distance, she spied mountains with snow-covered peaks. And through the windstorm and rain, Maglek still clung to the sword and the Shimmering shield, but when he spied solid ground, he released his grip and dropped to the dirt.

The Shimmering landed at the base of a megalith made of the same black polished stone as the *Zorash*'s cubed base. Clearly, the *Zorash* had brought them back to its home, where it belonged, where it could re-establish control of Farii's weather.

Release me.

Carefully, she set the *Zorash* on the platform designed to hold it and heard a whirring click. The *Zorash* glowed a dull orange.

Daveck, shaking and exhausted, finally dropped the Shimmering shield. Weapons fell to the dirt at their feet. Grabbing his opportunity, Maglek leaped forward to seize a blaster and a sword. But lightning popped in the air, a bolt from the *Zorash* directing fierce energy at the blaster. The scent of burning plastic combined with Maglek's howl of pain, and he dropped the scorched weapon. Frustrated and enraged, Maglek lunged at Daveck with his sword.

Drained from holding the shield for so long, Daveck scrambled to respond, his arm shaking, his fingers fumbling, his reflexes slow and clumsy. Terrified Maglek would strike before Daveck could defend himself, Sandra stuck out her foot, tripping Maglek and giving Daveck a precious second to retrieve a weapon.

Shaking off his stupor and exhaustion, Daveck shoved her behind him and met Maglek's blade with his own—just in time to defend himself. While Daveck was younger, bigger, and possessed more muscles, he'd just tapped all his energy by holding up the Shimmering shield. And Maglek's strength was fueled by anger at losing the *Zorash* and insane determination to recover it.

Heart thumping up her throat, Sandra feared that the longer the battle went on, the less likely were Daveck's chances of survival. Maglek fought hard, his rage making him stronger and faster than she'd have expected.

Scrambling on hands and knees, she searched for a functioning blaster, but the *Zorash* had melted all the weapons. And the swords were so heavy she could barely lift one, never mind use it. Above her head, she glimpsed Maglek's advancing lunges and Daveck's determination to hold position and protect her—but since he was clearly resolute on staying between her and Maglek, her current position was hampering Daveck's freedom of movement, making him an easier target.

She was about to scramble to her feet and move back to give Daveck maneuvering room, when she spied a dagger. Pulse racing, lungs tightening, she grabbed the dagger and rolled away. She didn't dare throw the weapon for fear of hitting Daveck by mistake.

Perhaps she could circle behind Maglek. She had no idea what she could do to help, but she waited, determined to do whatever she could. As Maglek advanced and the two men circled and their swords clanged, it became impossible for Daveck to stay between her and Maglek. She shifted position, first to Maglek's side, then to his back. When Daveck stumbled over a rock and Maglek surged forward, the older man's blade slashing Daveck's side, blood spouted and Daveck fell. He didn't get up. Didn't move. Blood welled along his side, indicating a long and severe gash.

Tears flooded her eyes and rage filled her heart. Maglek

raised his sword to strike the killing blow. Without thought to her own safety, Sandra lunged at his back with the dagger.

As if sensing danger, Maglek flinched away and she stabbed his shoulder. Her effort was enough to cause his sword to strike dirt instead of Daveck. But with a roar of pain Maglek spun, faced her, and raised his sword. She stared into his enraged eyes and realized she was about to die. Sickening fear sapped her strength, caused her knees to buckle.

But Maglek failed to account for her collapse and his sword, which he'd meant to separate her head from her shoulders, whistled over her head.

He wouldn't miss again. She scooted back on her butt, feeling for a rock, a stick, anything she could use as a weapon. But her hands came up empty, except for dirt. She flung the dirt into Maglek's face, knowing it wasn't enough, and waited for death to take her.

"Traitor," Maglek shouted, lifting the sword for a killing blow.

"She fights better than you," Daveck taunted, his voice racked with pain.

Maglek turned once again and Daveck's blade caught him between the ribs, a direct stab to the heart. He was dead before he sagged to the ground.

Relieved she'd survived and that Daveck was alive, she opened her mouth to thank him. But at the sight of so much blood, her relief turned to horror. Daveck had also fallen, his strength gone, the slash at his side enormous.

She crawled near him, terrified that he couldn't live, that she would lose him so soon. A lump rose in her throat and she swallowed back a choking sob. Even as she pleaded, "Daveck, stay with me," she knew he was losing his battle for life.

"Sorry." His eyes closed.

During the sword fight, the tornado had vanished. The gray sky cleared, the rain ceased, and the sun had come out as if to mock her grief. As if the *Zorash* had switched off the bad weather and regulated Farii's climate with one mighty thought, the weather turned balmy.

Desperate, she flung her thoughts at the *Zorash*. *Do something. He saved you. Now, you must save him.*

The breeze blew her hair. Birds flew over her head and cawed. The *Zorash* remained . . . silent.

And then the sphere shot an electric bolt at Daveck's side. Startled, she jerked, furious that after all he'd done, the Zorash would strike him. *You trying to kill him?*

The Zorash remained silent.

Daveck's breath grew faint. His eyes remained closed. The bleeding stopped and she feared these would be his last moments. He was so pale. He'd lost too much blood to recover. Even if Sandra had known what to do, she had no medical supplies and the wound was too severe for her to try to apply pressure to stop the bleeding—yet the bleeding seemed to have stopped on its own.

Numb, exhausted, grieving, she had no idea how long she sat beside Daveck. At one point during her vigil, she realized his breathing was less ragged. Even a bit of color returned to his cheeks. She was afraid to hope for a miracle. Yet the wound at his side seemed to be closing. The far edges possessed a fine pink scar, almost as if a magical zipper were closing his wound.

Lira's aura hovered and Sandra raised her eyes to the spirit whose body she inhabited. *You saved him?*

I encouraged his electromagnetic cell structure to heal itself.

Oh . . . my . . . God. *He's going to live?* The tears she'd held back brimmed over her eyelids. "Daveck, you're going to live."

His eyes fluttered open. He reached for her hand.

You are happy that he will live? Lira's astral aura vibrated with golden pink light, the woman's thoughts going directly into Sandra's mind.

Yes.

Then you wish to stay with him?

I do.

Then you will not mind if I visit your world, and merge with your body?

Of course I don't mind, but I thought you wanted to stay on the astral plane?

Lira's aura brightened. I have met a Romanian prince from Earth and he has convinced me to change my mind.

She sensed happiness in Lira's aura. *You've fallen in love?*

I think so . . . yes.

Good for you. And can I ask a favor? Sandra requested.

Of course.

Tell my friend Liza Mancuso what happened to me and that I am happy here.

Consider it done. Lira vanished.

And Sandra realized she would be happy here on Farii. As a reporter she'd ached to report the news, to change things, to make a difference. With the *Zorash* in place, prosperity would return and she wanted to be there to help steer this world into a more enlightened way of thinking. She wanted to enact laws to protect women, to give them a say in their government, to give them legal value beyond the length of their hair.

Together, she and Daveck could change things on Farii. And she wished Lira the best with her Romanian prince back on Earth. While she'd miss Liza, her friend—who was always telling her that a career was no substitute for a man—would understand. Farii was her home now.

Daveck's eyes searched hers as if sensing something important had happened. "Did you mean it when you said you loved me?"

She didn't have to search her heart. The answer automatically bubbled from her lips. "Yes, I love you."

"Does that mean you no longer resent our marriage?"

"My commitment to a career is no longer a problem."

"And why is that?"

"Because I've found the right man." And she had. She'd lost her career, but she'd found a calling. She wanted to improve the lot of women on this world. And without asking, she knew Daveck would support her efforts. She'd seen his innate sense of fairness during the Shimmering. A fairness that allowed him to accept her for what she was. A woman who only found life fulfilling when she had a cause. Yet a woman filled with love. Somehow the *Zorash* had found her a man to love, to live with for the rest of her days.

"You're certain you don't want to return to Earth? Suppose I agreed to go with you?"

His offer stole her breath. "You would do that? Leave your people for me?"

He nodded. "And not because I owe you." Daveck smiled, pulled her to him and whispered into her mouth, "I love you, too. And any world to your liking would suit me just fine."

She grinned. "There's more to fix here."

"True. But . . ."

"I'm sure." And she was. Daveck belonged on Farii with his people. With their people. Sandra had not just found a new home, but a friend. A partner. A lover. A husband. A whole new life waited for her. The *Zorash* had brought them together. Love would keep them together.

Heart full, Sandra sealed the deal with a kiss, knowing that she belonged here on this world with this man. "Kiss me, Daveck. And then . . ."

"And then?" he whispered, his voice husky with desire.

"Kiss me some more."

BEYOND DREAMS

Elaine Cunningham

*Many thanks to Anna Genoese for letting
a fantasy writer try her hand at romance, to Jozelle Dyer
for exceptionally keen-eyed editing, and to Susan Mates,
who read the manuscript and provided insight and
encouragement.*

*To Judie and Lisa, despite the fact that they're better
looking and more psychic than I am. Better sisters
would be hard to find.*

Chapter One

The woman was alone, just like the others had been, trapped in another small, well-hidden place.

The smell of damp earth gave her prison the feel of an abandoned well. Smooth concrete walls rose ten feet or more from the hard-packed dirt floor to the small wooden shed overhead. A flight of steep wooden stairs had once led up to the heavy door, but the old boards had long since fallen into a half-rotted pile. The only window was far out of reach, small and shuttered. Faint light from a full moon, visible through the shutters' broken slats, reached into the darkness with long, pale fingers, which seemed to linger on the young woman's upturned face.

She was short and curvy, bare-legged and beach-brown. Clad only in a bright pink tank top and matching bikini underwear, she looked like a college student just home from a tropical spring break. Her wavy brown hair hung in lank strands, as if she hadn't washed it for two or three days, but it looked as if it had been carefully finger-combed. A determined woman, judging from the set of her jaw and the rickety ladder she'd pieced together from the ruin of the old stairs and strips of multicolored fabric torn from her discarded skirt.

Her shoulders went back, and her chest rose and fell in a long, steadying breath. She started to climb, slowly and carefully, easing her weight from one creaking rung to the next.

The ladder fell a good three feet short of the window, but when she stretched, she could just reach the windowsill.

As her fingers closed on the old wood, a man's shout of protest rang through the cellar. A man's hands reached out to grab her. To stop her.

The windowsill gave way under her hands, crumbling into splinters and dust. She let out a startled cry and reached down for the ladder. The sudden shift of weight and balance pushed the ladder away from the wall, just as the rung under her feet cracked and sagged.

She tried to jump clear, but her foot caught in the tangle of wood and she succeeded only in changing the direction of the ladder's fall. It rode her down, slamming the back of her head into the concrete wall. Her scream broke off abruptly. She slid down the wall and lay still under the twisted wooden ruin.

In the silence that followed, dust motes and small splinters of wood spiraled lazily down the sloping moonbeams. A dark pool of blood crept out from behind the curtain of the woman's hair and began to spread across the hard-packed dirt floor.

A low, keening moan echoed through the small cellar. Then another, closer this time, followed by the insistent thump of a small, furry forehead against his and the rough, wet drag of a sandpaper tongue across his cheek—

The dream shattered, and suddenly Nick was sitting bolt upright in a tangle of sheets, gasping for breath. His lunge tumbled Cassie's cat off the bed. Swearing in fluent Siamese, the little animal hopped back up and settled down at the edge of the bed, the better to favor Nick with a baleful, blue-eyed glare.

"The girl fell," Nick murmured. "*Fell.* People dream about *falling* all the time, but not the moment of impact."

The Siamese, unimpressed, lifted his hind leg and began to wash—the feline equivalent of a one-fingered salute.

Nick gave the cat an absentminded ear scratch by way of apology, then swung out of bed and headed for the kitchen. His notebook computer was set up on the table there. He'd get no more sleep tonight, so he might as well record this latest dream while the details were still vivid.

He'd seen no reason to record his first nightmare of a woman imprisoned and left to die, but after the second, he wished he'd written down the details—and done so *before* they'd been confirmed by the local news. Only then could he be certain these remembered dreams had actually *been* dreams, and not something quite different.

Now, if only he could define "different."

Déjà vécu, perhaps?

He'd treated two or three people who'd suffered from this malady of memory, a condition that went far beyond the *déjà vu* moments most people experienced from time to time. It turned the mind into a hall of mirrors that projected the present moment back into some newly remembered past. People who developed *déjà vécu* spent much of their lives experiencing events they were *certain* had happened before.

A disturbing theory, but it would explain why the stories of those two abducted women had fit so precisely with Nick's "remembered" dreams. And given his family history, it wouldn't be too surprising if he developed some . . . cognitive anomalies.

But as Nick's fingers flew over the keyboard, his confidence in this tentative explanation faded. Not once had he experienced a waking moment as a replay of some past event. And he could remember thinking about those dreams several times before the details appeared on the news, which was not how *déjà vécu* presented. Also, tonight's dream was different from the first two, significantly so. There was a progression of sorts, a pattern he had yet to discern.

He'd seen the first two prisons through the women's eyes. Tonight he seemed to be standing off to one side, watching. The first two women had been alone, but the hands he'd seen reaching for the girl had been a man's hands.

He leaned back in his chair and considered this. A man's hands. Whose?

A new and terrible possibility struck him like a fist.

Several stunned moments passed before he realized he was shaking his head in mute denial.

No. Not that. It simply wasn't possible.

But it *was* logical, and try as he might, Nick could think of no better explanation. Why else had Hope Anders and Genna Rivers seemed so familiar when he saw their faces on the evening news? How else could he have known how those two women had died, and where their bodies would be found?

Nick pushed away from the table and went to the fridge for a bottle of water. He sipped it while he waited for his hands to stop shaking and his benumbed mind to return to something approaching its normal clarity.

His training told him that vivid, disturbing dreams were often the subconscious mind's attempt to bring something important to the dreamer's attention, but the message of tonight's nightmare eluded him. He stared idly out the window, running through the details again and again as he watched wind-driven clouds speed across a shining half-moon—

In his dream, the moon had been full.

He crossed the room with a few quick strides and checked the wall calendar. Yes, it showed the moon phases. Tonight's moon had just entered its second quarter; the full moon was nearly a week away.

That was the difference! He hadn't dreamed about the other women until after they were dead, but this dreamed-of death hadn't yet occurred.

He still had time to stop it.

Nick reached for his cell phone and asked the 411 operator to connect him to the Providence police.

"The nonemergency number?" she inquired.

He glanced toward the window, which neatly framed the waxing moon. The little brunette's death was still a week away. She hadn't even been abducted yet. Did that qualify as a "nonemergency"?

He settled for a simple "yes" and was connected to the police operator. His request to speak with the investigating officer in the oubliette murders led to several minutes of questions, followed by transfers to other lines and still more questions. Finally he was transferred to a Lieutenant Andreozzi.

"This is Andreozzi," announced a male voice, a young man's voice, blurred by fatigue and strongly flavored with the local accent.

For a moment Nick considered introducing himself as Dr. Romano, a title he seldom used outside of work. It lent an air of credibility, and he was going to need every scrap he could muster. On the other hand, he didn't want to give the impression that his "information" came at the expense of patient confidentiality. He'd rather be thought crazy than unethical.

Be careful what you wish for, warned a remembered voice—a slightly husky alto that even now brought a wistful smile to his face. One memory triggered another, and Nick glanced at the Siamese. The cat had hopped onto the table and was sprawled across the laptop's keyboard, regarding him with an insolent stare. Cassie had said the same thing about the cat, twelve years ago. When the sound of mice holding nocturnal footraces inside the walls had prompted Nick to wish for their eviction and a few quiet nights, Cassie had borrowed her sister Molly's best young mouser. Nimrod stayed; the mice moved out. Two months later, so did Cassie.

The smile dropped off Nick's face.

"Can I help you?" prompted the lieutenant.

Nick dragged himself back to the present. "My name is Nick Romano. I have some information concerning the oubliette murders."

"Go ahead," Andreozzi said wearily.

The detective's reaction didn't surprise Nick. No doubt the police had fielded dozens of crank calls over the past three weeks. Anonymity prompted people to do and say things they otherwise wouldn't. Maybe, Nick mused, Andreozzi would take him more seriously in a face-to-face meeting.

"Perhaps I should come to the station."

"That won't be necessary."

The detective's dismissive tone set Nick's teeth on edge. If he couldn't convince the police to take action *now,* a young woman would die in a few short days.

He took a deep breath and steeled himself for the ordeal to come. "I'm no legal expert, Lieutenant, but I'm fairly certain the D.A. would want you to read me my rights before you hear what I have to say. Can you do that over the phone?"

A short silence followed, interrupted by the soft crackle of the cell phone. "That sounded a lot like a confession."

"Unfortunately," Nick replied softly, "that's exactly what it was."

Chapter Two

Saturday morning was a picture-perfect spring day, and the view from the high school softball field was the sort of image usually found in coffee table books with titles like *Scenic New England.* The little town of East Bay had more than its share of charm, a fact that Cassie O'Malley, despite having been born and raised here, had only recently come to appreciate.

The river that ran through town lay just across the street, a silvery blue ribbon threading through old neighborhoods and shaded by older trees. On its banks stood a pretty wooden church, its tall steeple providing the only hint of white in a cloudless blue sky. A pair of large, sprawling cherry trees framed the walk to the old church, sending small flurries of fragrant pink snow adrift on the morning breeze.

The girls' softball team gathered around their star pitcher, laughing and chattering as they celebrated their latest win. In their bright green and gold uniforms, they resembled a flock of happy parakeets.

A rangy, too-tan blond woman broke away from the group of parents and strode over to Cassie, beaming with maternal pride.

"Kim pitched a good game." Cassie tipped her head toward the tall girl in the midst of the noisy throng.

"She takes after her mother," the woman replied, unconsciously flexing her pitching arm.

Cassie nodded her agreement. Donna Harper was a leftie with a wicked rising fastball. At forty-something, she was still the best pitcher on their church-run league, and for that matter, one of the best pitchers Cassie had ever caught.

Donna's gaze shifted to the short, slightly pudgy girl who was unbuckling her catcher's gear. Her smile dimmed, and she leaned closer to Cassie.

"I'm not going to tell you how to do your job—"

"That'd be a first," Cassie interjected dryly.

This prompted a fleeting grin. "Sports parents—gotta love us! Seriously now, Erica should be catching those low, outside pitches. Riverview scored two runs on passed balls."

Those two pitches had been *very* low and outside, but Donna already knew that. Cassie tried to ignore the welter of *un*-voiced criticism she sensed in Donna's thoughts. Apparently poor Kim was about to get an earful on the drive home.

Cassie shrugged. "Erica's only an inch or two over five feet. She doesn't have much of a stretch."

"You would have caught them, and you're not much taller," Kim's mother said tartly. "And you don't have a teenager's reflexes going for you."

"Also true, but I have to outplay the kids. It's the only way they'll take me seriously."

Donna lifted an eyebrow. "And that works?"

"Not so you'd notice."

The older woman chuckled. "You know I'm kidding about the reflex thing. Seriously, sometimes I think you know what I'm planning to throw before I do!"

Since this observation lay uncomfortably close to the truth, Cassie changed the subject. "You're pitching this Wednesday, right? Ready to kick some Episcopalian butt?"

"Not this week. That's the only night Kim has free, and I promised I'd take her shopping for a prom dress."

Her eyes met Cassie's, and her wistful smile, full of a mother's where-did-the-years-go nostalgia, suddenly froze. Her eyes widened and filled with guilt, and her smile slid away.

There was a reason, Cassie noted resignedly, why people say you can't go home again.

Too many people in the little seacoast town knew about the car crash nearly twenty years ago that had killed three high school seniors on their way home from the prom. Most townies remembered that Cassie was the only survivor.

To ease the moment, Cassie glanced pointedly at Donna's daughter, who was now supervising her teammates in collecting gear and picking up discarded sports drink bottles.

"Better get Kim a green and yellow dress. If she shows up out of uniform, no one will recognize her."

The woman's face relaxed into a smile that mingled relief and amusement. "She'll probably want her nails done in team colors, too."

Their shared chuckle was interrupted by Cassie's phone—the generic ring tone that signified a caller who wasn't in her address book.

"Go ahead and get that," Donna said. "I've got to run."

Cassie nodded acknowledgment, then flipped open the phone and gave her name.

"This is Lieutenant Mark Andreozzi, with the Providence police department," her caller announced. He pronounced his name "Mock," in keeping with the Rhode

Island custom of avoiding the letter "r" whenever possible. "You might not remember, but we met a while back, my first year on the force. I was one of the arresting officers at the back-to-school dance? The one with the keg party in the neighbor's driveway?"

"That was quite a night, even by East Bay standards," Cassie recalled. She flipped through her memory files, checking under "rookie," and came up with an image of a dark-haired man not many years out of high school. Layered beneath that memory was a younger version of Mark, a pudgy little kid whose biggest joy seemed to be tormenting his teenaged sister.

"You're Sandy Andreozzi's brother, right?"

He missed a couple of beats, then commented, "You've got a good memory, Ms. O'Malley."

Too good.

He didn't say the last two words out loud, but Cassie heard them anyway. Since his crisp, professional tone didn't invite reminiscences, Cassie responded in kind. "What can I do for you, Lieutenant?"

"Your name came up during a murder investigation, and we're wondering if you could come down to the station for a few questions."

An invisible fist closed over Cassie's heart. East Bay's quiet, small town pace could be tough on teenagers. Far too many of them turned to alcohol and drugs for entertainment. And with mom and dad both working long hours to pay for their waterfront lifestyle, kids frequently had too much money and too little supervision. Parties were common, and, as Cassie had reason to know, could turn deadly.

"Did something happen to one of my kids? Well, not *my* kids, genetically speaking. I teach at East Bay High."

"No, nothing like that. You're being called in because of your *past* job."

Cassie took a moment to absorb that. "I see," she said slowly.

But she didn't, not really. Several quiet years had

passed since the government's remote viewing program
had been declassified. Books had been written about psychic espionage, but Cassie never seriously expected anyone to make the connection between a small town teacher
and a former spy. That had been a brief interlude in her
life, and since she'd successfully hidden her "talent" for
years, she'd never really expected this day to come.

Andreozzi was waiting for her to continue, but she had
no idea what—

Realization hit her like a runaway SUV. "Oh, crap.
You're calling me about the oubliette murders."

"That's right," he said in a carefully expressionless
tone. Even over the phone, Cassie could sense that he was
trying not to sound as skeptical as he felt.

She took a deep, steadying breath. "And you want me to
consult on all three cases."

"There have only been two."

"Yes, but if the police are desperate enough to contact . . .
someone like me, that means a third woman has been reported missing."

"That's right," he said again. "Problem is, we don't
know who she is."

"How can someone report a woman missing if they
don't know who she is?"

"That's the problem," he agreed. "Well, it's *part* of the
problem. We have a guy here who confessed to the abduc-
tions."

Cassie's eyebrows lifted. "Well, that makes your job a
lot easier."

"You'd think. Problem is, he has alibis for both of the
murders, and he can't tell us who the next victim will be."

"Wait a minute—your guy confessed, but he has alibis?"

"Airtight," he confirmed. "He was out of town when the
first girl was snatched, and he was working round the
clock during the second abduction. But he came in with
this story, so we had to check him out."

She blew out a long breath. "So who is this guy?"

"Don't you know?"

A twinge of annoyance started to edge its way through her shock-fogged brain. "Nice," she observed coolly. "Have you heard the one about phone psychics? How if they were legit, *they* would be calling *you*?"

"Look, I didn't mean—"

"Sure you did." She impatiently dashed a stray curl off her forehead. "You called me, remember? You want my help, and you want me to work off the record, off the books, and on my own dime."

This earned a moment of silence, followed by a wry chuckle. "Huh. Looks like you *are* psychic."

"For this, I don't need to be. I work for the state, too. There's never enough money to go around, so we love volunteers. Never pay consultants unless we have to."

Another short pause followed. "So, you're saying you usually get paid for this sort of thing?"

Her fraying temper finally snapped. "I don't usually *do* 'this sort of thing'! I teach modern languages to high school kids. I coach softball. I live in the most boring town in the state and I fit right in, thank you very much. I have a golden retriever, for chrissakes! How freaking normal is that? So you can stop treating me like a low-budget circus act and—"

Anger had always been a trigger for her. It shut down her filters, lowered her shields, made her hear things she had no business knowing.

"Nick," she murmured.

She hadn't spoken his name aloud for over twelve years, not since she'd handed back his ring. Well, okay—*thrown* it back.

"Please?" inquired Andreozzi, employing the Rhode Island idiom for, "I didn't quite hear that."

Cassie cleared her throat. "Please tell me we're not talking about Dr. Nick Romano."

His silence was the only confirmation she needed.

"I'll be there in half an hour," she said.

She snapped her phone shut and glanced at the softball

field. Most of her girls had taken off, and a middle school team was already warming up. She hurried to her car and set out for the city, her mind racing at speeds her aging Miata could no longer hope to challenge.

This whole thing had to be some sort of misunderstanding. Sure, Nick could be a stubborn, single-minded pain in the ass, but he wasn't a killer. He wasn't. She couldn't have misjudged him that badly. She couldn't be that mistaken about someone she'd cared about.

Not twice.

She shoved painful memories to the back of her mind, figuring she had enough on her plate for one day. Nick was in trouble, and he'd asked for her.

He'd asked for her.

It was ridiculous, how happy that thought made her. She felt as if a door had cracked open in her heart, giving her a peep into a room as bright and full of joy as a childhood Christmas.

And *that* was a little frightening, even before she factored in the whole confessing-to-murder thing.

After all, Nick Romano had made it painfully clear he didn't want her. Her head knew there was no chance of a happy reunion, but apparently her heart and her hormones hadn't gotten that memo.

So what *did* he want? And for that matter, what the hell was he doing in Providence? Shouldn't he be living in that gorgeous Beacon Hill brownstone he'd inherited from his mother? By now, he should be department head at some Boston hospital. He probably had a leggy blond wife who shopped at Talbots and volunteered at the art museum, two kids in private schools, and a golf handicap. So why here, and why now, and *why her*?

Cassie made the twenty-minute drive in less than fifteen and found an illegal parking space not far from the police station. She was jogging up the broad, concrete stairs when it occurred to her that she was still dressed for softball: a green and yellow jersey tucked into a pair of well-worn jeans, an old pair of baseball cleats worn with one emerald green sock and one bright yellow. Her curly red hair had been skimmed back, given a couple of twists, then stuffed up into a green baseball cap. She didn't bother with makeup for a Saturday morning game. On the whole, it wasn't the look most women would have chosen for a reunion with a former fiancé.

You can take me as I am, or not at all.

Those words, the last words she'd said to Nick, echoed in her mind, nearly as loudly as when she'd first spoken them.

Nearly as loud as the silence that had followed.

It hit her then; they were about to break a silence that had lasted over a decade, and she had absolutely no idea what to say.

Cassie shrugged and pushed open the big glass door. Words would come to her. They always did, whether she wanted to hear them or not.

Chapter Three

Mark Andreozzi was waiting for Cassie at the front desk. He had put on a few pounds and grown a thick black mustache since she'd last seen him, and he'd cultivated the sort of bland, unreadable expression usually seen around a poker table. His thoughts, however, fizzled and flashed at her like a neon marquee with a faulty circuit.

He hadn't slept worth a damn since Thursday . . . all that bad coffee he'd been drinking was making him burp battery acid . . . he wished he could tell Sandy her old high school pal was a fake psychic, but his sister was the world's worst gossip and anything he told her had a way of coming back to bite him in the ass . . . he wouldn't have made this Nick Romano, who looked pretty much like a regular guy, for a doctor, much less a nutcase . . . he wondered if a better cop could tell just by looking that Romano was as crazy as a shithouse rat . . . he loved his wife, but damn, *he wished her ass looked half as good in blue jeans as the fake psychic's did . . . he really, really hoped the psychic* was *a fake, because the idea of someone hearing his thoughts creeped him the fuck out, but just in case maybe he'd "think out loud" some weird-ass word, like maybe "*hippopotamus!*" and silently dare her to work it into conversation . . .*

Cassie wasn't even slightly tempted. After she shook hands with Andreozzi and exchanged greetings that were entirely free of reference to African wildlife, they started walking down a series of corridors.

They didn't speak, but the detective's silent, increasingly fragmented commentary continued. When she couldn't stand the noise anymore, Cassie reached out and tapped the bright gold ring on his left hand.

"That looks new."

His face relaxed, softened. "Almost a year now."

"Congratulations. Local girl?"

He shook his head. "She's from Pawtucket."

Cassie suppressed a smile. Pawtucket was two or three towns to the north, which meant, by Rhode Island standards, the new Mrs. Andreozzi might as well have grown up in Nebraska.

"I've never worked with the police before," she confided. "You're going to have to tell me what you want me to do."

"Dr. Meyer—he's filling in for the house shrink—just wants you to talk to the guy. Ask him a few questions. See if you can, um, pick up anything."

Cassie's eyes widened and her legs abruptly ceased functioning. Andreozzi took a couple more steps before he realized she'd stopped. He turned back to face her, mild irritation seeping through his carefully neutral façade.

"Dr. Philip Meyer?" she demanded. "Tall, thin guy,

looks like he should be playing the German officer in a World War II movie?"

Andreozzi's lips twitched with amusement. "That sounds about right."

"*He* asked you to call me?"

"No offense, but it sure wasn't my idea. Is there a problem?"

Offhand, Cassie could think of several. Later she'd wonder why her former boss was working for the Providence police, but what rushed to the forefront of her mind was the realization that Nick hadn't asked for her, after all.

She tried to ignore the completely unreasonable stab of disappointment. "So Dr. Romano doesn't know I'm coming."

"He doesn't know about you, specifically. Meyer told him a specialist was coming in, a professional who had experience with cases like this." Andreozzi glanced at her bright green and yellow jersey, and repeated the word *professional* to himself with silent disdain.

Cassie's temper flared. "I'll tell you what; when women's softball goes 'professional,' I'll be sure to try out for the local team."

Geez. Bitchy much?

"Geez. Watch *Buffy* reruns much?" she shot back. Geekspeak was bad enough coming from her students, but if this cop kept it up she would, like, shoot him with his own gun.

Andreozzi's next utterance resembled an urgent request for the Heimlich maneuver. Cassie glanced at his stunned face and realized her mistake. Damn it! She hadn't responded to someone's unspoken comment for years.

Cassie sighed and started down a side corridor. Nick was in the fourth room on the left, and she was going to have to face him with her psychic shields shot all to hell.

She heard Andreozzi's footsteps behind her. He hurried to catch up, then slowed as he realized she'd taken the correct turn on her own. He desperately wanted her to pick the wrong door and prove she was a fake, but he was getting increasingly worried that she wouldn't, and wasn't.

Nick glanced up when she opened the door. Habitual good manners brought him to his feet, but his face was set with barely contained impatience, and his eyes were preoccupied and deeply shadowed with fatigue.

It wasn't fair, Cassie thought, fighting back a wave of emotion that mingled panic, resentment, and several others she didn't care to explore. No man had a right to look that good, not after a sleepless night. Not after twelve years. Not after, well, *everything*.

No hint of silver touched his thick, dark hair, and he still had the imposing physique that had won him a football scholarship. Not that he'd taken the scholarship or even needed it; his family had had pots of money. Old money, on his mother's side, but Nick's appearance was a throw-back to his father's working-class Italian roots. The only hint of his WASP heritage was the striking color of his eyes—a clear, light grey that in some lights and moods looked almost silver.

"Nick Romano," he said politely, holding out his hand.

His voice was just as gorgeous as she remembered: deep and resonant and thoroughly masculine, the sort of voice that reverberated through the female anatomy in interesting ways.

Cassie swept off her baseball cap and raised her eyes to his. "We've met."

For a long moment he stared at her, looking like a man who'd just been hit between the eyes with a two-by-four.

He lowered his hand, and his face took on an expression of well-practiced calm. His "doctor face," Cassie used to call it: pleasant, polite, professional. Detached.

"Cassie. It's good to see you."

She couldn't begin to tell what he was thinking—not from his voice, or from his face, or, to her surprise, from his thoughts. His mind was better shielded than most of the psychic experts who'd trained her.

Before the silence could get too awkward, Nick moved

to the table and pulled out one of the chairs for her. Cassie had almost forgotten men did that sort of thing. Still, she wasn't so lost in nostalgia she didn't notice Nick glance at Mark Andreozzi, eyebrows lifted in silent query. The detective's curt nod brought a flicker of emotion to Nick's face, difficult to read and quickly mastered.

He sat down across from Cassie. "Your family is well, I trust? All your siblings?"

The wistful note in his voice threatened to open doors she'd thought were long rusted shut. Nick had genuinely liked her big, noisy family. It was one of the things she'd loved about him.

"They're disgustingly healthy, every one of them, and doing pretty much what you might expect," she said briskly. Honesty prompted her to add, "All but Dez. Desmond became a priest, if you can imagine that."

A faint smile touched Nick's lips. "The mind boggles. I'll bet scores of young women wept over that decision."

"And a football coach or two. But enough about my brother the father." She folded her arms on the table and leaned forward. "Talk to me, Nick."

He regarded her for a long moment. "They said you've had experience in situations like this."

"In other words, what's my role here?" Cassie plucked at the sleeve of her softball jersey. "In this getup, I can carry a bat without raising eyebrows. And the best thing about the shirt? After I get the bad guy to confess, the blood washes right out. No lasting harm to the shirt. Too bad about the kneecaps, though."

To her surprise, he chuckled. She'd forgotten how that deep, intimate sound stirred things in her that had nothing to do with amusement.

"It's astonishing, how little you've changed," he said, still smiling. "You still look like an undergrad, and you're still . . ."

"A smartass?" she suggested.

"I was going for something more flattering, but sure, that works."

He was grinning now, a boyish expression that tugged dangerously at her heartstrings. Reach for the scissors, she told herself grimly, and cut yourself loose while you still can.

"*Everything's* still the same," she told him softly, "and that's why they called me here today."

The smile slid off his face, leaving his eyes bleak and distant. "Cassie, I appreciate you coming here, but there's really nothing you can do." He said this politely, but his tone was definite, final.

It took effort to meet his gaze with an easy smile, but Cassie managed to pull it off. "You won't get rid of me that easily, not after I got all dressed up to come to town."

His gaze dropped to her jersey, and memory flickered in his eyes. "Those are East Bay's colors."

She nodded. "I'm teaching at the high school."

"I'm glad to hear it. Your family's roots go deep. That's important."

The certainty in his voice pleased her. Nick had known and understood her so well . . . at least, up to a point.

"And what about you? Last I heard you were finishing up your residency. What route did you go? Hospital, private practice?"

"Some of both. I'm also teaching again, down in Newport. There's a serious shortage of teachers in the medical profession, nursing in particular. I took a year off to teach at Salve Regina."

The detective cleared his throat. "Maybe you folks could catch up later?"

"Yeah. Sorry," Cassie said. She took a long, calming breath, let it out slowly. "So, tell me why you confessed to murders you couldn't possibly have committed."

Nick sat in silence for several moments, deep in some private struggle. "I dreamed about those women," he said with obvious reluctance. "Vivid, detailed dreams."

"I can't say I'm surprised. The local news has been pretty relentless with the coverage."

"True, but the dreams preceded the discovery of the

victims, and they included information that didn't come out in the press. Since the city's finest haven't kicked me to the curb, it would appear some of this information was accurate."

"I see," she murmured.

And she did, all too well. They were back on familiar territory—or, more accurately, they were standing on a familiar patch of quicksand.

Thirteen years ago, Cassie had signed up for a psychology class for which Nick, then a graduate student, was the teaching assistant. A coffee date had turned into a conversation that lasted until sunrise. They'd shared an instant connection, one so intense it felt like recognition. Everything clicked: they were both athletes, happiest when in motion; they shared a love of quirky movies and the peculiar mixture of hope and heartbreak known to fans of New England sports teams. The core value that drove them both was the desire to save the world, and they were young and optimistic enough to believe it could be done. They pleased and surprised each other in bed. Family was important; they wanted children, and lots of them. He'd supported her dream of becoming a profiler for the FBI. Everything had been close to perfect until she'd been recruited by a very different government agency, and explained to Nick why they wanted her.

Up to that point, Cassie had seen no reason to tell Nick about her childhood "gift"; in fact, she'd believed that part of her had died in the car crash. The ability she'd lost at the age of seventeen had no part in the future they planned to share.

That was before her interview with the FBI recruiter. Before she was whisked away for a series of tests, before an impressive team of psychics and psychologists insisted the trauma of the car crash had only suppressed her ability. She could regain it, they assured her; she could use her gift to do interesting and important work.

The experience had been exhilarating, liberating. Life-changing. For the first time in years Cassie felt whole again.

She had been so sure Nick would understand, once he got used to the idea that his fiancée was a once-and-future psychic. She'd even thought the government-supported research would appeal to the scientist in him.

She'd been wrong. Nick's first response had been incredulity, swiftly followed by concern. No, "concern" was too pale a word. Cassie would never forget the flash of sheer panic in his eyes when he realized she was serious. Nick's training told him that "magical thinking" was a symptom of mental illness.

And now he'd turned that unyielding lens upon himself.

"So, let me get this straight," Cassie said briskly. "You dreamed about these women before they died, so you're somehow responsible for their deaths?"

"How else could I have known so much about them, if I wasn't involved?"

Cassie lifted one shoulder in a noncommittal shrug. "Something tells me you have a theory."

"You know about Jessica."

She nodded. Nick's older sister, his only sibling, had been diagnosed with schizophrenia when she was in college. Her illness had dropped a pall of shame and secrecy over the family, which, in Cassie's opinion, had probably contributed to her suicide. Nick had only been eight years old at the time.

"Certain disorders tend to be familial," he said calmly. "I may have developed a second personality, one capable of violence. It's not unknown," he added in response to Cassie's sigh.

"Nick, that's ridiculous. Unless 'stubborn and narrowminded' is considered a psychiatric diagnosis these days, you're perfectly sane."

"But what other explanation could there be?" He held up one hand to forestall her reply. "I don't want to talk about psychic phenomena. Dreams don't predict the future, or pick up other people's thoughts, or show you what's happening in the woods outside of Gloucester when you're miles away in your own bed."

"Okay, let's assume you're right, starting with the part about being miles away at the time."

"What if I have an accomplice?"

"An accomplice?" she echoed incredulously. "Yeah, I can see that. Salve Regina has always been a hotbed of criminal activity. Need a contract killer? Call the Sisters of Mercy—they'll set you up with a homicidal nursing student."

"Sarcasm aside, you may have a point," he admitted. "But I also spend two afternoons a week in a clinic in Providence. It has a . . . mixed clientele. Court-ordered treatment, for the most part."

Another corner of Cassie's heart melted. When it came to volunteer work, Nick used to say that the more frustrating the job, the greater the importance. Cassie hadn't fully understood this particular calculus until she'd started teaching teenagers.

"Have you been experiencing blackouts? Periods of time you can't account for?"

Nick shook his head. "But perhaps when I'm asleep . . ."

"So check your phone records for late-night calls. Construct a mileage log for your car to see if there's anything out of the ordinary," she suggested. "I'm willing to bet you won't find anything, but it might ease your mind."

"This isn't about me," he said quietly, "or more to the point, my peace of mind is not the issue here. Unless steps are taken now, another girl will be dead in less than a week."

"But you have no idea who she is."

"For good or ill, I'm sure I have that information. I just can't access it." He passed one hand wearily over his forehead. "I wish I could."

Suddenly Cassie understood why Philip Meyer had called her in.

A wave of anger swept over her, stealing the rhythm of her heart, stunning her with its force and fury.

She was dimly aware of one lost beat, perhaps two, followed by a quick skittering flutter in her chest as if her heart strove to catch up with her racing thoughts. Every scenario she could envision led to a single grim conclusion: Philip Meyer was about to make a Faustian bargain with another person's soul. And he wanted Cassie to help him close the deal.

Meyer wasn't psychic in any sense that Cassie could perceive, but in his hands, hypnosis became a tool that could uncover latent abilities. He'd helped peel away the layers of pain and guilt separating Cassie from her gift. He intended to do the same to Nick—without his knowledge or permission.

Of course Meyer had been listening in while Nick was questioned, so he knew Nick would reject any suggestion of psychic ability. But since hypnosis was also used in treating dissociative identity disorder, Nick would probably agree to it—as long as he didn't know the true purpose.

Meyer would record only a part of the session, leaving Cassie to convince Nick that nothing else had been said or done during hypnosis. That way Nick wouldn't write off future insights or dreams as "implanted." Eventually, he would have to believe.

Cassie glanced at the wall. No clocks. Nick wasn't wearing a watch, either. After being up all night, he'd probably lost track of time. This could be done.

But *should* it?

For a long moment Cassie wrestled with her tumbling thoughts. No one should make a decision like this for another person. Still, it beat the hell out of letting Nick go to jail for murders he didn't commit. It was far better than letting him believe he was following his older sister down a dark path to insanity. And what about the girl in Nick's dream? He was willing to confess to murders he didn't remember committing in the hope of saving her. Surely they should honor his intent.

"Have you thought about undergoing hypnosis?"

This prompted a snort of laughter from the cop. Cassie shot him a dirty look. "No, it isn't the least bit like that

stage show you saw at the Mohican Sun. And about that—
who the hell has a bachelor party in a casino?"

The color drained from Andreozzi's face. He cleared
his throat twice before pushing himself away from the
wall he'd been leaning against. "Should I get Dr. Meyer?"

Nick's eyebrows rose. "Dr. Philip Meyer?"

"Gets that a lot, does he?" the detective asked. "He's fa-
mous or something?"

"He wrote the textbook on diagnostic hypnosis, and I
mean that quite literally. I've read some of his work. I had
no idea he was in Providence, much less working with the
police. Yes, of course I'll talk with Dr. Meyer."

Cassie waited until Andreozzi made his escape. "So you
trust this guy's opinion?"

"Trust?" A wry smile lifted one corner of Nick's lips.
"That's not quite the word I'd use. Philip Meyer's credentials are impeccable, but I'm not entirely comfortable with
the idea of anyone walking around inside my head."

Cassie searched his face for any trace of irony or sarcasm, and found none. Nick wasn't referring to her. Apparently her psychic gift didn't make a big enough blip on
his mental radar for him to make that connection. As far as
he was concerned, it simply didn't exist.

Doubt and fear began to gnaw at her. This wouldn't be
easy for Nick.

There was a tap at the door, and Dr. Meyer came in without waiting for a reply. Nick rose to greet him; they all shook
hands and got the professional small talk out of the way.

"I'd like Ms. O'Malley to stay, if you don't mind," Meyer
said as he settled down at the table. He met Cassie's gaze,
and the expression in his pale blue eyes confirmed her suspicions about his intent. "The results of deep hypnosis can
be surprising to the subject. I will tape the session, of
course, but sometimes it helps to have someone you know
and trust present to verify the results."

Nick's eyes narrowed. "You know something of our
personal history. May I ask how?"

"I'd be surprised if you didn't. Over the years, I've consulted for various government agencies. Ms. O'Malley worked with me as a translator on several occasions, so I'm familiar with her file, which included names of family and associates. Your name sounded familiar to me, and upon consideration I remembered that you and she were once engaged. Can we begin now?"

Questions still clouded Nick's face, but he agreed and went through the steps Dr. Meyer described.

Meyer was good; no one knew that better than Cassie. But she was still a little surprised to see Nick sink into a deeply relaxed, receptive state. Some people were resistant to hypnotic suggestion, and everything she knew of Nick suggested that he would be at the top of that list.

For a while, the session was routine. When Meyer's methodical questioning became too much for Cassie, she got up and started to pace.

Over the next couple of hours, she learned things about Nick that she had never suspected, things he had long forgotten. Slowly, relentlessly, Philip Meyer took him back into a childhood when insight was first dismissed as imagination, and then as madness. Nick's sister had seen people who weren't there, heard voices no one else could hear. Her terror and denial became Nick's. The drugs she took to silence the voices, the dark abyss of depression that finally sucked her in—he'd experienced his sister's pain until he'd walled himself off in sheer self-preservation. And the guilt of that withdrawal locked the doors to memory.

When those long-closed portals were acknowledged, Meyer flipped on the recorder and turned his questions toward the oubliette murders.

Nick was describing his dream yet again when his words trailed into silence and something in his face changed. He turned to Cassie, and from his lips came a voice she'd never expected to hear again.

The blood rushed from Cassie's head with an almost audible *whoosh* and the room started to spin. She groped for a chair and sat down in it, hard.

Meyer turned off the recorder. "Are you all right, Cassandra?"

With difficulty, she focused on her former boss's face. "You son of a bitch."

He spread his hands, palms up. "How could I possibly know this was going to happen?"

"You know, that's a damn good question."

"I assure you, I had no idea—"

"Save it," she snapped. "Bring Nick back up. We're done here."

Meyer regarded her in silence for a long moment, then turned away and did as she asked. Nick took one look at Cassie and demanded to know what he had said.

Without a word, she hit the rewind button on the recorder and played back the last part of the tape. Nick's brow furrowed in puzzlement.

"That's not me."

"I don't disagree with you," she said.

"Then what—"

"That's the tape of your session."

Nick looked to Dr. Meyer for confirmation and received a somber nod. "How is that possible? I don't even speak . . ." His voice trailed off and he gestured to the recorder. "What the hell *was* that?"

"Farsi, with a French accent," Cassie told him.

He studied her in silence for several moments. "That's . . . very specific, even for someone with your gift for languages. The way you said that, without a moment's hesitation, suggests you had a particular person in mind."

Cassie had forgotten how perceptive Nick could be. "It sounded like someone I worked with several years back."

"I must have met him somewhere," Nick mused. "Under hypnosis, people can recall stray bits of information, things the conscious mind is barely aware of knowing. Who is he? Do you have any idea where he might be now?"

"His name was Armand Gaudine," she said, surprised that the name was still so difficult to say after a decade.

"And if you believe my brother the father, he's probably in hell."

Nick's brows lifted. "This man is dead? You're sure?"

"I ought to be," she said softly. "I'm the one who killed him."

Chapter Four

For a long moment Nick stared at Cassie, trying to assimilate what he'd just heard. The notion that he might speak Farsi under hypnosis, as impossible as that sounded, was easier for him to accept than the idea of Cassie killing another human being.

"You had a damn good reason," Nick said. "I might not know what it is, but I know you had one."

"Thanks. Appreciate the sentiment. And the way you avoid actually coming right out and asking? Impressive."

"I wasn't trying to be subtle. But fine, let's put this on the table." He tipped his head toward the tape recorder. "Since there seems to be a connection between what's happening in Providence and this former colleague, I'd appreciate anything you can tell me."

She glanced at Philip Meyer and got an almost imperceptible nod.

Occasional translator, my ass, Nick noted grimly. Cassie deferred to Meyer in a manner that suggested a well-established pattern. Most likely Meyer's claim of being a "consultant for various government agencies" was far from the whole truth.

"You know that I went into a branch of the intelligence service," Cassie said. "The work we did was very experimental, even for the far-seeing program. We didn't sit in a cloud of incense and read tea leaves all day; we were trained as field agents and expected to follow up on the leads we received. Armand was an experienced agent before he entered the program. He was my mentor. He was also a double agent. I didn't pick up on it."

"How could you have known?"

A small wry smile touched Cassie's lips. "My supervisor had her suspicions. I didn't believe her."

"What happened?" Nick asked softly.

"I almost got her killed. At my insistence, she set up a meeting with the three of us. I was late, but I got there in time to see him pull a gun on her. I killed him before he could get off a shot."

"You did your job," Philip Meyer said.

"So you've told me," she said without looking at Meyer. "I left the agency soon after that. I hung up my crystal ball, got my teaching credentials. Put it behind me."

Nick was starting to understand what this confrontation cost her. "Yet you came here today."

She lifted one shoulder in a studiously casual shrug. "I thought I was needed. But hey, what do you know—I was wrong again." She rose to leave. "Take care of yourself, Nick."

"Thank you for coming in, Cassandra," Meyer said.

Cassie paused, her hand on the doorknob. "You really want to show your appreciation, Meyer? Don't call me again."

She closed the door quietly behind her. To Nick, it seemed that most of the light and half the air in the room left with her.

"She's the real thing, Dr. Romano. Whether you choose to believe it or not."

Nick dragged his attention back to the psychologist. "Excuse me?"

"Cassandra was one of the most gifted people in the remote viewing program. And as you have no doubt surmised, I was the director of one of our field offices. She worked for me."

"As a psychic spy."

He shrugged. "If you like."

Nick shook his head in bewilderment. "That seems a strange career move for a man of your professional stature."

"Why so?"

"Psychic research? Not exactly hard science."

"Some would say the same of mainstream psychiatry."

"Many do," Nick admitted.

"It's not an exact science; you're quite right," Meyer said. "Cassandra never really accepted that. Most of the other people in the program were impressed with themselves when they got something right. She beat herself up when she got something wrong. I assume you know why."

Nick shook his head. He and Cassie didn't talk about that aspect of her life. Well, that wasn't entirely true. She had tried to tell him about it; he'd refused to listen.

"Are you aware of the accident that killed three of her high school friends?"

"She thought she should have seen that? Prevented it?"

"Our friend has high expectations of herself. She should. Her test scores are off the charts. Do you know how rare it is for psychic ability to show up consistently in a controlled lab situation?"

"I can guess," he said dryly.

A smile flickered across Meyer's face. "The sooner you're willing to entertain the possibility that psychic abilities do exist, the sooner you'll be able to help." He lifted one eyebrow. "Assuming that is your intention?"

"I'm here," Nick pointed out.

Meyer took a file from a leather case and pushed it across the table toward Nick. "Talk to the families and friends of the two victims, see if you can discern any patterns."

This, in Nick's opinion, was a strange way to treat a confessed murderer. "I assume the police have already done this."

"Yes, but *you* haven't. More to the point, neither has Cassandra. I want you to persuade her to go with you."

Nick smiled without humor. "I'm sure you do. And since you've worked with Cassie, you should know that once she makes up her mind about something, she's not easily persuaded to change it."

"It's spring break," Meyer said, as if he hadn't heard Nick's objections. "East Bay High School's out for the week. I believe that's true for the university, too. You've both got the time off."

"Cassie doesn't want to work with you. She was very clear about that."

"But she *will* work with you." Meyer gestured to the tape recorder. "I'm not sure what to make of this, but it's bound to raise questions Cassandra will want answered. Even if she's willing to keep a lid on her own curiosity, she'll respond to your need to figure out your part in all this."

That was probably true, Nick conceded. Cassie had come to his aid without question or hesitation. After all these years, that shouldn't have touched his heart so profoundly. Nor should being with her again have felt so natural. And he was fairly certain a softball jersey had never jump-started the male libido so effectively.

"About that recording," Nick said, starting with the easy issue first. "I'd like a copy."

Meyer took a thumb-sized device from his pocket and placed it on the table. "I thought you might. Take my back-up recorder. If I were in your position, I'd have a voiceprint done to make sure that really was me speaking. I'd also want a translation of the Farsi."

Since that summed up Nick's intentions precisely, he didn't bother to comment. He pocketed the little recorder and turned a searching gaze on the psychologist. "None of this makes sense, including your involvement. What are you doing here in Providence?"

The psychologist smiled. "One might also ask what you're doing working in a clinic and teaching basic psych classes to teenaged nursing students. From time to time, everyone needs to give back to the community."

"And it's just a coincidence that Cassie came into the picture?"

"Not at all. You merely provided an opportunity to contact her. If you hadn't come in, I would have found another way to reach out to her."

"So you're using me as bait to bring her into whatever it is you're doing."

"I thought I'd been very clear on that point," Meyer said calmly.

For a long moment, the two men regarded each other in silence.

"Have you considered the possibility that I might be telling the truth about those other women?" Nick demanded. "Did the risk to Cassie occur to you?"

"Of course, but Cassandra can handle herself. And tell me this, Dr. Romano; can you imagine yourself hurting her under any circumstances?"

He couldn't. Of course he couldn't. But neither could he imagine abducting two women and leaving them to a long, lonely death.

Soon to be three women, he noted. He'd come here to stop that, at any cost to himself.

But not to Cassie.

"If it will give you some peace of mind," Meyer offered, "one of the detectives will accompany you."

Nick nodded. That helped, if only a little. "And if I don't agree to do this?"

Meyer lifted both hands, palms up, in a gesture of dismissal. "Then you're free to go."

"Just like that?"

"The D.A. has enough to do without bringing obstruction of justice charges against every crackpot who confesses to a crime he couldn't possibly have committed. Surely you see how difficult it would be for me to justify detaining or observing you on the basis of some troubling dreams." Meyer tapped the file. "If you were working as a consultant, however, you stay on the radar and under scrutiny. We all get what we want."

Nick almost had to admire the way Meyer hit all the right buttons. "I've read several of your books. None of your bios mention that you're a brass-plated, manipulative bastard."

"An oversight, I'll grant you, but there's never enough space in an author bio to list all of one's credentials."

Nick debated, briefly, whether to be angry or amused by that. He let it go and gestured to the recorder on the table. "What do you and your myriad credentials make of that?"

Meyer folded his hands on the table. "In all candor, Dr. Romano, I'm not sure what to think. But I'm reminded of something President Johnson once said about his CIA director, J. Edgar Hoover—"

"That it was better to have him inside the tent pissing out, than outside the tent pissing in."

"Precisely," Meyer said. "If you are what you think you are, it would only be prudent to keep you close at hand. I happen to think you're wrong. I also think you could be useful."

As much as Nick hated to admit it, Meyer's proposal was better than any solution he could think of. He only hoped the man was right about Cassie's ability to handle this.

On impulse he asked, "Why do you call her Cassandra? Cassie's given name is Mary Catherine."

"Have you read the *Iliad,* Dr. Romano?"

"Back in high school, I suppose. At the time I was more interested in football than literature."

"Then let me refresh your memory. Cassandra was a prophet who lived in the city of Troy. No one wanted to hear what she had to say. They ignored her because they thought she was mad." He lifted one brow. "Food for thought, wouldn't you say?"

Chapter Five

A belated burst of feminine vanity prompted Cassie to linger over her shower and take extra care with her makeup. She dressed carefully, striving for a look that was casual but polished. Her favorite cotton sweater in a deep moss green, cream-colored slacks instead of faded-to-white-across-the-butt jeans, a glint of gold at her ears and throat: *this* was how she would have liked Nick to see her. This woman looked far more mature, confident, and, well, *normal*.

"Too late for that," she told her reflection. Snatching up her purse, she headed off to consult an expert. If anyone could make sense of the strange session in the police station, it would be her sister Molly.

East Bay's "downtown" was centered around three or four blocks of the main street, along with old homes on connecting streets that had been converted to shops over the years. Molly's house was a block or two past these shops, bigger than most and on a surprisingly large lot. Since her husband's disappearance several years back, Molly had pieced together a living from her home, her art, and her diverse hobbies.

These enterprises, collectively known as Molly-O's, took up most of the first floor of the sprawling old Victorian and the whole of the backyard. The latter was large enough for a long, narrow greenhouse and a fenced area that held several dog runs and a common doggy play area.

Cassie went out back first to check on Hannah. The golden retriever peeled away from the trio of dogs digging happily in a large pile of sand, pausing on the way to bend over a scattering of toys. She trotted over to the fence, dropped a tennis ball, and looked up expectantly.

"Hey, sweetie," Cassie murmured, reaching through the fence to scratch the dog's ears. Hannah responded with a happy yip. Cassie bent to retrieve the well-slobbered ball and lobbed it over the fence. The retriever galloped after it, wearing a broad doggy grin.

They went through this routine several times before Hannah returned to her friends. Assured that all was well at doggie daycare, Cassie circled around to the shop entrance.

The tinkle of chimes and the scent of herbs, both fresh and dried, welcomed her to Molly-O's. Three rooms opened up from the central hall. To the left was the herb shop, and beyond it Molly's art studio. In the larger room to the right was a pleasant jumble of books, candles, incense, jewelry, art, and assorted New Age paraphernalia. The whole was presided over by Molly's whimsical paintings of winged cats. An odd setting, perhaps, for one of the most sensible and pragmatic people Cassie knew.

The shop cat, one of Molly's beloved Siamese, slinked out from behind a potted lemon tree and wound around Cassie's ankles.

Molly poked her head out into the hall. She held an artist's brush in one hand, and a paint-daubed smock covered blue jeans and a faded green tee shirt. She'd pulled her long, red-brown hair back into a single braid, but as usual, there was a smear of paint just above one temple where she'd absently brushed back a loose strand. Her round, pretty face lit up at the sight of her visitor.

Almost immediately, her smile of welcome faded into sisterly concern. "What happened? What's wrong?"

Cassie couldn't quite repress a rueful smile. Most families quarreled over misunderstandings; the O'Malleys, on the other hand, knew each other far too well. Molly picked up emotions like a human barometer.

"I need your particular expertise. Or more accurately, one of them."

Molly's eyebrows rose. "Come on back. We can talk while I clean my brushes."

The cat bumped his head against Cassie's ankle and demanded attention with a loud, rusty-sounding meow. She scooped him up and draped him over her shoulder, giving him a brisk ear scratch as she walked down the hall.

Paintings lined the walls of Molly's studio, but Cassie's eyes went straight to a medium-sized canvas displayed on an easel. There stood Michael, the oldest of the O'Malley siblings, portrayed as a Celtic chieftain of some long ago time. His wind-blown cape was fastened at the neck with a finely wrought gold pin, and a small harp lay near his feet. Fanciful elements aside, this *was* Michael—the strong, intelligent face, the touch of humor in his eyes. He stood on a green hillside, arms folded across his chest, steadily meeting any gaze that fell upon him.

"What do you think?" asked Molly.

"Wow. Just . . . wow. Lord of all he surveys, isn't he?"

"Pretty much," her sister agreed as she poured turpentine over a pair of brushes. "Dee is over by the window."

Cassie glanced toward the large bay window that took up most of one wall. Leaning against the wall was another midsized canvas. This one portrayed their oldest sister, Deirdre, standing almost knee-deep in a woodland river. Her full skirt was hiked up and tucked into her belt, and a grinning toddler was perched on one hip. Her hair, as red and curly as Cassie's, was piled on her head in a loose knot, and her face was full of laughter as she shied playfully away from the water her six-year-old twins, Tommy and Tyler, splashed in her direction. Evan, who at ten thought himself above such antics, watched from the shore, looking both superior and wistful.

"It makes you want to join in," Cassie said with a smile. "What's with the family portraits?"

Molly capped the turpentine and put the can up on a shelf. "Christmas gift for the parents."

"You're thinking about Christmas in April?"

"Well, there *are* seven of us."

"Good point. So going by seniority, I guess a self-portrait would be next."

"Nope. I'm doing Laura." Molly nodded to her working easel.

Cassie moved over for a closer look. The mood of this painting was completely different from the first two. The youngest O'Malley sister stood to one side, her narrow form and sharp, unsmiling face half hidden in shadows. The background was a swirl of dark mist. The painting was still unfinished, but it struck Cassie as both apt and disturbing.

The Siamese, who had been purring sonorously throughout the impromptu art show, began to squirm and demand his freedom. Cassie put him down on an aging armchair. "What made you decide to skip over the middle sibs?"

"Don't worry, little sis—you'll get your turn."

Both women jumped and turned to face the real-life version of Laura.

Their younger sister stood a head taller than Cassie, and she was very slim and almost obsessively well-groomed. Her naturally curly hair had been tamed into glossy waves. She wore her nails a little longer than current fashion dictated, and her makeup was perhaps a little lavish for a Saturday morning. Silver spirals studded with amber swung from her ears, echoing the golden hue of her silk tee. Her slacks were a rich brown, and her slim-heeled shoes matched.

She looked Cassie up and down, and didn't appear particularly pleased by what she saw. "What are *you* all dressed up for?"

Cassie was spared from answering when Molly rushed forward and turned the unfinished canvas around. "I told you yours wouldn't be finished until Monday at the earliest," she scolded. You can see it when it's ready, and not before."

Laura shrugged and strode over to Michael's picture. "If I didn't know this guy, I'd say you were painting Lugh." She glanced over at Cassie. "Irish god. Warrior, physician, bard."

"Ah."

"And Deirdre might as well be Danu, the river goddess.

Summertime, fertility, all those good things." She turned to Molly and lifted one perfectly arched brow. "Are you doing this on purpose?"

"Painting the O'Malley family as the Celtic pantheon? No, that wasn't the plan."

"Damn. I was hoping I could be Aibell. She's in charge of making sure husbands are sexually satisfying their wives."

"There's a goddess for that?" Cassie asked.

Laura slanted another look in her direction. "Sweetie, there's a goddess for everything. Aibell has a better gig than most. Screw war and death and bringing in the harvest—she gets to sit around and dish."

"And what would you do with all those men who don't measure up?" Molly teased.

"Educate them. What else?"

"That's . . . a lot of work. Better you than me."

Laura's grin flashed. "Yeah, I've heard that."

Her sister gave her a good-natured swat on the arm. "Did you just drop by to insult me?"

"That's not a good enough reason? Nothing major—I stayed at the parents' last night, so I thought I'd stop by and say hello on my way home."

"But I'll still see you tomorrow for brunch?"

"Haven't missed one yet."

Laura gave them both a little wave and sailed out. Cassie watched her go, her expression wistful. "She seems so much more relaxed around you than me."

"That's because I wasn't held up to her as a blueprint."

Cassie's jaw dropped. "What? Who did that? Mom and Dad always made a point of not comparing us to each other."

"Laura did, though. It was a high school thing, mostly. She formed her image of what high school should be by watching you, and by that measure, she was always falling short."

"Impossible," Cassie protested. "She graduated at sixteen, for chrissakes."

"Exactly. You were always bringing friends home, she was two years younger than her classmates and never quite fit in. You had curves, she had angles. You had boyfriends, she had books. You made the varsity team for every girl's sport, set school and state track records that still stand, and went to college on an athletic scholarship. She tripped a lot. Teachers remembered you, and Laura always felt they were comparing her unfavorably."

"Even though she was such a good student."

Molly sighed. "Sometimes teachers resent students who are *too* good. And Laura's social skills weren't her strongest point at that age. She likes to be in charge, which is fine, but she can be a little bossy."

"Actually, Saddam Hussein was a little bossy. There's a difference."

Her sister didn't dispute the point. "Laura reinvented herself, inside and out. But where family is concerned, old patterns are hard to break."

"I suppose."

"But back to you." Molly gestured toward the shop. "Sit down, and I'll make us some tea."

She bustled off to the first-floor kitchen. Cassie headed into the gift shop and dropped into one of the two arm-chairs near the wall of bookshelves. As she waited, she idly scanned the titles. Molly prided herself on having read every book displayed for sale, on topics ranging from tarot cards to dowsing. Her view toward such things struck Cassie as a healthy balance of credulity and skepticism.

In moments Molly returned with a well-laden tray. She placed it on the little table between the two chairs and set-tled down across from Cassie.

"Earl Grey," she announced as she poured the steaming brew into delicate china cups. "I figured you'd want some-thing with caffeine."

That was a concession for Molly, who preferred herbal teas and sold her own blends. But not *much* of a concession, because Molly knew damn well Cassie was a degenerate coffee fiend. She disapproved of this habit, firmly and often.

"Okay, preemptive strike here: I'll give up caffeine when you start running with me every morning," Cassie offered.

Her sister shuddered. "While I'm recovering from that image, why don't you tell me what's on your mind."

Cassie went through the events of the morning, leaving out Philip Meyer's role in chipping away at Nick's mental shields. She also declined to mention just how Armand had met his death. Molly sipped tea and listened intently.

When at last Cassie paused to pick up her own cup, Molly suggested, "Maybe Nick is some sort of medium? That would explain the dreams, as well as channeling the dead French guy."

This was not the answer Cassie wanted to hear, but she had no argument stronger than, "But aren't mediums usually women?"

At least, that had been Philip Meyer's opinion. He'd done his best to get Cassie to conjure up the dead in the service of Uncle Sam. She'd just as adamantly insisted it was a foolish waste of time. He hadn't been happy about that. Knowing what a tenacious bastard Meyer could be, he was probably *still* unhappy about it.

"Earth to Cassie?"

"Sorry," she murmured. "Just running all this over in my mind."

"It's a lot to digest," Molly agreed. "To answer your question about mediums, I doubt women have more aptitude than men. It's just that women are more likely to, well, *tune in.* Men are usually too full of themselves. They barely listen to the living, much less the dead."

"Geez, not too cynical."

Molly shrugged away that observation. "Of course, Nick is a trained listener. Can you think of a reason why he'd start picking up a new channel, so to speak?"

"Before this morning, I hadn't talked to him in over twelve years. I have no idea what's been going on in his life." An evasion, yes, but even as she spoke, Cassie realized there was more truth in her words than she'd intended.

Nick had dreamed of those doomed women before his session with Philip Meyer.

"Hmmm." Molly looked unconvinced, but willing to let it pass. "But you *are* sure that Nick didn't kill those women."

Cassie blinked. "What the hell kind of question is that?"

"One you can't afford *not* to ask," Molly said. "Keep your mind and your options open. Look at every possibility, even those that seem impossible. Scratch that: *especially* those that seem impossible. People used to think multiple personalities occurred when someone was possessed by a spirit. Now no one believes in possession."

An icy shudder made its way down Cassie's spine. "But you do?"

"Show me the mother of a preteen daughter who doesn't," Molly said with a wry smile. "It's the only explanation that begins to cover the mood swings."

"All kidding aside, you really think I need to consider Nick's theory along with paranormal possibilities?"

"Sweetie, how can you *not* do that? If there are clear, solid lines dividing science and the paranormal—and I'm not convinced there are—people keep changing their minds about where those lines should be drawn."

"True enough." Cassie finally took a sip of her tea and managed, just barely, not to grimace. "But what possible connection could there be between Armand, Nick, and three young women in Rhode Island?"

"Apart from you?"

Cassie set her cup down with a clatter. Damn it, why hadn't she seen that herself?

Hormones. That was the only reasonable explanation. Seeing Nick had made her . . . yearn. That was the only way of putting it. Nick took up too much space in her head and her heart, and sent the rest of her into overdrive. Scientists should forget about cold fusion, Cassie concluded grimly, and work on harnessing the power of unrequited lust. What she had going on could probably keep most of Rhode Island humming along for a month or two.

"I don't know those women," she said. "I haven't seen Nick for years. How could this possibly be about me?"

"That's the question, isn't it?" Molly put down her teacup and leaned forward. "When we were talking about Laura earlier, I left out something that might shed some light, not only on her attitude toward you, but to this situation with Nick."

"Okay," Cassie said cautiously.

"Laura was still short of puberty when you were in the car accident, but she was already starting to pick up things. She can recognize psychic ability in other people, and she knew you were still strongly telepathic. And she said so, repeatedly."

"I never heard her."

"Everyone made sure you didn't. You had enough to deal with. People were tiptoeing around you, and she wasn't being heard. Not only does Laura dislike being ignored, but she also had to come to terms with her gift pretty much on her own."

"That goes a long way toward explaining our lack of connection, I guess, but what does it have to do with Nick?"

"I don't know," Molly said readily. "Maybe nothing. The point is, you repressed your ability for years, but you were able to recover it. Think about the recovery process, and you might get some insight into Nick's situation."

Cassie's heart leapt, so suddenly and hard that she almost heard it thump back down into place.

"Armand," she said. "He had a knack for helping people reconnect with repressed abilities. That's why I was assigned to him."

"Assuming this knack transcended death, that would go a long way toward explaining the tape recording. What did Nick-slash-Armand say when Nick was under hypnosis?"

She shrugged. "I don't speak Farsi; I just know the sound of it, and a few words. Armand and Selena—she was my supervisor—were both fluent."

"Well, getting a translation sounds like a good place to

start. In the meanwhile, think: what would Armand want? Closure, atonement?"

"Revenge, most likely."

"Yikes." Molly leaned back in her chair. "Is this a story you can tell me?"

"I guess. It has to do with the work I was doing right after college."

"The government job. The one you can't talk about."

"Couldn't," she said. "It's declassified now, and has been for a while. You probably know about the government's remote viewing program."

Molly's eyes widened. "My sister, a psychic spy! How cool is that?"

"Please. You sound like Tess."

"Oh, god—don't tell her that! The last thing any girl wants to hear is a comparison to her mother."

As if on cue, the front door banged open and a small, dark whirlwind blew into the hall. A moment passed before Cassie recognized her niece. Tess had cut her hair short and dyed it a solid, light-eating black. Her newly curvy figure was displayed by a brief black skirt and a black top that stopped two or three inches north of her navel. Her narrow, sharp-boned face was disguised by more makeup than most starlets wore to go clubbing. Cassie never would have guessed that Tess was just shy of thirteen.

"Men are pigs," Tess announced bitterly. She leveled a glare of laser-like intensity at her mother. "And don't say I'm asking for it by going around dressed like this."

Molly leaped to her feet, a warrior's light in her eyes. "Asking for what? What happened?"

Her daughter rolled her eyes. "Geez. Nothing *happened,*" she muttered. "Why do mothers always have to go all drama club about every little thing?"

She clumped up the stairs. Muffled thumps and bangs drifted down from her room.

Molly sank back in her chair as if exhausted. "Someone's in a snit today."

A particularly loud crash resounded through the house. Cassie winced. "Should we check on that?"

"Probably." Molly sighed, then shrugged. "She's been doing this a lot lately, but nothing much gets broken. I'm not happy about it, but I figure it's not the worst way a kid her age could act out."

Cassie's phone rang before she could respond. "Sorry," she murmured as she pulled it from her purse. She let out a little growl of annoyance when she recognized the number. "It's Mark Andreozzi again. I should probably take this."

When Molly nodded, she flipped open the phone. "What is it now, Lieutenant?" she asked resignedly.

"Dr. Meyer wants you to come back to the station."

Cassie closed her eyes and took a long, calming breath. It didn't help.

"For the record, I don't give a rat's ass what Meyer wants. Since you're apparently acting as his secretary, you can convey that message. Please add the appropriate hand gestures."

"It's about Romano."

She heard those words as she was snapping the phone shut. Gritting her teeth, she debated furiously for about five seconds before she hit the return button.

"What about him?" she asked when Andreozzi picked up the call.

"Looks like we got another expert consultant on the case," he said in a bland tone that didn't quite disguise the sarcasm. "*Doctor* Romano is going to interview the family and friends of the first two victims. Meyer wants you to go with him."

That, Cassie had not expected. "And if I don't?"

"He won't be alone, either way," the detective promised grimly. "I'll be along."

She shoved one hand into her hair and fisted it in the thick curls. Damn it, this was bad. Who knew what form Nick's emerging psychic abilities might take, or how he would react to them? Some people were dog-sick afterward. Andreozzi wouldn't know what to do. And what if

Nick was right about the source of his dreams? Or what if Molly was right, and he was able to channel the dead? If Nick succumbed to another personality—either his own or someone else's—he had a good chance of being arrested or committed.

"I'm on my way," Cassie said.

She threw the phone back into her purse. "That was a message from my former boss. He wants me to go with Nick and talk to the family and friends of the missing women."

"That sounds like a good idea."

"On the face of it, maybe, but nothing's straightforward and easy where Meyer's concerned. I wish I knew what he really wants me to do."

"Maybe this is about what Nick can do. Maybe you're going along to convince him of the possibilities."

A short, bitter laugh escaped Cassie. "I couldn't do it before. Why should anything be different now?"

"How about—oh, I don't know—two dead women and another soon to follow? If you need more motivation than that, there's a good chance Nick's status gets downgraded to prime suspect. Or more likely, he'll start thinking he's crazy, and keep thinking that way until his fears are supported by reality."

Cassie regarded her sister with a narrow-eyed glare. "You know, I really hate it when you're right."

Molly smirked. "You'd think you would have gotten used to it by now."

The creak of stairs drew their attention back to the hall. Tess crept past, cradling a Siamese kitten. Her face had been scrubbed clean, and she was wearing an oversized tee shirt and jeans. She looked years younger, and her eyes were huge and haunted.

The color drained from Molly's face. She reached out and touched Cassie's arm. "She's not just angry, she's terrified. I hate to intrude, but she's so afraid . . ."

After a moment, Cassie nodded. She reached out, gently probing the girl's thoughts for the source of her misery.

For a moment she got a glimpse of flying objects, a whirl of incomprehensible energy, a sense of abject helplessness. The next, she was flung out of Tess's mind with considerable power.

The front door banged shut, just as decisively. Cassie blinked several times and turned awed eyes toward her sister.

"Wow."

"What? *What*?"

"Tess. Apparently puberty is bringing on more than the usual changes."

Understanding flooded Molly's face, swiftly followed by maternal pride, which was promptly banished by concern.

"The poor kid. Turning thirteen is hard enough."

"No kidding." Cassie rose. "I'll get out of your hair so you two can talk."

"Actually," Molly said slowly, "I think it's you she wants to talk to."

Cassie absorbed that in silence. For as long as she could remember, Molly's role in the family had been that of peacekeeper, mediator, and all-around facilitator. Cassie had never given much thought to it—that's just how things worked. Molly always seemed to sense what people felt, what they wanted and needed. She took obvious pride in keeping her extended family close, happy, and more or less civil. That's what she did. That's who she was. Still, it couldn't be easy, stepping aside at a time like this.

"You sure?" Cassie asked.

"Go."

Cassie nodded and turned away, pretending she didn't notice the brightness in her sister's eyes.

She settled down on the porch step next to Tess and eyed the ball of cream-colored fuzz curled up on the girl's lap. The kitten's ears, tail, and paws were just beginning to darken, which probably put its age at about eight or nine weeks.

"I'm surprised you haven't found homes for all of Genevieve's litter yet."

Tess shot Cassie a suspicious glance—not an unusual teenage response to small talk. After a moment she muttered, "This one's the last." She shrugged. "Two other queens are expecting litters, so there will be more kittens soon."

It was an unusually long speech for Tess, and Cassie heard the wistful note in her niece's voice. She probably wouldn't get a better opening to talk about change, and growth, and the need to adapt.

Instead she said, "Remember when Emily was kicked out of boarding school?"

Tess nodded, and curiosity edged aside some of the misery on her face. Her cousin's disgrace had sent minor shockwaves through the extended O'Malley family. No one expected trouble from Emily, the firstborn grandchild, honor student, and all-around paragon. Her father, Cassie's oldest brother Michael, had hushed up the details of her expulsion, but Cassie had picked up enough to know what was what.

"Emily was doing great at school. She was getting good grades, had lots of friends, and made the lacrosse team. But one night she was upset about this guy she was crushing on, and some of the stuff in her room started moving around for no good reason. No hands, no strings, no obvious explanation. Her roommate was scared shitless—it freaked her out so badly she ended up leaving school. Rumors started spreading. Before you know it, people were saying Emily was playing mean tricks, or was a little crazy, or maybe just plain evil."

"People are stupid," muttered Tess.

"More often than not," Cassie agreed. "But you do understand that Emily was none of those things, right? She's just an O'Malley."

"Whatever that means."

"I didn't have this problem when I was your age," Cassie went on. "But then, I can't remember a time when I *wasn't* able to hear things people didn't say out loud. Sometimes, though, psychic ability develops later in life. And frankly, that sucks. Being almost thirteen is hard enough without the new challenges you're facing."

Cassie glanced down at the kitten, which was mewing and squirming in Tess's grip. "You're holding Arwen too tightly."

Tess released the kitten. Her gaze darted up to Cassie's face. An expression that mingled wariness, hope, and fascination crept into her eyes. Meanwhile, the kitten scrambled up Tess's shirt and nestled into the crook of her neck. The girl stroked the little creature absently and said, "When you live in a cattery, you never name the kittens. It's not good to get too attached."

Tess's tone was studiously casual, but Cassie knew a challenge when she "heard" one.

"That's a smart policy, I guess, but you *did* name this kitten. You named her Arwen, after the elf princess in *Lord of the Rings,* because in your opinion, cats and elves have a lot in common—the beauty, the grace, the attitude." On impulse she added, "And if it's okay with your mom, I'd like to buy Arwen for you. It'll save me the trouble of shopping for a birthday gift that you'll only return anyway."

The girl's face lit up. Clearly, Cassie had passed the test and scored serious extra credit. "Yeah, I think Mom will be okay with that," she said. Suddenly shy, she added, "And I only returned the sweater you got me for Christmas because I, you know, *grew.*"

Cassie nodded. "Seventh grade. Titty fairy. Gotcha."

"You're better at picking out stuff than most adults," Tess observed. "Is that because . . ."

"I know what people think? Sometimes. But that's not always a good thing, is it? I'm guessing you found that out today."

The girl averted her gaze. "So, do all guys . . ."

"Look at your boobs and think horny thoughts? Yeah, pretty much. Some are nicer about it than others. They can't help being curious, and they've got this hunting instinct going on. Just think of them as large cats, minus the tail and fur, and they'll start making a lot more sense to you."

Tess's smile made a brief, fierce appearance. "I'd like to neuter a couple of them. But not, you know, personally."

"I hear you." Cassie rose to leave. "I can teach you how to shield your mind so you're not bombarded with noise all the time, and how to focus and open up when you want to. Once you get the hang of it, it's really not so bad."

"And the . . . other stuff?"

"You mean things moving around for no good reason? That's just another form of psychic energy." Cassie was about to use the term for this phenomenon—*poltergeist*—but decided Hollywood had probably confused that issue beyond the possibility of easy explanation.

"It's a puberty thing, and it'll pass soon. In fact, just talking about it, just accepting that what's going on is perfectly normal for you, may take enough edge off the energy to put a stop to that."

"I hope so," Tess said fervently. "It's seriously freaking me out."

"Your mom can recommend some books for you to read. Also, maybe you should talk to Emily."

Tess dismissed that notion with an adamant shake of her head. "She's too freaking perfect." Her grim expression melted almost immediately into a look of resignation. "But once Mom finds out about all this, she'll probably set something up. Get Emily to take me out shopping or whatever."

"Go for it. The girl's got a driver's license, a Visa card, and great taste in shoes. And your Uncle Michael, bless his heart, understands the importance of retail therapy."

A grin ghosted across Tess's face, and she cast a quick glance up at Cassie. "Thanks. For Arwen and, you know, *stuff*."

"Any time you need 'stuff,' I'm your girl," Cassie promised.

Chapter Six

That promise echoed through Cassie's head the rest of the afternoon like a particularly annoying jingle. Like it or not, it seemed she was suddenly the go-to girl for all the psychic "stuff" in the bay area.

The prospect of being a mentor to a preteen psychic was daunting, but Tess was family, and that was all that needed to be said on the matter. Nick, on the other hand, was considerably more complicated.

Cassie slid a glance toward him, sitting inches and miles away from her in the back seat of Andreozzi's car. He seemed deeply preoccupied, and though he was gazing fixedly at the windshield, Cassie doubted he was actually registering the woodland scenery beyond.

Still, Cassie sensed an awareness between them, something so electric that she suspected they'd throw off sparks if they accidentally touched.

He turned to face her. The jolt of contact widened her eyes and shot her heart rate into the cardio training zone.

"I'm sorry you were brought into this," he said softly.

Cassie tore her gaze away. "Yeah, I got that."

She caught sight of his grimace from the corner of her eye. "That's not what I meant. You know that's not what I meant."

"Oh? And how could I possibly 'know' that?"

His expression changed from chagrin to exasperation. "People don't need a crystal ball to perceive meaning and nuance, especially two people who once knew each other very well. Things ended badly between us. I regret that, deeply. I know this is difficult for you. But sarcasm doesn't help."

"I beg to differ. Sarcasm is not only satisfying, it's also a socially acceptable alternative to ass-kicking."

Silence fell. Lingered. After a few moments the detective turned on the radio. He fiddled with the dial for a few moments, then began to hum tunelessly, more or less in time with the music.

"Considerate of him," Nick said softly, tipping his head toward Andreozzi. "I'd hoped we have a chance to talk in privacy."

Cassie's heart did a giddy little hop. She ignored it and kept her gaze forward. "What's on your mind?"

"Philip Meyer implied you were capable of dealing with any . . . trouble that might arise," he said hesitantly. "Physically, that is."

She turned back toward him, lifted one brow in a dangerous arc. "And that surprises you?"

"A little," he admitted. "You were always athletic, but never showed any interest in 'ass-kicking,' as you put it. In all candor, you seem too small, too feminine for that." His gazed skimmed over her as he spoke, warming as it went.

Warming *her* . . .

Cassie gave her libido a mental bitch-slap and smiled up at him sweetly. "Don't worry. Your ass is perfectly safe."

"I'm not worried about me."

His meaning hit her then, and she couldn't quite stop a snort of laughter. The notion that Nick would ever harm her was ludicrous, incomprehensible.

"Well, thanks for your concern," she told him. "The fact that Andreozzi came along tells me how much confidence you place in my ability to take care of myself."

"Dr. Meyer suggested sending the lieutenant, but it struck me as a sensible precaution."

"From his point of view? Absolutely. It was the quickest way to make sure I played along."

Nick's gaze sharpened. "Explain."

"People can develop their psychic potential at any point in their lives," she said. "It can be difficult at first. Even experienced and well-trained psychics often get sick or disoriented after a powerful vision."

He rubbed both hands over his face in a gesture of sheer frustration, then let them drop heavily to his lap. "Cassie, if the only tool you have is a hammer, every problem looks like a nail. Would you at least consider some other explanation than psychic phenomena?"

"Fine," she said evenly. "If you wig out, I promise to kick your ass. Happy now?"

His lips quirked in sudden amusement and a familiar gleam crept into his grey eyes. "Oddly enough, I probably would be."

Cassie remembered several good-natured wrestling matches, and the memory of how those sessions had ended sent an edgy, insistent heat shimmering through her. The intensity of her response, the immediacy of it, frightened her a little.

"Do you remember walking in the dunes at Plum Island?" Nick's voice had lowered, deepened, and the expression in his eyes left no doubt that his thoughts were taking a similar path to hers. Yet Cassie perceived a layer of concern under the steamy nostalgia: his smile was a little strained, his gaze a little too searching.

"Back then, I didn't put up much of a fight." She patted the purse sitting between them. "I didn't carry a gun at the time, either."

"I see," Nick said slowly, not taking his eyes from her face. "And you'd use it if you had to, to protect yourself and others?"

Oddly enough, he didn't sound angry, or hurt, or disbelieving. He sounded . . . relieved. Cassie's heart broke a little for him.

"Meyer sent you into a situation that's very likely to jump-start whatever it is you've been experiencing," she said, speaking more gently. "If you have a bad reaction, whatever the cause of it, Andreozzi might misinterpret what's going on."

Nick glanced at the detective. "And what would you do if he did?"

"Whatever I have to."

"And Meyer knows that," Nick said. Anger flashed into his eyes. "He'd put you between me and a police officer?"

BEYOND DREAMS 153

"If he saw it as a means to an end? In a heartbeat."

Nick shook his head in mingled disgust and disbelief. "Who *is* this guy?"

"And what the hell is he doing in Providence?" Cassie added. "Good questions both. I have no idea what interest Meyer has in this case, but I'm guessing he thinks you can solve it for him. So he's willing to use you. And, by extension, me."

Nick leaned in closer. "It might actually be the other way around," he murmured. "Meyer implied that he wanted you, not me. That I was bait to bring you into this."

Warning bells went off in the back of Cassie's mind. " 'This'? He wanted me for this case? Is that what he said?"

Nick's brow furrowed as he thought that over. "No," he said slowly. "He didn't refer specifically to the abducted women. What he *said* was that my coming in gave him an excuse to call you. Apparently he would have found another reason to approach you if this situation hadn't arisen."

Cassie hissed out an exasperated sigh. "Great. I should have figured he'd have a multilevel agenda."

They lapsed into silence. A *welcome* silence, for to Cassie's relief, Andreozzi wasn't broadcasting a barrage of mental noise. Either he was too exhausted to think, or Cassie's mental shields were much better than they'd been this morning. Since Andreozzi was driving, she sincerely hoped it was the latter.

Of course that was it. The prospect of seeing Nick again had rattled her, thrown her off her stride. But she was in control of her thoughts now. Her hormones . . . okay, not so much, but her mind was very, very firmly under control.

Maybe, she conceded, a little bit *too* much control. That could be a problem. Cassie didn't doubt for a second that Nick's dreams, all three of them, were genuine. If they were to save the third, unknown woman, Cassie had to be open to whatever information her particular gift could gather.

She closed her eyes and took a long, calming breath, then willed herself into the relaxation patterns that led to a deeply receptive state . . .

The vision slammed into her, suddenly, more vivid and immediate than anything she'd ever experienced.

As if she were there, Cassie saw Laura careening around a curve in her pride and joy—a black Mustang, which at the moment was going too damn fast even by Laura's hell-on-wheels standards.

Her sister's sharp-featured face was set in grim determination, and her hands clenched the steering wheel at precisely ten and two o'clock. Laura pumped the breaks, lightly, for what Cassie knew was not the first time. Then again, harder, and then she pushed the pedal all the way to the floor.

Nothing.

The car continued to pick up speed. Laura glanced at the control panel and reached for a lever on the steering column. Cruise control. She hadn't set it, but it was on. She jiggled the lever. Again, nothing.

Laura spat out a curse and slapped her right hand back onto the wheel. Not far ahead, a car was making a leisurely turn out of a side street. She swerved around it, directly into oncoming traffic. Horns blared as she swung back into her lane, tires screeching.

Her long, amber eyes narrowed as she scanned the road ahead. There was no place to pull over, not at this speed. The two-lane road was narrow, with no shoulder to speak off. Trees lined it on both sides, standing so close to the road that at times the branches met overhead. Laura muttered something that sounded like "*fucking shortcut*" and tried downshifting.

The engine screamed in protest, but the car slowed a little. Not much, but enough that Laura thought she might be able to pull off *this*—

She wrenched the steering wheel sharply to the right and felt the driver's side wheels leave the ground as the Mustang spun toward a narrow dirt drive. Immediately she corrected to the left to straighten out the car.

Not quickly enough—there was a sharp, metallic crack as her right mirror lost an argument with a tree, followed by a bad few moments as she fishtailed along the road, barely in control of the vehicle.

Just as the Mustang's tires started to grip the dirt road, she saw the turn coming. She slammed the palm of her hand onto the horn, blaring a warning in case anyone was up ahead. Fortunately the road was empty—

Damn it, no it wasn't! A pickup truck was blocking the ramp into the water, which Laura had planned to use to slow and stop her car. To the left of it stood two men, each holding a string of out-of-season fish and wearing identical stunned expressions.

She pulled to the right, barely missing the truck. There wasn't time to pull clear of the stout, waist-high piers framing the dock, nowhere to go but onto the dock itself.

The car rumbled along the wooden dock, then shot out over the water. For a moment it seemed to hang there, suspended between sky and sea. Along with Laura, Cassie braced herself for the impact—

"Cassie. *Cassie!*"

The fear in Nick's voice dragged her free, thrust her back into her own awareness. She shook off the vision and looked into his face, inches away from hers. He was leaning over her, his hands on her shoulders. The slight sting in one cheek suggested that he'd been trying to rouse her for a while.

Andreozzi had stopped the car alongside the road. Trees surrounded them; there was nothing to give Cassie a sense of her bearings.

"Where the hell are we?" she demanded.

"Just outside of Foster," the detective said. "The question is, where the hell were *you*?"

She waved his question away with an impatient flip of her hand. "Do you know the fire road off the north side of the reservoir?"

Before he could answer, she caught a glimpse of Andreozzi as a teenager, locked in a sweaty tangle with a plump blonde. They were in the back of a family van, parked alongside the dock she'd just seen in vision.

"Oh yeah, you know it. How fast can you get there?"

Nick tore his gaze from Cassie's face for a moment. "Please do as she asks."

The detective muttered, but he pulled into a U-turn and headed back toward the reservoir.

"What's going on, Cassie?" Nick asked softly, his hands still on her shoulders.

"It's Laura! She drove into the water. She's in the water *now*."

He studied her for a long moment. His face was carefully neutral, but his hands slowly fell away from her. "She drove into the water," he repeated.

Even in her panic, Cassie felt the sting of his withdrawal. "I guess she figured it was better than running into a freaking tree." She leaned forward and tapped Andreozzi on the shoulder, caught his eye in the rearview mirror. "Can't this car go any faster?"

The corners of the detective's mustache pulled down disapprovingly, but he sped up. To Cassie's surprise, he also picked up his radio and called in the accident.

The drive seemed to take forever. When at last they turned onto the dirt road, Cassie noted a faint haze low over the road. Some of the dust the Mustang's tires had kicked up still lingered in the air. Cassie took heart from that.

That hope faded a little when they rounded the turn and she saw that the truck was gone. Had they tried to get Laura out, or had they simply fled?

She was out of the car before it came to a complete stop, running for the water. Discarded beer bottles littered the ground and the dock, and she was vaguely aware of the crunch of broken glass underfoot and the sharp, bright pain as she turned an ankle on the loose stones. Cassie lost a half step, recovered her balance and her pace, and kept going. She was halfway down the dock before Nick caught up with her.

He grabbed her arm and spun her around. "Cassie, stop. Laura's not in the water."

She wrenched away. "Believe what you want. I know what I saw—"

"I believe you."

This stunned her into momentary silence. Nick took her by the shoulders and gently turned her back toward the shore.

"We'll talk later. Right now, we need to see to your sister."

An overturned rowboat was pulled up on the shore some hundred yards away. Beside it Andreozzi crouched over a dark, wet form. He was speaking into a cell phone.

To Cassie's immense relief, a slim, manicured hand slapped down on the boat's bottom and Laura hauled herself into a sitting position. Her long, thick hair, usually the rich mahogany hue of a pampered Irish setter and meticulously straightened and styled, hung over her shoulders in lank strands which were already beginning to curl.

Cassie broke into a run. She sprinted along the shore and dropped to her knees beside her sister. Her first impulse was to pull Laura into a hug, but as Laura turned toward her, Cassie saw the blood running down the far side of her face. She froze with her hands outstretched.

"Omigod! You've hurt your head."

"I'm fine," Laura muttered. "It's fine."

"It's bleeding! Right here." Cassie raised her hand to her own head to demonstrate.

Her sister slid exploring fingers into her sodden hair, grimacing as she did. "Hmmm. Must have cut it getting out of the car. Kicking out a window is harder than you'd think. The water comes in fast—must have washed some of the glass back at me."

"But you're okay?"

"Pretty much. Those air bags do the job." She gave her head an experimental shake, then lifted a hand to one ear. "Shit. Lost an earring."

"I'll buy you a new pair if you let me take a look at that cut," Nick offered as he strode toward them.

Laura looked up. "You again," she said, sounding neither

surprised nor impressed. After a moment she shrugged.
"Suit yourself."

Nick crouched beside her and probed her head with
deft, gentle hands. He accepted the first-aid kit Andreozzi
brought out of the car, used the penlight to check her eyes'
response to light.

"You're going to need a couple of stitches. The good
news is that the cut is just above the hairline, so you won't
have a visible scar. I'm going to put on a butterfly bandage."

He worked quickly, then folded some gauze and pressed
it against Laura's temple. "I want you to keep some light
pressure on, just like this."

The sisters' eyes met, and suddenly Cassie felt profoundly uncomfortable. Her vision had been unintentional,
but it still felt like an intrusion.

"It's lucky we came along just now," she babbled. "You
know, with a doctor and all."

Laura shot her a disgusted look. "Bitch, *please*. We can
do the dance of denial later, if you want, but give me a
freaking break. I just drowned my car."

Cassie's response was lost in the sound of an approaching siren. The local fire department pulled up behind
Andreozzi's car. When Nick went over to talk to the
emergency medical technician, Cassie leaned in closer to
Laura.

"You *know*. How?"

Her sister smirked. "You're not the only one in the family with red hair, a temper, and some extra circuits in the
mental wiring. You don't think I'd know when someone
snuck into my head?"

"It wasn't intentional."

Laura shrugged. "Maybe not, but I suppose it was in-
evitable. Molly's been after me to try to connect with you,
and you know how relentless she can be. That's what the
Sister Sunday brunch thing is about."

"Really."

"Well, that and waffles." She sent a quick, sidelong look
at Cassie. "It sucks to be me, right?"

"Not that I could see. You handled it like a pro. That said, I hope those two drunken bastards who ran off and left you in the water choke on those fish bones."

Some of the tension went out of Laura's shoulders. "Now you're talking. So. What's going on with the ex?"

"Long story. Oops, here comes the EMT. We can catch up on the way to the hospital."

Laura shook her head. "You two go ahead. Catch up. Fuck like bunnies. I'll be fine."

"But how will you get home?"

"I'll call a friend, okay? Stop fussing. And it's not like you have your car with you, anyway."

"Oh. Right."

"You can do one thing for me, though. Make sure they take my car to Jim Thorpe's garage in Smithfield."

Laura brushed aside the EMT's attempts to examine her and rose to her feet, unaided. The look she sent the man silenced him in mid-protest. He fell into step behind her as she walked over to the ambulance. She climbed into the back, then leaned out and repeated, "Jim Thorpe. No one else touches my car."

As the vehicle pulled away, Nick caught Cassie's eye. She wasn't aware of moving toward him, but suddenly there they were. His arms went around her, and she instinctively lifted her face to his.

As their lips met, a wave of emotion crashed over her: *awe, fear, curiosity, regret, loss*. And behind it, emerging tentatively into the light, were *joy, wonder, desire. Love*.

Shock froze Cassie in place for a moment. Never before had she sensed Nick's passing thoughts, much less anything like *this*.

The kiss ended before she could make sense of it all. But his arms were still around her, and a feeling of deep contentment enfolded them both. A moment passed before Cassie found a name for it:

Home.

She leaned her head against his chest and sank into the moment.

"I'm surprised Laura didn't insist on driving the ambulance," Nick murmured against her hair. From the tone of his voice, Cassie could tell he was smiling.

"They'd probably let her. It'd be easier than arguing."

He chuckled. "Not much changes. She was already running things when she was, what? Fifteen?"

"And now she's a college professor," Cassie said wistfully.

"A lot of time has passed," he agreed, echoing both her thought and her mood.

Someone cleared his throat pointedly. Cassie remembered Andreozzi and moved reluctantly out of Nick's arms.

"It's getting late," the detective said when he had their attention. He gestured toward the sunset clouds gathering over the reservoir. "I've still got the paperwork to do on this accident. If it's all the same to you, we can try again tomorrow. I'll take you back to the police station so you can pick up your cars."

They made the drive in silence. Once Andreozzi dropped them off, Nick fell into step beside Cassie. "Is there a place we could go to talk? Somewhere private?"

"If you don't mind following me to East Bay, sure."

His eyes widened when he saw her aging Miata. "This couldn't be the same car you had in Boston."

"Dez drove it while I was overseas."

"I'm amazed it still runs."

She cocked one eyebrow, and her smile held challenge. "Just try to keep up."

Fifteen minutes later, they pulled up outside the tiny bungalow Cassie called home. Nick took in the kelly green door, the exuberant spill of ivy and spring flowers tumbling from the window boxes, the softball cleats left on the porch.

"This is your place," he said.

"And as such, it's private."

He shook his head. "Cassie, I'm not sure this is a good idea."

"Oh, get over yourself," she told him. "You didn't kill those women, and you're not a danger to me." Not physically, at least, she added silently.

"I hope you're right. But if you are, that means I have to adjust my definition of reality. You finding Laura like that, the connection between us at the reservoir . . . I don't know what to make of any of this." He searched her face as if the answers might be written there. "Any of it."

"Then how about we go inside, make some coffee, and try to figure it out."

Cassie shut and locked the door behind them, then turned toward Nick. The raw emotion on his face stunned her.

"You know what the hardest thing about this is?" he said softly. "If I've been wrong all these years, I lost you for no reason. And when I saw you running for the water, hell-bent on diving in after your sister, all I could think about was losing you all over again."

"I know," she said softly. She brought her hands up to frame his face. "I felt it."

She held his gaze as she slowly, deliberately lowered her shields, focused on sending thought and emotion.

Suddenly they were open to each other in a way Cassie hadn't anticipated. Hadn't known was possible. She'd wondered from time to time how a man experienced desire and arousal. Now she knew.

Nick's eyes widened. "This isn't possible," he murmured. He skimmed his hands down her back, and the flicker in his eyes reflected the shimmer of lust that curled down her spine. "It's impossible to feel what another person is feeling. Do you—"

"Yes."

"Amazing. And the sensations are separate, distinct. Like holding ice in one hand and fire in another."

Cassie's wonderment matched his, but the spiraling rise of desire—hers, his, around and around—was far more compelling than intellectual curiosity. "I've never heard of this, either, but it does raise some interesting questions."

"That it does." Nick caught one of her hands and brought it to his lips. "Among other things."

She sent him a slow, wicked smile. "Show me."

He cupped her bottom with both hands and lifted her. Her legs went around his hips as he fitted her body to his. The pressure was exquisite, and the layers of clothing between them suddenly felt ridiculous, intolerable.

A tiny cry escaped her before Nick claimed her mouth. She wrapped her arms around his neck and sank into the kiss. When they finally drew apart, she nipped at his lower lip. She felt his libido register the slight sharpness of that bite, in much the same way her taste buds responded to good hot chili.

"Where's the bedroom?" he demanded.

Cassie wasn't sure she was capable of speech at that moment, so she merely pictured the way. Her house was tiny—just four rooms, with the bedroom directly off the living area. Nick turned toward the open door and crossed the distance with a few quick steps.

He hesitated beside the bed. Cassie could feel his attempt to slow down, to savor. Did he realize that at least half the impatience and urgency he was feeling was coming from her?

"The caveman approach," she assured him, "is a classic."

The sound he made was somewhere between a chuckle and a growl, and sexy as hell. He tossed her onto the bed and dove after her.

They rolled once so that Cassie was sprawled across him. She wanted to kiss him again, wanted the warmth and the intense connection, but she was so much shorter, and his face was a few inches out of reach. She wriggled her way up his body, drawing a heartfelt moan from him.

Nick fisted his hands in her hair, tightening just short of pain, and devoured her mouth. After a while his hands slid down her back, caressing, rediscovering, growing more insistent. He lingered, and Cassie felt his pleasure over the sensation of her firm, small curves filling his hands. He moved lower still to urge her legs apart and draw her into an even more intimate embrace. And everything—every shared sensation, every emotion—seemed magnified, multiplied. Cassie got a sudden image of making love in a hall of mirrors, seeing every movement reflected back, and back, and back. . . .

She pulled away suddenly and sat up on her knees, straddling him. Her sweater came off in one quick, impatient sweep. Nick pulled her back down, reached around to unhook her bra. He held onto the straps as she curled back up, revealing herself to him with teasing slowness.

Nick's hands were warm against her skin, his fingers gentle as they circled nipples that rose small and tight with desire.

"You look exactly as I remember you," he said in wondering tones. "Better, if that were possible."

His hands grew more insistent, drawing a gasp of pleasure from her. His eyes glazed, then widened with amazement, as he sensed what she was experiencing.

"Still an A-cup, though," she managed.

"Indeed you are," he said fervently. "I'm seeing a direct correlation between bra sizes and the academic grading system."

That amused and pleased her. "So I get top marks?"

"Oh yeah."

Her hands went to the fasteners on her slacks. "In that case, professor, you're going to love what I do for extra credit."

The doorbell jangled. Cassie froze for a moment, then shrugged. "They'll go away eventually."

It rang twice more, the buzzer long and insistent, while they were shedding the rest of their clothes. By the time it fell silent, they'd tumbled back into the bed. This time Nick rose over her, tracing a line of kisses down her throat. *Warmth,* she thought blissfully. His lips, her skin. He lingered at her breasts for several breathless moments, then moved down her flat belly. She felt his pleasure at the sight of the intimate vista before him, his amusement over the neatly trimmed little heart shape she'd adopted on a whim. His mouth traced the outline of that heart, then moved lower.

The first jolt of contact made her gasp—a quick, sudden breath that she expelled in a purr of contentment. He'd always been good at pleasuring her, but Cassie's awareness of *his* enjoyment added a whole new set of sensations. And his awareness of *hers* had much the same effect on him, which in turn . . .

All conscious thought dissolved in the growing maelstrom. There was so much to feel, so much. Too much. His urgency matched hers; his control maddened her. Desperate for fulfillment, Cassie pleaded—not with words, but with small, inarticulate cries.

Nick moved away from her, over her. The sudden physical distance gave her a moment's respite from the shared sensual storm. A moment's separation, no more, but it served to intensify the impact of his entrance into her body.

He moved surely, entering her with a single long stroke. She was ready for him, more than ready, but the explosion of shared pleasure tore a scream from her.

To her amazement, there was more. Neither of them had reached the precipice. Nick continued to move, and they found a rhythm that suited them both.

The climb was swift, the fall shattering.

Time passed in a glorious, languid haze. After several moments, or possibly an hour or two, Cassie became aware of Nick's weight pinning her to the bed. And close on the heels of that revelation came another:

There was another person in her house.

Rational thought returned with a rush. Cassie started to reach for the handgun in her bedside drawer, then realized that it was in her purse . . . which she'd dropped on the living room floor.

She reached out mentally, searching for any thread of thought or intent that would identify the intruder. There was nothing beyond her own faint awareness of a nearby presence.

"Nick," she said softly.

His response was a faint groan. She eased out from under him, found her clothes and dressed as quickly and quietly as she could.

The bedroom door was closed. Nick must have kicked it shut when he carried her in. Cassie slowly turned the knob, cracked it carefully open.

A woman sat on the sofa, leafing through a magazine Cassie had left on the table a week or so ago. A stranger.

The intruder's mink brown hair was short and stylish, her long, slim legs were crossed at the ankles in a lady-like fashion Cassie's mother would approve. She turned toward Cassie, revealing an interesting, sharply sculpted face. Her makeup was expert and her age impossible to guess, but the polish and style she exuded made such considerations seem minor. Her eyes looked familiar to Cassie, but only because of the warmth and lively intelligence in them. The color was not what she remembered, nor was the shape.

Even so, Cassie knew.

Selena Weis, the woman she'd killed Armand to protect, was sitting on her sofa.

Chapter Seven

Selena put down the magazine. "You're looking well, Cassie. You could use better locks, though."

"People in this town rarely use the ones they have."

"People, generally speaking, are idiots." Her gaze shifted to the bedroom door. "I've come at a bad time, haven't I?"

"Does it matter?"

Selena sighed. "Unfortunately, no. We need to talk. It's not something I care to discuss over the ridiculously insecure cell phones everyone insists upon using."

"Okay." Cassie sank down into the chair opposite her former supervisor. "So, what do I call you? I'm guessing you have a new name to go with the new face and the British accent. Nice job on both, by the way."

"Thanks. I'm known as Lea Morgan these days, but call me Selena if that's easier."

"You're probably here to complicate my life in some hideous fashion, but sure—not having to learn a new name for you will even things right out," Cassie said dryly. "What's going on, Selena?"

"After the program disbanded, I was determined to continue the work we'd been doing. The most interesting opportunity at the time was in the UK, a well-funded independent study. Unfortunately, my government work would not have been considered a bright spot on my resumé."

"Must have been one hell of a job to justify the name change and makeover."

"I was due for a new look. As for plastic surgery—" Selena paused for an eloquent shrug. "I would have done it sooner or later, regardless. So I called in some markers, built an identity that would withstand the security inquiries, and was accepted into the program. By the time that study ran its course, I'd established a history and credentials. It was more convenient to continue as Lea Morgan."

"Like a divorced woman keeping her married name."

"Very much like. Among other things, that name is attached to postgraduate degrees in psychology and parapsychology."

"University of Edinburgh," Nick said, "followed by a research fellowship at Princeton."

Both women glanced at the open doorway to Cassie's room. "Nick Romano," he said, offering his hand as he entered the room. "I've read some of your publications, Dr. Morgan, and I've seen your name mentioned in others."

Selena took his hand and gave him a thin smile. "Including the deconstructions of the remote viewing studies

at Princeton, no doubt. 'Statistical anomalies are not necessarily meaningful' was the general consensus."

Nick settled down beside Cassie. "What brings you to
Rhode Island, Dr. Morgan?"

"Please, call me Selena. As you know, I've been involved in research at various universities. Much of the
support for remote viewing dried up after the government
disbanded the program, but a few schools still offer parapsychology studies. Most of them are in the UK, some in
Germany. At present I'm doing a one-year teaching and
research fellowship at Remington College."

Cassie sat bolt upright. "My sister Laura teaches there."

"In the anthropology department," Selena acknowledged. "We've met, but I can't say I know her well. She can
be . . ." She trailed off uncertainly.

"A bitch?" Cassie suggested, since that was the label
Laura wore as a badge of honor.

"Forceful," Selena corrected with a smile. "And perhaps a little eccentric, but what I meant to say was that she
is very difficult to know."

Cassie nodded. Even as a child, Laura had been fiercely
private. Not everyone picked up on that, given her blunt
way of speaking, her circle of friends, and the number of
men who passed through her life. Selena, however, was
hardly a casual observer.

"I did talk to Laura often enough to learn that you were
her sister, and living locally. Something has been happening I think you ought to know about." She glanced at Nick,
narrowed her eyes and studied him intently. After a moment she said, "You're a doctor, are you not?"

"A psychiatrist, yes."

"Then you will understand the importance of what I
need to tell Cassie. In addition to teaching and research, I
have a private practice, very small and specialized. I treat
people whose psychic gifts have been misdiagnosed as
mental illness."

Nick went very still. Cassie reached for his hand, certain even before making contact that his thoughts had

turned to his sister. As she suspected, he was wondering whether just such a misdiagnosis had driven Jessica to despair and death.

"Most people in traditional medicine are skeptical of such things," Selena acknowledged, misunderstanding his reaction, "but consider the usual sequence: a child reports that he hears voices. An adolescent girl sees and hears things no one else can perceive. Worried parents of such children take them to 'experts,' who prescribe powerful drugs, sometimes in wildly inappropriate cocktails. These chemicals shape the growing mind, and the entire process distorts the child's self-image. Sometimes the mind splinters in an attempt to reconcile the reality it knows with the reality the rest of the world wishes to impose upon it."

"You're talking about dissociative identity disorder," Nick said cautiously. "In your opinion, this . . . misdiagnosis can be an underlying cause?"

"Not in every case, certainly, but some. This, however, is a debate for another time."

Selena hesitated, biting her lip in apparent consternation. She sent a brief, rueful smile in Nick's direction. "This is more difficult than I thought it would be. What I am about to tell you skirts the edges of professional ethics. Before you judge me, weigh the importance of this information against the cost of keeping silent."

Nick nodded cautiously. "There are times when patient confidentiality takes second place to preventing harm to other people, but it's never an easy decision to make."

"Never," she agreed fervently. She leaned forward, her gaze shifting between Nick and Cassie to include them both in the confidence to come. "I need to tell you about two of my patients: Faith Anders and Mita Patel. One of those names will almost certainly be familiar to you."

"Anders . . ." mused Cassie. "Wasn't Hope Anders one of the abducted women? The thirty-something blond woman with the twin sister?"

"Faith and Hope were twins, yes, identical in every regard

but the one that brought Faith to me. Her psychic ability emerged after a near-fatal swimming accident."

"And Mita Patel?" Nick asked.

"She was Genna Rivers's life partner."

"So there's a connection between the abducted women and two of your patients," Nick said. "Given the size of Rhode Island, that's not so difficult to believe."

"I only have seven clients, Dr. Romano, and all of them have demonstrated significant psychic ability. That is too small and specific a sample to explain this coincidence." Selena's gaze shifted to Cassie. "And there's more."

"There always seems to be," Cassie muttered.

"I've been involved in paranormal research since the program disbanded, so I . . . hear things."

"Comes with the territory."

Selena frowned, either missing the quip or disapproving of it. "That's not what I meant. I understand why you wanted to shut the door on that part of your life, Cassie, but did you ever think about what your colleagues might do after the remote viewing program was discontinued?"

"Any number of things, I guess. Some wrote books, others wrote books refuting their books, some moved into other branches of government service, some probably went into real estate." She sent Selena a grim little smile. "A couple of the channeling divas probably lost a shitload of money on the futures market."

The older woman laughed, not without malice. "If so, I sincerely hope Philip Meyer invested heavily."

"What's this about Meyer and channeling?" Nick asked.

"Office politics," Cassie said with a shrug. "Some of the remote viewers started claiming they were getting their information from spirit guides. Meyer was intrigued, and he pushed us all to try it. Selena and I were both dead-set against it. Me, because I didn't believe it was possible. Selena had her own reasons."

"When Meyer and others like him started going down this path, it was the beginning of the end," Selena explained.

"Remote viewing sounds vaguely scientific, so it's easy for the politicians to ignore these programs, but when you start talking about spirits and channeling you bump up too forcefully against conservative beliefs. But that's water long under the bridge. Back to my question, Cassie: don't you think that someone might have seen opportunity in all that suddenly available psychic talent?"

It hit her then. "Oh, crap. You're telling me some new organization snapped up unemployed government psychics."

"Two of them, actually. One is still under the government banner—deep, deep under. The other group provides guns for hire."

"Yikes." A shudder went through Cassie as she considered the implications. "Industrial espionage?"

"Among other things." Selena leaned back and hooked one arm over the back of the sofa. She studied Cassie for several moments. "This is all news to you."

"Well, *yeah*."

"So no one has tried to recruit you?"

Suddenly Philip Meyer's presence in Providence made a great deal of sense. "Not yet," Cassie said cautiously.

"Good." Selena sat up straight and knotted her hands in her lap—an uncharacteristically nervous gesture. "I don't mind telling you that I'm afraid of the forms this 'recruitment' might take. Or what might happen to people who resist. Someone is targeting psychics, Cassie, and not just here in Providence. I've been seeing this for several years now, but never in this particular form. Two women are dead, and I'm convinced there's a connection. I've closed my practice, destroyed my records, and warned my other clients to take extra precautions."

Nick cleared his throat. "And you're concerned about Cassie, because of the . . . psychic factor."

"It's not Cassie I'm worried about, at least not in the most immediate sense, but the people close to her," Selena said. "Faith and Mita are both very gifted women. I doubt it's a coincidence that one lost a twin, the other a lover."

Cassie sat bolt upright. "Omigod! Laura! She was in a

car accident this afternoon. She's okay, but her brakes went out and her cruise control locked up."

Selena looked very grave. "I'm sorry to hear that. She wasn't hurt, you said?"

"Not much." Cassie blew out a long breath. "I never thought I'd say this, but it's a good thing Laura drives like a freaking maniac on a regular basis. She handled it. This puts a very different spin on the accident. It may help us prevent another one."

"I hope so. Be careful, Cassie."

Selena rose to leave. Cassie walked with her out onto the porch, motioned for Nick to give them a minute. "One more thing," she said softly. "Do you know if anyone has been getting messages from Armand?"

For a long moment, the woman stared at her. "Messages. From Armand. You're talking about Armand Gaudine?"

"I know it sounds a little odd—"

"A *little odd*?" She shook her head in dismay. "Cassie, please tell me you're talking about letters and notes he left behind."

The wary disbelief on Selena's face was familiar. Selena, like Cassie, believed that the living mind was capable of far more than most people imagined.

The *living* mind.

Cassie gave herself a mental kick for bringing this up. Even assuming that it was possible to receive messages from beyond—and as far as Cassie was concerned, that was a very *big* if—and further assuming that Armand had broken through to psychics he'd known in life, no one who knew Selena's opinion on this matter was likely to tell her about it.

On the other hand, Selena's response raised another possibility.

"Has there been any? Information about Armand, I mean, recently coming to light?"

"Not that I'm aware of. Cassie, what's this about?"

"It's possible that there might be some connection between Armand and the two abducted women."

Selena's gaze sharpened. "Anything you want to share?"

"Not just yet."

The woman accepted this with a nod. "I'll see what I can find out. Most of the files have been declassified. I'll make a few calls to old friends, get someone started digging through the closed files."

"Thanks, Selena."

They did the hug and air kisses routine, and Selena walked off the porch, giving Cassie's aging Miata an approving nod and Nick's hybrid an amused smile. It occurred to Cassie, briefly, to wonder what kind of car Selena drove these days. Back in the day, her preferences—and her driving habits, for that matter—had been very similar to Laura's. Cassie grinned, trying to picture this newly sedate, polished Selena outrunning the Istanbul police in a "borrowed" Italian sports car.

The muffled ringing of a cell phone greeted Cassie as she walked back into the house. She picked her purse off the floor and dug out the phone.

"It's Molly," the caller announced in a voice stretched thin with worry. "Cassie, Tess is missing."

Chapter Eight

Nick saw the color drain from Cassie's face and instinctively reached out to catch her. No need; before he could get to her, she snatched up her purse and bolted for the door. Nick followed close on her heels. He didn't know what had brought that look to her face, but he'd be damned if he let her face it alone.

"I'll drive," he said firmly as he opened the passenger door of his car. "Where are we going?"

Cassie slid into the seat without argument and strapped on her seat belt with the air of one who expected rough road ahead. "Molly's house. Her daughter Tess is missing."

He remembered that name. Tess had been born shortly before Cassie left him. That would make Molly's daughter . . . dear God, almost thirteen! A girl that age was vulnerable in so many ways. The timing seemed particularly ominous, given the conversation they'd just had with the mysterious Selena.

"You don't think—"

"I hope not," Cassie said quickly. "Not that Tess can't handle herself. Or them. Whoever 'they' are. Assuming there *is* a 'them.' Which I hope there's not. God, I'm babbling."

"You're entitled."

She lapsed into silence. Nick was oddly pleased that she didn't point out the way to her sister's house. Perhaps she was just too preoccupied, but as it turned out, there was no need. His memories of East Bay's streets and landmarks fell readily into place.

Molly's sprawling Victorian was familiar, too, despite the addition of multihued trim and the wooden sign in the small front garden proclaiming the establishment to be Molly-O's Gallery and Gifts. Smaller signs hanging below the main one indicated that herbs and teas, doggie daycare, and Siamese cats were also available.

Nick pulled the car to a stop along the road. Molly came running out to meet them, her long red-brown hair flying loose over her shoulders. She hadn't changed much, either, other than the fact that the last time he'd seen her, she'd been exceedingly pregnant. When she flung her arms around Cassie, Nick noticed that her left hand was bare; the wedding ring she'd worn so proudly was gone. That surprised him. Jason and Molly had been crazy about each other, and nearly giddy about the coming baby.

As he came around the car the sisters broke apart, and suddenly his arms were full of Molly. He barely had time to give her an awkward pat on the back before she'd kissed his cheek and whirled back to Cassie, leaving him standing there feeling stunned and a little bit smitten.

Years ago, the O'Malley family had made room for him in their noisy, chaotic lives without seeming to break stride. That this matter-of-fact acceptance was still there for him struck him as nothing short of miraculous.

"Tess left right after you did." Molly's face was drawn with worry, and the words spilled out of her in a rush. "She said she needed to go for a walk. I knew what was on her mind, so I didn't press her. But that was hours ago, and it's dark, and she's not back, and I've called all her friends . . ."

Cassie slipped an arm around her sister's waist. "Let's go inside. If you'll make a pot of tea, I'll 'look' for Tess."

Molly's eyes lit up. "Sage tea—that will help, won't it?"

Nick had no idea what that meant, but Molly said it so hopefully he wasn't surprised when Cassie nodded.

A complex green scent hit him when they entered the house, and a Siamese cat who looked absurdly like Nimrod slinked over to inspect the newcomers.

Molly absently caught up the cat and tucked him under one arm. "I'll bring you something of hers to work with," she said as she hurried up the central stairs. "The top she was wearing earlier, maybe."

Cassie and Nick fell into step behind. "She seems to think you're a bloodhound," Nick murmured.

"It might sound odd, granted, but I get a lot of information through touch."

"I noticed."

She sent him a sidelong glance, and for a moment her eyes were heavy-lidded with sensual nostalgia. "Well, *that* was different. Definitely a first."

Molly motioned them into a small family room done in feminine shades of lavender and green. Two very plump female Siamese wandered into the room and regarded Nick with identical grave, blue-eyed stares. A sudden tug at the leg of his khakis startled him, and he glanced down at the cream-colored kitten that was about to climb him like a tree.

Cassie deftly plucked off the little cat before it got past Nick's knee. She casually stuck the kitten on the drapes, which it apparently found to be an acceptable substitute. Up it scrambled, nimble as a squirrel.

"Tess's shirt," Nick reminded her.

"Right. Some psychics are touch-sensitive. That's not my best skill, but I do find that holding a personal item helps focus my thoughts on that person."

"And the sage tea?"

Her smile was brief and wry. "If you believe the herbalists, it's supposed to enhance psychic energy."

"But if it's hot and in a cup, you'd prefer there be coffee beans involved."

"Oh, *hell* yeah."

But Cassie took the steaming mug Molly handed her and inhaled deeply. Nick watched as Cassie set the mug aside and picked up a scrap of stretchy black fabric. She closed her eyes and was suddenly . . . not there.

For a moment panic welled. Nick clenched his hands into fists to keep from reaching out to shake her back into herself. She'd looked just like this in Andreozzi's car. Despite her light, regular breathing, she looked like someone who'd been emptied by death, or whose mind had given way to madness. Nick wasn't sure which of those possibilities he found more devastating.

A lifetime of pain—his, his sister's, their parents, all his patients—flooded him. He couldn't do this. He couldn't watch this happen to Cassie day after day. He couldn't sit and wait, confident that she would be coming back unharmed, unchanged. He couldn't.

Nick sank into a chair and buried his face in his hands. What had he been thinking? How could he possibly have thought he could set aside reason and reality, ignore everything his training and his senses told him was possible?

There was no denying what had passed between him

and Cassie at her house, in her bed, but surely there was some rational way to explain that intense connection.

He scrubbed his hands briskly over his face and rose to pace. Maybe he'd been so convinced Cassie was the right woman for him that he'd held back from any real connection with other women. Perhaps his attraction to Cassie was so powerful, the difference between her and other women so vast, it suggested some extreme, irrational explanation.

"A dark car," Cassie said suddenly. "One of those retro sedans."

Relief flooded Molly's face. "I forgot about her friend Elise! She hasn't been around for a while, but her mother drives a PT Cruiser. The one you saw was dark blue?"

"Hard to say. It was just a glimpse, an impression."

But Molly was already dialing. "Deborah? This is Molly O'Malley, Tess's mom. Did she by any chance come home with Elise?"

The bright hope in Molly's eyes faded away. The short, one-sided conversation that followed confirmed what Nick saw in her face.

Cassie went over and put her hand on her sister's shoulder. "Tess knows better than to get into a car with strangers."

"Well, duh," announced a voice from the hall. Nick turned to see a slim girl with short, bottle-black hair walking into the room. She stopped dead when she saw the three adults staring at her, and her eyes widened when she took in the expression on her mother's face.

"Tess, where have you been?" Molly said in a carefully measured tone.

"Geez, Mom, take a pill! I was at the library. An old lady needed some help carrying a bunch of books to her car. She offered me a ride. If I *had* taken her up on it, I would have been home a lot sooner."

Nick recalled that the senior center was in the basement of East Bay's public library. Cassie's grandmother had been the ruling queen of that social set. He was impressed that a girl Tess's age would take the time to notice someone outside of her circle of friends.

Molly's faced softened a little. "That was a good thing to do, but next time you're going to be late, please call me."

The girl propped her hands on her hips, the picture of outraged dignity. "I *would,* if I had, you know, a *cell phone.* Like every *other* person in the known universe."

Cassie elbowed Nick. "I think our job here is done," she murmured.

But Tess, perhaps sensing what was to come, seemed in no hurry for them to leave. Her gaze shifted from Cassie to Nick. "Introductions, anyone? Or don't I rate?"

"This is Nick Romano, an old friend," Cassie supplied. "Nick, meet Tess."

"Dr. Romano," Molly corrected quietly.

The girl refrained, just barely, from rolling her eyes, but she politely extended her hand. As Nick shook it, her eyes widened. "Holy crap! You two guys are—"

"Lesson one," Cassie broke in: "Not everything that pops into your head needs to come out of your mouth."

If Tess heard, she gave no sign of it. "Wow. This is major. Cassie hasn't had a boyfriend since, you know, forever. It's got to where Father Dez is teasing her about being a 'stealth nun.' He's my uncle," she informed Nick, "and he's a priest, even if he is way too cute."

"Lesson two," Cassie said grimly, "is to review lesson one until it takes."

"Sorry." Tess scooped up her kitten, briefly buried her face in its fur. "So I guess you guys don't want to, you know, stick around a while."

"Another time," Nick said, smiling to take any possible sting out of the refusal. "It's been a long day, and I've got to drop Cassie off at her place before I drive down to Newport."

"That's where you live?"

"For now. I have an apartment there."

"We used to go down to Newport a lot," Tess said wistfully. "My dad took us sailing almost every weekend. Do you sail?"

Nick glanced at Molly. Her round, pretty face had gone white and still. "Not as much as I'd like to."

"Well, like anyone *could,*" Tess scoffed. "I'd live on a boat if I had half a choice."

"Tess," Molly said softly.

The girl blew out a sigh. "Okay. See you, Cassie. Nice to meet you, Dr. Romano."

The Nimrod clone was waiting for them at the head of the stairs. Nick saw several other furry shapes in the rooms beyond. "How many cats does Molly have?"

"Who knows?" Cassie said casually. "Careful going down the stairs. Sometimes they lie in ambush."

When they came outside, she turned to him. "What you said about driving to Newport tonight—was that for Tess's benefit?"

"Not entirely. I spent most of last night at the police station. As much as I hate to admit it, I'm getting too old to go without sleep."

Cassie bit her lip in chagrin. "That's right. Are you sure you want to drive all the way to Newport?"

"There should be plenty of dry food in the cat's dish, but Nimrod will be expecting his evening meal. If I don't show up, can opener in hand, he's likely to start destroying things just on principle."

A brilliant smile lit her face. "You kept him! Under all that bitching, I knew you liked that cat."

"Maybe," he conceded, "but don't tell him that. Annoying me seems to be his chief source of amusement."

"Well, sure. You're his human. Some Siamese pick one human as theirs, and you're Nimrod's."

"I'll have tee shirts made up," Nick said dryly.

Cassie laughed at that. She chatted amiably throughout the drive home—news of her family, for the most part. Nick registered the fact that she and her sisters met at Molly's house every Sunday morning for breakfast, but the rest of it went past him.

When they pulled up in front of her place, he noticed that she'd fallen silent. "You haven't heard a thing I've said, have you?"

"Not much," he admitted.

She grimaced and shook her head. "I'm such an idiot, going on and on like that when you're so tired. We'll catch up later. Get some sleep."

To Nick's relief, she hopped out of the car and waved him on his way without waiting for a kiss. He wasn't up to another bout of that intense sharing. The confusion he felt was nothing he wanted to inflict on Cassie.

He drove for several minutes, then pulled into the little downtown shopping center to check his phone messages. There was a missed call with a Boston area code. He hit the redial button and waited through several rings.

The sounds of clinking dishes, conversation, and laughter greeted him. "Nick!" sang out a familiar male voice. "Hang on, dude. I need to walk this outside."

Nick waited until the noise level faded. "I've interrupted your dinner."

"Don't worry about it. I've been waiting for your call so I could tell you how much I love you. We're talking totally straight, guy-love male bonding shit, but still."

"I take it the voiceprint was a match?"

"Dead on," his friend said proudly. "Dude, I should have thought of this myself. One voice, two languages—that'll make a great demo. Global market, am I right?"

"You're sure it's a match?"

"Hell yeah. I did a full-blown biometric scan. Hey, if a guy who speaks three languages is trilingual, and a guy who speaks two languages is bilingual, what do you call a guy who speaks one language?"

Nick suppressed a sigh. "An American?"

There was a moment of silence. "You've heard it."

"Probably. Thanks, Tom. I owe you one."

This time the silence lasted a bit longer. "Wait a minute—you owe me? Are you trying to tell me you didn't *know* it was your voice on that recording speaking . . . what the hell was that, anyway?"

"Farsi, with a French accent. I was fairly certain it was my voice, but I needed confirmation."

"You needed—Dude, I have *got* to hear this story."

"Another time," Nick promised. "Your dinner's getting cold."

"Yeah, there's that. I'll call you later this week."

The line went dead. Nick tossed his phone onto the passenger seat and pulled back onto the road.

He didn't doubt what Tom told him. His friend might still dress and talk like an MIT undergrad, but he ran his own business and was highly regarded for the complex business applications he programmed. His current software project was a voice recognition program that could match a customer's voiceprint to a sample on file, a security measure for phone and online sales. If Tom said that the voice on the digital recording Nick e-mailed him this morning was his, the discussion was over.

Nimrod met Nick at the apartment door, loudly demanding dinner and attention. Once the cat was settled, Nick turned on his notebook computer and checked his e-mail.

Yes, there was a message from Samirah, a former girlfriend and the only person Nick knew who spoke Farsi. He skimmed over the chatty e-mail, looking for the translation:

Listen to his dreams. They're only the beginning.

Nick leaned back in his chair and shoved both hands through his hair.

Was that a warning, or a threat? Either way, it had apparently come from a dead man, who had somehow managed to use Nick's voice to speak to Cassie.

"Only the beginning," he repeated. Did this refer to the continued abduction of young women, or was it more personal—a promise of more dreams to come, more messages from the dead?

Nick rose and began to pace. Could he do that? Assuming it was possible—and it was getting very difficult to deny that it was—could he face the night never knowing when the next visitation might come? Or would he succumb to insanity and despair, as his sister had done?

He walked over to the window and stared out into the night. A soft glow caught his eye, and firmed his resolve.

The moon was almost three-quarters full now, edging steadily toward the full moon . . . and the third woman's death.

Chapter Nine

Cassie rose with the sun the following morning and went straight to Molly's house to take Hannah for a walk. The dog's joyous welcome made Cassie feel a little guilty for leaving her overnight. Doggie daycare was, in Cassie's opinion, a better option that leaving Hannah alone in the tiny house when she was at work, but the golden retriever was accustomed to late afternoon runs and evenings at home with Cassie. To make up for it, Cassie took Hannah on an extra long walk, followed up with some Frisbee fetch in the town dog park.

She was returning Hannah to the doggie yard when she heard a car pull up in front of Molly's house. She hurried around front, rounding the corner just as Laura was climbing out of a rental car. Laura regarded the sedate white sedan for a moment, then kicked the tire.

Cassie grinned. "Back to your old self, I see."

"Why do people make cars like this?" she demanded. "See how the back is rounded off and then bulges out over the wheels? From behind, it looks like a fat woman in stretch pants."

"You'll have your car back in no time." Cassie took Laura's pointed chin in one hand, turned her face this way and that. "Wow. No bruises. And Nick was right about those stitches. They don't show."

"There's nothing wrong with my appetite, either," Laura announced as she pulled away. "Molly's done the full Irish breakfast thing, bless her heart."

How Laura could tell over the heady scent of daffodils and hyacinth from the front garden, Cassie would never know. But as soon as they entered the house, she realized Laura was right about the menu. The scents intensified as they climbed the stairs and walked down the hall to the kitchen in the upstairs apartment.

Molly was ladling Irish oatmeal into bowls. She handed one to Cassie by way of greeting. "Coffee's on the table. Help yourself."

"Where's Dee?"

"Sleeping, I hope. She was up most of the night with Adrian. He's teething and I guess he was pretty cranky."

The older siblings settled down while Laura loaded a plate with eggs and bacon and sausage and buttered toast. Cassie couldn't quite suppress a shudder.

"I'm a carnivore," Laura reminded her as she dropped into a chair. "Deal with it."

Molly plucked a couple of leaves from the potted stevia plant on the table and dropped them into her mug to sweeten her herbal tea. Cassie shuddered again.

"I heard about your accident," Molly said.

Laura snorted. "There's a shock. How many different family members called with the news?"

"Four," she admitted.

"Then the topic's been covered. Do you have any jam?"

Molly pushed a small crockery pot toward Laura. "Moving on, then. Still dating that gorgeous Pakistani grad student?"

"Unfortunately, no. There was a little mishap in the bedroom. I blame *Star Wars*."

"Of course you do," Molly said. She glanced at Cassie. "You know we're going to regret asking."

"Probably, but do you really want the question rattling around in your head?"

Laura ignored them both and reached for the ketchup

bottle. "Have you ever noticed," she began, "that from a certain angle a guy's equipment looks a lot like a side view of Darth Vader's helmet? I mean, put a black cape on one of those bad boys, and the resemblance would be uncanny."

Her sisters stared at her for a long moment. Finally Molly said, "Just so you know, I will curse you until the day I die for putting that image in my head."

"Yeah, well, imagine how *I* felt. The resemblance is funny enough when we're talking about white-ass Irish guys. I don't care what country you come from, once a woman points and laughs, it's game over."

Cassie cleared her throat. "I hate to change the subject—"

"No, you don't."

"True. But we should talk about your accident. Laura, it's very likely that someone tampered with your car."

"Gee, you think? Why do you think I insisted that the car be taken to someone I trusted?"

"Jim Thorpe," Cassie recalled. "If there was something to find, would he see it?"

"Oh, yeah. The man has more degrees than the three of us put together. Highly technical shit. Two years ago, he left some high-level forensics job in Virginia."

"Did he say why?"

"Sweetie, he didn't say anything. What do you think the Internet's for, if not to run background checks on cute auto mechanics?"

"So what *did* he say? About the car, I mean."

"Nothing yet." Laura emptied the cream pitcher into her oversized coffee mug and added three spoonfuls of sugar. "I called him yesterday from the hospital. The tow truck hadn't showed up with the car yet. He promised to call me as soon as he knew anything."

The back of Cassie's neck prickled with apprehension. "Here's my cell phone," she said as she handed it over. "Call him now."

For once, Laura didn't offer an argument. She took the

phone and called information for the number. Cassie heard the ringing, then the faint sound of a male response. Her sister asked about the car, said uh-huh a couple of times, and snapped the phone shut.

"Houston, we have a problem," she announced. "My car never made it to Jim's shop. Someone left a message on his machine saying the car would be towed to the police impound yard. Sweet dancing Jesus!" she burst out, slamming the table with one palm. "That Mark Andreozzi always *was* a flaming asswipe nitwit."

"I doubt this is his fault, but maybe he can find out what happened. I'll leave a message for him at the police station. Nick and I are supposed to meet him at ten."

Interest edged away the annoyance on Laura's face. "Oh?"

"Long story," Molly said. "And since it's not about you, you probably wouldn't be interested."

"Heh. Got me there. Make the call."

Cassie left a quick message and set her phone aside. She took a sip of her coffee and was relieved to find that it was the real thing. Molly was not above the occasional attempt to sneak healthy substitutes past her.

"I ran into a mutual acquaintance yesterday. Lea Morgan."

Laura scowled around a mouthful of eggs. "That must have been a rare treat."

"You don't like her."

"She's got rock-solid academic credentials and a great shoe collection. That much I'll say for her."

"Do you two ever talk about parapsychology?"

"God, not if I can help it! She's always after people to take tests, participate in her research. Not that I'd be of much interest to her." Laura cut a breakfast sausage in half and dragged one of the pieces through a pool of ketchup. "I'm a one-trick pony—the only thing I can do is perceive gifts in others."

She popped the sausage into her mouth. As she chewed, she stabbed the other half and waved it at Cassie. "Your primary talent, for example, is receiving and broadcasting information. You're a one-woman radio station. Tess is . . . well, I'm not exactly sure what all she is just yet, but she's going to be pretty freaking amazing."

"You could have warned me," Molly murmured.

"Oh, like you didn't know," Laura scoffed. She tipped her head to one side and considered. "Though come to think of it, she doesn't have *your* gift, so I guess I'm not all that surprised you didn't pick up on it."

Molly sat bolt upright. "*My* gift? I can pick up on emotions, sure, but a lot of people can do that. I have about as much psychic talent as a turnip."

Laura shrugged and glanced at Cassie. "Now you see why I don't do the diagnosis thing. It never goes well. That's why you didn't hear me blurt out, 'Holy crap, Nick—all of a sudden you're a medium? What's up with that?'"

Cassie's chest tightened. "Are you asking me that question?"

"With more subtlety than I'd intended, apparently."

"You're sure. About Nick."

Laura's gaze sharpened. "Hit a nerve, did I? Trust me, the man's a ghost magnet. Deal with it."

"That's surprisingly hard to do." Cassie paused for a wry smile. "I suppose it's ironic that I'm having problems with Nick's psychic ability, when we split up over his inability to accept mine."

"Apparently there are more things in heaven and earth than are dreamt of in *both* your philosophies. Where does this anti-afterlife stance come from? That accident you had as a kid?"

Cassie nodded. "I had nightmares for weeks," she said softly. "They were all more or less the same: looking for Stephanie and Allen and Dylan. Maybe I had to believe it wasn't possible to find them, so I could close that door." She shrugged. "And there might have been some youthful arrogance mixed in."

"Ah. If *you*, princess of the paranormal, couldn't contact the dead, they must be beyond reach."

"Pretty much."

"Bullshit," Molly said softly. Uncharacteristically.

Her sisters turned to stare at her.

"You were drinking that night," Molly said. "You felt guilty about it, even though you weren't behind the wheel."

After a moment, Cassie nodded. "If my head had been clear, I might have seen the accident coming. So yeah, I felt responsible for my friends' deaths. The idea of facing them again . . ."

"There you go," Molly said. "That's probably the main reason the notion of Armand contacting you is so troubling. I don't blame you. I wouldn't want to face a man I'd been forced to kill. And no, you didn't tell me that. You didn't have to."

Laura's eyes widened. "Hello? Left out of the loop here."

"Another long story." Cassie's phone rang. She flipped it open and checked the number, then held up one finger to indicate that she had to take the call.

"I checked with impound," Andreozzi said without preamble. "Your sister's car never made it in."

He sounded genuinely shaken. "You're sure?" Cassie pressed. "Maybe the car was taken to another station?"

"There's no paperwork in the system. Anywhere. I called the tow company I contacted from the site. They said they sent out a truck, but no one was there when they arrived. The dispatcher thought it was a prank call. He told me I should be careful, seeing as how someone had my badge number."

Cassie's brow furrowed. "That doesn't make sense. The truck came just as Nick and I were getting into your car. I heard you tell them to take Laura's car to Jim Thorpe's garage in Smithfield."

"Yeah. I'm still trying to sort all this out. Hopefully I'll have more answers by the time you and Romano get here. How's your sister?"

Cassie glanced at Laura, who was leaning in to catch

both sides of the conversation. "At the moment, I'd say she's pissed."

"Nailed it in one," Laura muttered as she slumped back in her chair. "So, I guess I should add 'deal with car-related clusterfuck' to this week's things-to-do list." Her scowl faded suddenly. "On the bright side, I've got a good reason to test-drive new transport. Want to come with?"

The doorbell rang. Cassie silently blessed Nick for his timing.

"Gee, if only I could. Nick's picking me up on the way to Providence. I told him to come right on up."

"Just like old times," Laura observed. An upward quirk of one mahogany-hued brow turned her words into a question.

"I'll bring you up to speed on everything as soon as I can," Cassie promised as she turned toward the hall.

Nick paused at the kitchen door, a wistful smile on his face. "A gathering of the O'Malley clan—that's a sight I've missed seeing. Not a single cat around, though."

"They scatter when they see me coming," Laura said, not without satisfaction.

"Speaking of which, whatever happened to Nimrod?" Molly asked. "I know you weren't keen on the idea of bring-ing in a mouser, so I never understood why Cassie didn't bring him back to me when she moved overseas. I assume you found a good home for him."

"That's debatable. He's still with me."

"Taxidermy?" inquired Laura.

Molly swatted her shoulder. "Stop that. Cats can live into their late teens, early twenties. The oldest cat on record was thirty-six."

"Yikes." Laura glanced at Nick and burst out laughing. "Look at him!" she hooted, pointing. "Swear to Christ, he just turned six shades whiter."

Molly sighed. "Would you like some coffee, Nick, or are you thinking more along the lines of a quick escape?"

"I'd love to stay, but we're expected in Providence shortly."

Cassie checked her watch, rose to leave. "Thanks for breakfast, Molly-O. Laura, I'll call you if I find out anything about your car."

She filled Nick in on this new development as they walked out to his car. His cell phone rang as they were settling in. He checked the number, then placed it in a small holder plugged into the dashboard and started the car.

"You're on speaker phone, Lieutenant," Nick said. "Cassie O'Malley is with me."

"Glad I caught you both."

Andreozzi's voice came from the car's stereo speakers. Cassie smiled. Boys and their toys.

"We got a missing persons call," Andreozzi said. "There's a match to the girl you described. Nancy Monaco, South Kingston address."

Nick's expression turned bleak. "I was hoping I was wrong about this."

"In that case, you're in luck," the lieutenant said. "Nancy Monaco *placed* the call. It's her boyfriend who's missing."

GETTING TO SOUTH Kingston meant driving north to Providence and down the other side of the Narragansett Bay. Nearly an hour, Nick estimated, enough time for him and Cassie to get a good start on the questions that had kept him up most of the night.

But Cassie's easy, chatty mood of the previous night had vanished. She seemed troubled, preoccupied. Nick drove in silence, giving her the space she apparently needed.

"So, did you voiceprint the recording Philip Meyer gave you?"

The question burst out of her suddenly. Nick slanted a quick look in her direction. "Yes, I did ask Meyer for a copy, and yes, I had it verified. Apparently I *was* speaking Farsi under hypnosis. I apologize for doubting what you told me."

"No, I'm glad you checked it out. You'll probably need a lot more evidence than that before you get your head around what's been happening. I assume you also got a translation?"

Telling her wasn't easy, but he passed along the warning.

She nodded as if she'd been expecting this. "It was your voice, yet it sounded exactly like Armand. The accent, the intonation. That's a little odd, don't you think?"

"Only a little?"

"I'm working my way up," she assured him. "You remember what I told you about Meyer and channeling?"

"You're starting to believe he might be right."

Cassie blinked at Nick's matter-of-fact tone. "What do you think about that?"

"I'm trying to keep an open mind," he told her. "A more immediate concern, however, involves the mix-up with Laura's car, and what it might mean."

Cassie nodded, her face somber. "Judging from what I saw, the cruise control wasn't just stuck; the car was accelerating. I don't have your fondness for gizmos, but it seems to me any device that could do something like that might be traceable."

"Andreozzi called the tow truck. He's the logical broken link in this chain."

"Agreed, but I didn't pick up anything like that from him. And I would have. He's a projector—he spills thoughts all over the place. He sounded really upset about the situation. I don't think he's responsible for Laura's accident."

"What about Meyer?"

Cassie whipped around to stare to him. "Meyer, behind Laura's accident? The oubliette murders?"

"The former head of a psychic espionage field office shows up in Providence. According to your friend Selena, there are two agencies recruiting psychics. If Selena is right, one of these agencies is auditioning unwitting prospects by seeing if they can find a loved one in trouble. You know Meyer. Would he do something like that?"

"There's not much he wouldn't do," Cassie said softly, "but that, I doubt. Not because I have a high opinion of his principles, but because it probably wouldn't work. Have you ever been able to read anything in a dream, or even seen the numbers on a clock? Psychic visions are similar to dreams. You generally don't come up with a street address and Yahoo driving directions. You get images, impressions, feelings. Sometimes that's enough to find someone. But only sometimes. Meyer knows this."

"You're still not seeing my point," Nick said. "Mita Patel couldn't find her lover; Faith Anders couldn't find her twin. *You found Laura.* You knew exactly where she was. If her accident was a test, you're the one who passed. That's bad news, no matter who is running the tests."

"Gotcha." Cassie's face turned grim. "If you're right, at least we know my family and friends are safe. If the price for that is playing psychic bloodhound for these people, so be it."

"Anyone who'd leave two women to die slowly and alone isn't likely to let you go with a handshake and a generous pension."

"All the more reason to find them and take them down."

Nick didn't doubt she'd try to do just that. The realization made something twist in his gut—

And made everything else fall into place.

This was the work Cassie was meant to do—what she'd intended to do since the day he'd met her. And one of the reasons he'd been so drawn to Cassie was that, at some level, he'd recognized a shared destiny.

Destiny—not a word Nick was accustomed to using. It was easier, at least at the moment, to put that notion aside and think in terms of details, practicalities. "Did you pick up anything from Meyer that would shed some light on this?"

"Nothing," Cassie admitted. "He's like Selena—impossible to read. You've talked to him, read some of his publications. What's your take on him?"

"Similar to yours—he's arrogant, intelligent, manipulative. I don't think there's much he wouldn't do to reach a desired end, but he strikes me as someone who likes to think of himself as working toward the greater good. I can't see Meyer working for a rogue organization. Clandestine government service is a perfect fit for his personality type. On the other hand," he concluded grimly, "I can't see him permitting *you* to work for one."

Cassie considered this in silence for a long moment. "Yeah. That could put a crimp in things, couldn't it?"

"We won't let it," he said. "I'm still not sure what this is about, but I'm in."

Her face lit up, and she reached for his hand. As Nick clasped it, he felt a surge of warmth and joy and—

Guilt?

"Cassie, you don't have anything to feel guilty about."

"Yeah, I do," she said in a flat tone. "You were under hypnosis for a lot longer than the recording suggests. Your dreams suggested that you had a gift, and Meyer thought it might be useful. He's really good at digging through the mental clutter to get to psychic gold."

Nick took a moment to absorb this. "He wanted you to lie for him, cover this up."

"Yeah."

"You didn't."

"No, but I went along with it." Her shoulders rose and fell in a heavy sigh. "I figured it was better than letting you think you were going insane. Still, I shouldn't have made that choice for you."

"I don't disagree," Nick said. "Putting that aside for the moment, the session with Meyer doesn't explain my dreams."

"That, I think, is where Armand comes in."

Nick flashed a look in her direction. "The man you were forced to kill. The voice on the recording."

"He was my first partner. We were also lovers, briefly. Bad judgment, granted, but for me it was a rebound thing.

Armand took it a lot more seriously. When I realized he was falling in love with me, I broke things off. It was only fair, since I couldn't possibly return his feelings. I also put up shields between us. Damn good ones, apparently, because I never got any sense that he was a traitor."

Cassie broke off and briefly buried her face in her hands. "This is hard."

"It's all right. Go on."

"Like Meyer, Armand had a knack for breaking through a psychic's repression. He didn't do hypnosis or counseling or anything like that. For some reason, he was a natural catalyst. And that, I think, is the connection."

"I'm not sure I follow."

"Judging from what I heard in your session with Meyer, you were pretty young when you started seeing and hearing things other people didn't. After Jessica was misdiagnosed, your abilities were suppressed."

"For precognitive dreams?"

"Maybe, but I don't think that's what's happening. You're a medium, Nick. You have an affinity for the dead. Believe it or not, I'm probably a bigger agnostic about that than you are."

His laugh was short and humorous. "Three days ago, I would have offered to arm wrestle you for that title."

"But now?"

"Let's say you're right about me being some sort of medium. Armand, being both dead and perceptive, would know this. And he'd work on bringing this ability to light."

"That's my theory."

They drove for quite a while in silence. Finally Nick asked, "To what end?"

"That, I couldn't tell you," Cassie admitted.

The street sign he'd been watching for was coming up on the right. Nick pulled into the parking lot of a brick apartment building. His gaze went to a small lawn, where a short, curvy young woman paced in apparent agitation.

It was the young woman he'd seen in his dream.

"That's her, isn't it?" Cassie said.

He nodded. "But as God is my witness, I have no idea what to say to her."

She unbuckled her seat belt and reached for the door handle. "Describe the place you saw in your dream. Maybe she'll recognize it."

She got out of the car and strode toward Nancy Monaco. Nick heard Cassie mention Lea Morgan, saw the panic flash across the girl's face.

Yes, he noted grimly, this abduction was very like the other two.

"Nancy, this is Nick Romano," Cassie said as he approached. "He's going to describe a place to you. Let us know if it rings any bells."

Nancy listened intently as Nick described the old shed and the cement-walled cellar below.

"That sounds like the old gin shed on the Everett place. That's my boyfriend's family," she explained. "Kevin's family has been on that land forever—they're swamp Yankees from way back. The cellar was built during Prohibition to store homemade alcohol. There used to be a false floor in the shed, but apparently it rotted away years ago."

"We'd like to check it out."

Nancy frowned, then shrugged. "Fine," she said shortly. "But it's a waste of time. Kevin has no reason to go there."

"I hope you're right," Cassie said.

As Nancy promised, the drive to the Everett place didn't take long. The old shed was situated well off the road, separated from the old farmhouse by a broad field and all but hidden in a copse of trees.

"Kevin's grandparents live here," Nancy said. "But they're snowbirds; they won't be back from Florida for another month or so."

She led them to a dirt path that skirted the field. When they were about halfway across, Nancy stopped suddenly, as if she'd run into a glass wall. The color drained from her face and her eyes rolled back. Nick caught her as she fell and eased her to the ground.

A spring breeze quickened, stirring the new leaves on

the trees surrounding the shed. It swept past them, carrying the leading edge of something unspeakably foul.

Nick recognized it at once: the odor of decay, thick and sickening, unmistakable to anyone who'd ever encountered death.

Chapter Ten

Cassie sat next to Nancy on the ambulance bench, rubbing the girl's back with one hand. Nancy clung to her other hand with a grip like a rock climber hanging onto a crumbling ledge. The young woman was wrapped in a blanket, and her eyes were red and swollen from weeping. A policewoman sat across from them, and Nick stood outside by the open door, his jaw set in barely contained anger and impatience.

"I just got back from spring break," Nancy told the policewoman for what seemed to be the tenth time. "Kevin had to stay and work. He didn't answer any of my calls. I thought he was pissed that I went off for the week with a bunch of girlfriends. But when I got back I still couldn't get hold of him."

"So you reported him missing."

"I spoke with the police," Nancy said. She sent an imploring glance at Nick. "When can I go home, Dr. Romano?"

"Soon," he promised. He turned a cool stare toward the officer. "Ms. Monaco has answered all your questions repeatedly."

The woman returned his gaze. "I'm still not clear on what part you two have in this. Consultants, you say."

"You've already contacted the Providence police and confirmed that," he said. "If you have specific questions about the investigation and our role in it, I'm sure they'll be happy to share information."

A wry smile twisted the woman's lips. "Yeah, I'm sure. All right, Miss Monaco, that's all for now."

Cassie waited until the officer left before gently disengaging her hand from Nancy's grasp. The girl leaned out and caught Nick's sleeve. "How did you know?" she whispered.

Nick was silent for a long moment. "I saw the shed and the cellar in a dream, with one difference: I saw you, not Kevin, imprisoned in the cellar."

Fresh tears filled Nancy's eyes. "When did you have this dream?"

"Friday night."

"Kevin was already dead."

"It would appear so. I know that might be hard for you to accept—"

"No, I believe you," Nancy said. "I read tarot to help pay the school bills. Every now and then I pick up some information that seems to come from someone who's passed on." Her eyes overflowed. "But why not this time? Why did Kevin reach out to you, and not me?"

"I don't pretend to understand any of this," Nick said. "The only explanation I can offer is that what Kevin felt for you was stronger than death. Maybe he was worried what might happen to you if you came looking for him. Maybe he was trying to make sure it didn't happen."

Nancy swiped the back of her hand across her eyes. "Yeah, maybe." She attempted to smile. "That does sound like him."

They left Nancy with her mother, then walked back to Nick's car in silence. He edged it out from between two close-parked emergency vehicles and swung into a U-turn.

"Nancy thinks well on her feet," Cassie observed. "She didn't say anything about Selena, or the psychic connection. 'Something Dr. Romano said made me think of the old shed at the Everett place.' That was nicely done. And the way she kept using your title, as if implying she was under a doctor's care—and needed to be."

"I agree. Did you notice how Nancy answered the question about calling in a missing person report?"

Cassie thought about it for a moment. "Come to think of it, she didn't answer directly. She said she 'talked to the police.' Do you think that's significant?"

"It could be. I think Andreozzi knows more about this case than he's letting on. That might explain why Meyer sent him along with us. After all, Andreozzi isn't exactly the only detective working on this case."

"Good point," Cassie conceded. "I didn't catch that. Geez, no wonder Molly said that it's not me that Meyer wants, but you."

"Maybe he'd like a package deal."

She snorted. "I'm sure he would."

"Would that be so bad?"

Cassie took a minute to absorb this. "You're serious," she marveled. "You'd work with me. With Meyer. Doing . . . this."

"We'll call him when we get back to your place. Lay out the cards, set some limits. Make a plan for moving forward."

She nodded slowly as the rightness of this sank in. "But just so you know, if he so much as *thinks* 'I told you so,' about the channeling thing, I'm going to deck him."

Nick chuckled. "Fair enough."

They swung by Molly's house so Cassie could pick up her car and her dog. Hannah took to Nick readily, but when they got to the door of Cassie's house, the dog shied back, whining.

Cassie and Nick exchanged a puzzled glance. "Intruder?" Nick asked softly.

She shook her head. "Hannah would be all over that. She takes the guard dog gig seriously. And I don't sense anyone here."

She leaned down to give the dog a reassuring pat, then squeezed past her into the house. "C'mon, girl," she said soothingly. "No bad guys in here."

Hannah didn't look convinced, but she edged into the room and trotted over to the sofa with the air of one determined to do her duty. She let out a whimper and pawed at the sofa cushion.

Nick picked it up and ran a hand under the crevices along the back and beneath the padded arms. "It's a good thing I just vacuumed," Cassie said. "Normally you'd find about seven dollars in change under there."

He lifted a finger to his lips to indicate silence, then held out a small, round metal object.

At first glance, Cassie thought it was a watch battery. Nick moved his hand closer to Hannah. The dog whined, then ran into Cassie's bedroom and hid under the bed.

Cassie's eyes widened, and she mouthed the words, *It's a bug*. Nick nodded grim agreement and dropped it into her outstretched hand.

A vivid image came to mind: Selena sitting on the sofa, her eyes full of warm concern. Swiftly following it, like a subtle second note in the taste of wine, was the suspicion that Selena's concern—and possibly much more than that—was a fraud.

Cassie set the device down on the sofa. "C'mon, Hannah. Time for your walk."

The golden retriever darted out the open door. Cassie caught up her purse on the way out and put the dog in the small, fenced backyard.

"Selena?" Nick asked.

"Pretty sure," Cassie said grimly. She dialed Laura's number and paced while she waited for her sister to pick up.

"You again?" Laura said by way of greeting.

"Tell me about Lea Morgan's psychic ability."

Her sister's snort of derision sounded like a burst of static. "Are you kidding me? She's almost a complete psychic null."

"Did you tell her you knew this?"

"Damn straight. I told you she was relentless about recruiting for her research. I figured that telling her I knew her little secret would get her off my back."

"And look where that got you."

"Oh." Static crackled for a moment as Laura thought this over. "You think Lea Morgan was behind the accident?"

"Hard to say. She has the best shields of anyone I know. In fact, she worked with new recruits to teach them how to shield their thoughts. But chances are she wouldn't want that bit of information getting to the wrong people. Listen, I've got to go. Watch your back."

"You, too."

As soon as she ended the call, Nick held out his phone. "I've got Philip Meyer on the line."

Cassie nodded her thanks. "Okay, Meyer, tell me about the new organization you're heading."

He actually chuckled. "If anyone else had asked me that, I'd be looking for a security leak. Well done, Cassie. Please tell me you're interested."

"Selena Weis—or perhaps I should say Lea Morgan—already covered the recruitment angle."

There was a long moment of silence. "Selena doesn't work for us. And trust me, she didn't learn of this agency from any inside source."

The implications of that were clear. So, suddenly, were many other things.

"Selena was a control, wasn't she?" asked Cassie. "A psychic null, placed in the remote viewing program for the same reason they use placebos in drug testing."

"Not to my knowledge," Meyer said slowly. "But now that you mention it, it's quite plausible that other branches of the intelligence service might do something of that nature. Why do you ask?"

Cassie told him about the bug. "I'm wondering if she was a spy three times over: for the remote viewing program, for another government agency evaluating the program, and for whoever paid her for information."

"That would explain a lot," Meyer admitted. "Selena 'found' a number of people no one else could get a fix on. And there were several occasions when important information gathered by other operatives turned out to be accurate, but a dollar short and a day late."

"Maybe her contacts set up scenarios that would make her look good, which ensured that she'd have access to still more information. Things they might find useful."

"It's possible. Selena has the strongest mental shields I've ever come across. No one in the program picked up on this."

"I'm not entirely sure about that," Cassie said slowly. "She worked with Armand Gaudine; he knew her pretty well."

"And you think he found out what she was doing?"

"It seems likely." Cassie had to take a moment to swallow hard. "And if that's true, Selena manipulated me into killing him for her. That way I was the one who'd face internal investigation. Her shields are good, but she might not have wanted to risk testing them against the inquest."

"You may be right," Meyer admitted.

Nick slid a steadying arm around Cassie's waist and took the phone from her. "You know Selena. What can we expect from her?"

"I suspect she's in Providence for the same reason I am. As Cassandra surmised, I'm recruiting. Since this has to be done quietly, I have several trusted people watching for unusual psychic potential. The police psychologist in Providence contacted me when you came in. She promptly developed a family emergency, and I flew in to 'cover for her.' Selena probably has her own contacts."

"Such as Mark Andreozzi," suggested Nick.

"Speak of the devil," Cassie murmured. She nodded toward the car pulling up in front of her house.

"We'll get back to you." Nick clicked his phone shut and strode toward the detective.

But the detective's gaze was fixed on Cassie, and he tried to swerve around Nick. Nick grabbed him by the collar and slammed him up against the house.

Andreozzi hardly seemed to notice. "Get hold of your family, your close friends," he told Cassie. "Tell them to stay home and lock their doors. If they see a dark blue PT Cruiser, they should call the police."

Fear struck Cassie like an icy fist. "Yesterday, when Tess was late coming home, I 'saw' one of those. But Tess said she was helping an old lady."

"Tess is not quite thirteen," Nick pointed out. He let go of Andreozzi and stepped away. "To her, everyone over the age of thirty is past their expiration date."

"True," Cassie admitted. "Who owns that car, Mark?"

The detective straightened out his shirt. "Her name is Lea Morgan. She's—"

"I know who she is. The question is, how do *you* know her?"

His expression turned bleak. "She came to me after the second woman was abducted. She told me the victims were connected to two of her patients and asked me to keep her informed. I told her I couldn't discuss an ongoing investigation."

"But she found a way to persuade you," Nick said.

"Yeah," he admitted. "Thing is, I was hitting the casinos pretty hard for a while. She found out somehow. I racked up some debts, took out a mortgage on the house my grandparents left me. Emily—that's my wife—she doesn't know. There wasn't enough equity in the house to cover what I owed, so I looked the other way a couple of times for some people. Dr. Morgan found out about that, too."

"Bottom line: she had you by the short and curlies, so you kept her informed," Cassie said. "So she knew about Nick? About me coming down to the station?"

He nodded, looking thoroughly miserable. "I don't mind telling you, you freaked me the hell out yesterday morning. It wasn't until after you left that I thought Dr. Morgan would want to hear about it, since she's into all that voodoo shit. No offense."

"Go on."

"So when I told her you were picking things right out of my head, she insisted I meet her at this motel. Nothing happened," he added hastily, "except she showed me how to sort of put up walls around my thoughts. It's hard to do—you have to keep thinking about it all the time. But Dr. Morgan had this girl with her—she wanted a second read on me, I guess—and the girl said I was a fast learner. 'The noise level dropped right off,' is how she put it."

"Good description," Cassie agreed. "Who was this girl? Did you get her name?"

"I'll get to that. After Laura's accident, I called Dr. Morgan from the scene. She must have set up the other tow truck. Maybe she even had one waiting nearby." He looked up at Cassie. "But I had nothing to do with what happened to your sister. You've got to believe that."

"Let's get back to the girl Dr. Morgan called in to test your shields. Nancy Monaco?"

The detective nodded. "I didn't get her name at the time, but I noticed her license number. Habit, I guess. She seemed familiar. I didn't figure out until today that she matched Romano's description of the third victim."

"There's a lot of short, brown-haired women," Cassie conceded.

"Anyway, I ran her plates, got her name and address. When I called her, it came out that she was looking for her boyfriend. I still figured she'd be the next to go, what with that dream of Romano's. So I sent you two down there, hoping you could warn her."

"And that's the whole story," Cassie said. "Everything you know."

Andreozzi hesitated. Cassie got a quick flash from him—the image of a black-haired girl with a frightened, furious face.

Tess.

Her response was instant, instinctual: she slammed her fist into the man's jaw.

"You son of a bitch," she said in tones rounded by rage and disbelief. "Selena—Lea Morgan—has Tess. You knew, all this time you were standing there whining out excuses. Where is she? Where's my niece?"

Andreozzi spat blood, and possibly also a tooth. "Can't you, like, tune in or something?" he pleaded. "Dr. Morgan didn't say. She wouldn't tell me anything, except that you and Romano had to come. No one else."

"Is he telling the truth?" Nick asked her.

Cassie shrugged helplessly. "People aren't open books. I can't always tell. And if he's shielding . . ."

Nick's silver eyes turned icy. "Would he be easier to read if he was distracted by a great deal of pain?"

"I'm a police officer," Andreozzi reminded them.

"You're a fucking disgrace," Cassie snapped. "You've said what you were sent to say. Just get out of my sight."

He didn't protest. After his car pulled away, Cassie slumped to the ground and dug both hands into her hair.

"Think, think," she chanted. "Where would Selena take Tess?"

"This might sound odd," Nick said hesitantly, "but has Tess said anything unusual recently, something that might shed some light? It seems likely that people with psychic ability will sense things, perhaps even say and do things, before they realize the significance."

Cassie looked up. "That's a good thought. Yesterday she mentioned her father. That was odd. She never talks about him."

"I gathered as much from Molly's reaction. And sailing—is that significant?"

"It could be," she mused. "Jason's sailboat is still in the slip. Molly has a hell of a time scraping together dock fees, but she refuses to sell it—couldn't if she wanted to, I guess, since it's in his name."

Nick extended a hand. Cassie took it and let him pull her to her feet. "It's me Selena wants," she began.

"Don't go there," he warned her. "I'm coming with you."

They arrived at the harbor in record time. Cassie hurried down the wharf to the slip where the *Grace O'Malley* was docked. The sailboat was gone; in its place was a small skiff with an outboard motor.

She climbed into the boat. Nick followed her and lowered the motor into the water while she untied the rope. The motor started on the second tug. He maneuvered the boat out of the dock area, then yielded his place to Cassie.

Following instinct, she headed south. They were almost to Prudence Island when she caught sight of the *Grace O'Malley*, with its distinctive green hull and the whimsical green skull-and-shamrocks version of the Jolly Roger on the foresail, a reference to the Irish "pirate queen" some four hundred years back in the family tree.

Selena stood on the deck, smiling and waving as if welcoming dinner guests. She lowered and tied off the foresail, then tossed them a line. Nick caught the rope and pulled the little boat up alongside.

They climbed the rope ladder and swung over the side. Selena turned to the two men coming up from the hold and indicated Cassie with a little flourish of one hand. "Here she is, gentlemen, as promised."

The younger of the two men eyed Cassie skeptically. "The boat belonged to the kid's father. She could have figured it out."

"True," Selena admitted, "but she also found her sister yesterday, and she wasn't supposed to."

"Laura wasn't a test. You just wanted her dead."

"And that surprises you?" the woman retorted. "But I suppose it's just as well the bitch survived. Another living relative gives us that much more insurance."

Her tone sent a shiver down Cassie's spine. "Where's Tess?"

Selena tipped her head toward the hold. "She's fine." The sound of an approaching motor brought a smile to her face. "But not for much longer, I'm afraid. It was very thoughtful of Dr. Romano to confess to the oubliette murders. He also knew where to find Kevin Everett. Helpful, but highly suspicious. And he'll be found on this boat with his fourth and final victim. Not counting you, of course, but then, your body won't be found, because you'll still be using it. Elsewhere, and in my employ."

Cassie leaped at Selena. The woman shifted, a classic aikido move that used Cassie's momentum to throw her to the deck. Cassie rolled onto one side and aimed a kick at Selena's knee. She connected hard, but a sudden roll of the boat spoiled her aim. The best she could hope for was a bruised shin—painful, but not debilitating. But it slowed Selena for a moment, buying Cassie enough time to get to her feet and jump onto the seat near the side.

She heard the thud of fists behind her, a shouted oath, a splash. Then more fighting.

One down, she noted. Nick was holding his own. She glanced back to see Selena lunging at her, determined to keep her from diving off the boat, leaving Nick and Tess behind.

As if, Cassie thought grimly.

She pivoted and kicked out hard, catching Selena just under the ribcage. The woman's breath wheezed out, and she staggered back and leaned against the mast as she struggled to breathe.

Cassie hopped down and headed for the hold. A hand clamped down on her shoulder, and before she could move, the cold barrel of a gun pressed under her jaw.

Nick froze, fist uplifted, his eyes on her face. He took a punch, shook it off, and started toward her.

"Stay right there," Mark Andreozzi warned. "You okay, Dr. Morgan?"

Selena pushed herself away from the mast, keeping one hand against it for balance. "You took long enough to get here."

"Maybe I could have gotten here sooner if you'd told me where I had to go," the detective retorted. "You said to follow these two, and I did."

"When dealing with a psychic of Cassie O'Malley's caliber, one does not take chances," Selena said—somewhat theatrically, it seemed to Cassie. She turned toward her client. "Are you convinced, or should we have her tell you where some of your associates' bodies are buried?"

"Fine," he snapped. "I'll take her, but it's on you if she can't find the guy we're looking for."

"Oh, she will," Selena said, smiling at Cassie. "She has a very large family, you see, and she's very fond of them all. So if you'd bring the girl up, Vince, we can get this done."

He disappeared into the hold, and returned with Tess slung over his shoulder. Her wrists were bound, and so were her ankles, but she still managed to kick and struggle. He threw her onto the deck. "Fucking brat," he muttered.

Cassie took heart from her niece's face. It was pale, but above her gag her eyes blazed with anger.

The boom began to shiver as if in a strong wind, straining against the ropes.

"Poltergeist," Andreozzi said softly, his breath brushing Cassie's ear. "Laura said something like that might happen."

NICK WATCHED, HELPLESS, as Mark Andreozzi marched Cassie over to the side of the boat and pushed her down on the seat. "Over here, Romano," he said, indicating the seat next to her. "Sit tight while I take care of the kid."

Nick did as he was told, but he watched Andreozzi, ready to leap if the detective took his gun off Tess for a moment.

Cassie touched his arm. *Wait.*

For a heartbeat or two, the shock of hearing her voice in his mind numbed his thoughts to all else. Then Andreozzi pulled the gag off Tess.

"Will somebody pay attention to the fucking French guy?" she shrieked. "I took, you know, *Spanish!*"

"French guy?" murmured Nick.

Armand. French father, Persian mother. See him, Nick; hear him. Show me.

In response to Cassie's unspoken plea, Nick followed the line of Tess's gaze. His eyes widened. There was a shadow of a man, no more, and a sound that might have been nothing but wind.

The rattling of the boom increased. Life jackets skidded out from under the seats. The wheel spun wildly.

"Cassie, what's going on?" There was fear in Selena's voice and a gun in her hand. She aimed it at Tess's bound ankles. "Tell me, or your niece will take a very long time to die."

From the corner of his eye, Nick saw the second man climbing over the side, dripping and furious. He was holding a knife; the older man now held a gun.

Nick turned his attention back to the shadowy form, willing himself to open his mind, to see and hear.

Shadow took on substance—a slim, handsome man of Middle Eastern heritage. His gaze was fixed on Cassie, and the expression on his face left no doubt in Nick's mind who this had been, or why he'd been able to break through.

Listen to his dreams, Armand had said, in a manner that Cassie could not possibly ignore, *they're only the beginning.* Not a threat, but a warning. Armand had truly loved Cassie, and some things were more important than death.

Nick reached for Cassie's hand as a flow of French words burst from Armand. He didn't understand. Cassie did.

"Now!" she shrieked.

Andreozzi spun and shot Selena, then turned the weapon toward the man Selena had called Vince. His shot went wide, caught the man in the shoulder and spun him around.

Another shot rang out, and Andreozzi jolted. Cassie darted forward, snatched the gun from his hand, and held it against the rope that held the jostling boom in place.

She fired and dropped to the deck, reaching for Tess as the boom swung over them, hard and fast.

It sent Vince staggering back and knocked the older man over the side. There was a thud as he hit the waiting skiff, then silence.

Cassie lifted the gun again and fired as Vince sighted down at her. The first shot stopped him; the next two sent him pitching to the deck.

Mark Andreozzi pulled himself to his feet, one hand clutching his bleeding shoulder. He walked over to the man and studied the three holes in the chest of his windbreaker. "Nice grouping," he observed.

The sound of sirens came from the shore, and a boat with flashing lights swept toward them.

"I called it in," Andreozzi said. He pulled a penknife from his pocket and handed it to Cassie, who was struggling with the knots on Tess's bindings. "This ends here. All of it ends here."

The bleak determination in his voice raised Nick's estimation of the man several notches. Accepting a difficult path was daunting, whether it resulted from fate or choice.

Nick glanced toward the shadowy form of Armand Gaudine. The man nodded to him, then blew a kiss toward Cassie.

"Actually, Lieutenant," Nick said slowly as he watched Armand's image fade away, "I have it on very good authority that this is just the beginning."

HILL AND SKY

Kassandra Sims

*To Jay-Jay and Holly and the greyhouse on Eastland.
To Miss Sparkle for existing. To Moriah and Chris
for making Nashville what it is.
To David for inspiration.*

*Nashville is as much a state of mind as a place. Any place
you can hear Waylan or Willie or a good indie singer-
songwriter, you've found NashVegas.*

Part One

It's not a stupid arbitrary ethical decision, Mom," Annika Madsen said into the receiver of her cell phone. She continued over the tired, put-upon sigh her mother issued. "I told you that I'm not working for The Office anymore. Pretty much the whole reason I moved away was, you know, to be away."

Her mother drew on her cigarette slowly, purposefully provocative in her utter disdain of her daughter's life choices. "You know, no one will judge you if you decide that Tennessee isn't right for you." By *right for you,* she clearly meant right for the family. "The Midwest is so bland, all Germans eating sausages and rusted steel mills." Annika's mother functioned under some strange misconceptions.

Annika barely managed to keep her eyes in her head, she rolled them so hard. "That's great, when I decide that, I'll let you know. Please don't judge me or try to pay for me to come home."

"Right, so the man from The Office is coming by in the next few days. You know how vague they always are." Her mother had moved on to filing her nails, with the phone obviously wedged between her chin and her shoulder.

"Uh, no. I just said no."

"So, you wouldn't even believe the outfit your sister was wearing yesterday . . ." Annika knew there wasn't much point in even breaking into the monologue, which was a long drone about the facts of her mother's daily life—who said what (misquoted), who wore what (with sartorial commentary), where she was forced to park. Used to such one-sided conversations, Annika was able to tune the soliloquy to just a hum of Seattle consonants and northwest vowels in her ear.

NASHVILLE HAD A well-established magical community, like most places in the eastern United States. Long settlement led to the entrenchment of magic and the folk who exercised magic. The first witches settled along the Atlantic, just like the first Others (or mundanes, depending on who was speaking and in what context). The largest magical populations weren't always in the biggest mundane cities—sometimes, but not always. New York, Miami, Boston—all had large, thriving magical communities that were barely or not at all hidden from the mundane population. In other, smaller cities, witches, sorcerers, alchemists, and arithmancers kept to themselves in a city within the city. Annika had contacts all over the country because of her family's business. Annika's family had facilitated transactions between two or more parties for time beyond time. But she hadn't moved to Tennessee to set up a satellite office, to bring the family business with its vast network of contacts to the East; she'd moved for change, just like the mundanes did. Of course, it helped that she knew people in the city, old friends from college, old friends who were tapped into the magical lay of the land in the East.

"They aren't all bad, really, I mean, bumblers and fuck-ups mainly," Stanzia said from behind the bar of The Unsaid Remark, the local coffeehouse/bar/music venue/magical shop that Annika worked at. It was before opening, so a nonemployee behind the bar making drinks was no big deal. Not that much was a big deal around The Remark. "Mostly they just stumble on things from what I can tell. I don't think there's a big conspiracy."

Annika took the beer and stared back at her friend. They'd known each other since college, when Stanzia had traveled west for school and fallen into Annika's life. That Stanzia had settled in Nashville had tipped Annika's decision to move to that particular place when she decided that Seattle and her family were just too much to bear, her whole life mapped out from birth and not an independent decision to be made by Annika herself. Tonight, Stanzia had her nearly black hair pulled back with hand-tooled black hair sticks adorned by red beads. The red matched the scoop-neck T-shirt she wore and made her dark gold skin look ruddy. Her face was sunburned. Overall it was a healthy-looking throwback to the days before skin cancer scares and UV-blocking sunscreen in everything from ChapStick to hair balm. Annika's own hair was also pulled back, but in a thick braid at the nape of her neck, her naturally light brown hair highlighted with several shades of blond. She was fair with a pale rose tan on top, mirroring her friend but several shades lighter on the scale. Their sunburns came as a result of tending the rambling herb garden they kept in their backyard—herbs treated, sorted, dried, steamed, boiled, and crushed for the other side of The Unsaid Remark, where the magical trade went down.

"Most of the people I've met who work for The Office were okay. They did catch that hedge mage who was extracting people's spleens and leaving them in cauldrons full of ice last year." Stanzia poured herself a beer.

"Whatever." Annika's issues with The Office were not about the organization itself—her opinion of their competency and intentions mostly agreed with her companion's—she just stubbornly refused to allow her mother to control her from all the way across the country. If she'd wanted to be guilted into being her mother's slave, she could have stayed in Seattle where her friends were. Stayed in her home and not set out on her own at thirty-two.

"Whatever, yourself," Stanzia replied. She flicked her rag with a snap and sauntered down the bar to talk to a couple of regulars who'd been admitted before opening hours, musicians from New Orleans who said The Unsaid

Remark came closer to the ambience of their home turf than any other place in Tennessee. The magic in the old, oak floorboards and yellowed stucco walls bled into the room, a flavor on the back of the tongue, like allspice and lemon. Sitting just off the nexus of a railroad track and a crossroads gave the location itself power. The building drew not only from the patrons and customers but also from the very soil beneath the structure.

Thursdays were Annika's evenings in the shop instead of hostessing in the bar. She sipped her beer and waited for the bell to chime on the other side of the wide arch leading from the bar into the shop proper. The building was constructed with a protective architecture. The entryway vestibule was blocked off: everyone entered through an outside door and traversed a fifteen-foot stretch of vibration-absorbing linoleum before walking into the bar through a second door. The vestibule worked as a holding cell for the undesirable element, a cleansing space for folks throwing off unwanted mojo, and a mental head-check that one was moving from the mundane world into a safe space for magic. Kitty-corner from the inner vestibule door, the bar ran along the wall—the usual dark, stained wood and stools, but cluttered with books and knickknacks—from a plastic Jesus statue to a set of carved stone votives that patrons wished on. Directly across from the inner vestibule door was the wide arch leading into the magic shop.

Annika sat at the very end of the bar, waiting as she enjoyed her malty adult beverage, and watched Stanzia engage in some sort of animated conversation with Jami, one of Annika's coworkers, a pretty girl with red hair and freckles who was always smiling or laughing. The high bell that only employees could hear chimed and Annika jumped off her stool—her feet didn't even touch the foot rung because of her short stature—and grabbed her beer.

When someone stood on the bar side of The Unsaid Remark, the archway into the shop displayed a large mirrored surface. This worked as both a decorative flare from

the bar—optically tricking the senses into imagining the
space as double its diminutive size—and also as a magical
barrier to those the protective spell deemed undesirable.
Annika personally had no idea what a desirable sort of
person, as opposed to an undesirable one, would be. Stepping across the threshold of the archway felt like cold cotton wrapping you from head to foot and releasing you
again. Not horrible, but not all that great either.

'Magic shops come in many varieties: the neat chrome
and glass, slick urban-inspired pseudo-scientific empori-
ums for people who chose to take all the wonder out of
magic; the specifically ethnic boutiques, Chinese, Hun-
garian, Maghrebi, Yoruban, you name it; but this particular shop was eclectic, democratic, able to provide for a
diverse, transient population. Someone could buy puka
shells or firebird feathers, a blessed canoe, or lampblack
from the studio of a bloody necromancer. Anything an al-
chemist, diviner, herbalist, doctor, astrologer, or even just
the modern witch on the go could need.

Unlike the rest of the building, which sat right where it
appeared to, Annika suspected that the magic shop actually
occupied physical space somewhere far away. She couldn't
have explained why except in the vaguest way; just a feeling she had. The room felt old, like oak tree roots clinging
to solid granite or sand spilling on the beach from the
deepest part of the ocean. The ceiling was divided into
eight sections with a peak at the center. From the center of
the ceiling hung a witch light—a ball of what appeared to
be amber glass—that illuminated the entire space. From
floor to ceiling on each of the eight walls ancient apothe-
cary cabinets with variously sized drawers stood like semi-
sentient sentinels waiting for witches and mages and
sorcerers to come and plunder their contents. Directly under the witch light sat a set of comfortable chairs, a couch,
a couple of rickety end tables, and a battered coffee table.
Between the furniture and the walls, tables and cabinets
sprawled haphazardly, stacked with odds and ends, objects
of power, tarot cards, crystals, thingamabobs, and whatsits.

A couple of middle-aged women in comfortably cut, brightly patterned clothes were chatting over a clockwork model of a bullring when Annika crossed the room to sit in her favorite gold damask Queen Anne chair and finish her beer. She waved her hand as she sat and the newest *Esquire* appeared on her lap. How the magic worked exactly, she had no real idea as she only devoted stray thoughts to the matter, not like Stanzia's constant musings on conservation of energy and the laws of thermody . . . whatever. Magic worked, and that was good enough for her.

A hum in the back of her teeth announced another customer was crossing the barrier between the bar and the shop. Annika registered it but didn't lift her eyes from the article about men's tennis shoes. Most of the shoes burned her eyes out with their neon contrasted with gray and black. Riveting reading.

Someone cleared his throat. She looked up, distracted. A guy stood with one hand on the back of a tan couch decorated with a cornucopia pattern. He smiled in what he probably hoped was a charmingly timid sort of way. The hair falling over his forehead was that strange color neither blond nor brown, called one or the other depending on the season, the light, or the observer. Even in the diffuse corona of the witch light, his eyes were clearly green above his ever-so-slight pug nose. He was schoolboy cute with dimples and shoulders slumping in a self-effacing way. At least, that's what he appeared to be selling as his first impression.

She wasn't buying it.

"Annika Madsen?" His smile grew wider, displaying even white teeth, deepening his dimples. He stepped closer, offering his hand, and his suit jacket drew tight over his biceps. His belt and shoes matched, perfect, shiny black with silver accents, complementing his dark charcoal suit and pristine white shirt. No tie, which was slightly incongruous.

He seemed to ping her exact thoughts, because he dropped his hand with a shrug and smoothed the fingers over the front of his shirt. "Dripped milkshake on my tie." He wagged his head with a rueful grin. "Eating in the car is only one of my bad habits." Patting his flat belly, he rocked back on his heels and glanced casually around the shop. "Been a while since I was here. Floating Eye of Horus is gone, hope that doesn't end up biting me in the ass." His eyes swung back to her as his hand went into his pockets. "Anyway, from your embarrassingly effusive greeting, I assume I am who you think I am." He flashed the even white teeth again. "Public displays of affection make me blush, really."

That amused an accidental smile out of her, and he plunged on like that was exactly what he'd expected and desired.

"Anyway," he stuck his hand back out again. "Tommy Brennan. You know who I work for. Do you mind if I take a load off? These shoes are killing me."

Annika shook his hand as he sat in the chair next to hers. "My mom said that someone was going to come, but she didn't say tomorrow."

"Technically, right now is today." His tone was smooth, calm, a quip pebble in a bullshit river. The mild Boston accent under the words might have made him sound less trustworthy if his face wasn't so choirboy-esque. She suspected that was why he was a first contact person with The Office.

"I don't know what my mother promised you guys, but I don't plan to continue the family tradition of helping out." She had nothing in particular against the organization that came the closest to a police force among the magically inclined. As a matter of fact there had been a time or two in her life—the rampaging djinn and the tommyknockers springing immediately to mind—when she'd been glad there had been someone who had to answer when called for help. But she'd moved away to sever the apron strings, not stretch them most of the way across the continent. Annika really felt like her mother attempting to involve her in more Office shenanigans was a way for her to assert control from a distance. Everyone has their issues.

Tommy Brennan propped his elbow on the arm of his chair and leaned closer to her. "Do you know why Nashville's a hub for musicians?"

That took her a bit off guard. She rapidly formulated a complex retort about the Grand Ole Opry and early music recording and record companies, but before she could reply, he went on.

"What do you know about the old myths?" A coffee service blipped into existence on the table in front of them and he leaned forward to pour a cup. He lifted his eyebrows at her questioningly, but she raised her beer towards him. "Shoulda thought of that." The coffee faded in a corona of black glitter and a pitcher of beer and two glasses appeared.

"Which old myths? Every culture has them. I'd say I know as much as most people, more than a lot of them." Her knowledge of Scandinavian and Eastern European traditions was best, being her own background, but Pacific Rim culture had also pervaded her life.

"Well, ones about music, naturally." He settled back sipping his beer.

One of the ladies who'd been shopping when Annika arrived approached them.

"Tommy," she said with laughter in her tone. "I thought you were in Salem."

Tommy stood up and kissed the lady on the cheek, all smiles and a deep rumble of laughter, the devil in his eyes. He embraced her, offered her a beer with a wave of his hand, and gestured at the couch for her to sit down. Effusive hospitality looked good on him.

"Hazel, it's been a lifetime. How's the garden?" The way his eyes blinked slowly seemed to say something, like a warning of sorts, subtle but there. Annika tilted her head and watched this man and wondered if he was more than just the pretty PR man used to lure in reluctant consultants.

Hazel's friendly expression pinched up a bit. "I haven't mistaken columbine for Circe's eggs lately." She turned her attention to Annika. "Lemon verbena, valerian, Pompey's fingers, comfrey . . ." As the list went on drawers in the cabinets along the walls opened and snapped shut again, bundles sailed through the air to land in neat stacks on the coffee table in alphabetical order—the alphabet being Persian, which was one of the reasons Annika was suspicious regarding the actual location of the shop. The list was addressed to Annika, but she had no physical control over the commerce in the shop. She was simply a conduit, a cipher through which the purchaser and that shop interacted. Without her, or the other employees, nothing could be bought or sold, like a key in a complex lock.

Gathering up her parcels, Hazel shot Tommy Brennan a sharp look. "I know you know what's on my mind, so you better not get on my nerves."

Tommy's smile dimmed a bit. "I have all the respect in the world for you, lady, don't be offended by my inability to tell a decent joke." He sipped his beer and called to her back, "And I'd be careful what I went around threatenin' and who exactly."

Hazel sniffed, collected her buddy, and exited the shop with a ripple in the surface of what on the shop side of the barrier looked like a whole lot of nothing. Sometimes Annika sat in the shop all night and watched the people in the bar getting drunker and drunker, unaware of her spying on them. It sounded a lot more fun than it was, really.

Tommy Brennan stared at her from just a couple feet away. The aw-shucks fell off and he looked ten years older. "I need your help. I know you have no love for The Office, and Hazel just made me look like a dick, so I suppose I won't be winning you over by personal charm, either. But all the same I need your particular talent. If this were just about me, though, it'd be a date I was after, not all this work nonsense." The smile popped back on his face, and against her best judgment, Annika blushed and felt as flattered as he intended her to. She met his eyes, green like hers but dark, undergrowth green where Annika's were mossy, and the *pop!* she'd felt all her life shuddered.

She blinked. "Oh," she said. His smile shut off like a switch as he smoothed the front of his shirt and slid to his feet.

"Yeah, oh." Glancing over his shoulder at her, he lifted an eyebrow. "Sorry for wasting your time, beautiful."

He was getting this all wrong. It's not like she cared. Shooting to her feet, Annika reached out to grab his elbow. He was even more solidly built than she'd thought, broad back and thick arms. "Why would I care if you're human or not? We're standing in the middle of a magic shop that's probably actually in medieval Samarkand." There had been other moments when Annika's ability had kicked her or someone else in the ass like this. Usually, she had more warning, a niggle about someone from quite a distance, which meant that Tommy Brennan had abilities of his own. The Remark itself hummed with so much magic that individuals usually didn't ping her inside its walls, the buzz of magic too strong to notice one person or another. But real power came with more of a wallop for her, a *pop!* or *zap!* that hit her behind her sternum or in her molars. Nonhumans all the more so. Tommy had been able to mask that for a while, and she hadn't ever met anyone who'd pulled one over on her before. His arm felt like a normal, human arm under her hand, but she knew better than to think in those terms.

Tommy's smile made a ghost of a reappearance. "You call me when you change your mind about the date or the freelance work." He paused. "Or if you want a full-time job. We could use you at The Office, sweetheart."

Usually, someone she didn't know calling her a pet name like that would have annoyed the ever-loving crap out of her, but something about this guy—the strange, sudden mood swings and the bone-deep feeling that he belonged in this room—made his comment seem like a true endearment. Annika dropped her hand from his arm and watched him run a hand through his hair, his back bunching and unbunching under his jacket, as he stepped across the barrier and into the bar.

The rest of the evening got lost in a few million beer bubbles and a mildewed treatise on lycanthropic physiology clearly written by someone who was demented and had a lot of time on his hands. The illustration of the third spleen was particularly amusing, with the *nodes of hornet* circled in yellow ink and the tiny devil sitting on a rock smirking.

FRIDAYS WERE USUALLY lost days for Annika in Nashville. She did yoga and sat in the sun if the weather suited, maybe went to lunch with Stanzia, maybe to coffee with one of their other friends. Her cell rang off the hook, and she seriously had to change her ringtone, because she must have been drunk when she picked "Back in Black." The first couple notes of the song made her grind her teeth.

That particular Friday was some sort of holiday for Stanzia, as her roommate and friend was busy setting up an altar in the dining room with action figures, small statues of various gods, rocks, and candles set in no pattern Annika could recognize. Annika grunted a greeting as she walked through the room to get coffee, the old floorboards of the prewar house groaning and squawking as she went.

Stanzia sang to herself off-key, in Spanish, maybe about a boat or something similar. Annika hadn't known any Maghrebis before she went to college in California and had met Constanzia Estrella. The largest ethnic groups in the Pacific Northwest were Chinese, Pacific Islander, and Nordic, naturally. Fluidity had always existed in the magical communities in the Americas, but some groups were more insular than others. Some groups came to the "New World" with long-entrenched traditions of secrecy and wagon circling, so the Welsh in New England and the Maghrebis of Florida and the West Indies were fairly scarcely flung over the rest of the map of the Americas, though majority populations in their home regions.

Annika sipped her coffee and watched her friend move the figures on the altar. Stanzia cracked her bare toes against the wooden floor. The bottoms of her feet were sandy and dark from foregoing shoes and her red, full hippie skirt tied in a knot high on her right thigh. Her hair, released from its sticks, almost reached her waist.

"Have you met Tommy Brennan before?" Annika asked, attempting for casual. The green of Tommy's eyes flashed through her mind.

"Oh really?" Stanzia laughed as she settled a Batman action figure against a fat, smiling Buddha.

"What?" Annika hadn't ever been slick when it came to her interest in men. Stanzia usually knew before Annika knew herself. That was part of the complex give and take of their relationship, predictable and sometimes grating like all long-term relationships from time to time.

"I didn't think you liked blonds," Stanzia replied, looking over her shoulder with a smirk.

"His hair's light brown."

Laughter flooded through the room, deep and bright like the flaming wicks of the candles flickering and guttering from the air conditioning.

"He works for The Office, what the hell?" The Kali scooted over to sit next to St. Brigid. Annika knew already that Stanzia didn't care one way or another about that, that she was voicing Annika's own opinions back to her in a convoluted attempt to be helpful.

She considered how to approach this that didn't make her look completely shallow. "He's not totally human."

"Huh. I thought this was because he's hot." Another round of laughter thundered out of her friend and Annika flipped her off and headed to the shower.

LATER, THEY SAT on ratty old lawn chairs on the deep, shaded front porch, drinking sangria and painting their toenails while Stanzia told Annika a story.

She sipped her drink as a guy on a moped zoomed by

them, honking his horn and waving. Annika wondered if any man in the history of motorized transport had ever picked up a girl by honking his horn at them.

This is the story Stanzia told:

One day, like all these things always happen, you know, just one day. (Here Stanzia smiled and Annika laughed along, amused because her friend was.) *So one day, a man came over the rise of the hill, stomping through the crocuses, spreading the sweet smell through the bright, fresh air without even pausing to appreciate it. This man looked down on a group of families with babies in their arms and was curious. He came closer and saw a baby popping whoosh! out of the crystal river and landing right in her father's arms, and he thought to himself, "I'm going to go down there to that river and I'm going to place the soles of my feet on the surface and I will fall down into the still water until just one hair on the top of my head is showing, and then I will be like these people." The families had left when he finally arrived on the dark, fragrant bank of the crystal river. He removed his shoes and placed his feet on the surface of the crystal, but nothing happened. He walked further out, to the very middle of the river, ridges smooth under his calloused feet. Still nothing. This man grew enraged. The babies had slipped right in and right back out! His anger grew in him like something ravenous. His heart shriveled in his breast and he thought to himself, "If I cannot sink beneath the surface of the crystal river and pop back up again into the bright sunlight, then no one ever shall again!" and he began to leap up and down. First one crack emerged under his pounding feet, then more and more, cracks radiating from beneath him in spider webs until finally the entire surface of the river, from its font to its delta, was dark with shattering cracks. Finally the man leapt one last time high in the air, and when he came back down, the crystal river splintered so that he fell down, down, down into a hole of jagged crystal knives. Even as he died, the man thought, "This is well, for*

*even if I die, no one else shall ever experience this river
which I could not."*

Stanzia finished the story with a wistful tone and
poured herself more wine. The sun barely peeked over the
roof of their neighbor's house, the day sliding down into
evening.

"Your stories make me want to cry," Annika sighed. She
knew they were just allegories, but that made the stories
worse, because the truths they hid were grimmer, more
brutal, rivers of blood and dead children, thousands of
years of repression of magic.

"That's the point. I mainly like the repetition in them.
My grandfather's really good at that. I think most of his
stories are self-invented, though." She lifted her feet to inspect her pedicure. Dark red verging on burgundy, which
suited her dark complexion. "So, you gonna call Tommy
and—" she curled her fingers like quote marks—"work on
the case?"

"Being a hypocrite doesn't bother me." The words slid
out on another sigh that was still more for Stanzia's story
than for what Annika was saying. "But it's giving my mom
the satisfaction of yanking my chain."

They didn't have to discuss how long it had taken Annika to finally leave Seattle and settle somewhere else or
how her mother had done everything short of tying her up
and storing her in the attic to keep her from going.

"He's really hot," Stanzia tossed out as she slapped a
mosquito on her arm. "Shit. Freakin' bugs." A blue light
flamed to life on the other side of the porch from where
they were nestled with their wine jug and nail paraphernalia. The light spun in a counterclockwise rotation and the
first insect victim went up in a hearty *ziiiiiiiizz* almost immediately.

Tommy Brennan definitely was really hot. Was Annika
shallow enough to bend her no Office work rule for that?
Did The Office send him specifically because they had a
file on her and knew she was that superficial?

"Or you could just agonize over it and overthink it and let him decide what's going to happen."

Annika looked over to see the smug look that Stanzia got when she thought she was totally right. "I need a new best friend. I hate you."

"La la," Stanzia replied. "I think I want tamales for supper." She gazed off towards a stand of bougainvillea and Annika knew the conversation was over.

ON SUNDAYS THE girls had a potluck dinner that started whenever people arrived. Sometimes that was four-thirty, sometimes that was eight. This particular Sunday, Stanzia sent Annika to Target for a couple extra chairs, some body wash, and tampons. It just so happened that Annika forgot every one of those items as soon as she got into Target, because that infernal store placed all of the cute clothes right next to the front doors. As she waded through the lagoon of kicky skirts and perfect tops, she was like a lost traveler wandering into Faerie.

An hour, a hundred and three dollars and forty-three cents later, she walked out of Target with bags of teal, white, and yellow outfits in a bubble of euphoria not unlike the afterglow of sex.

It was only as she pulled onto Chapel Avenue that she remembered she'd gone out for specific items that were expected when she returned. Turning the car around, she went the back way 'round and ended up in a grocery she hadn't ever been to before. The overhead lighting shone yellow on cracked linoleum and the other customers shuffled around with an air of dingy poverty. Amazingly, there was a display of lawn chairs by the narrow checkout counters. The soap aisle contained such strange items as "Mickey's Mugwort and Mint Manly Bar" and honeysuckle bubble bath. Annika found the tampons at least to be more standard. She pulled down Stanzia's brand and went back to ponder the soap selections. Sniffing a couple unfamiliar varieties didn't help her because each seemed as delicious as the one before. Realizing how long she'd been away, she picked up a bottle of thyme and lemon-scented body wash and shrugged. Stanzia liked lemon and she ate thyme a lot.

The clerk at the checkout had three teeth, was about five feet tall, skinny and bobbed his head up and down mumbling to himself. "Yup, yup, lemon, heehehheee, yup, Sunday, Sunday, know what that means!"

"Um," Annika began. "Uh, I want to get a couple of those lawn chairs over . . ."

"Lawn chairs, for the yard, HAHAHA!" the clerk said and rang up her other items without actually grabbing the lawn chairs. "Six dollars and thirty-three cents!" He stuck out a hand adorned with long, yellow fingernails. She didn't feel like arguing.

The exchanging of money took what seemed like a solid day and a half, and Annika's frustration grew and grew as her internal hum kept rising. She knew some of the store's denizens weren't human, but not which ones because the buzz of magic was so strong about the place. Finally, excruciatingly finally, she had her (mostly) exact change and she bugged out of the store, rolling her neck to crack it and hoping that all that sinning in your heart business wasn't really true.

In the parking lot, Tommy Brennan was sitting on a lawn chair next to her car, wearing a frayed Red Sox cap that was faded almost pink, ratty jeans, and a gray Berklee College of Music T-shirt. His ankle rested against his other knee and his flip-flop dangled half off. In the bright sunshine, Annika could see that he had a perfect spray of freckles high on his cheeks, apricot and gold blemishes that made him look even younger than he had in the dim witch light of the shop.

"Probably, in the future, you want to pay for your purchases in the little wooden box by the front door. I think the whole clerk setup is to amuse the regulars when a mundane wanders in off the street." He took off his cap and whacked it against his leg a couple times. His sweat-damp hair clung to the sides of his face. He squinted and hopped up. "Anyway, I got your chairs for ya."

She realized she hadn't said anything. She couldn't remember the last time she'd been struck dumb. What was he *doing* here? "Uh, thanks. You didn't have to do that." Rounding the car, she popped open the trunk and let him stack the collapsible chairs on top of the papers and books and random articles of clothing.

He slammed the lid closed and smiled down at her. He was probably pushing six foot or better, but he didn't wear his size in an intimidating way, more like in a spry, vital, jock sort of good-natured way.

"Anyway, if you change your mind about helping me out, pretty lady, you know where to find me." He winked and turned to walk away.

Annika squinted into the sun. "What do you mean?" she called at his back. "You didn't give me a card or anything!"

"You found me just now, didn't you?" His laughter broke apart the reflection of the sun on the black surface of her car, musical, but more like music taken shape.

She drove back to the house with a strange melody in her head, something familiar but not. Her abilities could seek out a specific person, but that took a focusing spell or an object. She'd never stumbled on someone after being drawn to them accidentally. That she knew of.

The smell of fried chicken greeted her as she climbed out of the car onto the oyster shell and gravel driveway. She grabbed the first load of stuff to take inside from the trunk. On the porch, several of her and Stanzia's friends played cards on the front steps, beer cans squeezed between their knees or sitting next to their legs. They waved and someone moved to grab the chairs out of the trunk without being asked.

People called to her and she smiled, but mostly Annika was preoccupied with Tommy Brennan. She couldn't tell if he was a mystery or she just wanted him to be. Being too self-aware often became a liability.

Stanzia stood in their high-ceilinged living room sipping from a blown crystal wineglass, gesturing emphatically at Rhys Cethin. The tall man stood next to her roommate wearing his usual sardonic expression, which when applied to Stanzia was actually an affectionate sort of sneer. His strange, changeable grey eyes watched Stanzia's movements precisely and he combed a hand through his longish dark brown hair when she finished her commentary on the cultlike tendencies of vegetarians. Sometimes Annika thought he looked like an Edward Gorey line drawing come to life.

"Weeeeeeeeellll," Rhys drawled out. "That's more fried chicken for us, huh?"

When Stanzia's face reconfigured into a scowl, he began to laugh and slap her on the back. They enjoyed annoying each other, and even when one seemed mad at the other, it was all an elaborate pantomime only they understood.

Once, Stanzia had explained it like this: There was once a family that had two children both born at the same time. One a boy and one a girl. When one would go outside, the other would stay inside. When one slept in the daytime, the other slept in the nighttime. When one would eat only bread, the other would eat only meat. (The list was longer than this, but no need to tell it all at once, save something for the retelling.) When one was in hiding, the other took to hunting. This story explains the Welsh and the Maghrebi coming to the New World, but you have to know the riddle to understand the lesson.

Annika didn't care what their deal was with each other, and she'd given up ever really getting the people in the East. She lived here now and people accepted her and loved her and didn't try to exclude her, but her home would always be the great north woods, the smell of pine sap and the ocean.

Rhys noticed Annika first and he loped over to fling an arm around her shoulders affectionately. "Where's my tampons, woman?" he barked out in a fake Southern accent.

"I knew you had PMS the other day when you were crying over that dog food commercial," Annika responded, whacking him on the belly with the flat of her hand. She pushed him away and forged ahead to the kitchen to find her chicken.

"Something happen while you were out?" Stanzia trailed behind and only sounded half-curious.

"Were you worried?" She was always worried.

"You need to talk to Rhys. Something strange is going on, and I assume it has to do with Tommy wanting your skanky ass to help him."

The chicken was juicy on the inside and crunchy on the outside, slightly spicy and salty. Annika moaned as she gobbled up a second piece.

When she swallowed down the last bite of the chicken she was inhaling, what Stanzia had said clicked together. Hunger sometimes made her a little frenzied. They watched each other for a few seconds, wordlessly communicating the way old friends do. "Sometimes I find animals more communicative than Rhys." Annika washed her hands in the sink.

"I think he has a crush on you, so he tries to be inscrutable," Stanzia said around the mouth of her wineglass. This was an old debate between them, so Annika just rolled her eyes and made a sign against the evil eye with her right hand.

"Irony's a bitch," Stanzia said and swaggered out of the room. Annika had come to pretty much the same conclusion about Rhys and his possible interest in her. Here was one of the best looking men Annika had known in a very long time pining after the one person who had less than no interest in a romantic relationship with him. He was too high-strung and moody and just flat-out strange. Annika already had his female version, Stanzia, to deal with. Annika also doubted Rhys's agenda was as uncomplicated as a romantic relationship.

The object of her reflection sat in the rocking chair in her living room with his feet up on the plaster griffin plinth they used as a side table, flipping the iPod from song to song with the remote. A whoop went up from outside.

His almond-shaped eyes turned to her and he smiled, displaying pointed canines. "Tommy Brennan, huh?" His smile appeared as genuine as ever, and he never seemed jealous of other guys, which was why they were able to be friends, good friends, despite his strangeness.

"Yeah. He wants me to help him with something." Which Annika was almost sure Rhys already knew. Rhys usually knew everything going on in Nashville.

"Yeah, I bet. Savin' his ass from getting killed." Point proven. Rhys cocked his head haughtily from side to side and ran his hand through his hair again to push it back from his face. The strands fell right back into perfect arrangement like a cartoon.

"Um, care to elaborate?" She picked up a random wineglass and poured herself a drink of the Malbec from the bottle on the table.

Rhys slitted his eyes and watched her for a few seconds. He was mercurial, the true definition of that, bubblingly happy one second, cruel the next, perhaps tortured by something she'd never get out of him, maybe just mentally unstable.

"Something's killing all the fey creatures in town." He cocked his head again and raised both eyebrows while biting his bottom lip. "You haven't heard about this?" The words spilled into the room, half genuine curiosity and half sarcasm.

She passed over about six responses, each less bitchy than the last. "Who would have told me? Tommy?"

"Well, your roommate maybe." Sarcasm dripped like acid off the words. When he said things inflected like that, Annika never knew if it was innuendo or something indigenous to his psyche she just had no access to. She generally ignored the parts of him with the sharpest points.

"What? I didn't know about that, dickhead!" Stanzia was passing through the room with a redheaded girl and a guy with a unicycle in tow. Rhys flipped her off with a smirk as Annika downed her glass of wine in three gulps.

"What's killing the fey?" Attempting to redirect the conversation might be absolutely pointless, but she tried all the same.

Rhys's eyes settled on her and he folded his hands over his belly. "I think that's what Tommy Brennan wants you to figure out." The cocky, endearing expression reemerged with a simple flick of his eyebrows. His smile could infect a whole room faster than a salamander's tail.

"You think, huh?" She poured herself more wine and wondered how far back in Rhys's bloodline the fey ancestor was. The DNA was written all over his appearance—from his height to his eyes to his suspiciously folded ears—and in his capricious nature. He had zapped her sixth sense hard the first time they'd met, but he'd never said word one about being anything other than just the run of the mill singer–songwriter from . . . come to think on it, she didn't know exactly where he was from. She opened her mouth to ask as he slinked out the room, calling *"Sly!"* to his buddy.

THE NEXT THURSDAY, after she'd facilitated the acquisition of a dozen clay lamassu to a nearly teenaged girl with pictogram tattoos all over her, Annika kicked her sandals off and settled in her chair just as Tommy Brennan strolled through the barrier into the shop. Instead of the suit, he was dressed in jeans and a short-sleeved pearl-snap cowboy shirt over a white T-shirt. His smile almost made sweat break out on her forehead.

"Thought you responded to the casual look better." He flopped down in the chair next to her with a thump.

"You looked good in the suit." Which was the truth. The suit just made him seem like a liar for some reason.

He batted his eyelashes at her in a joking way. "What's a fella gotta do to get some service around here?"

A loud pause resounded as the double entendre reverberated around the room. Annika thought about Sam

Adams and baseball and the beer appeared on the table next to a set of baseball cards. She blushed, not intending the baseball thing to be exposed. But every man she'd ever known from Boston was obsessed, and she found it quirkily charming even though she personally had no use for baseball.

"So, you wanna fill me in this time?" Annika watched as Tommy sipped his beer and scratched the side of his face.

He didn't turn to look at her. "Clearly, someone else has already told you. You must feel like you know enough to bargain or you wouldn't have broached the subject like that."

So. Tommy Brennan wasn't just a happy-go-lucky quasi-human haplessly appearing and disappearing according to no set schedule. Annika reassessed. She liked the idea of him as secretly gunpowder dangerous and glass-shard smart.

Resting his pint glass on his knee, he pivoted toward her, his jean-clad legs inches from her own jean-clad legs. His eyes flittered around her face—from her mouth to her light eyebrows to her cheeks. Annika looked like a debauched milkmaid most of the time—round rosy cheeks and dimples and huge green eyes that gave off the appearance of gentleness and innocence. She used that to her advantage often enough. The debauched part came from her wry facial expressions and the sleeve of tattoos on her left arm of a flock of ravens in flight. Ravens for wisdom.

Tommy Brennan seemed to look through her and at her at the same time, filing away secrets for himself that she probably would never know. "Do you remember when I asked you about the old myths the last time you graced me with your presence in this shop?"

Squinting her eyes, she wondered if how he was phrasing that was important. Words were often powerful. Magic came in many forms, many inherent to the user, others manipulated from outside forces. Annika had an innate knack for recognizing magic, magical users, and power points. Her people had been water witches, dowsers, architects, detectives, and investigators for as many generations as there was memory of and beyond. Personally, she found being born into a career a little limiting. All the same, her gift had brought her here to this room with Tommy Brennan asking her to use it to help the very people her mother had assisted for decades.

"How did you get involved with The Office? They don't recruit actively, do they?" She'd wondered that for years. She'd often thought of herself as the perfect magical policeperson. She had a skill that didn't have to be recharged or purchased, years of experience investigating this and that. The Office agents she'd come into contact with over the years always seemed so bizarre and ragtag. No one could ever explain where their so-called Office was, much less who financed them or directed them.

His eyes flew around the room, but it felt like a deliberate pause, not a real one to formulate a lie. "No, they don't actively recruit, and this is sort of on a need-to-know basis. Unless you want to fill out an employment application and join up."

She'd never in her life heard anyone really say "on a need-to-know basis." Whether hearing it said in earnest was amusing, cool, or annoying was hard to determine.

"I think you're the one with the need to know." Inside she leapt up and down at her clever zinger but kept a stoic expression on her face as Tommy Brennan laughed slightly and met her eyes.

"I got involved with them a few years ago when I was dating a girl who turned out to be a little darker than I had realized." He stopped and sipped his beer. She remained silent, letting the ambient sounds of the shop click and whir and chirp around them. Finally, he rubbed at his forehead and said "I thought she was into rough sex, really rough sex, granted, and what she was really into was human sacrifice."

"Huh."

"Yeah, huh." He leaned forward. "Look, my life history is on the table if you really want it, but the reason you don't ever hear anything about The Office isn't that no one wants to tell." He stared at her without blinking.

She supposed he was trying to tell her he wasn't refusing to speak so much as he was compelled not to. That sort of compulsion spell wasn't exactly simple, but if she was in charge of a shady, secret organization, she supposed she'd invest in that much time and effort to keep it sub-rosa as well.

He sat back in his chair and the witch light caught on the gold hair of his forearms, the tan skin sliding over solid muscle. Tommy Brennan was built like a football player, not a third baseman.

"So, have you ever heard any of the myths about non-human creatures and music?"

This seemed like a fluid continuation of the original conversation, in such a way that Annika felt certain this guy was used to being in control of most situations. Instead of being off-putting, his deft competency at getting what he wanted appealed on some subconscious level.

"Sure. Music attracts or repels certain nonhumans. But which stories are allegorical and which ones are literal—" She shrugged to indicate it was an eternal question.

"Did you ever wonder why certain places seem to collect artistic types for a while, maybe a decade, maybe longer?" His tone indicated he was utilizing the Socratic method so that she could come to all the correct conclusions on her own without him having to just give her a straight narration of the facts.

"No, not really." She hadn't and she didn't feel like making this a cakewalk for him.

He leaned his chin on his palm and stared into her eyes for a few seconds before springing to life and moving forward to get within a foot of her face. "Paris between the wars, London in the sixties, New York in the seventies, but on and off since settlement, there's always been something in this region, ebbing and flowing over the years, but distinctively real." He paused like he expected her to just leap up and supply the answer to this riddle.

Leaning back, he scratched his nose and cocked his head. "Euterpe has a vacation home on the river."

Euterpe, the muse of music? He had to be kidding.

Annika considered that for a few seconds as a couple in black T-shirts and leather pants crossed the barrier and disappeared behind a cherry wardrobe. "You mean the muses are real?" she finally asked, after he didn't elaborate any further.

"It always surprises me when people get surprised by anything anymore." Tommy Brennan rubbed his eyes with a thumb and forefinger and chugged his beer.

They sat in silence as the couple browsed for dried peacock feet or luminous amoeba or whatever was the hip, hot thing in the so-called right circles.

Greek deities were a couple of orders of magnitude above any sort of nonhuman Annika had ever heard confirmed absolutely. Magical people didn't tend to have stronger belief in higher powers than mundanes. Religion was tied to the same tags among witches as among those who had no access to magic—ethnicity, culture, whim, tradition. The muses were supposedly nymphs who embodied and propagated art and knowledge among the gods and humans. One for poetry, music, dancing, comedy . . . Annika couldn't remember them all.

"The name is probably putting you off. Think of her as more of a very strong magical focal point or conduit." Tommy Brennan broke into her thoughts. "What matters here is that other nonhuman creatures are drawn to her and her power and flock to places she is or has been. There're a wicked huge number of nonhumans in Nashville and its environs, and someone's picking them off. And they aren't starting with the little guys, either." All of the emotion had seeped out of his voice, he sounded like a blank page looked.

"What do you want me to do?" She felt like he'd told her as much as he had to lure her in, and it had worked just like the charm he knew it'd be.

"Help me stop the bad guy killing people, of course." He

stood up and stuck his hands in his front pockets. "Have a drink with me."

"We can have the drink now and I'll let you know about the other part."

When the hip couple stepped through the barrier, Annika and Tommy Brennan were a second behind.

THURSDAY NIGHTS AT The Remark tended to get a little rowdy. Some magical calendars coincide with mundane ones as far as days of the week, but many did not on the cycle of the months. Most witches kept lunar calendars. Many Asian communities had completely different concepts of time than those used in the Americas. A sort of cribbed, common calendar had come to be respected by most magical people in the Americas in the early part of the twentieth century. Why Thursday night had been declared a holiday was lost somewhere under a carpet or behind a drape.

Annika and Tommy Brennan sat at the end of the bar nearest the mirrored arch, their seats assured because the bar was always unspokenly reserved for employees and friends of such. Stanzia and Rhys were at a table in the back of the bar, clearly ridiculing the three-piece band on the stage.

The bar was a comfortable place, a second home, but faced with making non–work-related conversation with Tommy, Annika suddenly felt untethered and half-stupid. Usually she was cool and collected, she thought she could be charming when she wanted, but there were moments, like this one, when she felt bumbling and uncommunicative. She blamed Tommy. She fumbled for some vague middle ground of conversation.

"So, you like the Red Sox?" she blurted out, mentally kicking herself.

"Yeah! You like the Sox? Can you believe Francona switched Drew to the lead-off spot? I mean, the guy gets on base at a good clip, but we're paying that massive contract for his power, you know?"

He went on and on. Annika nodded but contributed nothing. She didn't know anything about baseball really, just knew a lot of people from Boston who for some reason wanted to tell her all about the Red Sox all the time. She didn't really listen, though, just let her mind wander.

She wasn't really paying attention to what fell out of her mouth when he fell silent and she said, "So, do you think about baseball all the time to fill in all the spaces when you're not thinking about sex?"

Tommy Brennan's smile sparkled and cracked almost viciously into a grin. "Are you propositioning me?" The grin became an attractive half-leer that made him seem dangerous in the way he'd hinted at a couple of times previously.

She blushed, feeling a little out of control. It had been a while since she'd actually met a man in whom she was interested intellectually, or even just physically.

"No, I was just teasing you," she answered lamely.

The silence that followed was almost unbearable, turning Annika introspective in the way that Stanzia said creeped her out, like Annika was absent from the room. Gradually she realized Tommy was talking. "What?" She blinked back to focus.

"I haven't ever heard a band in here that didn't make me want to throw myself in front of a rampaging catamount."

Two shots landed in front of them. Jami smiled from behind the bar. Tommy Brennan picked his up, waiting for her to do the same, and knocked his glass against hers. "Sláinte," he murmured brokenly.

The alcohol flamed down her throat, leaving a trail of pepper and cinnamon. She coughed once and pressed the back of her hand to her mouth. Tommy's eyes watered and one tear spilled down his cheek.

"Cheyenne Hauster!" Jami's huge eyes sparkled as she danced away. When Annika glanced over at Rhys and Stanzia's table, they were both deep in a conversation that included a lot of pointing and shouting at each other. That did not eliminate them from being the prime suspects. She could already feel the warmth seeping up from her stomach and from her fingertips and toes, down her arms and legs.

She pushed her hair from her face and slumped loose-limbed on the bar top to smile at Tommy, who returned the expression. His cheeks flamed bright pink, the same color as his mouth, and his posture could best be called a slink. When she went to push at her hair again, he beat her to it, the tip of one strong finger sweeping from her temple to the soft skin behind her ear and down the side of her neck. His eyes were three colors of green, light with flecks of almost black and lines of ivy.

Tommy's low laugh spun around the room in loops that ended by brushing against her face and exposed arms. "Let me tell you a story," he started.

This is the story that Tommy told:

Once there were two birds, a pure white hawk and pure black falcon. This was before there was strife in the world, no hunger or pain or sickness or hatred. One day the two birds both lit in the same tree. The hawk's pale eye met the black eye of the falcon and they spoke together in their minds. Let us merge as one and create gray, the hawk thought. Let us merge as one and create possibilities, the falcon thought. And the two birds disappeared to leave behind two mothers with eleven children each. The children were children both of each bird, darkness and light combined. Some of these children built shelters of shells and took to the sea in boats and pulled fish from the sea to eat. Some of the children took to the forests and built houses in which to live and pulled fruit from the trees to eat. For many generations, both families intermarried until neither knew from which mother any of them had sprung, because they had all come from both equally. Then, on the horizon one of the fishing people saw a thundercloud rolling across the vast gray sea. Then, on the horizon above the tree line, one of the forest-dwellers saw lightning crack across the sky. And thus were the two families split forever and combined forever with the coming of humans.

Annika felt lost for a second when Tommy stopped speaking. Black and white were easier than grey scale, one ending definitely where the other began. Grey was twilight where one's eyes struggled to make out distinct form from background. Grey meant always wondering what another person was thinking.

"So what am I thinking about?" Boston tinged his words until they flaked with salt.

Annika wondered vaguely what Tommy's abilities were, those thoughts skittering in between images of his green eyes in half-light, his bare shoulders limned by backlight. As she watched, the leer of earlier re-formed into something more secretive, something old like oak trees and the tide. He was black and white swirled until it appeared grey, an optical illusion.

"Definitely not baseball," she said.

His hand slid along the bar, blunt nails skimming her arm, which lay in a pool of condensation from the outside of her beer glass. She didn't know this man, and at the same time she felt she did. He seemed familiar in a way she couldn't name, in a way that seemed nameless. The band began to play a pipe and fiddle song and his voice joined with theirs in a strong hum. Somewhere on the edge of her hearing a sound at once ancient and new tugged her, pulling so that she lost focus on the room.

"It's the hauster." Tommy tapped the back of her hand, and she knew he was right, but she didn't care. "Your friends are bein' clowns."

She knew that, too. But she didn't care as she reached out to touch the freckles spread across the delicate skin under his eyes. His eyelashes flickered on her fingertips. His hand slid away from where it rested next to her arm on the bar. He left a fifty behind on the shiny wooden surface.

"Wanna hit the road, then?" There was laughter in his voice, something that made her feel that this wasn't some cheap encounter with a half-stranger—more a meeting between two people of like minds, something ancient, the acknowledgment of interest, of rain on a field and feet on a path. She knew at the same time the herbs in the elixir made her thoughts heavy with gravitas, the encounter seem vital and imperative. She just didn't care.

She was pretty sure they had planned to go somewhere when they stepped outside The Remark, maybe one of their respective residences, but they didn't make it farther than his car. Big, black SUV, the kind of car Annika usually mocked people for driving, but right now, struggling out of her shirt in the back seat, she was glad of its absurd size. She couldn't imagine where he lived anyway, a place full of beer cans and pizza boxes or antiques and ships in bottles?

The door barely slammed behind her when Tommy pulled her T-shirt over her head and tossed it casually aside. His hands and lips slid over where the fabric had covered.

"Beautiful," he murmured into her neck. "Someday I'm going to ask about all the tattoos," he said just below her ear. His hand twisted into her hair and pulled her mouth against his and they both tumbled down onto the wide back seat and Annika let the alcohol and the inevitability that was Tommy Brennan push her against the soft leather.

He loomed in the dark over her as he rose up to pull off his own shirt. Clothing did him an injustice. He looked good in it, but the muscles of his chest had the smooth beauty of rippled sand under soft waves. Not grossly chiseled, but manly, solid and comfortable. Annika pulled him down and made him flinch, biting his nipple before licking the smear of freckles hiding in his sparse, golden chest hair.

Annika moaned a little as his hands spanned over her ribs. They felt larger than they should and she fleetingly wondered if his physical appearance represented his true form, because he seemed to be made of the whole world. Tommy's knee slipped between her thighs and she pressed down, rubbing herself on him, unable to distinguish between the spark of his kiss and the shocks in her belly.

When he reached for the button on her jeans, Annika struggled to prop herself up on her elbows. "Condom," she scratched out, her voice almost failing her. Tommy sat up on his knees and rummaged in the console between the front seats, coming back toward her with a square of blue foil in his hand.

"Boy scout," she laughed, taking it from him.

"What?"

"Always be prepared. Take off those jeans, I can't do it at this angle."

He managed to strip them both of the denim keeping their skin apart. If she'd been the one to remove their clothes she would have just used magic.

"It's more fun to do it the Other way," he whispered in her ear.

Annika laughed and reached a hand between their bodies, finding him hard. She stroked the solid weight of his erection, with his hands pressing heavily against her breasts.

She brought her other hand down by her hip, ripped the foil open, and stretched the condom over him. She pictured his head disappearing between her thighs, just the top of his hair visible, him kneeling in the sun and biting the inside of her knee; of him by candlelight with a book falling from his left hand, holding her against him with one arm and his mouth pressed to her throat.

"Oh, God, stop thinking—" His voice broke as he moved over her, pushing the blunt head of his cock against her wetness.

"Oh. Oh, you feel so good," she whispered unintentionally before coherent thought and speech left her completely.

Later what she would remember most was how the tension in his body solidified his muscles, making him seem vast and otherworldly. He rolled like the rough waves of the Pacific Ocean and she felt at home again, just for a second before she came.

THEY DIDN'T TALK much after, although he was solicitous and gave her a handkerchief he assured her was clean, and turned his back rather chivalrously while she struggled back into her clothes in the back seat of the car. Luckily, she was still in a haze from the drink foisted on her by her "friends."

When he dropped her off at home she was torn between relief at not having to try and make conversation after what they had just done and disappointment that she wouldn't wake up next to him.

SINCE THURSDAY NIGHTS were abused so roundly, Fridays were often the day of recovery in Nashville, as was usually the case for Annika and her household (however many people that happened to be at the time). This particular Friday, Annika slept until two in the afternoon. She woke up only because Rhys's voice clearly barked out from the living room, "I did *not* say that!" in tones of belligerent outrage. She rolled out of bed, sore in that pleasant sort of day-after way, and slid on her house shoes: flip-flops with happy sushi emblazoned on them.

Even with teeth brushed and face washed, she felt like she'd gone ten rounds on a broom and impacted red clay on every dislodging. She slouched into the living room to find Rhys writing on the wall with a finger, glowing letters burning her retinas and leaving black afterimages as she blinked. She didn't bother to ask, just walked straight through and on to the kitchen to pour a cup of cold coffee. Out the kitchen window, she saw Stanzia in the backyard collecting herbs. Annika picked through the pantry and settled on a cold sausage for brunch. She stood in the middle of the kitchen with her cup in one hand, gnawing on the sausage held in the other, trying not to feel too humiliated when she flashed on what she'd done the night before. Her face burned and she jumped a little when Stanzia banged open the back door, woven basket in hand and a smirk on her face.

"That bad, huh? Embarrassing yourself even thinking about it?" She bustled past, knocking everything on the dining room table to the side and lining up the herbs in some arcane order understandable only by the slightly unhinged. "I didn't hear you come in, but that could be whatever Rhys did to my room. He said he soundproofed it for me. As a favor." She made a sound in the back of her throat, something between a cluck and a growl. "I'm going to do him a favor in return, I swear."

"I just want to sit in the yard and sweat the alcohol out. Maybe get a liver transplant." The whine refused to be suppressed.

"You didn't have that much at the bar, so you must have come home and had some more, to drink the shame away." Annika had no comment on that. Stanzia went to the fridge and came back with an ice pack that she handed over. "The worst pains are the self-inflicted ones because there's no one else to blame." That totally brushed under the rug the fact that she and Rhys were probably behind the inhibition-lowering potion shot.

"Oh, more backwoods witchy wisdom, I can't ever get enough!" Rhys called from the other room.

Both women rolled their eyes—Annika instantly regretting it as her head throbbed in double time.

She shuffled out to the backyard and laid on one of the reclining lawn chairs in the sun, the scents of verbena and lavender strong, underpinned by hot earth and the green of the grass. Moths landed on her arms and took off again, and she lost consciousness only to wake again with the sun hidden behind the horizon.

Annika was just beginning to wonder why she wasn't sunburned when she saw the note written in the air: *That was me! Rhys*. The words were in the same fiery letters he had painted earlier on the walls of the living room. She'd never thought too much about his abilities because he'd never evidenced any before, other than a simple fire-lighting spell and a facility for unknotting yarn with a couple flicks of his wrist.

She stripped and stood under the showerhead, unmoving for a solid fifteen minutes before bothering to wash her hair. There was a note taped to the door of her bedroom when she wandered that way, wrapped in a towel, intending to get dressed in ugly Mom clothes and lay on the couch to watch the DVR for the rest of the night. Then she hoped to sleep another ten hours or however long it took for her hips to snap back into proper alignment.

Nice try. Tommy called five times while you were asleep. Call him back or tell him to stop calling. S

Her closet thwarted her, though, and she ended up dressed in a plain, burgundy cotton A-line skirt and a matching T-shirt just in case. The couch part did happen, though. "Law & Order" marathon. She was asleep in ten minutes.

"CAN WE WATCH something besides "COPS" for fucking once?" Rhys's voice woke her again. Her eyes refused to open for long moments while she listened to the back and forth of the conversation.

"The last time you chose, we ended up watching some nature show about snow leopards."

"Yeah, because that's cool." This followed by rumbly laughter.

"You could go to your house and annoy Sly for a while and leave me alone to be happy in my own home."

"I don't have cable."

"You don't have electricity, do you?"

"Not exactly."

"You realize you're retardedly superstitious, right?"

"Shut up."

"You drive a car, but no electricity; seriously, does that logically follow?"

"Did you losing another shoe yesterday logically follow from being sober?"

"Oh, God, you two, shut the hell up!" Annika rubbed a hand across her sticky face and moaned.

"I thought you'd sleep through the night," a third, crisply accented voice said.

"You owe me twenty bucks," Rhys said as Annika's blood pressure bottomed out and she hoped if she prayed hard enough to the norns she could just expire on the spot.

People showing up uninvited was common around her house. Partially, this was an extension of the overall culture that dictated that hospitality had to be extended or the spurned party could call on the rights of an enemy. No one wanted more sworn enemies than strictly necessary, so unless someone was really heinous (or insane), hospitality was offered whether the resident wanted to or not. This was always good for free meals for freeloaders and the lonely.

"I told them I'd come back, but . . ." He let that dangle. Annika could imagine that Rhys took perverse pleasure in inviting him to stay, thus forcing Stanzia to invite him to stay even though she mainly wanted to get rid of everyone in the house at a given time. Annika had become a victim of the sideshow her friends couldn't help themselves from putting on.

She sat up and ran a hand over her hair. Tommy looked as put together as ever, hair brushed and soft T-shirt clinging to the muscles of his arms and chest. Another Berklee shirt, leading her to conclude he probably went to school there, which was a little strange for a fey. Sitting next to Rhys, they looked like a matched set of the different mundane versions of elves: one golden and almost too bright to look on, the other dark and clearly possessing secret knowledge from the pleased twist of his lips.

Stanzia was ignoring all of them, flicking through some book written in chicken scratch characters. Hopefully, not the demonology thing again.

Stanzia had been right, though; sometimes the self-inflicted wounds really were the worst because there was no one else to blame. Particularly when you wanted to hurt yourself all over again the next day. Swift attachment and a short attention span had cost Annika in the past, not that she thought she was going to just wake up one day reformed and only seek out the "right" kind of person. Who even knew what *right* was from day to day. Sometimes Annika believed in fate, in an orderly universe controlled by rational rules, and sometimes she believed that magic really was an unexplained form of science and that every good act took a bad act off the other side of the ledger. But on other days, she believed the world was made of chaos and disorder, entropy, the fabric of reality unraveling in a looser and looser ball, eventually dispersing into nothing, to Ragnarok and unreality. When she was hung over, she wished Ragnarok would just get here already.

She brushed her teeth, washed her face, and stumbled into the bedroom to change her clothes. The tang of coffee tangled around her as she made her way back to the living room. The old, battered samovar-like coffeepot Stanzia brought out on holidays and for family sat on the table with chipped mugs next to it. There were even cookies: mint chocolate, lemon zingers, and oatmeal.

Tommy chewed on a mint chocolate wafer, seemingly riveted by "COPS" as she slouched back into the room and sat on the couch next to Stanzia, who handed her a cup adorned with a nodding dodo and full of heavily milked coffee.

"This show is stupid. Why don't they go arrest the real criminals, lawyers and politicians and companies that dump hazardous waste into water systems?" Rhys bit angrily into an oatmeal cookie and chomped bleakly.

"The point of this show is social engineering to make middle-class people feel pleased with themselves that they aren't like these people." Stanzia answered in a distant sort of way, still flipping through her book and making notes.

"Whatever," Rhys scoffed.

Annika noticed the way Tommy's hair was darker at the

crown and progressively lighter as it grew on the sides of his head and down to his neck. The hair at the nape of his neck was a distinct gold reflecting the overhead lights. His fingernails were perfectly manicured but stained in places, as if they'd been sprayed with henna or something like it. After a few seconds, she noticed he was watching her, too, with a serious sort of expression she hadn't seen him wear before. Her magical detection sense sang through her like a plucked guitar string, reverberating in a loop the longer she stared at him.

"Anyway," Rhys said abruptly, pointedly, as though he knew what was happening. Annika looked up, embarrassed, surprised, to see him wearing his sardonic face. "Aren't you two supposed to be out saving all the fairies from being trampled on? When you come back bring me a roast beef sandwich." He lifted an eyebrow and smirked in the cocky way he managed without being a total prick.

"Yeah, we should go." Tommy pushed himself to his feet.

When Annika turned to say good-bye, her mouth only opened halfway because Stanzia was staring at her with an unreadable face, which could mean anything from that she already knew the end of this story or that she'd heard a distant bell chiming.

Part Two

Nashville rolled by through tinted glass: cracked cement with grass growing up through the interstices, the hope of the earth struggling through the barren landscape of technology. Tommy's stereo played "Mountain Stage" on NPR, probably a podcast, Gillian Welch singing an old, old ballad whose words didn't even register. Annika was a grown-up; she'd slept with people before and been forced to endure torturous close contact afterwards that made her want to scratch her face off or run away from home (however, that's not why she finally did run away). Tension tapped on her stomach and made her avert her eyes out the window, but she didn't feel any bone-deep regret or shame, just the uneasiness of wondering what was on Tommy's mind.

She really did sort of like him. Which was hardly surprising considering that she found it easy to fall in love and he was easy on the eyes. She would also be lying to herself if she said the man of mystery act didn't intrigue, whatever her moral compass said about The Office.

"Where're we going?" She tapped a fingernail against the glass of the window and thanked Buddha for air conditioning. Magic hadn't ever managed to solve that particular problem because of, well, lack of logical thinking among witches. That was one of the many reasons Annika had a hard time with the theory that magic was really some part of what the Others called science. There were some superficial similarities between the two forces, but there were superficial similarities between an apple and a tomato, too.

Tommy drove with one hand resting on his knee, loosely

holding the bottom of the steering wheel with a couple fingers, his body slung back in the seat. He shifted gears fluidly, as if thought had long since passed necessity. He was totally on reflex.

Slowly winking one eye, he smiled and the years fell off him. He looked every day of eighteen. "I thought I'd take my girl on a proper date. We'll have a time, don't worry about that." His smile took on an edge, his eyes hidden in the dark as a car's lights strobed over his face. "Your hair looks good pulled back like that."

Resisting the urge to smile at his compliment or to touch her braided hair, she asked, "A time? Are we going to a party?"

"Nah, on the clock, we're goin' where the wild things are." His accent reduced *are* to *ahh* and a smile, totally unexpected, lit up her face.

The Gateway Bridge crosses the Cumberland River on Shelby Avenue, carrying people from east Nashville (which is really north Nashville) into the heart of downtown. The foot of the bridge stands a block from the mundane tourist mecca of Broadway, the mythical street of honkytonks and Fan Fair, as gaudy as the tackiest tourist destinations in the United States. If you go in the opposite direction from Broadway after you cross the Gateway Bridge, however, turn left instead of right, you land in an area of genuine music full of great venues and locals out for a good time. Tommy turned left off the bridge and Annika thought the night was already looking promising.

Down the numbered streets in the direction they took, office buildings sat cheek by jowl with bars and clubs, some refurbished and gentrified, others pocked seventies cement and siding. Parking was a problem, and Tommy and Annika drove around for a long time before they happened on a spot on 3rd Avenue between a Yaris and an eighties-era Caddy.

"Where're we going?" Annika asked again, after she'd hopped out of the car and Tommy had closed her door for her. Belatedly, she realized he had intended to open it.

"Rutledge." He offered her his arm with the elbow thrust out, and she took it with a slow blink and a grin. The skin on the inside of his arm was baby soft and the thick veins just underneath felt fragile, like bright, unprotected flowers reaching up to the sky—waiting to be trampled or withered by the sun.

The Rutledge was a music venue on 4th Avenue that alternated between being a party zone for overeager college kids out for Jager bombs and hook-ups and a refuge for serious musicians drawn by the amazing acoustics. The front wall in the bar section was all windows, and as Tommy and Annika passed by she could see a crowd already bumped up against one another by the bar, arms flailing over heads and mouths open around straining voices.

On the glass front door, a poster for the main act of the night caught Annika's attention. *Turpentine on a Brush Fire* was emblazoned at the top of the poster. An illustration occupied most of the five by three paper, a desert scene cut by a scraggly bush. On one side of the bush the face of an agitated old man with emphatic eyebrows shouted while on the other side another figure in a robe and sandals poured liquid out of a jerry can labeled TURPENTINE onto the bush. In the robed guy's other hand was a Zippo reading MOSES. As Tommy reached to open the door, Annika thought she saw the flames engulfing the bush flicker.

The sound immediately swept over them when Tommy flung open the door and tugged her inside. Annika hardly noticed because her sixth sense spun around like a compass needle drawn by a lodestone. All she could sense was power, something like bass notes radiating from the ground and up her legs and into her bones. She reeled a bit and Tommy tucked her closer to his side. He glanced down at her, quickly flicking his eyebrows up and down with mischievousness, dimples and gleaming eyes alerting her to trouble ahead. Maybe the good kind of trouble.

She winked back up at him, causing him to toss his head back to let out a huge, thrilling laugh.

His laughter turned heads. Annika became slightly self-conscious that she and her companion had suddenly become the focus of attention of many of the outliers of the mob frantically trying to solicit more alcohol for further inebriation. The Rutledge was a mixed crowd, meaning witches and other magical types frequented it alongside mundanes. Generally, alcohol covered a multitude of sins. If a mundane woke the day after a bender and recalled seeing someone surrounded by a corona of sparkles, or a guy with goat feet, he could chalk that up to hallucinations or vivid dreams. Some people used actual defensive spells to cover their tracks, but Annika had never bothered with all that. Though, to be honest, she tended not to mix all that much. She had enough problems without having to worry about being an emissary for her entire community; better to leave that to the activists.

Tommy pulled her through the crowd with a hand pressing her fingers into the crook of his arm. She recognized a couple regulars from The Remark, who lifted their drinks or tried to press forward to get near her. They made their way up some wide stairs that brought them into the upper section of the venue, where high-top tables sat cluttering up the space in no particular pattern. Along the cast iron railing that fringed the front of the balcony, most of the tables had been pushed together and an eclectic crowd smooshed together sloshing drinks over each other as they weaved in and around one another.

Sitting in the middle of the crowd, facing the room instead of the stage, a short, round girl with glossy ringlet curls wearing a hippy smock shirt displaying her braless cleavage smoked a bidi and gulped a golden drink. She seemed to give off some kind of pulsing charm, magic but more. All the other people at the table were arrayed around her like a *Last Supper* tableau. Next to her, on her right hand, was Sly, Rhys's roommate of all people. His impish smile beamed when he saw Annika. Pulling his cigarette out of his mouth, he waved her over, calling her name above the sound of the crowd. His wiry frame was animated with pleasure and good will.

Annika had liked Sly from the first time she'd met him. He'd been hauling wood out of the back of his battered seventies pickup a few logs at a time. She only later found out that the wood was to fuel the stove in the kitchen because of Rhys's aversion to having electricity in the house. Sly had given off the low-level thrum of a backwoods herbalist, and she'd taken to him immediately. He was charming with his bright caramel eyes and hazelnut brown skin and tawny beard.

"Whazzuh, girl?" he shouted as she disengaged from Tommy to lean across the table to hug him. "What's doin', lady?" His effervescent charm always set her at ease. How he and Rhys cohabitated, or were even the sort of friends they were, had never really fallen together for her. Some things in life, though, were inexplicable.

The people occupying the stools directly across from the hippie girl and Sly moved aside to let Annika and Tommy sit. Annika turned to thank the man on her right, but she hesitated when he stared back at her with an unfathomable expression, placid and removed, cold maybe. Her sense was so overwhelmed in the building that she couldn't pick out specific threads, to feel for malignancy or benignity.

"Hey, I know you!"

Annika turned back to the girl next to Sly. The girl's shoulders and Sly's pressed together and they seemed to match each other in a way Annika had no words to express. Sly's companion reached her hand across the table and grabbed Annika's wrist. Bass lines of magic pulsing up from the ground, wave after wave resolved into threads, something like harmonics, each thread bisecting and trisecting perfectly into octaves and progressions. Every thread began at some point on this girl's skin, filaments finer or thicker blanketing the entire room. Sly was cocooned, Annika could clearly see between the snapping closed of her eyelids in a blink and the reopening of them.

The girl removed her hand and smiled with glossy bowed lips. "I'm Brandi!" She said with an East Tennessee accent. "With an *i*!"

She offered her glass to Annika. "Southern Comfort, want some?"

An immediate refusal rolled from the back of her tongue, only to be caught behind her teeth when Tommy touched her leg under the table. She nodded her head instead and took the glass from Brandi's hand. A conversational hush fell across the balcony, leaving in Annika's ears the eerie sound of leaves crunching underfoot as she lifted the glass to her lips and let half a mouthful of the sweet alcohol roll across her tongue and down her throat.

A collective sigh drifted through the bar and the conversation started back up around them. Tommy's hand rested on her thigh halfway between the knee and hip. If he spread his hand his fingers would span almost the entire length. Annika handed the glass back to Brandi, who looked as sweet as the drink she favored. Her spaghetti strap dress sported a white lace bodice and a red and white polka-dot tentlike bottom.

Sly passed her another glass and as she hesitated, he smiled so big his eyes closed all the way. "Don't worry, girl, nothin' in there but scotch and soda. Would old Sly Dog hurt ya?"

Annika sipped her drink and as the last of the Southern Comfort was chased into her belly, she became aware that the overwhelming sense of magic in the room no longer was such. She could pick out individual strands. Tommy's was thick and bright, represented by something like the white-hot heart of a flame. Sly's was more complex, represented by the sound of a G chord.

Wait, she didn't know what a G chord sounded like!

But as she focused back on Sly fully, Annika realized she did know what a G chord sounded like, and that sound represented Sly totally.

When she tried to focus this sieving of magic on Brandi, all she got was the web of lines running through the room and out the windows and doors. No neat picture resolved itself.

Brandi tapped the back of Annika's hand with a smile and all of Annika's attention immediately tunneled onto her. "So, do you like music?" She was chewing gum, and she smacked it between draws on her bidi. Which might not have been a bidi by the sweet floral tones of the smoke she exhaled.

"Sure, of course." Annika wasn't sure she was ready to discuss music with the actual muse of music.

"Oh now, baby, don't put my girl on the spot like that." Sly wrapped his arm around Brandi and pulled her against him. She smiled up at him with what Annika would have read as sappy love on anyone else, but on someone worshipped as a demigod, who knew what the expression meant?

"Do you like old-time music, Annika?" Brandi tilted her head to the side and her hair fell over her shoulder, catching the light. Her heart-shaped face and pixie mouth reminded Annika of the lyrics to "Girl From the North Country" by Bob Dylan.

"Ohhhhhhhhh," Brandi sighed with a smile. "I love Bob Dylan!" She hopped in her seat and laughed, setting off a chain of laughter down the table. Tommy's hand left her thigh to land in the middle of her back, rocking her with the force.

Tommy let out a low *hmmmmmm* in perfect pitch and broke into the first couple lines of the exact song Annika had been thinking of. The rest of the balcony soon joined in, either harmonizing or playing improvised accompaniment. On the second verse, Annika couldn't help joining in even though she'd never been able to hold a tune in a bucket. Bob hadn't ever been much of a singer himself, so no real loss. Feet pounded and tables shook with clattering glasses and palms. The room vibrated with laughter and the song morphed into "Scarborough Fair" rearranged with an old-time feel, more mountain holla and less Ye Olde Folke Toure.

The balcony faded into clapping and swaying as the stage called sound check and the artist on stage finished up the second song along with the impromptu chorus. When the exuberant impromptu concert came to a close the artist, a youngish guy in standard Nashville uniform of white T-shirt and thin cotton pearl-snap plaid overshirt and jeans, tuned his guitar and checked the monitors. During the pause Brandi leaned forward, pressing her breast against Annika's arm, and motioned for Annika to lean closer. Her soft face took on what had to be the most severe expression she could produce.

"The music's dying," she sighed.

Annika wasn't sure what kind of response she could give to that. She'd lived around magic all her life and had known some really strange individuals. Sometimes it was best not to engage.

"The music's dying," Brandi repeated and her eyes welled up with tears.

Unlike a hero in an epic tale, Annika knew before she said it that she was committing herself to something insane or dangerous. "What can I do to help?" She didn't usually like to get involved with drama not directly related to herself or her loved ones, but "the music's dying" sounded like it could affect a whole lot more than just the people here in this room.

"You have to find him."

There was a finality to the remark that reminded Annika of Stanzia saying "It's like a bell ringing far off, you know?" Up until that moment, no, she really had not known.

The guy on stage stepped up to the mike again and picked out a three-chord progression intro on his guitar before kicking into the lyrics of his song.

"You took my favorite shirt, did you have to smash my heart for effect?" he sang. Annika didn't see any hidden meaning there. Most songs were about heartbreak or its prelude.

The guy was as good as you'd expect of someone playing for a Muse. She drank her scotch, which progressed from singles to doubles, and watched Tommy watching her. He was manipulating her. She'd known that from the first time she'd seen him. What she hadn't expected was to enjoy the ride. Most people delude themselves, thinking they're in total control of their lives. Annika's father was a numerologist and astrologer. She'd been raised with a dubious attitude towards free will. That was partially what had kept her on the West Coast so long. What was the point of making a large change when the outcome was already foretold? Everyone has internal battles; one of hers was against her inbred inclination to trust in fate.

From what Annika knew of most fey, they seemed to believe in fate even more seriously than humans did. What she knew about fey, though, was mostly secondhand or through books. She wasn't the kind of person who pried into people's lives with no invitation and nonhumans had codes about how they gave up information.

Tommy clearly had a plan, and he seemed competent enough. That didn't mean she would blindly follow, but she would at least let him explain himself, give his reasons, explain his plan. She hadn't been doing much of anything anyway—he wasn't disturbing her life any more than she had done when she moved to Nashville. She'd moved for a change; meeting demigods was definitely a change.

Four drinks in, she was ready to crash again. She tugged on Tommy's sleeve and he helped her off her stool. She really enjoyed that. Getting used to his constant babying wouldn't kill her. Sly made an elaborate pained face that she was leaving, but she mouthed *tired* and he shrugged and turned back to the music. Brandi didn't take her eyes off the stage. She was slung all over Sly, with both her arms clinging to him and her head on his chest.

On the stairs, she was glad she'd worn a denim skirt and a pair of Chucks, because she was too tired and drunk to have walked back to the car in heels or even flip-flops.

They stepped out of the air conditioning into the embrace of the humidity and heat. As the summer progressed in Tennessee, the heat became a living thing with a life cycle and a heartbeat.

"That went well." Tommy pushed his hair off his face and looked down at her with a grin.

"What's your deal anyway?" The words popped out before she really thought them.

"What?" Tommy's smile flattened out as they rounded the corner towards the car.

"What sort of fey creature are you? You have to be something strong. Because of the flame in my head." That made sense to her. Maybe not to anyone else on the planet.

"Flame?" He hit the automatic lock on the SUV on her side and opened the door for her. He offered a hand because of the height, and she took it, letting him half lift her into her seat. Leaning over her, he also buckled her in. Once that was done, he paused and stared into her eyes. "Do you really want to ask me this stuff?"

"What do you mean?" Embarrassment was going to make her belligerent. She didn't mean to turn angry most of the time she did, it just came out of nowhere and she rode it.

"You know exactly what I mean." His tone was full of the sort of command and authority he did everything in his power to mask most of the time. She focused on him and saw his flame again. He slammed the door.

She stared out the window at the passing streets as they drove home. When they pulled into her driveway, she opened her door and hopped out of the car before he could get out himself. She slammed the front door harder than she'd intended behind her. What her problem was, she wasn't exactly sure. Maybe she was disconcerted about Brandi and Sly. That felt like a cop-out, though, because *weird* was the theme of her life. What wasn't weird? She felt scorched by the mild rebuke from Tommy, humiliated like a child caught out lying in front of a group of respected adults. She wanted to punch him in the face for making her feel that way, but she also wished she could take back breaking the rules with him, too. Both feelings were equally ridiculous since she barely knew him. The real problem was, she hated herself for wanting his attention and not knowing why.

SATURDAY AROUND NOON when Annika got up, the house was empty. She put her iPod in the dock and listened to Lucinda Williams at top volume as she made herself some eggs and toast. It was only after she got out of the shower and was opening her bedroom door to get dressed that she found the note from Stanzia: *Gone to market with idiot. S*

That explained where those two were. Annika laid on her bed wrapped in a damp towel, thinking about Tommy and her habit of getting overly attached to inaccessible men, until she was forced to get up and get dressed for work.

The act at The Remark that night was a regular who had a theme album revolving around the traditional Celtic calendar. If that wasn't bad enough, she was working with the two servers who both fought over who got to work the least on any given shift. This intrusion of the humdrum felt like a thin veneer over her real life, something she had to overcome to get back to the good bit.

A couple hours into her shift, she stood by the end of the bar, pushing her hair back up into a chignon with bobby pins, when a Dale Watson song began to thrum out of the sound system. She hummed along until the lyrics began. As she started to sing, her broodiness fell away and she felt connected to all the other people in the room, vitally and deeply connected by something ineffable and ultimate. Her voice lifted a little higher and one of the women at the table next to where she stood picked up the next line and sang along. They gave a sort of impromptu karaoke performance for the rest of the song, and when it ended, the people in earshot clapped and whistled. Blood hit her face and she started sweating. She covered her face with a hand and laughed with embarrassment.

Jami, who was bartending, handed her a beer when she walked back to her usual post at the end of the bar. "I didn't know you could sing!" She was thrilled. Jami was always happy for other people. She was charming, hickory eyes and sienna hair and the kind of grounding that manifested itself as earth magic in so many of the people in this region. Jami had the kind of green thumb that had started legends in the preindustrial age.

"I can't," Annika said without thinking as she sipped her beer. Jami wrinkled her nose, and when Annika focused on her, she saw a climbing vine with bright, multicolored blooms in her mind representing Jami.

"Whoever told you that was just jealous!" Jami smiled and flounced away. People being jealous was her usual explanation for most ill will.

A ripple of power ebbed to her left and flowed back towards her. Before she even turned, she knew who had sat down next to her.

"So, you didn't ask me about my plan." Tommy paused. "I'll have a Black Cat."

Jami had the beer poured before Annika could tell Tommy where to shove his beer. Placidly, she turned his way. He had the baseball cap back on, a faded Red Sox T-shirt to go with it this time. She didn't think he could wear anything badly.

"Clearly you're here to impart deep insights. Wow me."

He chuckled. "You're just too pretty to pull off bitchy, you know. Doesn't work for you." She was considering a retort, but he plowed right on. "I've already figured out the M.O. I just don't know why."

She hopped up on the seat next to him so she didn't have to strain her neck to look up at him. "I feel like there should be more in the explanation phase."

"Oh, sweetheart, I feel like there should be more to a lot of things." His smile faded until he wore the serious, authority face that she realized was probably his regular, unguarded expression.

"If you know what he's doing, why can't you catch him?" She also wanted to know why there was an assumption the bad guy was a he. Also, what exactly was happening, and how about that whole images in her head thing?

"You only project your thoughts when you're angry. That's pretty awesome. Did you learn that somewhere?" His knuckle knocked against the bar as Annika's whole body flooded with adrenaline, ice zapped down her spine, followed by a full body blush. "You're probably screaming the alphabet in your head now, no point. You're not angry now. I'll bet embarrassed." He paused and sighed, rubbing his eyes.

"You read minds?"

"No. I pick up projected thoughts. If I want to. To answer your other questions: most bad guys are male so I figure this one probably is, too. What exactly is happening isn't a paint by numbers, sweetheart, but from what I've pieced together by the bullshit information I've gotten from the community, people stronger than humans are being killed or consumed by something that's circling in closer to Brandi. Like a noose. That's bad, because if something very bad were to get at her, well, I don't know what the fuck exactly would happen, but something awful. Maybe something people would call an apocalypse, maybe just all the music would die in Nashville and surrounding areas—which could mean all of the East. I don't really know. Could be anything." He drank half his beer while she sat there grinding her teeth. "Mainly, and here I'm going to be fucking frank, I don't want to die. I'm not tooting my own horn when I say that I'm not your run of the mill wood witch brewing up bark tea and selling tourists love charms made outta unicorn piss."

She opened her mouth to object there, because she wasn't stupid. He tossed up a hand, palm out.

"I don't know shit about the images in your head. I'm sure you can thank Brandi for that. She must have taken a liking to you." His eyes flicked around her face. "Beware Greeks bearing gifts and all that shinola."

Jami wandered over and smiled big and bright at Tommy. "Hey there, handsome!" Her enthusiasm was usually a force of nature, but Annika wasn't in the mood for much more than laying in the dark and pretending the world away. "I'm glad you like my girl here. She's special!" Most people would sound as fake as Atlantis if they chirped sentiments like that; on Jami, they came out ebullient and sweet.

"Yes, she's certainly that." His laugh set Jami off in return. She leaned back, holding a hand on her flat belly.

"Oh, you!" She wagged a finger at him and just shook her head when he motioned for the tab. "You can give me a kiss for it, though." Her wink said something that Annika couldn't read.

To her shock, Tommy stood on the rungs of his stool, planted the palms of his hands on the bartop, and leaned in to give Jami a nuzzled kiss on her cheek. She blushed brick red and fanned herself with her hand.

"Good luck for him to kiss you, you know," she said in a low, conspiratorial tone. Dancing away, giggling to herself, Jami sighed under her breath.

"The fuck?" Annika tried to pin Tommy in place with her eyes.

"Jealous?" His expression began flirtatious and eroded second by second. It landed on dangerous, and her heart vacated her chest and started to beat in the back of her throat.

"Did you think I was inflating my self-worth when I put myself only a rung down the annihilation ladder from Brandi?" He dropped his eyes and brushed the front of his shirt with the palm of his hand. "I'll give you a ride home. Jami was coming over to tell you that your shift was over, but she got distracted."

RHYS RARELY EVER told stories—another odd thing about him. But one Saturday night when he was extremely drunk, he told Annika and Stanzia a story as they sat on the front porch of their house, drinking water and watching the Perseid meteor shower.

This is the story that Rhys told:

Forget all that once there was crap. *A fox and an owl both lived in the same tree, one in the roots and the other in the branches. One was wise and one was crafty. Which was which? If you assume that the owl couldn't burrow and the fox couldn't climb, then you already told yourself a different story from the one I'm telling now. The crafty owl hunted by night and burrowed in the roots of the tree to sleep during the heat of the day. The wise fox lived in the hollow of a tree branch and let the birds nest in the branches and bring his meals right to his door. Our own assumptions usually blind us to what's right in front of our faces.*

This particular Saturday night, Rhys was sitting on the front porch of Annika's house when she and Tommy pulled up. Rhys had his feet on the wooden railing nestled into the ivy vines that grew all the way around the balustrade and sides of the house. His bare toes peeked out white among the dark leaves. On his head was an ivy crown and on his lap his old battered guitar.

Tommy stopped on the stairs and stuck his hands in his pockets, watching Rhys for a few seconds. "Mind if I go inside?"

Rhys smiled and ducked his head, a casual, commonplace gesture from him. Annika almost pointed out this was her house, not his, but Rhys cut her off.

"Yeah, sure, why not?" He laughed and lifted a can of beer to his mouth.

When she focused on him, the image of a wave, tall as a house and about to crest, appeared in her mind. He lifted an eyebrow at her and quirked the side of his mouth.

"Yeeeeeeeeees?" His stare felt the same as ever, not any more loaded than it was yesterday.

"Whatever," she said, walking towards the front door.

"Whatever, yourself!" he answered.

The living room was strewn with its usual Saturday night chaos of people, musical instruments, alcohol bottles, and dishes. Sly sat on the couch with his fiddle in his lap next to one of the neighbors, an Indian girl with short hair whom Annika had only met a couple times.

"What say you, girl?" Sly hopped up and tossed his arms around her. Leaves crunched somewhere nearby.

Annika drew back and was about to ask after Stanzia when Tommy walked back in the room with two beers in his hand. He offered her one and as she took it said, "She's in the backyard doing something you don't want to know about."

Her mouth only got half-open before he lifted one side of his mouth and the matching eyebrow. "She told me, obviously."

Annika didn't think he had been gone long enough to go outside and confab with her roommate. So. Well, that was interesting. But not pressing at the present.

The Indian girl drew Sly's attention and he started picking out a song on his fiddle.

"Outside?" Annika walked back out onto the porch without waiting for affirmation.

Rhys was in the same place, idly picking at his guitar strings.

"So, what's the plan?" She parked herself on a step and waited for Tommy to cough up the goods.

His eyes fell on Rhys, who ignored him for several seconds.

Finally, Rhys rolled his eyes and glared at Tommy. "Dude, really? Don't you have some kind of serious issue to deal with? Don't worry about me. I think you already know where I stand."

"We'll see," Tommy said with a tone that would have made Annika beg for forgiveness, but Rhys just laughed in a bright run of arpeggio.

"Whatever, man."

"Do you two have some kind of history?" Annika didn't really want to even ask that much. The last couple days had been pretty nuts without stepping into a feud between two people she wouldn't want to piss off.

Rhys made a half-barked scoff. "Shhhyeah!"

"Back to the matter at hand." Tommy sat on the step below hers. Annika rolled her eyes at his blatant sidestepping of the situation. "I have a plan."

"Oh, this should be good." Rhys played an accompanying chord progression on his guitar. Tommy cut his eyes at him but didn't reply.

"We should play a couple open mike nights and draw him to us and once we have him where we want him, we spring."

Rhys's laughter startled a flock of crows out of a nearby tree. Their wings beat almost in time, shaking the leaves of the oleander and the camellia in the front yard.

"Yeah, the perilous downfall of this plan is that I can't play an instrument and I can't sing." Annika was sort of glad about that for the first time in her life. When she'd first moved to Nashville, she'd felt that lack like an ache, unable to participate when her friends were swept up in the ecstasy of communal playing. She'd learned soon enough that once everyone was drunk enough, talent doesn't matter as much as enthusiasm.

The silence on the porch was cut by the songs of crickets and bullfrogs and the muffled bleed-over from inside the house. Annika looked from Tommy to Rhys and they both stared back at her. Rhys began to pick through a familiar tune.

"When first I came to Louisville, some pleasure there to find, I met a maid from Lexington whose beauty filled my mind."

Tommy nudged her leg. "Sing along." He picked up on the next line himself and sang under Rhys, their voices both growing stronger and somehow better when twisting together. Annika joined in timidly on ". . . the lily of the West." When no one's ears seemed to bleed, she grew bolder and pitched her volume up to meet theirs. Tommy smiled and winked at her and Rhys flipped his hair in his face with pleasure.

They sang five verses or so of the song and Rhys finished up with a quick run over the neck of his guitar with his thumbnail. She was flushed, ebullient, ready to sing more.

Sly busted open the front door with his fiddle in his hand. "What's this here, then? A porch party?"

Other people filtered out, the Indian girl Gita, Peg and Mike from behind them. Stanzia wasn't there, but that didn't mean much on a full moon. They switched from traditional American tunes to "The Four Marys" with Sly and Gita on fiddle and a call and response on the chorus, and on to Irish sing-alongs and sea shanties. Rhys led a timber-rattling version of "Spanish Ladies."

The evening felt encased in a bubble of eternity, as if the minutes bleeding into other minutes were just one long moment that would never end. The night would hold onto them and keep them like this forever, alive, young, vibrant, free. Tommy pressed his leg against hers and she knew she could take him to bed now, but she also knew she didn't have to. In some way, the give and take of music felt more intimate than rushed kisses in the back of a car, more real than the press of skin against skin that ended in an abruptly in-drawn breath and a bitten-off curse. Music was eternal. Like Saturday night.

"I can sing because of Brandi?" She really had no other explanation for her sudden perfect pitch. She didn't figure that was some kind of sudden-onset adult skill or anything. Tommy winked at her and pinched her cheek.

"Her drink." His smile made her feel fifteen again, silly and awkward and full of possibility.

"Which I assume wasn't actually Southern Comfort." It wasn't a question.

"Some people call it soma, some call it ambrosia, depends on who you ask. She gave you a great gift."

"But why?" That was really the part she wasn't getting. At all.

"There used to be a saying, 'the gods are fickle.' I'm not a theologian, and I don't know what makes a person a god, but I do know that sometimes great power makes people act . . . irrationally and according to some impulse the rest of the world doesn't comprehend."

Sort of like you, she thought, but just held his hand instead of saying anything.

Much later, as the chariot of the sun strained at its gates, Annika pressed a hand under Tommy's sweaty T-shirt against the slick skin of his belly and licked the salt off his bottom lip before tucking herself face first into her cool sheets.

SUNDAY MORNINGISH, ANNIKA and Stanzia discussed what the duo should be called and what the set list should be over bread pudding flavored with orange peel and some flower Stanzia's mother grew.

"If you call it 'breakfast blah' you can eat dessert in the morning. Like coffee cake. You add coffee to cake and *voilà,* instant breakfast acceptableness." She flourished her fork.

Annika swiped her bread pudding through the caramel sauce Stanzia had whipped up to go with the breakfast dessert. "Since we're doing cover songs, maybe we should stick to sing-alongs and crowd pleasers." She wasn't shy and didn't have stage fright, but she hadn't performed in public since theater in college.

"Did you even ask Tommy what instrument he plays?"

"He can play anything," Rhys said as he wandered into the living room with a plate of food. Neither woman bothered to ask where he'd come from since he just appeared at will wherever he pleased. He sat on the couch close enough to crowd Stanzia and she moved over slightly to accommodate him. He smirked and moved with her, so she just gave up and let him wedge himself next to her, eating off of her plate instead of his own.

Annika pondered whether Tommy could literally play

anything or if Rhys just meant anything she might want him to play.

"I think you missed my whole point." Stanzia pushed all the raisins to the side of her plate and Rhys scooped them up. "She's not *talking* to him."

"I love it when you talk about me like I'm not in the room. Really. Please continue." Annika felt her eye twitch.

Rhys sighed long and put upon. "You should just stick to the oldies. 'Yn Nyffryn Clwyd' and 'Danny Boy' or whatever other lame things the Irish go in for."

"Um." Annika looked at Stanzia, who was rolling her eyes. "Yn Nyff . . . what?"

"It means 'The Missing Boat.'" His tone was definitely saying "Well, duh!"

"Just play some Dylan and Waylon Jennings, that kind of thing. The Irish ballads idea isn't horrible." Stanzia said this with an expression of exaggerated innocence.

Rhys looked like he was two seconds from stabbing her roommate with his fork. "Oh, so it's war?"

"Play 'Tangled Up in Blue' for me." Stanzia ate around the dried fruit in her bread pudding, leaving that for Rhys, who ate each piece she exposed. His expression didn't lighten its murderous scowl, but nothing exploded for the moment.

"What about the name of the band?" That one really escaped her.

"Oh, that's simple," Stanzia said in the sort of bored, reflective tone she used when discussing issues other people found complex. It was keeping her shoes on and remembering how to drive that Stanzia found difficult.

"Yeah?" Annika was doubtful, but she'd been friends with this woman for long enough to at least hear her out.

"Hill and Sky."

Rhys grunted agreement. "Hmm."

Annika was at a loss. "Fill me in?"

"The fairies in the old Irish folktales lived in mounds, hills."

So far so good. "Yes?"

"And Scandinavian witches traditionally flew—sky." She handed her plate to Rhys, who finished her bread pudding. He handed her his coffee and Stanzia finished that.

The whole flying thing was sometimes a pain in the ass. "You know that's a stereotype." She resisted the urge to give a lecture on the prejudice associated with inflicting all of the culpability for the witchhunters accusing all witches of flying, of the broom fixation by the mundanes, and all the attendant rigamarole on Nordic witches.

"And the living in dirt mounds under the earth and dancing the night away thing isn't?" Stanzia said off-handedly.

Point. "Point," she acknowledged. She rolled the name around in her head a couple times as Rhys and Stanzia began to snipe about the television.

"OK, I like the name. Hill and Sky it is!" She was pretty pleased. Having the name in place made everything else seem simpler. She wondered if Tommy would like it. He didn't strike her as the kind of person who would care one way or another about the name of the fake duo they were putting together for a sting, but on the other hand names were often highly symbolic and full of possible pitfalls.

"Yeah, I know." Stanzia wandered out of the room with the plates in her hands.

"What do you mean?" Annika called after her.

Rhys cut his eyes away from a panda documentary on the television to lift his eyebrows at her. "She means—" he cleared his throat—"she already knew the name when she told you. You just think you chose."

That was why Annika had issues with free will and fate. Rhys was obnoxiously disinterested in her existential crisis, bamboo being far more fascinating. She chose to ignore him in favor of printing out lyrics for their set from the Internet.

AFTER A LONGISH nap, Annika woke up feeling like her life was a soap bubble and she was navigating from within the fragile surface. She heard guitar picking from the porch and found Tommy sitting in one of the rocking chairs under the bay tree. He smiled up at her but didn't say anything. He had a pitcher of tea at his feet and several glasses. She poured herself a glass to find the subtle flavor of bimini leaf, apricot, mango, and nutmeg under the crisp taste of the bright, sweet tea. Condensation beaded on the side of her fragile blue Turkish glass as a mockingbird castigated another bird in the magnolia in the neighbor's yard.

Tommy's hum of magic felt like part of the landscape, natural like the sun creeping across the flaking grey boards of the porch, familiar like the smell of grass. She glanced at him to find him watching her with his mouth partially open. For half a heartbeat she had some deep insight, some transcendent knowledge of this person, and then, just as swiftly, he broke into a lopsided smile and it was gone.

Tommy lifted an eyebrow and started sketching out a real song. He picked over "Girl from the North Country" and she sang around his tenor in counterpoint. The garden bloomed with late lilies and the jungle of medicinal plants Stanzia kept in the front yard: primrose, angelica, motherwort, hyssop, peony, rue, yarrow, ginko, ginseng, aloe, damiana. The bay tree waved in the sun, fragrant and sweet.

"I guess it's convenient that the act playing tomorrow night at The Remark canceled, huh?" Annika watched a starling tossing water over his head with a wing in the mermaid-shaped birdbath at the side of the house.

"Convenience can be bought or obtained by other means." The words were light, even if the meaning was somewhat ominous.

"How did you end up working for The Office?" She thought randomly asking might produce results if she kept at it.

"Nice try."

The front door banged open and Stanzia stood there barefooted with her hair down her back, covered in soil and sweat.

"Of course," Tommy sighed.

"What?" Annika looked from one of them to the other. Neither said anything, but Tommy pivoted to glare at Stanzia.

"If you think that, why did you let me in the house?"

"What's going on?" Annika stood up so fast her chair toppled over.

"The bad guy has Jami. Or . . ." Stanzia broke off.

"Had her." Annika finished. The expression on her friend's face, the furrow between her eyebrows, and her hard mouth told her more eloquently than words that the answer was yes.

"Shut up!" Tommy shouted at Stanzia, who flipped him off and stomped off into the house.

He rubbed a hand over his forehead, eyes squeezed closed. "She was shouting in my head."

"Oh." Annika had never heard that her best friend could shout in anyone's mind, but, then again, it was turning out to be a strange week.

"I think your dark friend told her how to do it." He looked beat down, tired, smudged at the edges. He looked more human than he ever had before.

Her dark friend? "Rhys?"

No answer.

She had no suggestions about what to do. She wasn't a heroine. She didn't even feel particularly grown up most of the time. Annika waited for Tommy to tell her what they were going to do and hated herself for it. If she were The Office agent, she'd rush in and save Jami, even if she'd probably get herself killed doing it. They sat in silence for almost an hour before Sly bounded up the front steps on the balls of his feet, followed by a slinking Rhys. Neither of them seemed as cheerful as usual, but neither of them said anything about Jami either. In the distance, a church bell tolled. The sun streaked the sky vermilion, coral, and egg yolk.

People filed in for supper in singles and doubles and trios. Annika and Stanzia's weekly Sunday dinner was canceled for the Wake of Jami Eclat.

American witches have as many traditions as do their nonmagical fellow citizens—a myriad of religions and spiritual paths, sometimes (often) idiosyncratic, sometimes common or popular. This riot of beliefs and symbolism created somewhat bizarre rites of passing. The Unsaid Remark was closed to the public for Jami's wake. "Wake" tended to be the most common term applied to funerals in the East; why this was so was never really examined by anyone but scholars. If there were any scholars at Jami's wake, they were as drunk as everyone else and probably boring each other over the provenance of the use of the term.

Stanzia dressed head to toe in white and made Annika do the same. Before heading to the bar, she hung their household altar with a large piece of white bunting. They walked over to The Unsaid Remark in the midst of all the other dinner guests, with Sly at the head of the crowd playing a mournful fiddle tune the whole way. Once they reached the bar, Sly's fiddle was joined by another playing some kind of Appalachian dirge, all slow bowing and drawn-out chords. Instead of the stage, the musicians arrayed themselves around the room and played from tables or the bar, each picking up and playing part or all of a tune at will.

The Remark burst at the seams. The perimeter of the bar was set with small altars bedecked in ribbons and smoking incense, fake paper money, golden coins, splashes of wine and spirits, and more arcane offerings. Annika had never been close to Jami, but they were friends, and she felt adrift and confused by this sudden loss. Food began to appear, piles of hard-boiled eggs and salt, caraway bread, ears of corn, barley cakes, chicken legs, funeral pie, and shortbread were what Annika saw when she glanced over the bar.

Tommy took up a fiddle from one of the Korean guys from the West End and put his ear to the body to tune it for a few seconds before joining in "Black Velvet Band." His downy eyelashes brushed the tops of his cheeks and caught the light, fracturing it into gold and white. He swayed with his chin tucked down low, the instrument played at a strange angle. As the tune he'd begun with ended, he picked out a familiar melody and Annika's heart tightened. The rest of the musicians joined in on the fourth bar or so and they all played the intro, but when the first line of lyrics should have kicked in, no one sang. Before she even thought about it, she started on the second line of the lyrics as they went on. Tommy turned his body towards her but didn't open his eyes. Her voice got stronger and the rest of the bar began to sing along on the chorus.

It was only fitting that everyone who knew her would wake Jami with "Ripple" by the Grateful Dead. Annika hadn't ever thought there would be a day that she'd be bawling her eyes out over a damned Grateful Dead song, but there you have it. Stanzia surprised her by joining in and even knowing the words. They swayed together, the whole bar calling out strongly on the la, la, la, de, da, finale before Sly kicked into "Sugar Magnolia."

Tommy walked her home some time later, after she'd eaten a plate of kugel and been careful to pick out the raisins and leave them on the side of her plate for Rhys. Tommy's arm on her back was strong, reassuring even though she knew he couldn't protect her from anything that counted.

Sitting under the bay tree, Tommy looked almost scared in the darkness. "Jami's innocence was powerful. Way more than you can imagine." There was a tremor in his voice she'd never heard before. Annika reached out a hand and gripped Tommy's in it.

"We're going to be OK."

He looked up at her, the green in his eyes hidden by the night.

"I hope you're right, *a ghrá.*"

THIS IS A story Annika's mother told her:

In the bad old days, before our ancestors were blessed with the intelligence to escape from Europe, the Others attributed all sorts of ills to us. One that endured was that our powers were diabolical. We often lived apart then, but close enough to the Others to be known. Mothers among the Others would dress their children up like our own children the day before Easter and leave them on our doorsteps. Because of our rules of hospitality and because of our compassion, we would take these children into our homes. But our good will was our own undoing because of the fact that the day before Easter every fourth year coincided with our own Spring Festival. On the Spring Festival, we taught our children to fly. Because the children of the Others were mixed in with our own children, often an Other child would sit astride a broom and learn the freedom of leaving the earth for the buoyant potency of the air. These children passed from the mundane world into our realm, and we were forced to keep them. Thus comes the enduring myth of witches eating children.

Annika's mother could sometimes be hysterical, in the sense of fainting spells and the vapors. Many of the older Nordic witches were paranoid. Probably because the persecutions lasted until so recently in their history. For whatever reason, Annika sometimes was more frightened of mundanes than was strictly warranted, even if she doubted the causal chain of events that led from abandonment to child eating. The feeling of being terrified of another witch was new. She hadn't ever experienced a renegade wizard or a sorcerer with a vengeance scheme.

"Why do you think this bad guy is killing our people?" she whispered to Tommy as they lay in bed early on Monday morning. They were both clothed, because they'd had little energy to do more than lay awake and stare balefully at each other until they had passed out the night before.

"To stop the music."

"What does that have to do with you or with Jami?" The light filtered through the shutters over her bedroom window, patterning Tommy's face with narrow stripes. He lay on his back, her on her side next to him.

"You don't have many fey in the West, do you?"

Wasn't that the truth? Or maybe they hid better. She'd never met anyone even claiming to be of mixed race before she came to the East. All of this was new for her.

"The Rockies were somewhat insurmountable for a lot of folks, so I'm told," he said, sucking in a breath and sighing it out again. "Music has its own magic. It draws fey creatures to it. Whether music makes magic, magic makes music, whether they are two sides of the same coin, I don't know. You'd have to ask Stanzia or your dark friend. All I know is that if you kill enough fey here in Nashville, enough with enough power, then the music will die. The real music, not that industry garbage."

"Oh." The picture was snapping together for her now. The differentiation of "real" music from pop music, manufactured music, was interesting. That made sense if you believed that music was an extension of magic, which was a natural system, a sort of life force. That made real music alive, an outgrowth of someone's essence, her soul. Manufactured music was just a commodity, a way to make money, often for people who already had a lot of money to begin with. "You think that's what's happening?"

"One theory, anyway." He rolled over and shoved her on her other side to wrap around her back, mashing her pillow so they could share it. "It's Sly's theory, and I have reason to trust his judgment. Brandi's been in Austin a lot over the last couple years, weakened the magic already. Maybe someone got ambitious, thought taking out some other strategic players might tip the scales in the favor of autotuned vocals and meaningless lyrics."

"Hmrph," Annika grunted as she settled into blissful comfort, thinking of the difference between the music on the radio and the music made on her front porch or at The Remark. They were worlds apart.

Tommy began to hum, his voice wrapping around her the same way his body did. She drifted off to sleep with a golden buzz outside and inside her skin. Annika dreamed of bumblebees flying in and out of mounds in the earth and of perfectly tuned harps.

MONDAYS, STANZIA HAD office hours, which meant the front bedroom had a string of unlikely individuals outside, filling the hallway and living room. Slouching students in jeans and battered T-shirts with notebooks in their hands, matrons with bouquets of plants, elderly sorcerers with scrolls or metal objects in hand. Most of them knew Annika or Tommy or both. None of them commented when they both emerged from the same bedroom. Who they were afraid of offending didn't matter, all that mattered was that they were silently disapproving or approving.

Breakfast was coffee and orange scones, alfresco in the back garden with the bees and the butterflies and the birds that Annika fed. The petitioners and querents stayed out of the garden when they poked their heads in to find it occupied by a resident and Tommy.

"How do you two know each other?" Tommy asked, lounging in his chaise by the bird feeder where two larks were puffing up their chests over some grain.

"College." The sun was already bright and Annika would have given anything for Rhys's sunblock spell.

"Encanto?" He used the nickname the Californian Institute for Sorcererous Studies was called by alumnae and everyone else. She nodded.

"What did you study?"

"History, Law. Stanzia was in Theory."

Tommy wiped crumbs off the front of the Hodgepodge T-shirt he'd found in her clean laundry. "I hope so."

They both laughed, thinking about the people in the house.

"You went to one of their schools?" She didn't really want to bring it up, because sometimes people got touchy about contact with the mundanes. That is, the whole subject was very political with activists on both sides.

He didn't seem put off. "To a music college, yeah. Not really that big of a deal."

She let that pass. For the majority of people, yeah, that was still a very big deal. Going to one of their colleges was close to integration, which was one of those incendiary topics best left to twenty year olds and policy wonks.

Rhys breezed in the back gate and across the yard, tossing off a "How many idiots are in there? I want to watch 'Deadwood' on the DVR."

"Do you mind if I ask you how you know him?" Tommy sat up and swung his legs over the side of his chair to face her. His serious business face firmly wedged itself across his features.

Annika had wondered where Rhys had come from a few times over the year or so she'd been in Nashville. "To the best I can ascertain, he just showed up one day. It was before I moved here."

"Probably came with the house, then," Tommy growled.

"What?" Rhys wasn't a brownie.

He got up and walked into the kitchen without responding.

In the living room, Rhys was reading the tarot of an old lady with a ferret on her shoulder with the help of a four-year-old girl standing solemnly by his chair.

"Hanged man," the girl intoned.

"Yup," Rhys confirmed.

"But what does it mean?" the old lady practically had a coronary.

"The liminal space, the time between, the moment of clarity, the space between one way of being and another," Rhys said without his usual bored tone. Annika turned to see him looking at the wall between himself and Stanzia's office.

"But what does it mean?" the old lady asked again.

"That a choice has been made and the consequences have yet to befall," he replied, lost in thought, his eyes still on the wall. The hair on Annika's body all stood on end and sweat pricked on her forehead and upper lip. That reading was not for the old lady. Rhys's eyes flicked from the wall to her face.

"Hmm," Rhys said with the sort of deep meaning that most sages usually fail to impart with their obtuseness.

Tommy rearranged the tableau by emerging from the dining room with a guitar case and a frown.

ANNIKA DIDN'T FEEL as nervous as she figured she should have, walking on stage at The Remark and sitting on the little stool she'd seen so many other singers sit on before. She was still numb regarding her gift from Brandi, to be honest. Suddenly having a new skill was probably like any other rapid alteration in life: the loss of a loved one, falling in love, moving a great distance. She had experienced all of those in her life, and she knew that transition took time. Sometimes a person didn't even know they had moved on until far down the line from actually doing it. Maybe the day would come when she would burst into song without regard for who was in the room, no self-consciousness retained from her previous life as a tone-deaf singing gimp, but that day lay long in the future. For now, she didn't trust that the gift had stuck and expected to open her mouth and hear her old, reasonable but nothing special voice reaching out to a room full of people.

And the room was definitely full. The memorials to Jami were still smoking and swirling with color and light. The food on the bar still kept coming, now with added Lane cake and macaroons and haystacks. There was the sort of holiday spirit in the air that often accompanies tragedy, people wanting to band together to curse the darkness. Annika wanted to perform a fitting tribute to her friend, and she wanted to lure the person who killed her out into the open. It was the second part of the plan, and the subsequent capturing of said culprit, she was still not clear on. Tommy had been characteristically vague.

The house lights flickered and Tommy bounded onto the stage and sat on a matching stool next to her, pulled his guitar out of its case without bothering to tune it, and smiled brightly as he smoothed his Sox T-shirt down the front. He swung his guitar up onto his leg.

"Ready?"

She opened her mouth to respond as he opened his and boomed out, "Hello, Nashville!"

Lots of good-natured booing followed.

"Come on, give a guy a break, will ya?" He ducked his head and laughed at himself. "I've been waiting years to use that crummy line."

Annika watched him silently, all too aware that she had a stupid grin smacked all over her face just from looking at him, from being close enough to him that his shoulder bumped hers when he tilted from side to side. Stanzia waved to her from the back, a huge glass of wine in one hand and Rhys's shoulder in the other. Rhys looked neither unhappy nor pleased in particular. She knew she'd never be able to read his mind, so she might as well give up trying. He had creeped her out pretty hard earlier, but that happened sometimes with powerful people; they were unknowable, even when you thought you knew them intimately.

Her mind came back to the task at hand as Tommy played the opening bars of Lucinda Williams's "Fancy Funeral."

"This is for Jami," Annika whispered, the sound carried throughout the room by the spell cast on the stage. Tommy's head bent over his guitar and as Annika's voice slipped out it seemed made of something besides air and vibration, something that disintegrated her own thought and re-formed as the meaning behind the words of the song: regret over unlived moments, loss of a potential future, the way we never say the things we should.

The room fell away and Annika's life was a garden of memory, a slow ride in a limousine to a humid, bug-swarmed cemetery in the glare of midday, umbrellas used to keep the sun off instead of the rain bobbing over mourners' heads and the sound of pebbles hitting a casket lid.

They were singing "Fake Plastic Trees" before she even realized they had switched songs. That was four or five songs down the set list. Tommy was watching her instead of the crowd, his eyes verdant, making her think of the smell of newly mown grass and the taste of aloe. He added a flourish at the end of the song.

"We'll be takin' a break now. Feel free to buy us a drink!" Standing up, he propped his guitar next to his stool and offered her a hand.

The next few minutes were a swirl of colors bleeding into each other, the world trying to slot back into its regular pattern.

"You look high," Stanzia said at her elbow as Annika picked up a cool, damp pint glass at the bar.

"I feel high," she replied in her normal speaking voice.

"Well, because you are high, just not in a way you're used to. We'll talk later. I have theories."

Then she was gone and a man Annika didn't know was next to her, pressing a card into her hand.

". . . representation? If not, that's fine, too. We deal with a lot of unagented acts."

Annika looked at him but couldn't really focus on his face. He seemed . . . average. Brown hair, undistinguished eyes, thin, white.

". . . one of the largest labels in the world. You'd be amazed what we could do to your sound. You wouldn't even recognize yourself!"

Someone jostled her from behind and when she looked up, Rhys was between her and the average man, smirking at him with his most condescending smile, like when he just made a point off Stanzia about alchemy. His arms were crossed over his chest.

"Huh," Rhys said, like always.

Tommy said her name, and around then she must have passed out.

Part Three

This is a story that many people tell:

Long ago, before your time, our people came across oceans to live in the East and the West. Some went far south where summer was winter and winter was summer. Some went down rivers as wide as oceans to live scattered amongst the trees. Some sat in aeries and nested with birds. Some sat on beaches and their feet dug deep in the sand. Some dug beneath the earth to twist roots in their hair. Then the Others followed. First a few and they vanished. Then more and we hid. But like the way magic soaks through the pores in wood, the Others soaked through the East and the West and soon the fires were lit and the drownings began. Some say the Office arose then, to protect our kind from the Other kind. Some say the Office arose when the Others' wars threatened our children with hot metal and hungry bellies. Some say the Office arose when we fell on our own and discord pulled apart East and West, the people in the forests from the people in the aeries, the sandy-toed from the root-haired. In the end, they exist, and if the need is truly dire, the Office is only a fervent wish away.

Annika woke to complete silence. She felt for the pillow that had to be over her head, muffling out the sounds of the house, and found none. There was no traffic noise. The birds in the laurel tree outside her room must have undergone an avian genocide. No cats cried for scraps in the garden. The television had been switched off. She swung her legs over the side of her bed to find her flip-flops right where they should have been. She was dressed as usual for bed in a tank top and boxer shorts. Something, however, was very wrong.

Shuffling over the few feet to her bedroom door, she turned the knob and cracked it open. Noise flooded in like a radio suddenly switched on to ten stations at once. Cars braked suddenly in a tossing of gravel and screeching of metal on metal, dogs barked in the distance, cats screamed, the bird revolution continued unabated in the trees around the house, the television blared out the "COPS" theme song. Pulling the door all the way open caused the volume to rise precipitously. She experimented by closing the door slightly and opening it wider, and found that the more the door was closed, the quieter the inside of her room was.

Rhys's soundproofing spell. Well, Annika wasn't going to complain about that one. She wondered if it was one-way only. That would be like him, to charm her room so she couldn't hear anything outside of it, but anyone else in the house could hear her in her room . . . doing whatever it is grown people do in their bedrooms.

The hallway was dark, none of the wall sconces on since it was broad daylight, but sun barely penetrated the far end of the hall where Annika's room was. She felt a heavy foreboding as she stepped through the open pocket doors into the living room, but no one was in there either. Nor in the dining room. Nor the kitchen. She walked out onto the porch only to find one of Stanzia's stray cats sprawled in the sun, his white belly rising and falling contentedly.

She called out then. "Stanz?"

Nothing.

She tried again. "Rhys?"

Again, nothing.

Which could really only mean one thing: the cellar. Annika avoided the cellar with a single-mindedness that sometimes resulted in her forgetting they even *had* a cellar. Their bungalow sat on what appeared from the outside to be a stone foundation. The stones actually formed the outer wall to a sunlight basement that was the first level of a series of cellars. The sunlight basement was pretty much as advertised: a room as large as the house itself with old, wavy glass windows set at odd intervals in the outer stone wall, allowing light inside. Stanzia used the space to dry flowers and herbs and the underside of the house served as rafters for the space, bunches of fragrant plants hung in bundles and groups according to color, length of stem, family, purpose—who knew with her. The household also used the back portion of the room as a storage area for odds and ends, holiday gear, old kettles and cauldrons and broken furniture. Light filtered in through the waving bouquets and dust motes, sometimes thin and sickly, other times oddly robust. The place creeped Annika out.

The sunlight basement, though, had nothing on the true cellar beneath it. Under a rug wrought with an elaborate mermaid pattern done in shades of aqua and teal and jade, stood a trapdoor leading to a set of rickety steps that granted access to the dungeon. OK, not really, but sometimes Annika had nightmares that maybe the cellar really was a dungeon. On this particular Tuesday, the rug lay rumpled in a heap and the hole for the trapdoor yawned open. When she peered down into the maw of the cellar, Annika saw the room was illuminated by flickering witch light.

"Stanz?" she called down, standing at least a foot from the top step.

"Yeah, Annika, we're down here, but you don't gotta come down. We'll be up after a while."

"What?" Rhys scoffed. "How were you planning to get that to work? Get down here."

All in all, Annika wished she'd stayed in bed. She sucked in a breath, made a sign against the evil eye, and started down the steps. The walls of the cellar proper were probably once neat granite and limestone blocks, but over the years they had been eroded so that nooks and crannies of various sizes had formed between the stones. Stuck in these interstices were all forms of papers and whirligigs, broken astrolabes and stuffed peacocks in bottles, crystals and diodes, powders, tinctures, bones, and salves. At all four corners of the large room were witch balls glowing with light, amber at two corners and pure white at the other two. In the middle of the room hung a chandelier of four more witch balls, all white light. Annika's fear wasn't of the dark, because there was hardly any to be had in the cellar. Her fear was based on the primal apprehension of the lurking thing. The unknown *whatever* lurking just out of your peripheral vision. The cellar was full of lurking things—she was sure of it. As much as Annika's mother called it a stereotype, Annika's people had been folks of the air, of the open spaces, of the outdoors. Being underground, being pinned down by the weight of the house, squeezed by the weight of the stone walls, pressed against by the scents of decay and mildew, made her anxious.

She crept down the stairs to find an unlikely scene. Stanzia sat on the top of her battered, sea captain's desk with a map in her hand wearing a long smock-style apron over her dress. Tommy stood next to her in dirty jeans and a shirt she recognized as another random shirt found in her laundry—her dad's old Captain Marvel shirt—pointing at something on Stanzia's map. Rhys was playing a Game Boy while leaning against a table on the opposite wall; at his feet was a sleazy-looking guy sitting cross-legged and eating a scone. Everyone looked up when she neared the bottom of the stairs.

"I left breakfast out for you," Stanzia said over the top of her map.

"What's going on?" That seemed like the best first question.

"What do you mean?" Tommy focused his attention firmly on her. "Do you have memory loss? A headache? Do you remember what day it is?"

"What?" She should have had some coffee.

"That's the guy from The Remark last night." Stanzia lifted her chin towards the guy with the scone, who waved and continued to eat. "There's coffee over here." She pulled her skirt in tighter to reveal a carafe on the desk next to her. Annika skirted the area directly under the central chandelier, hugging the wall as she scrambled to get her coffee. Even if nothing currently occupied that middle of the room, the space held residual magic strong enough to give someone a jolt. Her favorite coffee cup—the one with the winged hippos—sat next to the Spanish-style, inlaid coffeepot.

"So. What's going on?" She used the false casual voice she employed on crazed exs, wild animals and her mother. "And what is that guy doing here?"

"We're going to project a map," Stanzia said as though that explained everything. Which, all in all, was pretty typical. "And that's the guy who was trying to lure you to the bad guy. To do to you what he did to Jami. And everyone else."

"A map of what?" They had a whole script. "They sent an agent to lure me?"

"A map of Tennessee." Stanzia made a pinched face. "It's Nashville, who else would a bad guy send besides an agent or a PR rep to lure someone to their demise?"

OK, that was getting closer to some kind of substantive information. "How about you just explain to me exactly what's going on."

"Oh, just kill me now," Rhys groaned from across the room without pausing his frantic thumb movements.

Stanzia pushed her hair back and pointed to the map. "Right, you know how representational magic works?"

She did. "You use something else to stand in for something you don't have in order to affect action on the thing you don't have."

"So, what we don't have is the entire state of Tennessee. Instead, what we have is a map of Tennessee."

So far so good. "So the map stands in for the state. And? What are we looking for?"

"We're looking for an anomaly," Tommy piped up, his smile sliding onto his face when Annika looked over at him.

Annika rolled her eyes and lifted a hand to indicate further explanation would be wonderful. She sipped her coffee.

"I was thinking . . ." Stanzia said in a voice Annika recognized as one that would lead to tangents and nonsalient points. Rhys sighed pointedly. "If you could focus your ability on a magically imbued representation of a location you could find hot spots."

Oh. "Hey, yeah, that's a *great* idea!" Stanzia did talk about that sometimes, about making a diorama or some other model with little figures of people, automatons, affixed to it that Annika could use to represent some place rather than having to go out looking for magical creatures or people. This lazy way definitely appealed to Annika. Normally, she had to have some object of the person she was seeking or a location to go to in order to track them down. This way was far more efficient.

"Anyway, I figured maybe with a map of Nashville and the surrounding area we could locate focal points faster."

Annika didn't bother to ask why they hadn't ever tried this before. The answer was that Annika was trying to stay out of the family business and refinement of her skills was the last undertaking she'd been interested in since moving to Nashville. Besides, Stanzia talked about a lot of concepts she never took any further than musings.

"OK, so what's up with . . ." she nodded towards the guy sitting on the floor.

"We thought it best not to release that specimen back into the wild until we've obtained further intel." Tommy delivered his comment with a straight face but ruined the effect by smiling sarcastically afterward.

"Hey, my name's Clay!" the specimen said with much more dignity than you would expect from a guy in a grimy button-down black shirt and a bandana around his head, sitting on a dusty Persian rug in a cellar next to Rhys's scuffed-up leather tennis shoes.

"Pipe down," Rhys gave him a shove with one of said scuffed-up tennis shoes.

"Y'all suck," their kidnap victim mumbled.

"Isn't your job to keep people from absconding with other people?" Annika was feeling much more like herself after her coffee.

Tommy stuck a finger to his temple and screwed his face up in a parody of deep thinking. Dropping his hand rapidly, he shook his head. "Now that you mention it . . . no. My writ is to stop the bleeding of magic from Nashville, and in the course of executing said writ I have personal discretion."

Oh, that sounded *great*.

"You cops are all the same, The Office, the FBI, no one got no rights no more." Clay, the collateral damage, tossed in his shekel.

A clock appeared on the wall behind Rhys's head and disappeared again. "I don't have time for this." Stanzia jumped down off the table and pulled a plumb line and a bag out of one of the pockets of her apron. She tossed her left hand high and the plumb line sailed through the air to hang suspended under the exact center of the chandelier. The plumb line swung in a widdershins arc, each rotation fractionally tightening the described circle. As the plumb line moved, it left behind lines on the floor that as the circle tightened and tightened resolved into a map. When the plumb line hung still, pointing to the dead center of the map, Annika noticed the indicated location was their street, probably their house.

Stanzia smiled and reached back to pull her hair up in a knot and simultaneously pulled a nautical compass out of one of the pockets of her apron. She snapped it open, scrutinized it for a couple seconds, and snapped it shut. "Just feel over the map and you should find what you're looking for." She handed the compass to Annika. "This will lead you directly to the person you're seeking when the time comes."

"What am I looking for?" Annika searched her friend's face for further clues.

"That part I've been thinking over," Tommy said from behind her. He stepped up to stand at her shoulder. "If this guy consumes power . . ."

"There should be an absence of magic in his general vicinity, a static place or a null area." Stanzia sighed. Tommy stared at her with his mouth slightly open and Rhys laughed maliciously.

"It's pretty obvious," Rhys sing-songed.

"I thought so." Stanzia, though, just sounded surprised anyone would think otherwise.

Right.

"You two get into a lot of trouble, don't you?" Tommy's tone indicated amused interest instead of his usual wariness when dealing with Rhys.

"You don't even want to know what they get up to." Annika winked at him before turning back to Stanzia, who was growing impatient, which was obvious by the way she was touching her hair and looking towards the door to the sunlit basement. "What?"

"What, what?" Stanzia looked like she'd been caught out at something.

Which concerned Annika because a distracted Stanzia could mean the room might blow up at any second. "What're you in a hurry for?"

"She's got to use the bathroom, too much coffee," Rhys supplied.

"Pretty much." Confirmation from the afflicted who just looked quizzically at Annika.

Annika rubbed her forehead. She loved her friends, she truly did, but sometimes she would have preferred to just sit in the dark by herself pondering the merits of springtime. "How does this work?"

"OK," Stanzia said and knelt down on the floorboards at the edge of the map. She motioned for Annika to do the same. When they were kneeling side by side, the old wood cutting into Annika's bare knees, Stanzia took her hand and pulled a pincushion out of a pocket in her apron.

"Huh-uh." Annika tried to tug away and Tommy stepped forward to intervene, but before either of them could say or do more than hesitate, Stanzia pricked Annika's finger with a silver needle. She held the bleeding finger over the map and squeezed out four drops of blood in a row, took a blink's worth of a pause, and one more drop of blood after that.

"For the cardinal directions and the center of everything," Stanzia explained.

Annika reached out to steady herself as she was overcome with a head-spinning bout of vertigo. The room tilted like a four-point see-saw and she rolled with it, coffee taste bitter in the back of her throat and her vision bobbing as she tried to ascertain a horizon. Just as rapidly as the dizziness set on, it vanished, leaving her aware in a curiously natural way of the map. She gazed down at the streets cross-hatching one another, at the Cumberland River running through the center of town, at the green arrows representing trees, and the miniature Parthenon glowing in Centennial Park. When she waved a hand over her neighborhood, she felt heat over her house, hot with magic, with recent spell casting, with the deep thrum of constant power seepage imbuing the very house with the spice of sorcery.

She began at the bottom of the map and worked across in a grid. In some places, the heat spiked. Above the Parthenon she had to draw her hand back as what felt like the touch of a flame licked at the center of her palm. East Nashville was a banked fire, constant, warmer in places, but not even cool in the smallest part. Music Row hid the secret cold heart of the absence of magic, working outward from it, the heat dissipated and cooled until right over a particular building there was nothing but cold like an ice cube.

"Here." Annika put her finger on the center of the cold spot.

"Huh," Rhys glanced up from his Game Boy. "Shoulda known."

"What's there?" Stanzia stared at the map with only mild interest; now that the spell itself was executed, her focus was elsewhere.

"IFB, song publishers. They pay songwriters to write for other artists. Top Ten stuff. Radio music," Rhys answered with a bored tone. Annika didn't really feel like taking on a mundane corporation.

Tommy was silent. Annika looked over her shoulder to ask him what was next on the agenda, but he was gone.

"What the hell?"

"What?" Stanzia said as she started up the stairs to the basement.

"Where did Tommy go?" Annika twisted her head from side to side but saw nothing.

Stanzia looked around and shrugged. "Disappeared, I guess."

"*What?*" She'd really had enough craziness for, oh, at least a year.

"Didn't you ever notice Rhys doing it?" Stanzia asked vaguely over her shoulder.

Rhys, when Annika looked over at him, was smirking with his arms crossed over his chest. "What?" he asked with a broad smile and a lift of his chin.

"Can I go now?" Clay the hostage asked.

"Why not?" Rhys flicked his hair out of his face and walked past Annika like nothing out of the ordinary was happening. She was starting to suspect that maybe for him, that was actually the case.

As she made a fist of frustration, she noticed the nautical compass wasn't in her hand anymore. She watched as Clay scrambled up the stairs to the basement, leaving Annika standing next to the map under the deathly still plumb line in the creepy cellar whose lights were beginning to fade without Stanzia in the room. She scuttled up the stairs, following everyone else and wishing that wasn't such an apt metaphor for her life.

STANZIA WAS IN her office, which looked much like the basement but with far more windows, and shelves for squirreling away booty.

"How did Tommy take the compass out of my hand and get up the stairs without anyone noticing?" Sometimes, not often with the people she knew, but sometimes the best course of action was direct questioning.

Stanzia looked up from the pile of papers she was sorting through and seemed to consider the answer for a few seconds. "I'm still not completely clear on what his deal is."

"Deal?" She asked, but she already knew that answer, really. Annika had seen the flame of him in her mind, just like she saw Stanzia's arrow.

Stanzia blinked at her and narrowed her eyes. "You know he's not human . . ." she trailed off, either waiting for Annika to fill in more or expecting a thought of her own that didn't arrive on time. When Annika just rolled her hand for Stanzia to go on, she obliged. "Who knows what sort of abilities fey and other nonhumans have? I don't trust the written accounts."

"You can be pretty irrational." Between two people who weren't as close, that could have sounded cruel or callous. As it stood with them, it was just a statement of fact.

Stanzia let out a full-body laugh that left her holding a hand to her chest. "I don't deny that."

Annika plopped down in the overstuffed chair sitting in front of the ancient cherry desk and frowned. "Why did he leave me here?" The words came on a whine, even though she was trying to use her big girl voice.

"Because you're just a consultant." She said it matter of factly, clearly not intending hurt feelings, but sometimes Stanzia could be like that, cutting by accident.

"I'm *just a consultant*?" That really galled.

"Oh." Stanzia finally tuned into the conversation and used a thumb to mark her place in the book she'd been paging through furiously. "I meant as far as the work thing went." She paused. "I thought we'd talk about all this when everything was done. You know, get a bottle of whiskey and sit on the porch and drink all the secrets out."

Which was their normal habit, so that was fair, but sometimes Annika didn't feel like being very fair. "I *like* him."

Stanzia just sat on the edge of her desk and waited.

"Do you think he likes me?" There, she said it and she felt stupid, but so what?

"He's braving Rhys for you, so I assume so." Stanzia's smile said she meant it as a compliment.

That wasn't the sort of answer she wanted. At all.

Stanzia tugged her hair down and knotted it back up again. "I don't know this guy. I mean, I've known him sorta for ages, but you want me to pass judgment and give you the all's clear on someone you met in a time of duress. I'm reserving judgment."

Annika scowled. Reserving judgment never meant an all's clear later.

"Getting wrapped up with a fey is never a good idea. Don't you read fairy tales?"

Annika glared some more. "What about Rhys? He's not human, exactly, is he?"

Stanzia put her book down completely then and stood up. She smiled a smile that felt like parental approval and an unasked-for holiday. "That you'll have to ask him about." Then she left the room.

"Hey, you're not going to tell me yourself? Backstabber!" Annika called after her, but she didn't mean it. There was humor in her tone. There were some rules that a person didn't break, not because of The Office, but because there were older, darker, more twisted and frightening penalties for breaking them. Contravening the fey never seemed to turn out on the plus side for humans.

THE SUN WAS struggling to pull its panoply of tangerine and bubble gum pink along with it as it retired for the night when Tommy pulled up in front of the house in his sleek, black SUV. Annika was sitting with her feet up on the railing of the porch, nursing a grudge and a Blue Moon. He looked no worse for wear, cleaner jeans than earlier, but these still stained from something like black ichor. He wore a jersey-style T-shirt with white stitching around the sleeves and neck. The material looked like it felt soft. The last of the sunlight caught in his hair, burnishing it bronze and gold.

His expression screamed contrite, but Annika was old enough to know an act when she saw one. Tommy was pleased with himself. So, he'd triumphed and saved the day while he left the little woman behind safely, confused and out of the know.

"I know you're pissed at me," he began as he hit the bottom step of the porch. "You have every reason to be."

That was a good tactic. Someone else might have bought it. But Annika just gave him a hard look, the one that had made the boys cry when she was in her early twenties.

His expression rearranged itself into an echoing hard look. "The bottom line is that you don't get a say. This was my game to play and I played it." He pointed into the distance, his face reddening from anger or embarrassment, or some emotion she couldn't identify. "This is my job, and I might not like it, might even fucking hate it, but it's what it is. I do what I have to, and if that means wrecking anything I have with you before it gets off the ground, well, I guess what's done is done."

The last bit was delivered while standing on the porch proper with his hands on his hips, shouting. His eyes stood open so wide she could see the whites all around his irises. Rocking her chair back and forth with one toe on the ground, she stared up at his looming figure. Annika realized that the grass smell she associated with thinking of his eyes actually was his smell. He gave off something *green*, chlorophyll and fresh pine sap.

"So, I guess you like me, huh?" She said this with a smile, a small laugh burbling up to underline that remark.

He stared for a couple more seconds, dropped his arms from his hips, and ran a hand over his head. "Well, yeah." A smile poked its way around his anger and a dimple peeked out. "You're not pissed off?"

"Oh, yeah, I'm pissed off. And you also didn't tell me how much you'd be paying me to consult on this case, either. Do you pay in currency or something else?" Her tone turned earnest and his smile slithered away.

"Are you serious?" He sounded like he might choke. "The Office paid your mother upfront."

"What?" It was her turn to choke. "She what?" There was murder in her future, her immediate future.

"Forget I said anything." Tommy stepped over her out-stretched leg and parked himself in the rocking chair next to hers.

Annika worked through Lull's Stages of Precipitation to calm herself down. "You got the bad guy?"

"Official business." He said it in a no-nonsense tone, as though she was just going to accept that as an answer.

"What? Are you kidding me?" She stared at him with her mouth half-open.

He sighed. "You're either in or you're out. I don't make these rules. I don't even know how to *bend* the rules. I have so many hexes and bindings on me I wouldn't even know where to start untangling."

"You're claiming you're physically unable to tell me what happened?" This was stretching believability.

"I'm physically and metaphysically unable."

"Right. Wanting to seem aloof and enigmatic has noth-ing to do with it." Annika hated the part of her that couldn't leave a challenge alone.

Tommy laughed and reached out a hand to run his thumb over the back of her hand. "I never said that wasn't a benefit. Is it working?"

"I go for dependable and hot." She grabbed his hand and held on to it.

"Well, one out of two is better than being a Yankees fan."

She actually laughed at the Yankees joke. That was the moment she knew she was truly doomed.

"Are you safe? Is Brandi and everyone else safe? Can you at least tell me that?" Most witches know that even the best compulsions had backdoors, secret keys, circumnavi-gatory routes.

"No one else is going to be consumed." There was a

finality to the clipped delivery that made Annika believe him. She watched him in the soft glow of the witch light that appeared on the porch as the sun disappeared, his winged eyebrows and pug nose and pink, mischievous mouth, and she knew if he asked her for a boon, she'd give it.

"There's a way I could tell you everything." He attempted to sound flip, but she was getting to know him too well for that—he just sounded like a pleased kid with a secret.

"Do tell." She already knew.

"You could join The Office, become an agent."

The birds in the bay tree began a pitched warbling battle that rattled the leaves and released the spicy scent of the tree into the summer humidity.

"I guess you got your job in a similar fashion."

"You guess right. But there wasn't a pretty girl in my story." His thumb rubbed over the soft skin of her palm.

"A pretty boy?" She waggled an eyebrow at him and he laughed loud and hard with his head back.

"I guess you'll just have to take me up on the job offer to find out, huh?"

THIS IS THE story that Annika told at some point in her long life:

Once there was a girl who lived on a rocky shore lined with tall pine trees. She was a happy girl full of curiosity. She was also a loyal girl full of filial duty. The girl said to her family, I want to taste the dew on the clouds. The girl's family said, we cannot spare you. The girl said to her family, I want to sing with the birds in their nests. The girl's family said, we cannot spare you. The girl said, I want to taste the green of the earth. The girl's family said, we cannot spare you. One day the girl stole away in the night on the back of someone else's prayer as it passed by her window. She landed far from the rocky shoreline and the tall pine trees. One day the girl said, I have seen all I came for and my curiosity is quenched. On that day, she turned her face up and tasted the dew of the clouds. A bird snatched her up to sing a duet in his nest. And the very green of the earth reached up to beckon her to come within. The girl stepped into the green of the earth and realized curiosity is only as large as the world of which you're aware.

Love is magic

Upcoming Paranormal Romances
FROM TOR

Fallen

Claire Delacroix
978-0-7653-5949-0 • 0-7653-5949-9
OCTOBER 2008

Red

Jordan Summers
978-0-7653-5914-8 • 0-7653-5914-6
NOVEMBER 2008

Cursed

Jamie Leigh Hansen
978-0-7653-5721-2 • 0-7653-5721-6
DECEMBER 2008

Magic's Design

Cat Adams
978-0-7653-5963-6 • 0-7653-5963-4
FEBRUARY 2009

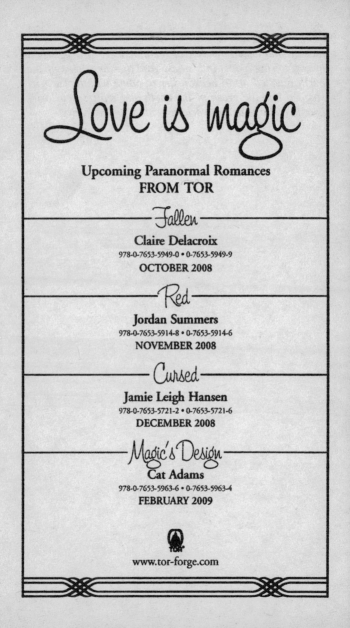

TOR

www.tor-forge.com